the Suffragette Scandal

COURTNEY MILAN

The Suffragette ' dal: © 2014 by Courtney Milan.
Cover design © C   ·y Milar
Cover photographs   ' Dreamstime.com.

Print Edition 2.0

For everyone who has carried water
in thimbles and teaspoons throughout the centuries.
And for all those who continue to do so.
For as many centuries as it takes.

Chapter One

Cambridgeshire, March 1877

EDWARD CLARK WAS DISGUSTED with himself.

It was one thing to do a man a favor. It was another entirely to take it this far—for Edward to shoulder his way through the shouting crowd on the banks of the river, jostling with other men for position. And for what purpose? So he could see a pair of boats come around the bend of the Thames? He hadn't even known he was acquainted with a member of the Cambridge crew until he'd glanced at a newspaper this morning.

And yet here he was. Waiting. Like everyone around him, he leaned forward intently. Like them, he caught his breath when he glimpsed the first boat. But the crew on board was attired in dark blue, and cries of "Oxford, Oxford!" rose in a tumultuous roar around him. He sank back on his heels— but before he had a chance to relax, another boat came into view, rowed by men in light blue. Competing shouts rang out.

Edward didn't cheer. He focused on the Cambridge boat intently.

It had been almost a decade since he'd seen Stephen Shaughnessy. Back then, Stephen had been a boy. An annoyance, as ever-present as a mosquito. Edward had expected to feel a wave of nostalgia when the man came into sight. Maybe the bitter tug of guilt.

But he couldn't put a name to the feelings that assailed him—dark, indistinct things that pulled at him uncomfortably, leaving his muscles tensed and a phantom itch in his smallest finger. They weren't proper emotions at all. He had only the sense that it was about to storm, and yet there wasn't a cloud in the sky.

Stephen—Edward knew he was the third man in the Cambridge boat from the papers—was nothing but an indistinct blot of dark hair and moving muscle. Scarcely a reason for Edward to leave his comfortable home in Toulouse, to risk the complacent life he'd fashioned for himself.

He'd done it anyway. He'd tried to eradicate all his idealism, but apparently he *did* still hold on to a few foolish principles.

Around him, the crowd's expectant cheers grew louder, more boisterous. The race was close; the light blue Cambridge shirts crept up on Oxford. Edward felt like a dark rock, solid and unmoving in the midst of a froth of excitement.

Nothing represented his former brave, irrelevant principles more completely than the people mustered along the banks of the river. Everyone else concentrated on what was—for the moment—the most important thing in the universe: the men in their boats, struggling for speed in the choppy water. Here, there were no ethical morasses. In a universe of uncertainty, this one contest was set in stone. There was only black and white, right and wrong, Cambridge and Oxford.

And Oxford was ahead by a quarter length.

Not everyone was excited. To his right, back a few paces, a woman stood, scarcely hiding her boredom. She was dressed in a fussy, lacy gown that made her look like a sugar-spun confection. Pretty enough to look at, but he suspected she would hurt his teeth if he tried to partake. She clung to the arm of a florid-faced man, and glanced riverward every half minute or so—the certain look of a woman who'd been dragged out here and was doing her best to feign interest.

Most of the people standing back from the riverbank weren't even trying to hide their boredom. The race was the place to be, so they'd come to see and be seen. He should join them, leave this prime position at the water's edge for someone who cared.

But that was when his eye landed on one particular woman. She wasn't standing behind the crowd out of ennui; she was perched on a stool, the better to see the proceedings. She wore a dark skirt and a white shirtwaist. But her jacket had a decidedly mannish flair to it—strong lines, military braid at the cuffs, and epaulettes at the shoulders. She wore a man's bowler hat. A length of fabric in that odd shade of light bluish-green that was known as Cambridge Blue was knotted around her neck in a fair imitation of a cravat. She wasn't feigning interest in the race; she *was* interested. She leaned forward, every bit as intent as the most avid student, as if she could push the craft forward with the power of her mind.

Edward had intended to drop back, but when he picked his way through the crowds at the banks, it turned out to not be a retreat. He found himself drifting toward the woman as if he were a satellite being drawn into orbit around her. As he got closer, he saw wisps of auburn hair peeking out from under her hat.

She watched the proceedings with a concentration so intent that she didn't even notice him coming to stand a few feet from her. She simply pushed up on her tiptoes, fists clenched at her side, eyes fixed on the race.

He could see the river from the corner of his eye. The rowers were closing in on the finish. The woman leaned forward, raising a fist as if to cheer—and then gasped in sudden surprise.

Edward turned back to the river. He scarcely had a chance to see what happened. A dark object flew through the air from the opposite bank; the shouts of encouragement turned to outrage. And then the thing—whatever it was—hit the Cambridge boat right on Stephen's position. It burst apart, and Edward saw a splash of vivid orange.

He'd been right. There *was* a storm coming. Edward stepped forward, his jaw clenched, a rising fury encompassing him. But there was nothing he could do—not here, not on the banks of the river.

Now he remembered why he hated England. He hadn't felt this helpless in almost a decade, not since his father had ordered Stephen and Patrick stripped to the waist and whipped in front of him. *This* was why he'd come back. After all these years, he finally had a chance to do something about the anger he'd buried.

The boat was close enough now that Edward could see Stephen miss a beat, wipe his face. Some kind of an orange dye in a brittle shell had been lobbed at him.

"Oh, infamous!" shouted the woman in the cravat. "Don't let them take you down, Stephen. Show them!"

He turned back to her. *She* knew Stephen? The mystery deepened. Here she was, rigged out in Cambridge colors, cheering for Stephen as if she had every right to do so. He had no idea who she was. She might be his fiancée, although he'd not heard of a betrothal. She wasn't family; that he knew for certain.

Edward couldn't make out Stephen's expression at this distance, but he didn't need to. There was a determination to the set of his shoulders, one Edward recognized all too well.

He'd been best friends with Stephen's elder brother. Stephen had been five years younger—a persistent extra at best, an annoying hanger-on at worst. He'd followed the older boys around looking precisely as he did now: determined that he would not be excluded. The harder they had tried to leave him, the more he'd attached himself. Apparently that stubbornness hadn't changed, because now he pulled harder. The Cambridge boat slid ahead a quarter of a length, and then another. And then they were in the lead, sliding past the judge's boat to the roar of the crowd.

"That'll show those bloody bounders," the woman next to him muttered. She put two fingers to her lips and gave a sharp, piercing whistle of approval.

Nothing demure about her at all. Ladies in England *had* changed since he'd been gone. He found them much improved.

She removed her fingers and, for the first time, she noticed him. She raised an eyebrow, as if daring him to remonstrate with her.

Not a chance. He turned to her.

"Let me guess. Your brother?" He gestured toward Stephen. He knew she was no relation, but he had no wish to reveal his own connection. "What a disgrace that was."

Her nostrils flared. "No more than some of the other things... Well, never mind."

Other things? So Patrick *had* been right. Stephen was in trouble, and there might be something Edward could do about it.

"And no," the woman continued, "he's not my brother."

There was no ring on her finger. "There must be a brother somewhere," he mused. "Someone is responsible for all this Cambridge spirit." He gestured to her cravat.

The corner of her mouth tilted up, as if he'd said something extremely funny, and she was afraid to laugh for fear of hurting his feelings.

"My brother *did* go to Cambridge," she admitted. "But that was decades ago. I don't cheer on his behalf."

"So you developed a taste for sport while your brother was..." He stopped. He wasn't good at judging age; he never had been. But he doubted she'd been anything other than a tiny child decades ago.

She did snicker at that.

He tried again. "You know one of the rowers, the one who was spattered with dye. You shouted his name...?"

"Oh, yes. Stephen Shaughnessy. We Cambridge misfits ought to keep some kind of camaraderie."

"Misfits?" He frowned, and then realized that was not the most surprising word she'd used. "*We?*"

"You saw what they did." A hand went to her hip, resting against the white brocade of her jacket. "If you know the name Stephen Shaughnessy, you can guess why he's not universally admired. As for me, you can stop gently probing. I'm technically *not* a Cambridge misfit—not any longer. I graduated from the Girton College for Women a few years back."

It had been a long time since he'd been taken by surprise. He knew, vaguely, that Girton existed and women had graduated from it. But there weren't many of them; the number was so small as to be almost nonexistent. He blinked and took her in again—that mannish blazer, that cravat knotted around her neck. Oh, women *had* changed since he'd left England.

"You're a suffragette," he said flatly.

She blew out a puff of air, and he felt an almost physical blow. The wind had blown strands of her hair loose from under her hat. It shone a brilliant auburn in the sun. That blazer ought to have made her look masculine. Instead, the cut accentuated her curves rather than hiding them, bringing every last difference between her body and a man's into prominence. But it was her smile that made her dangerous— a smile that said she could take on the entire world, and she'd do it twice before breakfast.

She wagged a finger at him. "You're mispronouncing that word."

"Your pardon?" He groped, trying to remember what he'd said. "Suffragette? How does one pronounce it, then?"

"Suffragette," she said, "is pronounced with an exclamation point at the end. Like this: 'Huzzah! Suffragettes!'"

The moon could ignore the earth more easily than he could turn away from her. It took every ounce of willpower he had not to smile at that. Instead, he gave her a level look. "I don't pronounce anything with exclamation points."

"No?" She shrugged this away. "Then there's no time like the present to start. Repeat after me: 'Let's hear three cheers for the women's vote!'"

He could feel his amusement spilling out on his face despite his best efforts. He clamped his lips into a straight line and lowered his voice. "No," he told her. "Cheering is entirely beyond my capabilities."

"Oh, too bad." Her tone was sympathetic, but her eyes were mocking. "I see now. You're a womanthrope."

He'd never heard the word before, but the meaning was all too clear. She'd judged him to be just like every other man in England. Foolish to protest that he was different. Foolish to care what this unknown woman thought of him.

He spoke anyway. "No. I am a realist. Likely you've never met my sort before."

"Oh, I'm sure I have." She rolled her eyes. "I've heard everything. Let me see. You believe that women will vote for the handsomest candidates without using their faculties of reason. Is that the size of your *realism?*"

He met her accusing gaze with an annoyed look of his own. "Do I look like a fool? I don't see any reason for women not to vote; you're no stupider, on average, than the typical man. If there were any fairness in the world, suffragettes would succeed in all their political aims. But the world is not fair. You're going to spend your entire life fighting for gains that will be lost in political bickering ten years after they've been achieved. That's why I won't spare you three cheers. They'll serve no purpose but to waste my breath."

She looked at him for a moment. Really looked at him, as if she were seeing him for the first time rather than imagining a man-shaped…womanthrope in his stead.

"Good heavens." She reached into a pocket in her skirt. "You're right. I haven't met anyone like you."

She looked him over again, and this time there was no mistaking that slow head-to-toe perusal. His heart gave an odd little thump.

And then she smiled at him. "Well, Monsieur le Realist. Call on me if you ever find yourself in need of an exclamation point. I have an entire box of them."

It took him a moment to realize she was handing him a card. She slipped it between the gloved fingers of his right hand; he caught it with his left before it could fall to the ground. The type was plain and unassuming, with none of the little decorations or curly scripts one expected from a woman's calling card. But then, this was a card of business; no woman had ever given him one of those before.

Frederica Marshall, B.A.
Owner and Editrix-in-Chief
Women's Free Press
By women—for women—about women

When he looked up, she'd already gone. He caught a glimpse of her yards away, wending her way through the crowds, her stool under her arm.

And then the swirling throng swallowed her and he was left with nothing but her card.

Chapter Two

Kent, later that evening

THE HOME WHERE EDWARD had grown up hadn't changed at all.

A deer track ran through a nearby wood; a windswept meadow of wild grasses, carefully constructed so as to give a natural appearance, abutted the south wing. The river, a quarter mile distant from the house, made scarcely more than a comfortable murmur of passing water from here.

The house stood at the end of a long road a mile from the center of town. The ruins of a onetime fortress, the gray stones silver in the moonlight, loomed from the swell of a hill. A battle had once been fought here; he and Patrick had always been unearthing bits of armor and decaying sword hilts. Now there was little left but the battlements up high and, down by the river, a collection of stones that had once been a ferry. Those sad remains guarded a sandy ford that had long since been replaced by the bridge a mile upstream. After nearly ten years of absence, Edward was about as relevant to this scene as those abandoned battlements.

The modern house lay before him, the picture of utter tranquility.

That tranquility was a lie. On that field near the stable—that was the place where Edward's father had ordered Patrick and Stephen whipped.

The windows of the house cast a golden, illusory light on the scene of that memory. Edward shook his head, dispelling his grisly thoughts, and stole his way to a glassed side door.

Moonlight spilled into the library. Through the windows, he could make out a desk stacked high with papers. Edward had received his share of reprimands in that room. He'd held his head proudly there, refusing to break, refusing to *lie,* no matter what the consequences.

Pah. He'd learned better now. The notion of morality was relative. For instance, he intended to break into this house. Some might call that "burglary."

It would be, in the moral sense: The current residents of the house would not welcome his intrusion.

From a legal perspective, however, there was one small and yet salient difference: This house, and everything in it, still belonged to him. It would be his for four more months, until he was declared dead once and for all.

He couldn't wait.

He pulled a thin piece of steel from its hiding place in his coat sleeve, crouched beside the lock, and listened for the telltale click. He'd known a man who could open any door in a few seconds flat. Edward, by contrast, had only rarely needed to break and enter, and so the skill was all too rusty. It took him three uncomfortable minutes to persuade the door to let him in.

The scent of old cigar smoke assailed him immediately— dark and pungent, a rancid smell that had seeped into the curtains, into the walls. It was an old smell, as if nobody had smoked in the room in months. Edward found the matches, lit an oil lamp on the desk, and turned the screw until a dull glow illuminated the desk. There were stacks and stacks of papers to go through. If Patrick was right, the proof would be here.

Proof was one of the two reasons he'd come.

The file he was looking for turned out to be hidden in the leftmost drawer, underneath a sheaf of mortgages. Edward untied the twine wrapped around the papers and sorted through a mess of little notes and tantalizing bits of correspondence. But the series of newspaper clippings particularly caught his eye.

The first was just over six months old.

Ask a Man, he read. *The inaugural release of a column of weekly advice by Stephen Shaughnessy.*

So. Patrick had the right of it. Someone here *was* paying attention to Stephen. His friend had mentioned that Stephen wrote for a paper, but Edward hadn't realized he had a regular column—and a column of advice, at that.

Frankly, the thought of taking advice from the twelve-year-old he'd once known sounded rather horrifying. But even Stephen must have matured somewhat in the intervening years.

There was a note of explanation before the column started.

It has come to the attention of the editorial staff that our newspaper, with its determination to be "by women, about women, and for women," cannot possibly impress anyone as we lack the imprimatur of a man to validate our thoughts. To that end, we have procured an Actual Man to answer questions. Please address all inquiries to Man, care of Women's Free Press, *Cambridge, Cambridgeshire. —F.M.*

It took Edward a moment to check the head of the paper. Indeed. *Women's Free Press,* it read. That was the name of the business on the card he'd received that morning. *F.M.* was almost certainly Frederica Marshall, the spitfire he'd met on the banks of the Thames. It made sudden sense of her behavior. She was Stephen's *employer.* There was no reason that should make Edward feel glad; he was unlikely to ever see her again, and even if he did, he'd no intention of entangling himself in any sense. A kiss, a cuddle, a quick farewell—that's all a man like him ever hoped for.

Still.

He shook his head and read on.

Dear Man, someone had written. *I have heard that women are capable of rational thought. Is this true? What is your opinion on the matter?*

Breathlessly awaiting your manly thoughts,

A woman

Edward tilted his head and shifted the paper so that the answer lay in the dim circle of lamplight.

Dear Woman,
If I were a woman, I would have to cite examples of rational thought on the part of women, which would be awfully tiresome. Once we got through the example of the ancient Greeks, matriarchal rulers in China, Africa, and our own country, once we passed from Aglaonike the astronomer, to Cleopatra the alchemist, and on through our very modern Countess of Chromosome, we'd scarcely have time to talk about how great men are. That simply won't do.
Luckily, I am a man, so my mere proclamation is sufficient. Women can think. This is true because a man has said it.
Yours,
Stephen Shaughnessy
Certified Man

God. Edward stifled laughter. Stephen hadn't changed one bit. It had been years since he'd seen him, but Edward could still hear his voice, irrepressible as ever, always arguing, always *winning*, pushing everyone to the very brink of rage and then defusing the anger he'd aroused with a joke.

It was good to know that Edward's father hadn't managed to completely crush his spirit.

It was even more interesting that Miss Marshall had chosen to print this particular column.

He flipped to the next clipping, dated one week later.

Dear Man,
Is this column a joke? I cannot honestly tell.
Signed,
Another Man
Dear Other Man,
Why would you think my column a joke? A paper written by women, for women, and about women obviously needs a man to speak

*on its behalf. If it is a joke for men to speak on behalf of women, then
our country, our laws, and our customs must all be jokes, too.*

Surely you are not so unpatriotic as to suggest that, sir.
Yours in one-hundred-percent-certified seriousness,
Stephen Shaughnessy
Verified Man

Ah, he was going to enjoy reading these. Edward flipped
to the next page. This would be an excellent way to pass the
time while he waited.

Dear Man—

The door to the room opened. Edward's pulse leapt—
this was, after all, the second reason he had paid this visit—
but he did not move. He sat in the chair that had once
belonged to his father and waited.

"What is this?" The man in the doorway was just a
silhouette, but his voice was achingly familiar. "How did you
get in?"

Edward didn't say anything. Instead he turned up the
lamp, letting the light flood the room.

The other man simply frowned. "Who the devil are
you?"

For a moment, Edward was taken by surprise. He'd been
gone more than nine years, and he'd been thought dead for
the last seven. But he had always assumed that his own brother
would at least *recognize* him. They'd had their differences, more
than most brothers did. The years that passed had severed any
sickly bond that might have subsisted between them, leaving
them to wobble away on their own separate paths. But until
this moment, Edward hadn't realized how physical those
differences had become.

Once, they'd looked much alike. James Delacey had
been a shorter, younger version of himself. James's hair was
still dark and glossy and his face was soft and smooth. By
contrast, Edward's once-dark hair was shot through with
strands of white. His hands were all calluses; he suspected that
the only skin on his brother's hand that wasn't soft was a little
rough mark from holding a pen.

And then there was the fact that Edward had spent his last years at manual labor and had gained the shoulders to match.

James wore sober black. He was in mourning, Edward realized with surprise. Odd. Edward's father had been lost to him years ago. For James, it had only been nine months.

"The last time I saw you," Edward said gravely, "was on the London docks. You told me that it was for the best that I left and that you'd keep Wolf exercised until I changed my mind and was allowed back."

Silence met this proclamation.

"Well?" Edward leaned back in the chair, affecting laziness. "It's been almost a decade since then. How is my horse, James?"

James set his hand against the doorway as if to hold himself upright. "Ned?" His voice shook. "My God, Ned. I must be dreaming this. You're not here."

Edward grimaced. "How many times have I told you? I prefer Edward. For God's sake, James, come in and shut the door."

After a moment's hesitation, James did just that. Of course he wouldn't call the servants. Not now, not with a handful of months remaining. It had been six years and some eight months since last he'd written to his family. At the seven-year mark, James would officially inherit everything. He probably had the date marked with stars and rainbows on his calendar.

"Ned." James stumbled forward, fell into a chair. He was shaking his head in confusion. "My God. You're *dead*. We had a ceremony." He looked up, his eyes dark with some unspoken emotion. "We sold your horse. I'm sorry."

Of all the things his brother had to apologize for, selling an unused stallion seemed the most foolish.

James frowned. "We put up a monument, too, at some bloody expense. If you were going to turn up alive, could you not have done so in a respectable time?"

Edward could not help but smile. Yes, he had heard that correctly. His brother had just complained to him about the expense associated with his death.

"I just visited my grave," Edward assured him. "The monument is lovely. I'm sure it was worth every penny."

"What have you been doing with yourself? Why haven't you said anything? By God, if you'd only known how I have suffered these last years. I've been telling myself that I sentenced you to death."

Edward's hands twitched. How *James* had suffered? His brother sat across from him, whole and hearty. His suffering had involved neither missing meals nor cowering under military bombardments. He'd not been kept in a basement, hadn't had everything taken from him in one long, unending nightmare. He was sleek and handsome, a version of Edward who hadn't walked through hell.

"I'm sorry," Edward said dryly, "for any discomfort I caused you."

"Yes." James frowned. "And it's not over yet, is it? This is damned inconvenient."

Personally, Edward would have found it more inconvenient to be dead. But he could hardly begrudge his younger brother his point of view. "Do say why."

"This will be the most immense scandal." James looked at the desk, drew a deep breath. "You'll want the title, then. That's why you've come." His hands clenched in his lap, as if he were preparing himself for a fight.

Ah, yes. Another thing James had that Edward lacked: the illusion that this family had some semblance of honor. Edward could remember believing that. Barely.

"If I had wanted to be Claridge," Edward said, "I'd have returned the day I heard of Father's death. No, James. Keep the title. It's yours."

James frowned, as if he could not believe his ears. No doubt he couldn't conceive of a world in which a man walked away from a viscountcy. "Speaking of the city, how did you ever survive?"

There were a great many things his brother might have meant by that question. *How did you get on after Father left you stranded?* Or, perhaps: *Did you by any chance go to the British Consul before the siege started?*

How had he survived? He'd survived any way he could.

But he simply smiled at his brother. "I survived by luck," Edward told him. "When I had it."

James's eyes widened. "Was it bad?"

"No," Edward lied. "But only because I learned to be worse in response. Trust me, James. I'm no longer fit company. I know who Viscount Claridge is supposed to be. I had enough lectures on the meaning of our family honor to recall that. I can't be him."

He'd had enough of people making him into someone else, and the boy who had grown up in this house might as well stay dead, for all the use he'd been.

"You, on the other hand," he finished smoothly, "can. You will."

James blinked, taken aback, but seemed to take this as simple truth. He seemed, even, to think that Edward had given him a compliment. He nodded, looking faintly relieved to discover that his entire world was not going to be upended.

God, James was so simple to read. Relief was evident first in the slump of his shoulders. That was followed by an intake of breath and a narrowing of his eyes. He looked at Edward in sudden suspicion. He was no doubt wondering why his brother had returned from the dead after all these years if not to claim the title. Soon enough, James would realize this was a negotiation, not a reunion.

"You need an allowance, then." James sounded resigned.

"God, no." Ongoing blackmail was never his preference. There were too many opportunities to get caught. Edward thought of the file underneath his fingertips. "There's only one thing I want from you."

James leaned forward. "Well?"

Edward flattened his hand on the newspaper clippings. "You're going to leave off whatever it is you're plotting to do to Stephen Shaughnessy."

James let out a long, slow breath. He reached up and rubbed his forehead. "I see."

"Your word that you won't hurt him, directly or indirectly. That's all I want; give me that, and I'll let you live out your life in peace."

"I see," James repeated more sharply. "It was his fault you were sent away in the first place, or have you forgotten? But that's how it is. You've been alive these last seven years. In all that time, you've sent not one note to your own brother, not one *word* indicating that you were alive. But I can see you've spoken with Shaughnessy. Regularly enough to know that his little brother has landed himself in water too hot for his taste. That does rather clarify matters."

"You left me to die," Edward heard himself snap out. "You can hardly complain because I chose to gratify your desires."

James paled. "I didn't," he said too swiftly. "You must know I didn't. What I told the British Consul… It was true, in a sense."

A sense. When the declaration of war had come, Edward had written to his father, asking for the means to return to England. It had been a blow when his father refused. He'd said that if Edward didn't believe in the family honor, he needn't rely on the family's help.

But it was James who had taken matters two steps further. When Edward had arrived at the British Consulate in Strasbourg two steps ahead of the advancing army, the consular secretary had declared him an impostor. The secretary had received a letter to that effect, after all—a letter signed by James himself. Edward had been called a liar and a profiteer and he'd been tossed out on his ear.

With that had vanished Edward's last hope of financial assistance or a pass of safe-conduct.

Old news, now. They'd both been little more than boys when that happened. Edward steepled his fingers. "What you told the British Consul," he repeated calmly. "It was true. In a sense." He didn't make the words a question. He didn't need to.

"It was just that you were singularly unrepentant, Ned, and—"

"I prefer *Edward.*"

James swallowed. "Yes. Edward. I didn't think... That is, it was for your own good, and..." He seemed to realize that this was not a fruitful line of argument. He shook his head, as if he could shake off what had happened to his brother with so simple a motion. "You're not dead after all. So..." He let out a long breath. "All's well that ends well, eh?"

Too bad for James that Edward was not the sort to be won over with meaningless platitudes.

"I agree," he said smoothly. "All's well that ends well. These are old events, and you and I find ourselves in agreement after all these years. It's in everyone's best interests that I remain dead. Yours. Mine."

He smiled and waited for that threat to sink in. His brother shifted uneasily on the seat across from him.

"So once again, I ask you: Will you leave off plotting against Stephen Shaughnessy?"

James let out a long, shaky breath. "It's not that simple. I have a place in this world. If I am going to be Viscount Claridge for the rest of my life, I'll need to maintain a certain reputation." He pressed his lips together. "It's like with dogs. If you don't give them a good slap on the head from time to time, they'll never think you're in charge."

"Are we still talking about Stephen Shaughnessy? He's a boy with a silly column, not a dog."

"Yes," James said flatly. "He's completely unimportant on his own. But you asked me not to hurt him *indirectly* either, and I can't do that unless I let Miss Marshall and her damned paper alone."

Edward inhaled and thought of the card in his pocket. But he didn't let his brother see that his interest was piqued. He managed a dubious frown instead. "Who is Miss Marshall? Am I supposed to care about her?"

James's lips thinned. "She is the prime example of everything that is wrong with England. Writing those damned reports, getting the women all heated up, forcing Parliament to spend valuable time on irrelevant matters. Do you know how much *time* was wasted on the inquiry she forced regarding the government lock hospitals?" His brother made a disgusted noise. "Decades ago, a pretty girl with pleasant conversation, a mild competence, and a taste for independence would have set herself up in London as some man's mistress. Look at her now." There was an angry edge to James's voice. "Beholden to no man, putting her nose in where it's not needed, setting wife against husband, servant against master. Most of these women, well…" He shrugged. "They're relatively harmless. Let them natter on; it gives them something to occupy their time. But Marshall? She's real trouble."

It was interesting to know his brother so well and yet not know him at all. Edward could still tell when James protested too much. "When did you ask her to be your mistress?"

His brother flushed crimson. "It was a generous offer! The best that someone of her breeding could expect. And she turned me down without any consideration for my feelings. In any event, that's years in the past—hardly relevant now—and I wouldn't have her at this point, not if she begged me."

Strange that he and James had that much in common. It might have been the only thing. Miss Marshall was precisely his sort, too.

"I understand," Edward said mildly. "She sounds a right terror."

James wouldn't know that he intended that as a compliment.

Indeed, his brother nodded in relief. "This thing with Miss Marshall… Well, we're months into the planning. Father started it. It was one of his grand plans—you should see what she wrote about him. I can't see it left undone." He frowned. "If you'd like me to leave Stephen alone, you could convince him to separate himself from Miss Marshall."

"I could." Edward pretended to consider this. "That might be an acceptable compromise."

But then he would have to talk to Stephen directly. He'd have to reveal the truth of his continued existence, and that was far too dangerous. The more people who knew of him, the greater the likelihood that someone would tell. And once the secret was out, Edward would be forced to come forward. It was one thing to abandon the viscountcy to his brother, who would see to the estates. It was another entirely to leave the properties uncared for. Even Edward was not so vile a scoundrel as to accept that. If the truth came out, he'd have no choice but to take James's place here. He'd spend the rest of his days in this cloying, smelly room, suffocated by his father's title.

Besides, knowing Stephen, a simple confrontation wouldn't do any good; the boy he'd known would never leave a friend—or an employer—in the lurch simply because he was threatened.

And more importantly… Asking Stephen to run away went very much against Edward's grain.

Edward could threaten his brother with ease. But helping him to achieve his goals? After what James had done? No. Everything in Edward revolted at that.

He scarcely knew Miss Marshall. She had struck him as naïve and optimistic. She was not the sort of ally he would normally seek out; he generally preferred to work with more cynical types.

But—not entirely irrelevantly—he'd liked her. He couldn't say the same for James.

"There are a few small things already in motion," his brother said airily, "but they're of little consequence, and I'll try to make sure they don't hurt Stephen more than they must. Will that do?"

"Is that port over there?" Edward motioned to the other side of the room.

His brother turned away. "Why—no. It's brandy."

"Just as good. Pour us a glass, then, and we'll drink to our accord."

His brother crossed the room, a pleased smile on his face. No doubt he thought the whole thing had been worked out.

While James's back was turned, Edward rolled the contents of the thick file he'd been perusing before James came in—newspaper clippings, letters, and all—into a bundle and stashed it inside his coat. He'd go through it all and slip it back in place by morning. James would never know.

All things being equal, Edward would rather not betray his little brother. Even after what James had done. But then, life was a series of hard choices. He could walk away from England and leave his best friend's younger brother to the mercy of his family's plan. Or he could make Miss Marshall's better acquaintance and upset the whole thing.

He could see her in his mind's eye for a moment—that all too delightful smile on her face. *Call on me if you ever find yourself in need of an exclamation point.*

No exclamation points.

But then, he'd never needed punctuation to get his revenge. He'd found lies and forgery to be much more effective tools.

Hell, he'd be doing Miss Marshall a favor. She didn't need to know any of the details—and maybe, if he was lucky, he'd get that cuddle after all.

Chapter Three

Cambridge, a few days later

"ONCE IS COINCIDENCE. Twice is suspicious. Three times?" Frederica Marshall tapped her pen viciously against the pages of newsprint in front of her. "Three times demands an explanation. Well, my dears?"

Two women sat beside her, examining the pages for themselves. The room was warm—almost overly so—but they were all used to that by now. Lady Amanda Ellisford, one of Free's dearest friends, sat on her right, frowning, her eyes darting back and forth between the two columns. Mrs. Alice Halifax, Free's cousin, sat on the other side. Alice's lips moved slightly; she took longer to read the words. Rather unsurprising as she'd only learned to read three years ago. But her face darkened as she did.

"It's like looking at two gowns made from the same pattern," Alice said. "Different cloth, different seamstress. But it's still a copy."

The headline of the article Free had written was "Why Women Should Vote." The headline of the article opposite was "Why Women Shouldn't Vote."

Same number of paragraphs. Same arguments addressed in each paragraph—raised in hers, discarded in the opinion piece printed in the *London Star*. But the piece in the *Star* had been printed nine hours before Free's newspaper had gone to press.

"Someone is going to notice," Amanda said quietly. She chewed her lip nervously, and then sighed. "More than one someone. Once they do notice, they'll talk."

Well might Amanda be nervous. This was the third time that something like this had happened in the last month. The first, Free had dismissed as coincidence. The second had left her suspicious. But this? This looked like confirmation.

"I know just what they'll say," Alice said. "They'll say women are capable of only aping men, that we do nothing but take the words that men write and put 'not' in front of them. They say it enough as it is."

They'd say it in public this time though, with something that looked like proof. Free would get another spate of angry, accusing letters. Some of them would no doubt be ugly indeed. She shook her head, dispelling that thought. Ugly letters were inevitable. They came no matter what she did; they were the price for accomplishing anything. There was no point worrying about them.

"We need to figure out how this is happening. Three different papers echoing words that I've written, printing counterpoints to my pieces before we've even gone to press." Free shook her head. "If it's not a coincidence, it's a deliberate attack. And if it's a deliberate attack, someone has access to what I've written."

"It could be someone going through our rubbish," Amanda said. "Finding your drafts—that would do it."

It would.

"Could be one of the staff," Alice suggested.

"It could be anyone who comes through the building." Amanda looked down. "Or anyone who gets one of our advance proofs. None of us have made an attempt to hide our work."

No, they hadn't. Free sighed and put her head in her hands, rubbing at her aching temples. Why *should* she have acted so mistrustfully? She didn't want to suspect the women who worked with her, didn't want to turn the friendly business that she had painstakingly built into a place of wariness and disbelief. It was hard work, making a place where women felt safe enough to trust one another. This sort of black suspicion could ruin everything they had accomplished.

No doubt that was why someone had done it.

"We'll need stricter rules," Amanda was saying. "Keep your drafts locked up, Free. No more circulating of the opinion pieces for wide comment among the women."

"Make a list of people who might be responsible," Alice said. "And we'll think about how to determine who's at fault. Once we know that, we can decide how to proceed."

The door behind them opened, and a gust of wind entered the room. Free set her hand on the papers, holding them in place. The incoming air was fresh and sweet; they'd printed proofs that morning, and the steam engine had warmed the room enough that the breeze was welcome.

She recognized the man standing in the doorway. She'd spoken with him at the race the other day. He was tall, his hair salt-and-pepper, his eyes dark, moving about the room before coming to rest on her. Hard to judge his age; by his hair, she might have guessed as high as forty. But he hadn't spoken like a man in the middle of his years. And he had a handsome bravado that would better fit a younger man.

He looked around the room with an air of interest, glancing from the tables in the front, where Free and her chief editors stood, to the troughs on the side of the room where they wet the paper, from the drums of press ink to the dark metal of the silent rotary press. One eyebrow rose, ever so slowly, in question.

Free straightened and came forward, holding out her hand. Not palm down, like a lady angling for a dance, but as a gentleman would under similar circumstances. Would he try to wring her bones to dust, to demonstrate his strength? Would he take her hand as if they were about to dance together? It was a test of sorts.

This man didn't hesitate at all. He took her hand in his and gave it a firm pump.

"Mr. Edward Clark," he told her.

She tried not to raise her eyebrows. *Edward Clark* was a solidly English name; his speech, while perfectly fluent, was tinged with the mildest hint of a French accent. She'd assumed he'd been born in France, but had lived in England long enough to lose all but the slightest hint of his native tongue. Maybe that was wrong.

"Miss Frederica Marshall," she responded, although if he'd found his way to her place of business, he likely knew that already. "Can I help you?"

His gaze traveled to the table behind her. They'd been poring over the inner page of the newspaper; the printer's plates sat on the table next to the proofs for anyone to see.

Amanda was right. Their next issue of the paper was hardly shrouded in secrecy. Anyone really could walk in and see it. But Mr. Clark didn't remark on the paper. Instead, his mouth quirked up at the corner.

"You were being literal," he said, gesturing at the cart that stood beside the table. "You do have a box of exclamation points."

Now that he'd spoken a bit more, she found herself thinking him English. An Englishman who had lived in France awhile, perhaps?

She smiled. "Along with colons, semicolons, and commas. All the punctuation a girl can dream of. But let's start with the question mark. Surely you didn't come here to ogle my movable type. Is there some way I might be of service?"

He looked back at her. She had the feeling that he knew precisely what he was doing—that when his eyes twinkled at her so merrily, he knew exactly the effect it had deep in her stomach.

Free rather enjoyed the feeling. There was nothing wrong with a man who enjoyed a light flirtation, and Mr. Clark was no hardship to look at. So long as he understood that it would go no further, they'd get on famously.

But he simply said, "I have a business proposition to put to you."

She pursed her lips. "As a preliminary... This is a newspaper by women, for women, and about women. I'm unlikely to hire you to write a column."

"I don't write columns," he said. "I can do some creditable illustrations, but I would make a dreadful employee. It's not that sort of proposition. Is there somewhere we might discuss this in private?"

She gestured to the side of the room. "I have an office in here."

He followed her. Her office was nothing more than a converted storage room—one where she'd had a portion of the wall adjoining the main room knocked out and replaced with glass, so that she might be able to have privacy for business meetings precisely like this while still leaving her safely in her employees' view. He took in the surroundings—the old, chipped desk that she placed herself behind, the stack of grammatical texts and population reports on the bookshelf behind her. She realized, with a hint of chagrin, that a draft of yet another column—one that was scheduled to appear in three days' time—sat out in plain sight. She placed a stack of blank paper on top of it and sat behind her desk.

But he was looking through the window out to the floor of her business. "The lady in the light blue," he said in an idle tone, "I presume is Lady Amanda. And the woman with the pinched expression must be Mrs. Halifax."

"Should I have performed introductions?"

"No," he said. "I'm only making a point. I've done my research over the last few days. I know who you are." Those last words came out low, and his eyes cut back to her as he spoke. They had a startling effect on Free—as if he were making a declaration, one that made her feel just a little fluttery inside.

It had been so long since anyone had made her feel fluttery. It felt like winter sunshine—something to be savored because it surely wouldn't last. She hoped he didn't say something awful to ruin it.

"Consider your point made," she said with a nod. "You know who I am."

"And when I came in," he said, "the three of you were no doubt discussing the plot to discredit you. You've at least discovered what they're doing with your editorials, then. Good for you, Miss Marshall. You've made my work that much easier."

Free winced. "So you've noticed as well." If he—a random man off the street—had made the connection, others would, too. It would only be a matter of time until someone wrote about it. She would have to figure out a course of action, and she had no time to waste.

"Noticed it?" He shook his head. "No, Miss Marshall. I was apprised of it."

"So it's already being discussed in public." Damn it all. She didn't need more to do. "Well, thank you for letting me know. We've no acquaintance to speak of, and I appreciate the warning. Now, if you'll excuse me—" She began to rise.

"I won't excuse you." He gestured at her. "Sit down. This is not a matter of public discussion. My information comes directly from the man responsible for the copying."

She paused, halfway frozen between sitting and standing.

"Directly from him?" she repeated.

"Yes," he said. "I know many of his plans. He thinks I'm on his side. And it's a lucky thing that I'm not, because if I actually were, you'd have no advance notice of what is about to happen. And that would be very, very bad for you."

Free sank back into her chair.

"Shall we fetch your box of question marks?" he inquired. "It's quite simple. There is a man who wants to do you harm. He trusts me enough to disclose his plans. As I don't wish for him to do you harm, I offer you my help."

He had such a lovely smile, such a warm manner. It was really too bad that it was all a lie.

Free shook her head. "Your story does not inspire trust. You don't know me, and so I can't believe you care what happens to me. A tale of some shadowy man who wishes me harm is entirely plausible. Half of England wishes me harm. Yet you offer no proof except information that I have already discovered. You claim that this man trusts you, but you've just offered to betray that trust. That tells me you are not trustworthy. I don't know what you're about, Mr. Clark, but go about it elsewhere."

She expected that he would get a little angry in response. Men didn't like to be called liars, especially when they were lying.

But he simply smiled and leaned back in his chair. "Good. You're not as foolishly naïve as I'd originally supposed. That will make things a little easier. Let's start with the basics. You're right. I don't know you, and I don't give a damn what happens to you." He said that with a brilliant smile on his face, one so at odds with his words that she had to remind herself what he'd said. He'd said it charmingly, sweetly, seductively even: He didn't give a damn about her.

"That," Free said, "is very likely the first true thing you've told me. If I can see through the flimsy allure of your charisma, I suspect others can, too. Why would anyone trust you enough to divulge their secret plots?"

He leaned forward. "Ah, that's the thing, Miss Marshall. I come with sterling references."

She looked him over dubiously. His jacket was not firmly pressed; it had been a few too many hours since his last shave. His hair was disreputably long. Those things could be fixed by a maid and a razor, but nonetheless… "You've just offered to double-cross the men you're working with. What sort of references can you possibly have?"

"Well, that's the beauty of it. I can have any references I want. Shall I show you one of my best ones?"

"By all means. I doubt it will change my mind."

Instead of producing a letter from a pocket, he reached across her desk and filched a blank piece of paper from her stack. Then, before she could protest, he swiped her pen and inkwell.

"Let us see." He looked off into the distance, tapping one end of the pen against his lip. And then he began to write. "To whom it may concern: I have had the opportunity to work with Edward Clark for many years. He is honest, upright, and intelligent. He will serve you well in all things." He shrugged.

"Normally, of course, I would be more effusive and specific. Specificity is the trick to a good forgery. But in this instance, the substance of the reference is not the point. It's about the form." He signed the paper with a flourish and slid it across the table to her with an easy grace.

"I just saw you write this myself," she said. "Why would I believe…" And then she looked at the page. Really looked at it—at the letters before her, at the signature that he'd dashed off with such easy confidence. Her mouth went dry.

"Precisely the point," he said. "You shouldn't believe me. But perhaps, looking over this particular reference, you can understand why people rely on me."

If she hadn't seen him write it just now, she would have thought she had written it herself. That was her handwriting, her name. That precise carefree curve of the F, the casual loops of her last name… He'd captured them perfectly.

"I'm wanted by two governments for forgery," he said cheerfully. "Luckily for me, one of them no longer exists. And the other, in case you are wondering, is not part of the British Commonwealth. You would not be harboring a known fugitive."

"That may be so." She pushed the paper away from her. "Maybe you could convince someone else to trust you. But after that demonstration, I am rather less likely to trust you than the reverse."

"Excellent," he said cheerily. "I'm not a trustworthy man. I've lied to you a half-dozen times over the course of this conversation, and I'll no doubt do it again. For instance, the name I was born with is not Edward Clark—although I have used that name regularly for the last six years or so, and I think of it as mine now. By all means, Miss Marshall, don't trust me. But do work with me. On this, our interests are aligned. You don't want to be ruined, and I'd rather your enemy not ruin you either."

"Why? You don't give a damn about me."

His smile didn't slip, but it grew just a touch darker. "You're right," he said. "But as it turns out, my indifference to you is overbalanced by my dislike of him."

Or—equally likely—he'd been tasked with charming her, learning her plans.

"No, thank you." She smoothed her skirts over her lap and met his gaze directly. "I'll take my chances on my own. I do not need help from a self-professed liar who might betray me at any moment."

He sighed. "This would be far easier if you were less clever." It sounded like a complaint, but he winked at her at the end. "Damn it, Miss Marshall, I'm trying to be a little honorable. But very well. Since I must." He raised his eyes to her. "You need to work with me because I *will* betray you."

She sucked her breath in. "Pardon?"

"How precarious is your position in society, Miss Marshall? You're young, unmarried, and reasonably good-looking." He said the last with no emotion, as if he were just reciting facts.

He was. She had to remember that. No matter how flirtatious his tone, that was all she meant to him: a collection of facts.

"I have two possible plans to foil my enemy. One is to work with you to defeat him. The other is to shut down your operations here so thoroughly that he doesn't get the pleasure of doing it himself. A forged letter of credit sold to your enemy? A missive in your handwriting, written to a lover and indiscreetly left for someone else to find?" He shrugged. "It would take me half an afternoon to make your life utterly miserable and maybe a few days to make it impossible."

Her heart had begun to thud in a low, heavy rhythm. Strange, how the system of nerves could so overtake the mind, that a man sitting before her and speaking in such an easy tone could make her feel as if she were a hare faced by a pack of wolves. He looked at her with a small smile on his face. It seemed as if he could hear her pulse, and its thready beat was music to his ears.

She wasn't going to rabbit away. This was *her* business, her life, and she wasn't about to let this man ruin it for her. She steepled her fingers, willing them not to tremble, and gave her best impression of a bored sigh. "So this is blackmail."

The smile Mr. Clark gave her felt like a weapon—one that he'd chosen carefully from his massive arsenal. It was the smile of a man who knew that he could charm and devastate, and he employed it with the precision of a master. He leaned forward. "Miss Marshall, I believe you are mispronouncing that word."

She looked over at him.

"You should pronounce it like this: 'Huzzah! Blackmail!'"

Her eyebrows rose. "How extraordinary, Mr. Clark. I thought you didn't use exclamation points."

"I don't." He smiled at her. "But you do, and there's no need to be parsimonious."

"Huzzah." Free met his gaze with a flat stare. "Crime! Right now, that crime is blackmail, but it won't be blackmail much longer."

"No? How do you figure?"

"With luck and a good quantity of arsenic…?" She gave him a smile of her own. "Soon it will be: 'Huzzah! Murder!' Now there's a cause that deserves my exclamation points."

She'd meant to confound him. Instead, his smile tilted, and all that calculated charm disappeared in a wash of real laughter. He leaned back in his chair, shaking his head. Somehow, it was even more unnerving to realize that he found her amusing. And entirely unfair that some small part of her wanted to make him laugh again.

She raised an eyebrow and regulated her voice to honeyed sweetness. "Would you care for some tea, Mr. Clark? I'll prepare a pot of my very special recipe. Just for you."

He waved a hand at her. "Save it. You see, Miss Marshall, I don't wish to ruin the future you've so carefully built. I'm going to play the scoundrel here. All things considered, I'd rather be your scoundrel."

She sat back. "Go ahead, Mr. Clark. Do your worst. I am inured to baseless threats. I don't need your lies."

He leaned back in his chair, a look of dissatisfaction on his face.

Of *course* he was glaring at her. She huffed in annoyance. "Yes, I am a terrible person. I refuse to give in to intimidation. I don't need a scoundrel, thank you very much. Now good-bye."

"Yes," he said. "You do. Bugger it all." He shut his eyes and placed his fingers against his temples. "I was hoping not to have to do this, but…"

Free narrowed her gaze at him. They'd run through lies, forgery, and blackmail. What was next? Physical threats?

"I'm going to have to tell you the truth," he said with great reluctance. "Some of it. And I'm going to have to tell you enough to convince you I know what I'm doing."

She didn't believe that for one second.

"The person who is intent on destroying you is none other than the Honorable James Delacey."

Free went very still. Delacey was also Viscount Claridge—or at least, he would be soon; there was some technical holdup in confirming him, although she gathered it was a simple procedural matter. Other than actually taking his seat in the House of Lords, he was afforded all the other social privileges of peerage. She'd met the man two years ago. Their acquaintance had been fortunately brief, and she had no wish to pursue it further. She set her hands on the table, pushing them flat against the cool surface.

The man in front of her did not mark her unease. "I would say that Delacey has no love for suffragettes, but it's more complicated than that. His father never liked you; you shut down a factory that he'd invested in and lost him a great deal of money. And Delacey himself asked you to be his mistress some time ago, and you turned him down. He's held a grudge ever since."

If Clark knew *that*, he did stand high in the man's counsel. It didn't make him a friend; it didn't mean he planned to help her. But he at least knew *something*.

"Delacey plans to discredit you completely," he said. "He's going to have one of your writers arrested this weekend on suspicion of theft, and while you're still reeling from the scandal of that, he'll point out that several of your recent essays have been drawn from other papers. Your advertisers will withdraw and your subscription numbers will plummet." Mr. Clark gave her a brilliant smile. "As I'm sure you can see, you are at something of a disadvantage. You don't have to trust me, Miss Marshall. You don't even have to like me. But if you don't listen to me, you'll regret it."

"Why?" She speared him with her gaze. "Why are you doing this?"

He shrugged nonchalantly, but his fingers curled on the desk a little too tightly. "Because Delacey and I have an old score that needs to be settled." Mr. Clark's lips thinned and he looked out the window again, over her press. "It's that simple. Delacey wants you hurt, and I will not forgive him. So we have a mutual enemy. I don't pretend that we will be friends, you and I—but I came here to present myself as an ally. I didn't have to tell you that I was capable of blackmail. I didn't have to demonstrate my skill at forgery. If I had wanted to, I would have delivered you a recommendation from Queen Victoria herself. And—Miss Marshall—"

He leaned toward her, gesturing her close as if he wished to impart a great secret.

She couldn't help herself. She leaned in.

"You know," he said simply, "that if I'd wanted to be gentlemanly and agreeable, I could have charmed you. In an instant."

A wash of heat passed through her, a flush that was half embarrassment and half acknowledgment of the truth. A beat passed while his eyes held hers. Oh, he was good at that—at giving her just that hint of attraction. Not so much as to put her off; just enough to intrigue her.

Free refused to be intrigued. "You could have," she told him. "But charmed or not, I would still have been thinking."

"I'm dishonorable and disreputable. I lie and I cheat, and I am telling you plainly that you are only a means to an end for me. I'm not telling you the truth, but overall, I'm not playing you false. You may not know the exact cards I hold, but you will know the score. I promise you that much."

She didn't trust him or his promises—not an inch. And yet he was right. He might be a dishonest man, but he'd not pretended to be anything else. It was a curious sort of honor.

"I am not playing you false," he repeated. "Delacey is trying to ruin your reputation. Delacey intends to do far, far more, with lasting consequences. Tell me the truth, Miss Marshall. If you had the opportunity to beat Delacey, would you take it?"

She thought of her editorials, so painstakingly written—stolen from her, her heartfelt words twisted and butchered to serve causes that she hated. She thought of all the things that she'd heard Delacey say about her, coming to her on whispers and innuendo.

Every last ugly letter she'd received, every cowardly anonymous threat that she'd shoved in her rubbish bin, every sleepless night after he'd propositioned her.

She couldn't lay all those terrible letters at Delacey's door. But if he planned even a fraction of what Mr. Clark claimed, she wanted him held responsible.

He was trying to take what was hers. He was trying to beat her down, to make an example of her to all the women who looked to her and thought, "Well, *she* did it, so why can't I?"

And he'd singled her out because she'd said no.

"Do I want Delacey held responsible?" she heard herself say. "Yes. Yes, I do."

Mr. Clark nodded. "Then, Miss Marshall, you're in need of a scoundrel." He spread his hands, palms up. "And here I am."

⌘ ⌘ ⌘

EDWARD LOUNGED IN HIS SEAT, letting Miss Marshall contemplate him. She'd leaned forward an inch, her nose wrinkling. Those things should have signified unease, but paired with the clear, calm gray of her eyes, they gave him no idea what she was thinking.

He had thought she would be easy to read. Ha. He had thought she'd be easy to manipulate. Another ha. She'd not bent an inch. He'd been wrong on both counts, and as confounding as this conversation had become, at least these next few weeks would be exciting.

Miss Marshall, he silently admitted, hadn't needed to be any more exciting.

Her eyes focused on him unblinking. She tapped her lovely lips with a thumb. "What does Delacey have planned next?" she finally asked. "You said he was going to have one of my writers discredited. Which one?"

She hadn't agreed yet to work with him, he noted. He'd been furious when he went through his brother's notes and pieced together the extent of what James had planned. *A few things still in motion,* his brother had told him, with an airy wave of his hand. No doubt he thought those *few things* unimportant.

Miss Marshall leaned forward. "Amanda? Alice?" There was a ferocity in her tone, almost a growl at the back of her throat as if she were a mother wolf protecting her cubs.

"Not that I know of." Edward frowned. "He wants Stephen Shaughnessy."

She blinked and sat back. "Stephen? He writes one column a week. It's purely for amusement."

"Yes, but he's a man."

She snorted.

He tried again. "Shaughnessy is an excellent target because so many dislike him."

Her jaw squared. "Only idiots dislike him."

Protective and loyal, too. "Ah, but there are a great many idiots," Edward told her, "and he inspires so many of them. He writes a column making fun of men. He's Catholic. He's Irish. He doesn't know how to keep his mouth shut. You saw it yourself—matters are bad enough that his *own classmates* pelted him with dye."

Miss Marshall winced. "That was one of his classmates?"

"Yes. There are a great many who are primed to believe the worst of him. And Delacey knows him—his father was a servant on his family's estate. There's some sort of bad blood there. I'm sure if you asked Shaughnessy, he could explain the details."

She didn't nod. Instead, she set her chin even more mulishly. "So what is Delacey planning to do to him?"

"Tonight, someone is going to remove a family possession from another student's room and place it among Shaughnessy's belongings."

Her expression grew dark indeed. He smiled at her languidly, refusing to let her see the fury he still felt at that.

Having Stephen charged with theft, and likely removed from school, was what his brother had dismissed as *a few small things*, ones that need not concern either of them overly much.

Miss Marshall considered this. "What do you propose to do about it?"

"I'll follow the man in, take the item, hide it somewhere outside," Edward said. "I could do all that without you. But it would be best if Shaughnessy had an unassailable alibi for the evening. I trust you can make that happen."

"I can get him away," she said slowly.

"Excellent. Then we're in agreement."

She held out a quelling hand. "Not yet. I still don't trust you, Mr. Clark. For all I know, you're planning to arrange the particulars of this as soon as you've gained my compliance. And since you propose to go alone, there will be nobody to gainsay your word about what you discover. Convenient for you."

That sense of excitement returned, prickling Edward's palms. "What do you suggest instead?"

She gave him a brilliant smile. "You may remain as my guest here throughout the day. You'll be a guest who never leaves, who interacts with no one else. That way, I'll know you've not sent any messages arranging anything."

"That's a great deal to ask of a man who is offering to help you."

She glanced over at him. "But then, you're not offering to help me. You don't give a damn about me. You want *me* to help *you* achieve revenge. You'll surely put up with a little inconvenience for that, won't you?"

She hadn't missed a thing. Edward conceded this with a wave of his hand. "Continue on. I stay here all day. And then what will happen?"

"I'll accompany you to Shaughnessy's room this night," she said. "I'll search it. We'll see if that item is there together."

"And if it is, you'll trust me?"

She tapped the forged reference he'd left on her desk and smiled even more brilliantly. "If it's there, I won't turn you over to the authorities. It was good of you to demonstrate your skill with forgery so beautifully in front of me. You've even left me evidence. So if you're telling the truth about this, I suppose I'll let you go free. For now."

He absolutely *should* have been annoyed with her. Instead, he wanted to laugh—and to shake her hand and tell her that she played a jolly good game.

Come to think of it, he didn't precisely want to let go of her hand, once he'd given it a shake.

"Miss Marshall," he said, "are you blackmailing me with my attempt to blackmail you? Can I now threaten to go to the authorities and turn this convoluted double blackmail plot into triple blackmail?"

She leaned forward, gesturing him to come close with a finger. He set his hands on the desk and leaned in close. They were separated by twelve inches and an expanse of wood. She licked her lips, and he felt his mouth go dry. Oh, no. There was nothing boring about her. He was riveted, in fact.

She smiled at him, and then spoke in a low voice. "You said you'd done your research, Mr. Clark. You said you knew who I was. You obviously didn't look very hard. A woman doesn't run a newspaper and perform her own investigations without learning how to deal with scoundrels. You think you can push me around, that you can traipse in here and take charge. You can't. If you really want your revenge, you're going to have to work for it."

He tried to muster up a sense of annoyance. She was complicating everything. She watched with an expression that struck him as halfway between severe and impish. But—alas—he couldn't come up with even a trace of exasperation.

It was going to be downright *fun* working with her.

So instead of agreeing, he picked up her pen again and pulled the letter he'd forged back from her.

"Postscript," he narrated aloud as he wrote. "Don't let Edward Clark's patent humility fool you. He is maddeningly brilliant. Beware. It will creep up on you over time." He passed the letter back to her. "There. That makes it rather better, don't you think?"

She perused the line he'd added with a dubious raising of her eyebrows. "Not particularly, no."

"Should I have underlined *maddeningly?*" he asked. "Or *brilliant?* I ask because if you're going to have me up for forgery, I want to make sure you have a perfect specimen to present to the court. A man has his pride."

"Underline neither," she said calmly. "I'll let you know when you've earned my italics. For now, you may only lay claim to regular type and full stops."

He couldn't outblackmail her, outthink her, or outcharm her. He couldn't even outbrazen her.

"Tell me, Miss Marshall," he said. "Do you ever bend to anyone?"

She shook her head. "Only if it will get me what I want. I'm a very determined woman."

He could believe it now. He'd been misled by her idealism, her smile. A man might see her trim form seated at her desk, her fingers slightly stained with ink, poised above the letter he'd written, and see only a small, lovely woman. He might see that and completely miss the steel in her character.

Edward wouldn't make that mistake again. A hint of a smile touched her lips as she looked down. She was maddeningly…everything. This entire endeavor had tilted, and now, like a cart on a hill without a driver, it was careening away. He didn't know when the crash would come, but he wasn't about to jump off.

This was so terribly bad that it had actually come full circle round to something…enticingly good.

"Well, then." He stood. "Lead on, Miss Marshall. If you're to keep me under lock and key, I suppose you must let me know where I will be staying."

Chapter Four

Miss Marshall put Edward in something she called the archive room. In actuality, it was little better than a dusty closet. A single high slit of a window allowed barely enough daylight through to illuminate a chair, a spindly desk, and a mass of cabinets.

"Mr. Clark is considering advertising with us," she told the other women in the main room. "He wants to look through the archives of the paper."

Which, actually, was not a bad idea. He thought he'd done the necessary research, but he'd had only the vaguest notion of what Miss Marshall was like when he arrived here—and that had been gleaned from five minutes in her company and the combination of notes in his brother's file. The reality of her had smashed all his dimly held expectations to bits.

He started reading her paper from the first issue.

It took only four issues for Miss Marshall's thrice-weekly paper to leave him properly terrified. She'd had herself committed to a government-operated lock hospital—one of those dreadful institutions established for the protection of the Royal Navy, where they held prostitutes suspected of carrying venereal diseases. Miss Marshall had stayed for twenty-six days. She'd been examined, mistreated, starved, and frozen. When she'd finally been sprung by her brother, she'd written a scathing report on the conditions inside.

Nobody had been willing to print it, so she'd started her own newspaper.

Her report on the mistreatment of suspected prostitutes gave her material for her first week in operation. In subsequent weeks, she'd taken work in a cotton factory. She'd worked as a maid in the home of a peer rumored to despoil the virtue of his servants. She'd interviewed courtesans and prostitutes on the one hand, and the great dames of society on the other. She wrote about all these things in plain, simple, damning language.

Over the years, she'd added on writers, a second page to her paper. Her newspaper featured pieces from female thinkers like Emily Davies and Josephine Butler. Advertisements had bloomed. The columns covered everything from mundane advice on how to grow a few extra vegetables in a tenement to biting criticism of the newly-established colony on the Gold Coast. And it was all written by—and about—women. Stephen Shaughnessy's acerbic column on Wednesdays was matched against a woman by the name of Sophronia Speakwell, who gave equally biting advice on Saturday.

No wonder his brother was targeting Miss Marshall.

And no wonder Edward had failed to convince her. He'd huffed internally when she'd called him a womanthrope—but he'd underestimated her so badly that he had to wonder if he *was* the sort of person who couldn't give a woman her due simply because of her sex.

A mistake he needed to correct instantly, if he was to deal with her at all.

Hell, he'd threatened to ruin her reputation as if she were a fussy, prim little debutante. No wonder she hadn't blinked. It had been rather like waving a butter knife at an accomplished swordsman.

The door to the little room was open; he could see her flitting about as the day progressed. She and the other women spent much of the afternoon laying out type, sending a few sheets through the machine, and then poring over the resultant copy. He could hear them arguing over antecedents, a friendly little squabble. Miss Marshall left shortly thereafter.

Instead of turning back to the archives, Edward opened his small sketchbook. Other men kept journals; Edward kept drawings. There was something about reducing an experience to a sketch or two that engaged his memory of details.

He tried to recall her office as best as he could. He could envision every last scratch on her desk, could remember the exact stack of papers, the position of the inkwell and pen. These things he penciled with swift, sure lines.

But when he tried to draw Miss Marshall, his memory was not so good. She'd had her auburn hair up in a simple bun; she'd worn a plain gown of dark gray with black cuffs. But none of the lines he put on paper seemed to capture her. He was leaving something out—something vital. He didn't know what it was.

At three in the afternoon, she returned. He shut his notebook, picked up another newspaper—he was nine months in, now—and pretended to be absorbed in it.

She came to his door. She was carrying a paper sack, which she held up.

"Sandwich, Mr. Clark?"

He set the newspaper down. "And you're feeding me, too? Why, Miss Marshall. I could almost imagine that you care."

"I have an older brother." She came into the room. "He complains bitterly if he misses a meal. I've no desire to hear you whine all evening."

He snorted. "I don't whine. Ever."

"Well, we can be sure you won't now." She handed him the sack. "There's water and soap up front, if you care to…" She stopped and frowned. "You never removed your gloves. I should have warned you. It's easier to wash ink off hands than fabric."

"Really?" He looked at her. "Miss Marshall, I have seen your hands. Do you ever get all the ink off?"

She smiled proudly at him. "No. I'm marked for life."

"I thought as much."

"We have a paper that needs to be on the 4 a.m. mail train. If you'll excuse me." She gave him a nod in acknowledgment and then ducked away.

He flipped his notebook open again. The sketch was definitely missing... *something*. There must be some trick of the light or expression that had failed him. His drawing of her seemed pallid and insubstantial in comparison with the reality of Miss Marshall in the flesh. He'd underestimated her once; it would be poor tactics to do it a second time.

He was trying to figure out what was missing, when the main door to the business opened and a man walked in.

Edward's attention was instantly riveted. He kept his gaze firmly on his notebook, but he could not help but watch out of the periphery of his vision. The man who went up to Miss Marshall was taller now than Edward remembered. Those muscles he'd developed rowing were new. But it was, without a doubt, Stephen Shaughnessy. Edward could hear the tone of his speech from here. His voice had deepened, but it had that same lilting sound to it, that touch of Irish, a hint of his mother's accent softened by a life lived in England. It brought back a rush of unwelcome emotion.

Little Stephen. Annoying Stephen. *The clod,* he and Patrick had called him, when he was particularly amusing and they'd not wanted to admit it. He hadn't become any *less* clod-like if his columns proved anything.

Calling the other man names didn't change a thing. Edward still yearned. He didn't even know what he was yearning for. He'd told himself a million times after he was thrown out of the consulate that he didn't have a brother, that he didn't have a family.

The sight of Stephen put the lie to that. Edward had a little brother after all—maybe not one who was related to him by blood, but a brother nonetheless.

Stephen bent his head to Miss Marshall. They stood close together, Miss Marshall barely coming up to Stephen's chin. She tilted her head and pointed a finger at him, and slowly, Stephen raised his hands in surrender. He said something; she laughed.

Edward looked down and turned the page in his notebook. Every one of Stephen's features was burned in his mind—that sharp nose, those mischievous eyes, the tilt of his smile. He could almost see him reduced to pencil marks on the blank page before him.

He wouldn't sketch him. He sketched to remember, and this was hard enough as it was.

Get on with you, he thought. *Go away. Be safe. I'm dead, but I won't let my family hurt you again.*

But he didn't look up at Stephen as he thought that. Instead, Edward shook his head, took out the newspaper, and went back to reading.

⌘　⌘　⌘

STEPHEN HAD A ROOM on a building that backed onto the River Cam.

From the bank of the river, huddled in a bush along a pedestrian footpath, an opera glass in hand, Free could see inside. Mr. Clark had posed no objection to sitting in the leaves and twigs with her.

She could make no sense of him. He'd lied to her—and he'd cheerfully admitted as much with a smile. He'd tried to blackmail her—but had shrugged complacently when she'd refused to be blackmailed. He was no doubt an utter scoundrel, but he was the best-natured scoundrel she'd ever had call to work with.

"Did you go to Cambridge?" she asked him.

He gave her an incredulous look. "What do you take me for? One of those prancing dandies arguing over Latin clauses?" He shrugged. "If you're going to hold the glasses, keep your eyes on the room. We don't want to miss anything."

He didn't try to take the glasses from her, though. Free sighed and trained them on Stephen's room. He'd left a lamp lit, but it was still dark enough that she could miss something if she didn't pay attention.

"You've been *somewhere*," she said. "Somewhere before you lived in France is my guess. Harrow, perhaps? You have that hint of something to your speech."

He snorted and looked away. "Eton."

She snorted right back at him. "My brother went to Eton. I'd recognize *that*. You're lying to me."

"Of course I am. We're reluctant partners, Miss Marshall, not friends swapping childhood stories." Another man might have snapped out those words. He said them with a trace of humor, as if it were a great joke that they were forced to be in each other's company.

"Ah. Shall we sit in stony silence, then?"

"No," he said. "I'm perfectly happy to have you entertain me, if you prefer. Tell me, what was the result of the Hammersmith-Choworth match that took place this morning? I was rather isolated this afternoon and hadn't the chance to find out."

Free let the glasses fall and turned to him. "We're reluctant partners, Mr. Clark," she mimicked. "I'm not your secretary to relay the news to you."

He shrugged. "How like a woman. You don't know. Do you think pugilism is too violent, that it's beneath you?"

Free burst into laughter. "Oh, no. If you think you can set me off with a poorly placed 'how like a woman', you're much mistaken. It's terribly unoriginal. Everyone does it. I had thought better of you than that."

There was a short pause. Then he shook his head ruefully. "You're right. That was a dreadful cliché. Next time I attempt to provoke you to respond, I'll do better."

Free took pity on him. She raised the glasses once more and trained them on the lighted window. "Choworth fell after twelve rounds to Hammersmith."

"Hammersmith won! You're making that up. Did he manage to outdodge him, then? I know Hammersmith is faster, but Choworth has the punch. And the strength! I've seen him—"

"Careful, Mr. Clark." Free smiled. "You're using exclamation points."

There was a pause. "So I am." He sighed. "Do you know, boxing is the only thing I missed about England? I'd track down English papers just so I could find the results of my favorites. I was mad about fighting as a boy. I think it's the only thing that hasn't changed."

"Choworth apparently landed a few cuts to the right in the ninth round," Free said after a pause. "Hammersmith was down; he struggled to his feet, but the account in the afternoon *Times* said the onlookers thought he was done for."

He tilted his head at her. "Do you know that because you read all your rival papers as a matter of course, or because you actually follow the sport?"

"My father used to take me to matches when I was a child." Free smiled. "We still go together. Take from that what you will."

"Hmm." Mr. Clark snorted. "Unfair."

Before she could ask what he meant by that though, the door to Stephen's room opened. Free waved him to silence and focused her glasses on the window. A man was slipping inside. He wore a dark, knit cap pulled low over his head.

"There's someone there," she told Mr. Clark.

"Damn."

She had wondered if all his good humor was a deception—if, perhaps, he hated her and was just extremely good at hiding it.

That one syllable convinced her otherwise. There was a quiet fury in it. Beside her, he tensed, his eyes glittering.

"Damn," he repeated. "I was hoping—*really* hoping—that he'd call it off."

This, too, might be an act. This was, after all, the man who had dashed off a brazen forgery in front of her without blinking an eye.

Free kept her gaze trained on the man in Stephen's room. The fellow stopped in front of Stephen's dresser, turned toward his desk, and then, after another pause, slipped out the door once again.

She stood. "Let's go."

They scrambled down the path over the bridge. He didn't try to outrun her—even though it would have been an easy prospect with her in heavy skirts and a corset. He kept pace with her instead, jogging easily at her side. When they came to the outer wall of the dormitory, he paused.

"If I give you a lift, can you get up to his window?"

She didn't even hesitate. "Of course."

Before she could ready herself, he took hold of her by the waist and swung her up. She had only the briefest sensation of his strength, the power of his muscles, before her fingertips caught the edge of Stephen's windowsill. She scrabbled for a firm hold; his grip on her shifted, sliding down. One hand came under her foot as support. Then he boosted her up, and she pulled herself into Stephen's room.

"Do you need me to help you up?" she whispered out the window.

"You're too precious," came the reply. And so saying, he swung himself up, finding a foothold here, a handhold there. Before she knew it, he was hauling himself over the sill of the window, scarcely out of breath.

Her eyes widened.

"I can tell you're not a gentleman," she said as he pulled himself into the room. "You're far too strong."

"Ah, you noticed." He straightened, brushing his hands off, and gave her a wicked smile. "I've done some metalwork. But we can talk about how attractive my muscles are at some time when we are *not* illicitly entering a building."

From another man, that casual boast would have been downright disturbing. But Mr. Clark didn't leer or wink. He didn't waggle his brows to make sure she'd understood his lewd implications. He simply turned away and studied the room as if he hadn't been outrageous at all. As if he'd spoken the simple truth.

And maybe he had.

Free covered her mouth to keep from laughing.

"You'd better search," he said. "That way, you can be sure I didn't place anything. I'll keep watch."

It felt odd, rifling through Stephen's chest of drawers. Even though he'd given her permission, it felt like an invasion on her part. She finally found a ring—an ugly thing of tarnished gold and amber—among his cravats.

"There," she said. "That's it. You were right about that much."

She still wasn't going to trust him.

He gestured. "Take it. Let's get out of here before we're discovered."

She didn't trust him, but if she let herself, she could like him. He was clever, easygoing, and utterly unoffended by her intelligence.

It was such a shame that she was going to have to ruin their temporary camaraderie.

Free went to the door. "There's one last thing I need to do." They'd spoken all this time in hushed whispers; this time, she didn't bother to moderate her tone.

He made a face. "Hush. You'll be heard."

That was rather the point. Free raised her hand. Mr. Clark took a step forward, but before he could reach her, she'd rapped—hard—on the inside of Stephen's door.

"You can come in now, Mrs. Simms," Free said in a carrying voice. "Let's see what we have."

Chapter Five

EDWARD HAD SWUNG HIMSELF out the window before he even had a chance to think what Miss Marshall was doing. His heart was pounding; his hands were clammy.

But instead of dropping to the ground immediately, he held on, his heels finding purchase against the rough rock of the building, his hands wrapped in the ivy.

"Well, dearie," he heard an older voice saying. "Is it as you thought?"

"I'm afraid so. There's a ring in here."

The old woman—Mrs. Simms—clucked. "An ugly business, Miss Marshall. An ugly business. Good thing you caught wind of it. Stephen's a dear."

Not everyone hated him, then. Edward hadn't spoken to Stephen in years, and yet he was unsurprised to discover that he was still winning women over.

This other woman was sniffing distastefully. "I can vouch for the fact that he's not been in all evening. I went through his things at three this afternoon as he was leaving, and I saw nothing."

Ah. Edward leaned his forehead against the cool stone. She'd arranged for a backup plan, in the event that they'd failed in their objective. Clever.

She hadn't told him about that, of course. That was more clever still; he certainly wouldn't have told himself, either. That must have been when she left her paper—she'd made certain that if he was lying to her, Stephen was protected anyway. And then she'd brought him a sandwich.

Damn, but he respected that.

"I'll take it, then," Mrs. Simms said. "And when the cry goes up about *missing things,* I'll disclose everything. You can't be found in here, Miss Marshall. You know what they'll say. Go on."

"You're a dear. Have Mr. Simms send a message if there's anything else I need to know."

He could hear her coming to the window as she spoke. He dropped to the ground and waited.

She clambered over the edge, looked down, and caught sight of him. "You're still here," she said in surprised tones.

"Hang," he told her in a low voice. "I'll catch you."

She didn't hesitate. She swung her legs over the sill. He caught a flash of stockinged ankles and white petticoats—and then she lowered herself down. He wrapped his arms around her.

It was a little uncomfortable to let her slide down him. Uncomfortable for him in the best way possible: He was aware of every last shift of fabric. She had a lovely scent to her, something sweet and wild, like lavender on an empty hillside. He almost didn't want to let her go when her toes touched the ground.

He did anyway, taking a few steps back.

When he glanced at her, she was smiling. "Are you angry at me?" she asked sweetly.

"Of course not. I told you not to trust me, and you didn't."

Every time he thought he knew what to expect from her, she upset his expectations. He felt buffeted about, unsure of his footing.

Also, she liked boxing.

God, this was bad. Very, very bad.

"Well," she said with a shrug, "we have to talk."

Bad went instantly to worse. Talking was never a good thing. He glanced at her warily. "We do?"

"Yes." She gave him a sudden grin. "But don't give me that look. You're the one who suggested it, after all. We're supposed to talk about how attractive I find your muscles."

His mouth went dry. No use pretending anymore. He wanted her—everything about her—from that saucy smile to the inner workings of her clever mind. He wanted her badly.

He took one step toward her.

"Alas," she said, "we'll have to postpone that discussion. After all, I have a newspaper that must be out with the 4 a.m. mail."

He couldn't believe it. She'd…toyed with him. Incomprehensibly, ridiculously, damnably. *He* was supposed to be the scoundrel here. *He* was supposed to be putting her on edge.

"No wonder you weren't prepared to give me italics on either maddening or brilliant this afternoon," he told her. "You were hoarding them all for yourself. Well played, Miss Marshall. Very well played."

She gave him a smile—he could only call it maddeningly arousing—and then turned away. Her skirts swished around her ankles. She walked away from him with swift, sure strides, as if she knew her destination. As if it had nothing to do with him.

Edward had the odd notion that after years of drab motionlessness, his entire world had suddenly begun to spin about him. He'd had that feeling ever since he'd been pulled into her orbit on the bank of the Thames.

She gave him the most astonishing vertigo. He should have hated it.

But he didn't—not one bit.

⌘ ⌘ ⌘

EDWARD HAD NEVER BEEN in Baron Lowery's stable before, but he was struck by a sense of aching familiarity from the moment he entered. The tack hanging against the wall, the smell of oil and herbs, the arrangement of the tools… The best moments of his childhood had been spent in a stable laid out like this.

Familiarity was good after the extremely odd events of the last evening.

As he walked down the aisle, a groom popped up from a nearby stall, a puzzled expression on his face.

"May I help you?" The boy's voice broke on the last syllable.

"I'm looking for Shaughnessy," Edward said. He kept his expression calm and easy, even though his heart was racing. He hadn't seen Patrick in years and years.

"He's expecting you, then?" This was said dubiously.

"No, but he'll want to see me."

"Now?" The boy frowned. "Day's almost over. Can the business wait?"

"I'm not here on business."

There was a longer pause. The boy opened the stall door and shut it carefully behind him. Edward knew that gesture—this was a boy who'd been admonished to check the latch, to make sure. He knew that admonishment, too.

The boy brushed his hands together. "I'll go see if he'll come. Who should I say is calling?"

"Mr. Clark."

Not a flicker of recognition. The boy shrugged and disappeared, and Edward waited.

It had been years since he'd imposed on Patrick. His friend had never breathed a word of the debt that Edward had incurred. He wouldn't—Patrick wasn't the sort to parcel out who owed what to whom. That's why Edward had to keep score on his behalf. Those debts would never balance. All Edward could hope was to keep them at bay.

The door behind him opened.

"Edward, you great oaf," a man said.

Edward turned. Before he could catch a glimpse of his friend, Patrick was on him, wrapping his arms around him.

"Not a word in response to my letter," Patrick said, "not a telegram, not a note, not even so much as a semaphore flag waved at a hazy distance. I thought you would—"

"You thought I wouldn't help?" Edward asked gravely.

Patrick pulled away, holding Edward at arm's length. "Don't be ridiculous. I knew you'd come through for me. But when I realized you must be in England, I thought perhaps you wouldn't visit."

Edward had considered it. There wasn't a person on the planet who knew him as Patrick did, and Patrick had an unreasonably rosy outlook on Edward's flaws. It made him uncomfortable being around the man. It wasn't just the things Edward had done; it was the way Patrick was. Patrick didn't lie. He didn't cheat. He was honorable, fair, and reliable—everything that Edward was not.

It was only an accident of history that they were friends at all—history, and Patrick's staunch refusal to turn his back on his onetime friend. Edward felt almost guilty about maintaining that friendship. His very presence was corrupting.

He'd eradicated guilt from every other aspect of his life, but he couldn't be rid of it here. He loved his friend far too well to let a little guilt stop him.

"I was in the vicinity," Edward said idly. "I thought I'd stop by."

"Oh, the *vicinity.*" Patrick smiled knowingly. "You're here on a whim, then?"

It had been several hours by railway.

Patrick punched Edward in the shoulder. "Idiot. At least this way I can thank you in person. It's late enough that I might consider knocking off work. Come have supper with me."

"You're knocking off?" Edward raised an eyebrow in mock incredulousness and took out a pocket watch. He examined this in mock seriousness. "But it's not quite six. Do you dare leave a full *nine minutes* early?"

Patrick's face sobered in contemplation of this. "No, no. You're right. I should do one last set of rounds, make sure everything is in proper order."

"I'm joking."

Patrick shook his head ruefully. "I'm not."

So Edward waited while his friend puttered about, conscientiously checking oats and water. That was Patrick. That had been Patrick's father, too—the stable master on the estate where Edward had grown up.

Strange that the lessons Edward had learned from that man had made him into such a competent scoundrel. *Do everything in your search for perfection. Think about matters from everyone's point of view. A few seconds spent checking can forestall a day of disaster.* It didn't matter if it was forgery or horse trading; it was still excellent advice.

When Patrick was finished—at sixteen minutes after six—he conducted Edward to his quarters, a small two-room cottage half a mile from the stables. He washed his hands and then put a kettle on the hob.

"You still have the miniature," Edward said.

The painting sat on a shelf over the hearth—two boys sitting on the banks of a river, the branches of trees behind them rendered inexpertly in oil. The younger version of Patrick—short and wiry, brown-haired, pointed up at the sky. Edward had painted himself looking at the viewer.

That had been from a lack of imagination—he'd been looking in the mirror as he painted—rather than artistic choice.

Looking into the eyes of the child he'd once been gave him a strange feeling. That boy had dark, innocent eyes and a smile that had nothing of cynicism to it. Those eyes belonged to some other person. They were an illustration of a story he'd once been told about himself—too simple and sweet to be real. He wished he could blot himself out of the picture.

"Of course I have the miniature," Patrick said. "Why would I get rid of it?"

He disappeared momentarily into a cellar and came back with a pair of sausages. He set these to roast over the fire.

Edward looked away with a shake of his head. "I don't suppose you have my other painting."

"What, the one of Byron the Bear being taken down by the Wolf?" It was a prizefight that they'd read about in one of the books they'd devoured. It had captured both their imaginations. They'd reenacted it many a time, and when Edward had graduated to painting on full canvases, capturing that moment had been one of his first triumphs.

"No," Patrick said softly. "I couldn't take that one with me when we…left."

When Edward's father had him whipped, Patrick meant, because Edward had coaxed him into speaking up when he shouldn't have. When his family had been thrown out after twelve years of service.

"But enough of old times." Patrick straightened from turning the sausages on the fire. "I only asked you to speak with your brother after Baron Lowery told me he'd overheard some disturbing things from him. But I detect your hand in the latest round."

"Stephen told you already, did he?"

Patrick blinked. "Uh. No. I read it in the paper."

Edward's eyes widened. "You *read* about *me* in the paper? Oh, for G—" He remembered, just in time, that Patrick didn't curse, and he covered his blasphemy with a cough. "For good George's sake," he continued more mildly, even though he knew he wasn't fooling his friend. "What did the paper say?"

"It wasn't about you," Patrick said slowly. He crossed the room to his desk and opened the drawer. "Ah. Here. Read it for yourself."

Edward went to him. It was a two-inch column on the second page of the *Women's Free Press*, and it was sparse on details. A charwoman had seen a man slipping into a student's room. She'd helped that very student pack for a sudden visit that afternoon, so her suspicions were roused. Upon further inspection, she found that the man had left behind a ring—which she knew had not been present when the student quit his room, as she'd examined his drawers herself while packing the bags.

We do not speculate as to the motive of those who attempted to falsely lay the blame on the innocent student, the paper ended piously. *We note, however, that said student is known to our readers as Stephen Shaughnessy, the author of a regular column in this paper.*

Miss Marshall had said nothing to him about reporting the event in her paper. Of course it was a brilliant idea. She'd obtained witnesses to Stephen's innocence. And her story had been released first; future attempts to implicate Stephen would be colored by this and met with greater skepticism. She'd not been lying when she left him last night: She did have a paper to get out.

Of course, it was also her way of letting Edward know that she would not do his bidding quietly, that whatever he tried, she could do better. She had a circulation of—he flipped the paper over and checked—some fifty thousand subscribers. She had years of using her business as a weapon, and if he crossed her, that weapon would be at his throat.

And he'd foolishly thought that he could walk into her life and dictate to her what to do.

"You're smiling," Patrick said.

"Of course I'm smiling." Edward set the paper down. "You subscribe to a paper that advertises itself as being *by women, for women, and about women.*"

Patrick's nose wrinkled.

"That wasn't meant as an aspersion on your tastes," Edward hastened to add.

"You may recall that my brother writes for said paper," his friend said stiffly. "I subscribe out of fraternal pride."

"Indeed."

"And Miss Marshall is exceedingly clever," Patrick said. "The fact that she is a woman, writing for women, doesn't change that."

That, Edward was beginning to realize, was an understatement. "Indeed," he said shortly.

"I met her once," Patrick continued. "I gather that now you have as well. I *like* her. Have you told her who you are?"

"A woman who ferrets out secrets for public consumption? Of course I haven't told her. I lie to everyone. In another few months, the whole matter will be moot anyway. Edward Delacey will be officially dead, and James will be the viscount. If I keep lying long enough, it won't even be a lie."

Patrick's lips pinched. Of course he didn't approve. But he'd come for Edward after Strasbourg, and he understood.

Patrick knew James had lied to the Consul, leaving Edward in the path of the advancing army. He'd been told about the shells and percussion fuses, about the weeks on the fire brigade. That would have been enough to torment any man, but then, there'd been what happened after the city was surrendered. Patrick might not approve of Edward's lie, but he understood why he didn't wish to go back.

Patrick sighed now. "At least let me tell Baron Lowery—"

"No." Edward stood. "That would be almost as bad as telling Miss Marshall. I don't care how deep your…friendship is with him, how much you trust him. Your employer sits on the Committee for Privileges. James must present his petition to join the House of Lords to them before he can address the entire body. Do you think Lowery will remain silent when James states that his elder brother must be presumed dead?"

Patrick looked away. "It's unlikely. That's precisely why I think you should tell him."

"Oh, no. No. I won't."

"You'll let James be the next viscount, knowing that *this*"—Patrick smacked his hand against the paper—"is how he'll use that power? I know the idea of taking over is anathema to you, but Edward, you could do some good. Think about it."

"You think about it," Edward snarled. "You, of all people, should understand. I don't do good."

Patrick tapped the paper once more. "What was this, then?"

Edward felt his throat close. He'd planned to steal into a room like a thief, to simply foil his brother. It was Miss Marshall who'd enlisted others. She had chosen to make their private choices into a public maneuver, designed to shield Stephen.

Edward? Well, he'd tried to blackmail her.

"Your sausages are burning," he said instead.

They were. They'd lain too long on one side. The casing had charred, peeling away from the innards. Patrick made an annoyed noise in his throat and rescued the meat.

"What would be the point?" Edward asked. "Do good? We both know better than that. I'm no longer a hotheaded idealist, and even if I were, I'd be suffocated in a sea of old men determined to protect their prerogatives. I have no desire to spend my life railing against that particular futility."

Patrick speared the sausages on a fork. "You don't really believe that."

"Look at what I've done with my life, Patrick, and tell me I don't believe that."

His friend glared at him.

And that's when the door to the cottage opened. Edward didn't know the man who stood there, looking at him, but he could guess his identity by the tight expression that crept over the man's face.

"Oh," the newcomer said. "Uh. Mr. Shaughnessy. I'm…interrupting something, then? I…had a question about the gray mare."

Patrick's nostrils flared. He set his besausaged fork on a table. "Hello, George," he said. "This is Edward Clark." He cast Edward an annoyed look. "I was *so* hoping to introduce you two. Might I do it *properly?*"

That emphasis on the last word left little question as to what he meant. It no doubt rankled Patrick to lie at all. To tell such a lie to Baron Lowery, of all people, must have burned him.

"I'm sorry," Edward said. "There's nothing proper about me."

Baron Lowery was blinking at Edward, a quizzical look on his face. "So. The mythical friend is real."

"Not at all," Edward said lightly. "I'm like a unicorn: You'll convince yourself in a few days that I was nothing but a horse, misapprehended in dim light. I must be leaving."

"Edward." Patrick sighed. "You just *got* here. You can't—"

"I can. I must get back to my latest task, after all. We haven't reached the end of it."

"Yes, but—"

"You asked me to help. I can't do anything else you asked for, but this…" Edward smiled sadly. "This task needs someone like me. Don't worry about Stephen. I'll make sure he's safe." Edward nodded. "Baron. Patrick."

He slipped through the door before he could think better of it. Dark had come, a thick gloom that was broken only by faint, indistinct starlight. Edward stumbled down the path, making his way toward the main drive as best as he could in the dusk.

He heard footsteps behind him, coming after him. He didn't look back, not until a hand grabbed his wrist and forcibly turned him around.

But it wasn't Patrick. It was Baron Lowery, glowering at him.

"See here," the man said. "I don't understand a thing about your friendship with Patrick. I don't know who you are. But if you hurt him, I will hunt you down and *pulverize* you."

The man was shorter than Edward, and Edward had spent the last years at manual labor. He simply drew himself up to his full height and looked down at the baron.

"*You'll* protect *him?*" Edward rumbled.

Even in the starlight, he could see the other man flush. Lowery had to know what he was revealing. A baron didn't fight to save his stable master from a hint of insult. He certainly didn't take on a big man like Edward.

"Yes," Lowery said in a low voice. "I will."

Edward couldn't do any good, and thus far, his friendship hadn't benefited Patrick much. The best thing he could do for his friend was to leave.

And so he reached out and put his hand on the other man's shoulder. "Good. I'll hold you to that."

Before Lowery could do more than blink, Edward turned and left.

❋ ❋ ❋

THE FLOWERS WERE COMING UP cheerfully yellow in their boxes, the window was open a few inches, and the spring breeze that filtered in was sweet and refreshing. Tea and toast were laid out on the table, and Free was surrounded by her best friends. Two nights ago, she'd achieved a complete and total victory.

Despite all that, this morning felt rather less victorious.

"Another column was copied," Alice said, laying her clipping out. "The *Manchester Times*. Here. It's almost exactly your discussion of Reed's bill. There are entire sentences duplicated."

Free frowned. "How is that even possible? I didn't let any of you see the column until it was proofed. I was careful this time."

"Then it must be the proofs." Alice shrugged. "If that's the only option."

Alice Halifax was Free's cousin through her father. Her family had grown up mining coal until the mine's production faltered. In the panic of '73, she and her husband had fallen on even harder times. Free had known Alice only dimly at the time of the panic, but she'd needed someone to help out, and so she'd asked. It was the best decision she could have made. Alice was straightforward and direct, telling Free and Amanda when the paper went astray, when they were too theoretical. She also told them when they were condescending to women who knew the confines of their station better than they did. She grounded the entire paper. If *Alice* thought this would make trouble, this would undoubtedly make trouble.

Free sighed. "You are no doubt right, Alice. If you say it must be the proofs, it must be the proofs." She put her head in her hands. "But I don't want it to be the proofs." If that was the case, secrets weren't being sold by some stranger going through her rubbish.

Alice shrugged, unmoved. "You don't get to be stubborn about this, Free. Reality is what it is."

Amanda, who had been sitting at Free's left, was more gentle. "It's likely not what you're imagining," she said. "You're supposing that Aunt Violet or one of the other people we send complimentary proofs to is chuckling evilly while she hands them off to your enemies. But just think rationally. It's much more likely to be a servant filching the household papers."

Free let out a long breath. Amanda was right, and it was a calming thought. But then Amanda always was a calming influence. They'd met almost a decade before, when Amanda's Aunt Violet—Violet Malheur now, the former Countess of Cambury, and a brilliant, successful woman—had announced a series of scientific discoveries, upsetting all of England in the best way possible. Amanda had attended Girton a year behind Free. After years of being friends, it had seemed easy to ask Amanda to join her when she started her newspaper. Now Amanda reported on various Acts of Parliament. She spent half her time in London, taking notes in the Ladies' Gallery.

When she was here, though, she and Amanda shared this house and a charwoman. The land they had built the house on—leased for as many years as Free had been able to get—had once been a cow pasture on the edge of Cambridge. The space also housed the building where her press stood, some fifty feet away. That way, when the press was running late at night, they'd not be bothered by the noise. Her dwelling was scarcely a cottage—three small rooms—but she felt secure here, surrounded by her friends.

She shook her head. "Then we'll figure out who is doing it, and we'll stop them." She hesitated. "In fact... Along those lines, do you recall the man who was here the other day?"

"Mr. Clark." Amanda frowned. "Is that right? Is he advertising with us?"

"Yes. Well." Free grimaced. "He wasn't really here about advertising."

"What a shame. With Gillam's pulling out—"

"He was here because he claims that the Honorable James Delacey"—Free gave the word *Honorable* a sarcastic twist as she spoke—"is behind the copying. I'm not sure we can trust Mr. Clark. In fact, I'm certain we can't. But he may be telling the truth about that."

She spilled the whole story. Almost the whole story. She left off mention of the blackmail and the forgery. She also—somehow—didn't mention the compliments he'd given her or the solid feel of Mr. Clark's hands on her waist as he'd boosted her to the window.

Amanda listened with increasing disapproval. "Free," she finally interrupted, "whatever were you thinking? Going off alone at night with a strange man? What if—"

"She's taken bigger risks," Alice said with less rancor.

"I told Mrs. Simms where I would be," Free said. "I left a letter, so if anything happened to me—"

"Oh, good." Amanda rolled her eyes. "If my best friend had been killed, I could have avenged her death. What a comfort that would be! You have to be more careful, Free. I've seen some of the letters sent to you. There was that incident two years ago with the lantern, and just three weeks ago, those letters painted on our door in the dead of night."

"Well, nothing happened." Free looked away. "As Alice says, I've done more dangerous things for a story. If I went into hiding just because people sent me vile threats, I'd spend my entire life cowering beneath a blanket."

"Oh, don't do this." Amanda huffed. "There's a massive difference between *hiding beneath a blanket* and *slipping out at night with a man you just met*. I don't care how sterling his credentials were."

"Oh, they weren't sterling at all," Free said. "I'd never have trusted him if they were. They were more like tarnished brass, and we laughed at them together."

"Even worse. You have to stop taking risks, Free. Learn to be afraid for once."

As if that was a skill she had to learn. Free's nostrils flared. "My entire life is a risk. That's what it means when I put my name on a masthead and speak up. If someone decides to make an end of me, there's nothing I can do about it—nothing at all but surround myself with the illusion of safety.

If Mr. Clark had wanted to kill me, he could have simply crept into my room in the middle of the night with a garrote."

That brought to mind a memory of one of Free's nightmares, a dark, lurid image that lurked at the edge of her conscious thought. Oh, she was afraid. She never stopped being afraid. She just tried not to let it stop her in turn.

Years ago, her aunt had passed away, leaving Free a surprising legacy. But the money she'd received was not the most valuable thing her aunt had left her. Her Aunt Freddy had also written her a letter. *One of these days,* her aunt had written, *you are going to learn to be afraid. I hope that what I've managed to save for you will help you move on from that in some small degree.*

Free kept that letter on the table next to her bed. Freddy had been right; she had learned to be afraid. Sometimes, if a nightmare was particularly bad, Free took the paper out and held it, and it kept the worst of her fears at bay.

She shook her head, shoving this all away. "We can argue about the past all we like. But the truth is that nothing I did could have stopped a determined assailant—not my good sense, not my most demure choices."

"Free," Amanda protested.

But Alice leaned over the table and patted Amanda's hand. "She's right, Amanda. If she didn't take risks, then she'd be a lot less like herself, and a lot more like…" She trailed off, perhaps realizing what she'd been about to say.

"Like me," Amanda said bitterly.

"No," Alice said. "You take risks. In your own way."

Free wished she could say something in response to that. Instead, she swallowed and looked at her hands. Time for a change of subject. "You're going down to London next week, aren't you?"

Amanda gave her a jerky nod.

"Then I'd like you to take something to Jane, if you could."

"I suppose. If you think you can manage to keep yourself from getting killed without a housemate," Amanda muttered with ill grace. "Are you going to keep away from Mr. Clark?"

Free sighed. "There's no point in promising. He won't be back." Yes, he'd flirted with her. He'd been shameless about it. But after the way she'd altered their plan and then put everything in the newspaper? It was unlikely. Even if he'd told her the truth, and she very much doubted that, men didn't like women taking charge.

"Free," Amanda said in exasperation. "Stop evading my question."

"No," Free said, rubbing her temples. "I won't promise. He'd be a useful tool, if he did come back. But he won't."

Chapter Six

FREE HAD BEEN CERTAIN—almost certain—that she'd seen the last of Mr. Clark two weeks ago, on that night in March. As the days went on, she did her best to convince herself that it was true. Every time the door opened, she turned, her breath catching. Every time someone other than Mr. Clark entered, her heart sank. Foolishly, she told herself—entirely foolishly. After all, there was no reason to look forward to his return. Matching wits with him once had been enough for a lifetime.

And besides, the only man her paper really needed around was Stephen Shaughnessy. Free was sure that *he* was on her side, at least.

That incident involving him had sobered everyone, making them realize what was at stake. It had driven Stephen to write even more outrageous columns—and everyone else had followed suit, throwing themselves into their work.

No, they didn't need Mr. Clark.

April was well and truly started. Amanda had gone down to London to report on the latest sessions of Parliament, and Free had stopped glancing up when the door to her business opened. She'd shrunk the foolish impulse to no more than a touch of interest—one she could push away, concentrating on the papers before her instead.

And then...

"Hullo, Miss Marshall," someone said from the doorway of her office. Someone with a rich, dark voice, one that spoke of amusement and danger all in one breath.

Free jumped, dropping her pen and spattering ink across her sleeve. Not that it mattered; all her day gowns were well-inked.

She blotted at the stain anyway. "Mr. Clark. How do you do?"

He smiled at her, and she did her best to remember all the reasons she shouldn't like him. She didn't know his real name. He'd tried to blackmail her. He'd disappeared for weeks with no explanation.

But he had a very nice smile, and he seemed truly pleased to see her.

Damn him.

She tried not to smile back. "And here I thought that you took the piece I wrote about the events of the other night for what it was—a threat to expose you publicly. I thought you'd absconded in response."

"Of course not." He leaned against her doorframe. "I did take your warning. It was clever of you, Miss Marshall, to make it clear that you have yet another hold over me. I can hardly begrudge you that."

He appeared to be serious about that.

Free shook her head. "On the contrary. That seems precisely the sort of thing a person usually holds a grudge about."

"Ah, but if I were that sort of man, you wouldn't find me nearly so compelling." Without being invited, he walked into her office. He didn't seat himself at one of her chairs; he leaned against her desk, as if he had every right to come so close. "A man must make choices: He can become enraged for no reason on the one hand, or he might impress men and women on the other." He shrugged. "I've chosen to be charming. Is it working?"

God, she'd forgotten how utterly outrageous he was. Time to wrestle this conversation back under her control.

"Mr. Clark," she said as sternly as she could manage, "never tell me that you're doing *that* again."

"Which of my myriad flaws is making you uneasy, Miss Marshall?" He gave her a long, slow smile. "Is it my arrogant conceit or my wicked sense of humor?"

"Neither," Free answered. "I rather like both of those. It's just that you're trying to use my attraction to you to set me on edge." She smiled at him. "It won't work. I've been attracted to you since the moment I laid eyes on you, and it hasn't made me stupid once."

He froze, his hand on the edge of her desk.

"Did you expect me to deny it?" Free shrugged as complacently as she could. "You should read more of my newspaper. I published an excellent essay by Josephine Butler on this very subject. Men use sexuality as a tool to shut up women. We are not allowed to speak on matters that touch on sexual intercourse—even if they concern our own bodies and our own freedom—for fear of being labeled indelicate. Any time a man wishes to scare a woman into submission, he need only add the question of sexual attraction, leaving the virtuous woman with no choice but to blush and fall silent. You should know, Mr. Clark, that I don't intend to fall silent. I have already been labeled indelicate; there is nothing you can add to that chorus."

His mouth had dropped open on *sexuality*; it opened wider on *intercourse,* and wider still on *attraction.*

"I've found," Free said, "although Mrs. Butler would hardly agree, that the best way to deal with the tactic is to speak of sexual attraction in terms of clear, unquestionable facts. The same men who try to make me feel uneasy by hinting at an attraction can never live up to their own innuendos. Once I show that I will not be cowed, that facts are facts and I will not hide from them, *they're* always the ones who blush and fall silent."

"I've mentioned before that I'm not like the rest of them." He shifted on her desk, turning to face her. "I have only fallen silent because listening to you admit an attraction to me is far more pleasant than speaking myself." He gestured. "Please continue on. What else do you like about me?"

There was something about him that made her feel daring.

"Alas," Free said briskly. "There's nothing more. I've run through all the praise I can muster. You have an admittedly splendid physique, but it is unfortunately wasted on a man burdened with your abysmal personality."

He laughed at that. "Brava, Miss Marshall. That *is* my besetting sin, is it not?"

He was the only man she'd ever met who was stymied by compliments and yet accepted her worst insults as his due.

"So you see," Free said, "we're all better off if we can just admit these things without putting too much significance on the matter. Let's skip that rigmarole and get down to business. Why are you here, Mr. Clark?"

"Does anyone *ever* get the best of you?"

"Yes," she returned, "but only when I choose to give it to them."

"Ah."

"Now, tell me, Mr. Clark. Did you come here to allow me the chance to once again demonstrate my intellectual superiority, or did you have some actual business?"

"You don't need to demonstrate your superiority to me. I take it as a given on all fronts." He reached into his coat, removed a notebook, and began to flip through it.

He *was* arrogant. And conceited. And yet… He had never denied her credit for any thought she'd had. It was hard to remind herself that she didn't dare like him.

He creased the spine of his notebook. "I've not been idle these last weeks. I've been doing some work on your behalf. Here we are. I introduced myself to Mr. Calledon, owner of the *Portsmouth Herald*, and asked him how he came to write that extraordinary column mirroring yours."

"And he simply told you?"

"After that glowing letter of reference I gave him from his former mentor at the *London Times?* Of course he did, Miss Marshall. He practically fell over himself to do so."

Free raised an eyebrow. "Somehow, I suspect that his former mentor wrote no such letter."

He winked at her. "And yet if you showed it to him, he'd find the writing so achingly familiar that he'd be hard-pressed to disavow it. I *am* good."

"Bad," she corrected. "We might recall, from time to time, that forgery is generally not accounted *good.*"

His smile widened. "Then I am excellent at being bad. In any event, Calledon admitted that he had been paid a sum to run the article. The text was provided by a solicitor shortly before press time. I even managed to obtain this."

He took a folded piece of paper from his notebook and set it before her.

She unfolded it. It was a typewritten page containing the text of an article. Free recognized it as her own. A handwritten note atop offered it with the sender's compliments.

Free narrowed her eyes. "Is that real?"

He shrugged. "Real enough that the participants themselves wouldn't know the difference. With this in hand, we could, ah...*convince* Calledon to publicly admit that he'd copied you. Surely you can see the benefit in that. But then, perhaps you're too *good* to put pressure on others."

"Mr. Clark." Free almost wanted to laugh. "Do you suppose I had myself committed to a hospital for prostitutes afflicted with venereal disease by telling everyone the truth all the time? Sometimes, the truth needs a little assistance."

He smiled in satisfaction. "Precisely. No wonder we get along so well, Miss Marshall."

"So is that what you've been doing all this time?"

He flipped the page back. "You must think me the most inefficient fellow. Here's Lorring of the *Charingford Times*." He held up another bit of paper. "Chandley of the *Manchester Star*." Yet another note. "Peters from the *Edinburgh Review*. Have I impressed you yet, Miss Marshall? I may have an abysmal personality, but I do have my advantages."

"I'll grant you that." She leaned forward, thinking about those bits of paper he'd showed her. She could use them—but at this point, nobody had yet noticed the duplications. Was it better to point them out herself and thus forestall the inevitable story? If she did, she might lose all chance at catching her enemy publicly. And without proof of a motive, the copying might seem a mere childish prank.

That was when she caught a glimpse of Mr. Clark's notebook. She had expected a few notes, perhaps a page in some scrawled code that only he could unravel.

But she saw nothing like that.

She reached over the table and plucked the book from his hands.

"What are you doing?" he growled.

There were no words at all in his notebook—just a simple drawing of a bearded man in an office. "That is exactly Peters from the *Review*," she breathed.

"Yes." His hands twitched. "I make sketches. It helps my memory."

"You're good." Free turned the page. There was a penciled drawing of a café in Edinburgh, gray clouds threatening overhead.

"Of course I'm good," he told her. "I'm excellent. I should think you would have noticed by now. Might I have that back, or are you not done violating my privacy yet?"

"When you put it that way, then… No. I am not finished. Ah, here's Chandley." She smiled. "Oh, you got his mustache just right." She flipped the next page. "And here's a train car." She flipped it again and then stopped. The next page was *her*—a pencil sketch of her standing on a stool, wearing one of her favorite walking gowns, and leaning forward.

She swallowed. "Right. This." She flipped the page again.

But that was her, too, head bent over her metal type, her fingers closing around an exclamation point. The next was her gesturing at some unknown person, smiling. And the next was her, too.

He reached forward and smoothly took the notebook from her. "I had to keep sketching you," he told her, his tone mild. "I never could get any of them to look right, and I do hate failing at any endeavor."

Her mouth was dry. "On the contrary." She did her best not to sound shaken. "They seemed…very well done, to my eye."

"Yes." His mouth twitched up. "Of course they are. I am something of a genius, after all. Likely the only reason I found the drawings inadequate is the sexual attraction."

She felt her stomach twist. His eyes met hers, held them for far too long. But no, she wasn't looking away.

"It's rather more difficult for me to grapple with than it is for you," he said politely, almost courteously. "You see, you *don't* have an abysmal personality."

She'd heard the expression *playing with fire* before. She'd never before been tempted to employ the expression. Fire was a dangerous enough tool; any reasonable person kept it safely locked away when they could. But this was a heat she could enjoy.

She had to say something, anything, to bring back that necessary distance between them. It was a game between them, nothing more. She'd challenged him, and naturally he'd responded.

"You're right," she heard herself say. "That must be difficult for you. I'm pretty brilliant myself."

"I had noticed. You're both pretty and brilliant."

She shook her head, clearing away all that heat. "All of this is why we need more proof." She let out a breath. "We need to embarrass Delacey. Publicly. And to do that, we need to demonstrate conclusively that he has been deliberately trying to discredit me for his own purposes."

He didn't argue. He simply nodded. Free could get used to the notion of having a scoundrel to help out around here.

"And luckily for us," she said, "I know just how to do that."

⌘ ⌘ ⌘

IT WAS THREE IN THE MORNING by the time Free cut the last sheet off the press. The pages were still wet, and the ink that had been transferred to them was still susceptible to smearing. She handed the paper to Alice, who took it from her and hung it up to dry. Behind her, Mr. Clark unlatched the drum that held the type. He'd remained behind, lifting and carrying without complaint. He set the drum to the side, removed the roll of heavy paper from the press, and hung it over the trough to drip dry.

"They're going to be shipped still damp," Alice warned.

There was nothing Free could do about that. So the sheets would be a little wrinkled on arrival. It didn't matter.

"Go home," Free said wearily, letting her head sink into her hands. "Go home and go to sleep. We've still to produce the paper itself tomorrow." After that, it would be Sunday and they could all sleep.

She'd never thought her twenty-six years made her old, but she felt old now. Five years ago, she'd thought nothing of staying up till all hours, talking with her fellow students about anything. But if she wanted to figure out how Delacey was obtaining her advance proofs, first she had to figure out which one of them was going awry. They'd taken to burning the sheets that Free and Amanda marked up, but Free had been in the habit of printing off a few extras, sending out early copies to friends and family.

Only one way to know which was going astray—and that was to send out three different proofs to the people who received them. She'd made small changes only—a misspelled word in one, transposed sentences in another.

Still, making those false proofs—setting up the machinery for each one—had been exhausting.

"Thank you all," she finished with a yawn.

"It's our press, too," Alice told her.

Free felt her cousin's hand on her shoulder, a brief touch. She reached up blindly and held it for a moment.

"I'll go home soon," she said. "I'll just wait for the sheets to dry a little, and then pack them up for the mails. I can rest my eyes here."

Alice and her husband lived in the attached building behind the press. Alice usually supervised the running of the press at night; she was never asleep when the press was running. That also meant she was near enough that Free could call out if anything went wrong. The errand boy would come by in half an hour for the mails, which he'd cycle down to the train for later delivery. She buried her head in her arms, almost drifting off. She could hear the others gathering their things, feet shuffling against the floor. Then a cool draft of night air came as the door opened, cutting through the humid steam let off by the press's engine.

"Oh, that's nice," Free said. "Leave the door open."

They must have done so, because that lovely breeze kept on.

She dozed off—her thoughts became blurry and indistinct—but not for long. Slowly, she came back to consciousness, remembered why she was still here. She opened her eyes.

But she was not in an empty room. Sitting some three feet away from her was Edward Clark. She blinked, but the image of him didn't alter.

"Why are you still here?"

He shrugged. "I didn't think it was right to leave you alone, asleep, in the middle of the night with the door open."

She raised an eyebrow.

"I know," he said. "You're thinking that between the certainty of me and the unknown dark, you'd rather have the dark. Not that you have any reason to believe me, but I'm not *that* sort of scoundrel."

She rubbed her eyes, coming to herself. "That's not what I was thinking. My cousin is near enough that she'd come on a scream. I was thinking that it was an absurdly protective gesture."

He'd said he felt sexual attraction, and she didn't doubt he did. But that could mean anything. He might feel the stirrings of lust toward a thousand women a day. No, she was safer remembering his first words to her. He didn't give a damn about her.

Impossible to think that while remembering the sketches he'd made of her.

He looked away from her, glancing at the sheets that hung from large wooden rods. "Tell me what needs to be done, Miss Marshall. I'll do it, and then you can head off to bed."

"Check to see if the ink still smears."

He stood and crossed to the sheets that were hanging. "The pages are still damp, but the ink is fast."

Under her direction, they got the proofs ready for the mails. He worked with her, fetching envelopes and ink, folding the sheets of newsprint.

He talked as he worked. "Tonight was interesting. I always imagined that a printing press used wet ink, like from an inkwell."

"This press can put off twenty thousand sheets per hour. It cost me five hundred pounds. You can't get that sort of speed with wet ink without smearing it. So instead, you wet the paper and use lampblack..." Free smiled. "Now listen to me babble on."

"I like hearing you babble." He wasn't looking at her as he spoke, just folding up sheets. "This is as far from that first press as a chisel and stone tablet are from a fountain pen. Twenty thousand sheets in an hour, and every one of them a weapon. I wonder if Gutenberg imagined *this* when he made that first Bible."

She wondered if Mr. Clark saw the same thing she did when she looked at her press. It wasn't just a thing of metal and gears, a machine that chopped and printed at an astonishing rate. It was a web of connections, from the account of life in the mines from a woman in Cornwall, to the description of the latest parliamentary machinations.

But no. No matter what he said, how charming he was, she had to remember who he was. A liar. A realist. He might care about her in the casual way that men cared about women they wanted, but he didn't care about anything she did.

Such a shame.

He watched her address the envelopes. "Do you really know Violet Malheur? And is that *the* Violet Malheur? The one they call the Countess of Chromosome now?"

Free smiled dreamily. "A little known fact: I invented the word chromosome. Also, Lady Amanda is her niece. So, yes, we do know her. She's penned a few essays for us on female education and vocation." Free scrawled a brief note to Violet and folded it in with the proof.

"Is there anything you *don't* do?" he asked.

"Sleep."

He laughed softly. Free could almost have forgotten that he'd threatened her with blackmail, that he couldn't bother to spare a single cheer for her future. She could almost believe that he was a friend.

They packaged the proofs and added them to the mailbag left on the stoop.

He took his scarf from the hooks at the door; she took a light cloak.

He went outside, but waited on the stoop for her to lock up. "Do you need someone to walk you home?"

Free pointed fifty feet down to her house. "I live there. I can manage that on my own."

"Ah." But he didn't move, and for some reason, she didn't either.

"Right," she heard herself say. "Good night, then, Mr. Clark. Go get some sleep."

He smiled wearily. "Not yet. I'll be watching the mailbag, to make sure that our culprit isn't interfering at this point. You go, Miss Marshall."

Still she didn't. "Why are you doing all this? You say it's revenge, but I can't make sense of you."

He looked down the street, away from her. "Just…wrestling with my conscience."

"What?" She gasped in fake shock. "Mr. Clark! I didn't know you *had* one of those."

"I didn't think I did, either," he said wryly. "That's why it's proven so hard to defeat. I'm out of practice." He sighed. "Very well, then. A while back, I told you that you would always know the score between us, even if you didn't know the details."

She turned toward him. "And now you want to tell me details."

"God, no." He looked disgusted. "Now I'm debating if I should tell you that the score has changed."

The air shifted subtly between them. She turned to him. "You've given up on revenge, then."

"No, Miss Marshall." His voice was low and warm, so warm she could have sunk into it, let it enfold her. "I told you that I didn't give a damn about you."

Her breath stopped in her lungs. He was watching her ever so intently, so intently that she shut her eyes, unable to meet his gaze. "Oh?"

"That has changed. I find myself giving a damn. It's an unfamiliar experience, to say the least."

Free let her breath cycle in and out, in and out. But it was the sound of his breathing that she listened for, as if his inhalations might provide some clue to untangle what he meant.

She kept her eyes shut. "Well, Mr. Clark. You have not given me enough information to proceed. Precisely what sort of a damn are we talking about here? Is it a little damn? A big damn? Do you give more than one damn, or are we talking of damnation in the singular?"

She could hear his shoes scuff against the ground, taking him closer. Closer to her. She couldn't see him, and that made the moment all the more intimate. She could imagine the look in his eyes, faintly approving.

"Free." His voice dropped low, so low that she could almost feel the rumble of it in her chest. And then she felt it— not his hand, but a waft of air brushing her cheek, and then the absence of any draft. The warmth of him heating the space next to her.

"This," he said, "is about the shape of it."

She couldn't help herself. She leaned forward, letting his hand brush against her jaw. His finger ran along her chin; his thumb brushed against her lips. Her eyes fluttered open.

She'd imagined him intent on her, watching her ever so closely. But she hadn't expected that look in his eyes, hadn't expected him to exhale when she finally looked at him. She hadn't expected him to move closer still, as if he'd spent long years alone and only she could fill that hollowness inside him.

He leaned forward. His lips were close to hers, so close that she might have stretched up the barest inch and kissed him. But she wasn't going to close that gap. She willed it into existence, demanded that it stay there. And he didn't move any nearer.

"How deceptive," he remarked.

It was such an odd thing to say; she blinked and looked up at him.

"It's some kind of illusion," he said. "Or a painter's trick. Until this moment, I had the distinct impression that you were a lady of ordinary dimensions." His fingers stroked her cheek with a gentle brush. "But now you're close and you're not moving, and I can see the truth. You're tiny."

"I am small," she said, "but mighty."

His touch was warm on her jaw. "Have you ever watched ants? They scurry about carrying crumbs three times their size. You've no need to remind me of your strength. It's great big fellows like me who crack under the strain."

He *was* great. And big. He was touching her as if she were some delicate thing.

"Tell me, Miss Marshall," he said. "As unconventional as you are… Hypothetically speaking, have you ever considered taking a lover?"

As he spoke his fingers slid down her neck, resting briefly against her pulse. He must feel it hammering away, must know the effect he was having on her.

"As we are speaking hypothetically," she told him, "I suppose that a woman can only break so many rules. I've chosen the ones that I shatter very, very carefully."

"Ah," he said. But he didn't move away.

"I tell myself all those things," she said, "but I'm a suffragette, not a statue. I have the same desires as any person.

I want to touch and be touched, hold and be held. So yes, Mr. Clark. I have, hypothetically, thought of taking lovers."

His eyes darkened. But perhaps he could tell that there was more to come.

"But we are speaking hypothetically. I don't think I would do it in truth unless one thing were true."

"Yes?"

"I would have to trust the man."

His fingers came to a standstill on her throat. His eyes sought hers. For a long, fraught moment, he didn't say anything. He didn't protest. He didn't demand an explanation. He didn't erupt in anger.

Instead, ever so slowly, his mouth tilted up in a sardonic smile. "Well." He spoke quietly. "That rather rules me out."

She hadn't known she was holding her breath until she let it out. "Yes. It does."

"Just as well," he returned. "I wouldn't like you half so much if you let yourself spin breathless fantasies about me."

Oh, she'd spun breathless fantasies. She was spinning one now, damning herself for having good sense when she could be getting a proper kiss instead. Later, she'd think back on this moment and imagine a thousand different endings.

For now, she swallowed back all that ill-advised want. She smiled at him—teasingly, she hoped, with no limpid doe-eyed desire—and shrugged a shoulder. "Oh, look at that. I *am* coming up in the world. I have graduated from mild indifference to a moderate preference."

But she couldn't trust even that assertion on his part. He was charming, but he was a terrible scoundrel. And if he intended to seduce her… Well, he was doing a bang-up job of it. How she wished her foolish reason didn't assert itself over her desire. She suspected he was the kind of bounder who could make her feel very, very good before he casually destroyed her life.

"If ever you change your mind," he said, "do let me know."

"You mean, if I decide to trust you?"

For a moment, his eyes grew dark. His fingers tapped against her cheek. And then he moved away. "I'm a realist, Miss Marshall. I don't hope for things that can never be. I meant that you might one day relax your requirements." He turned away. "Now go home and sleep. I'll watch the mails."

Chapter Seven

"IT'S SO GOOD TO SEE YOU, Lady Amanda."

Lady Amanda Ellisford sat, her hands clasped around a saucer, trying to remember why she was doing this again. Oh, yes. That was it. She was doing this because apparently, she loved pain.

Not that there was anything inherently painful about visiting Free's sister in law. Nothing at all. Mrs. Jane Marshall was perfectly lovely. Her secretary was…more than that.

Once, Amanda had made morning and afternoon visits alike with no sense of unease. Now, though, the trappings of the social call—the plate of biscuits and sandwiches, the clink of cup and saucer—served as an ever-present reminder of what she no longer was.

She was no longer the girl who sat in pink-papered drawing rooms yearning for more.

And yet here she was. Sitting. In a drawing room.

"Just Amanda will do," she said, trying not to sound stiff. "There's no need to *Lady Amanda* me."

Time was, there'd been nothing stiff about her under circumstances like these. She'd known how to make small talk about nothing at all for hours on end—a consequence of having had nothing in her life to talk about. But the skill had atrophied after years of disuse, and now, it seemed as if it had been some other girl who had been able to chatter away without flinching.

Today, even the tick of the clock behind them seemed to reprimand her. *You no longer belong here. You walked away. Why do you think you can simply come back?*

It echoed a long-remembered voice. *You went away once. I wish you'd do it again, and never come back.*

Mrs. Jane Marshall obviously had never known what it meant to be conscious of her every move. She wore a day gown of pink-and-orange checks, trimmed with yellow lace. It would have been a hideous combination on another woman—like imagining flamingo feathers stuck haphazardly in a chicken's tail. On her, it just...*was.*

Amanda felt like the badly feathered one in the room.

"I'm only in London a few more days," she said. "Free asked if I would bring by a few letters—and this for the boys." She held out an envelope and a brightly wrapped package.

"She spoils them," Jane said, but she smiled as she took the package. "I'll be sure to write her a thank-you. And thank *you* so much for bringing it by."

"I have no wish to bother you," Amanda said, making sure to look at Mrs. Marshall directly and at her secretary not at all. "I'll be out of your hair in a twinkling."

"But you're never a bother to us." Those words, said in so sweet a tone, did not come from Mrs. Marshall. Amanda turned—mostly reluctantly—to take in her secretary.

If Mrs. Jane Marshall was a flamingo, her social secretary, Miss Genevieve Johnson, was a perfect little turtledove. Or—to use another, not quite inappropriate example—she was like a china doll. She was perfectly proportioned. Her skin was a flawless porcelain, her eyes brilliantly blue. If there were any justice in the world, she would be stupid or unfriendly. But she wasn't; she had always been perfectly kind to Amanda, and her intelligence was obvious to anyone who listened to her for any length of time.

She was exactly the sort of woman whom Amanda would have stood in awe of, when she'd had her Season nearly a decade past—the sort of brilliant, shining social diamond that Amanda would have watched breathlessly from afar.

In those ten years, Amanda had figured out exactly why she'd watched women like her with such avid intent. But understanding why Miss Johnson made her uneasy made her feel more in doubt, rather than less.

When uncertain about a conversation, ask a question requiring a long answer. That was what her grandmother would say.

Amanda struggled to think of something appropriate. "So… How much do you two still have to do for your spring benefit? The last Free told me, you were up to your ears."

Miss Johnson's perfectly shaped eyebrows rose. Not so high as to be rude; it seemed an involuntary response on her part, and Amanda realized she had misstepped somehow.

"We only have to send the thank-yous for attendance," Mrs. Marshall said. "But there *was* a great deal that had to be done."

Oh, God. It had already happened. Amanda felt herself blush fiercely. Of course it had. Miss Johnson would never have made so horrible a blunder. If Miss Johnson was a china doll, Amanda felt like the proverbial bull entering the shop where she was kept. She was outsized and clumsy, capable of smashing everything around her with one misplaced flick of her ungainly tail. She felt both awkward and stupid.

"But tell us why you're in town," Miss Johnson said. "Are you visiting your sisters?"

"My sisters don't see me." Her response was too curt, too bitter.

Miss Johnson drew back, and Amanda could practically hear china plates crashing around her, breaking to smithereens.

"I'm here to talk to Rickard about his suffrage bill," she continued. "He's been circulating it, trying to get anyone else to sign on."

"And how is he doing?"

About as badly as Amanda was managing now. "The radicals hate it," she said. "It limits voting to a small minority of married women. Everyone else hates it because, well…" Amanda shrugged once again. "It's a terrible bill. But it's a bill at least."

"I'll have to ask Oliver what he thinks of it," Mrs. Marshall said. Oliver was her husband and Free's half-brother. He was a Member of Parliament—and through a set of circumstances that Amanda had found it polite not to understand, also the half-brother of a duke. He was usually conversant in these affairs.

"Oh, he's opposed, I'm sure," Amanda said. "He's part of the set that says the next suffrage bill must be the universal one. It's the most dreadful mess."

"Why is that?" Miss Johnson asked.

Amanda recognized this tactic from her youth. She was being *drawn out*—by an expert no less. She flushed.

"Well. There's an argument about who ought to be allowed to vote. All women? Just women who own property? Or maybe only married women. Of course, almost every group favors a bill that allows only *their* ilk to vote. They all promise they'll circle back eventually and include the rest— but there's very little trust that those representations are true." She considered that. "The mistrust is not unwarranted, given, um, the things that some have said." No need to go into those. In the beginning, Amanda herself had been one of those women who shied away from universal suffrage. Women, yes, but *poor* women?

It had taken some interesting conversations with Alice Halifax before Amanda had come around, and she was still embarrassed with herself for her earlier stance.

"Universal suffrage," she continued, "is a harder task to achieve, but if we'd insisted on it back in 1832…"

She trailed off, realizing that she was the only one talking. Once again, she felt herself flush. When she was seventeen, she'd thought that she could leave the drawing rooms she inhabited. She'd imagined learning more, becoming a larger person. She hadn't understood that the process of leaving meant that she would never fit in her old life again.

She understood the rules just well enough to remember them a minute too late.

"But," she said, feeling her cheeks heat, "we needn't talk politics." God. It was the most dreadful of drawing-room missteps. How gauche of her. She was so used to being able to say anything that she'd forgotten how to hold her tongue.

She made a great show of checking the clock on the wall. "Dear me. I must be off, or I'll be late for my appointment with Rickard." It was in two hours, but no point in mentioning that. She could look over her notes again.

"But we *like* hearing you talk of politics," Miss Johnson said gently. "Haven't you a few more moments?"

Too bad that Amanda knew that tactic, too. You were always supposed to set the other person at ease, no matter how badly she was doing. That left you free to gossip about her in good conscience afterward.

Amanda frowned repressively. "I'm afraid I don't."

She'd accepted reality for what it was years ago. She'd no interest in being a proper lady. She was a bull; her place was in a field, flicking flies off with her tail, or—if need be—charging her enemies with horns lowered.

But Miss Johnson sighed almost regretfully. "Do come back," she said, a pattern card of politeness.

That's all it was: politeness. If Amanda had been an artist, she'd have painted a swirl of butterflies around Miss Johnson, dancing gently around her. But she wasn't, and instead, every one of those butterflies seemed to be lodged in her stomach, fluttering in protest.

It didn't matter. If you were a bull and you happened to find yourself in a china shop, there was nothing to do but head for the exit and try not to knock over any of the displays on your way out. Amanda had understood that years ago, and nothing had changed since then.

"I will," Amanda said.

It wasn't precisely a lie. She was sure that Free would send another package one day, that Amanda would be forced to return.

And Miss Johnson and Mrs. Marshall would likely get a good day's worth of gossip abusing her manners afterward, so it was a fair trade for all the broken china. She might have been able to shrug it off.

But there was one small thing that made this all more than humiliating. Miss Johnson smiled as if she had meant her invitation. Her flaxen hair shone in the morning sun, and her lips were perfectly pink as she said her good-byes.

Things would be bad enough as they were. But it was just Amanda's bad luck that she had a taste for porcelain dolls.

⌘ ⌘ ⌘

SEVERAL WEEKS AGO, EDWARD had visited his brother. Tonight, he returned to James's office once more. The room was almost precisely as it had been when last he'd come. Papers were strewn across the desk; volumes on land care and finance sat on the bookshelves lining the walls. The day's newspapers had been stuffed in the rubbish bin.

This time though, he found James already in their father's place at the desk. His brother opened the glassed door to the outside with a suspicious frown and gestured for Edward to sit across from him. "Why are you here, Ned?" he asked skeptically.

"I still prefer Edward," Edward managed mildly. "But never mind that. I haven't come back to bicker. I realized that I owe you an apology."

If anything, that made James more suspicious. His nose wrinkled in obvious distrust. But what he said instead was, "Nonsense. Water under the bridge and all that, surely."

"No." Edward put on his best false earnestness. "It's not nonsense. I assumed that you'd not want to see or hear from me based on your actions seven years ago. But I feel I have misjudged you. I never gave you a chance to tell me why you did what you did. That was unfair. Unbrotherly, even. I assumed the worst of you, but I can see now that I was mistaken."

His brother was still suspicious; Edward could tell from the set of his jaw, the flare of his nostrils. But James was too rooted in the rules of polite conversation to accuse Edward of lying, and that meant he responded to his words at face value.

Good. Making a man speak a lie was the first step toward making him believe a lie.

"Right." James blinked. "Yes." His words came reluctantly. "Of course I never wanted you...harmed. Ahem." He steepled his fingers. "It was for your good, you understand? It was only for your good. You sent that urgent letter stating that there was an army marching on the scene, that you needed our assistance to get away. And Father had sent you there for punishment, right? You hadn't come around yet. That was all that was on my mind. I promise, I never, absolutely *never*, intended you to perish."

The hell of it was, Edward suspected James was telling something that looked suspiciously like the truth. He had no doubt studiously told himself that he didn't intend for his brother to die. He'd justified it all to himself—saying that Edward, by refusing to bow to their father, had essentially made himself an outcast. He was just *like* an impostor.

No doubt he'd justified his lie to the consul a hundred times over the years. The fact that Edward could have died, and James stood to inherit the viscountcy as a result... No doubt, he'd told himself that those things did not matter to him.

It was a lie, of course. But men lied to themselves all the time, telling themselves they were far better than they were.

Edward tried not to fall into that same trap.

"I understand that," Edward said with what he hoped was an approximation of brotherly warmth.

"I wept when you could not be recovered," James told him.

Edward was sure that was true, too. James would no doubt have felt very sorry. If he hadn't, he would have been forced to admit he was a vile betrayer who'd secretly hoped his brother would die. No man saw himself as a villain. James had done what he'd needed to do, and then he'd lied to himself about his actions.

"I haven't been fair to you." Edward reached across the table and clasped his brother's hand in his. James's hands were bare; Edward hadn't removed his glove, and the contrast of pale skin against black leather, of bumbling incompetence against smooth, slick falsehoods, seemed to set the mood for what was to come.

"I realized my mistake," Edward said, "when I read about Stephen Shaughnessy in the paper."

His brother's mouth twitched slightly.

"You really *did* have a plan for him. But you went to all that trouble to undo it, just for me. Because I asked."

Edward knew that James had done nothing to undo his plans. *James* knew that James had done nothing. But James didn't know that Edward knew. It took James all of three seconds, spent blinking wide-eyed at that canard, to swallow up the bait.

"Why, yes," James said. "Yes, I did."

Lies worked best when you could invest the target in the lie itself. James wanted to believe he was a good person. He wanted to believe he could be forgiven for abandoning Edward on the eve of war. He wanted to believe himself an honorable fellow who would never welsh on an agreement—and so when Edward handed him the chance to believe it, he grasped hold of the possibility.

But telling oneself lies was a dangerous business. One started to believe them. In James's case, believing that Edward was his brother in anything but blood would be the most foolish lie of all.

"It was difficult," James said. "You and the Shaughnessys... I always felt that they stole my older brother from me." That was said so bitterly that Edward suspected it was true. "Giving up on my plans for Stephen was difficult. But if it would bring my brother back, well, there's a pleasant symmetry to it, eh?"

There was no symmetry, pleasant or otherwise. Even if James had been telling the truth, he'd have acted because he wished to keep Edward away and take what should have been his birthright.

But Edward smiled and pretended to be touched. "That means a great deal to me, James. A great deal. I've not been fair to you. Listen to me now—all these years spent apart, and

I never even asked after your situation. I hope my absence hasn't posed too many problems for you."

"Oh, not too many." James leaned back.

"You're being too kind to me," Edward said. "Come. Tell me how things have *really* been."

Getting a man to lie to himself was a peculiar sort of black magic. One had only to whisper the faintest praise in his ear, and he'd invent the rest. He'd make himself out to be a hero, beset by villains and calamity.

"Well," James said slowly. "I didn't want to make too much of it, but there have been some difficulties."

"Ah, I thought so." Edward smiled.

"I don't have full control over the finances yet, and I can't sit in Parliament. That's delayed many a plan of mine." James frowned. "And when I was looking for a wife, I'd have been able to do better had there not been that cloud over the title."

Edward *tsked* in sympathy. "How dreadful for you. I hope you're not too unhappy on that score?"

"It all turned out for the best," James said heartily. "Annie had a decent portion, and she's pretty enough. She eases me when we're alone in the country together and doesn't mind what I do in town. I couldn't ask for a better wife."

"Indeed. What more could a man want?" Edward asked. He even managed to sound sincere saying it.

But the answer to his rhetorical question rose unbidden in his mind. It was ridiculous to want Frederica Marshall. It didn't matter how he dreamed of her at night; it didn't even matter that he, apparently, did not disgust her, either. She was too intelligent to entangle herself with a man like him—and he was just foolish enough to want her anyway.

He was already in over his head. He didn't mind that.

The danger was in telling himself lies. And the notion that he might have Frederica Marshall was the sweetest, most seductive lie he might have told himself. He wouldn't give into that.

His brother burbled on—about his sons, his friends, about nothing in particular, helped on by a few judicious comments on Edward's part. After a full quarter hour, James seemed to realize that he'd been monopolizing the conversation.

James took a long swallow of brandy and finally looked at Edward, squinting. "So," he said. "What *have* you been doing with yourself all these years?"

"Running a metalworks in Toulouse," Edward said smoothly. That much was true if James ever cared to look into the matter. His brother didn't need to know any of the other things Edward had done.

But apparently, that was enough. James looked thunderstruck. "A metalworks! When you say *running* it—you mean you own it, but…"

"A fancy metalworks," Edward smiled faintly. "If it makes you feel better. We do ornamental gates, fences, gratings for chapels. That sort of thing. And yes, I run it. I'm involved in all aspects of it."

"You don't actually mean that *you* do some of the…" James gestured futilely. "You know. The *working*. With metal."

"Of course I do. I've always been artistically minded, and metal is just another medium."

James did not ask any of the questions that Edward might have found uncomfortable, questions like *How did you come to own a metalworks?*

Instead, he took a long swallow of his brandy. "No wonder you disappeared. You told me you'd done things that reflected poorly on your honor, but I'd never imagined that you would take up a trade. Why, metalworking is practically…manual labor." This was followed by another swallow of liquor, as if spirits were the only thing that could make metalworking tolerable.

"It *is* manual labor." Edward tried not to let his amusement show. "However fancy the product might be."

"Good God." James drained his glass, frowned at the bottom of it.

"Here," Edward said, reaching forward and picking up the glass. "Allow me to do the honors." For one thing, standing and turning his back on his brother meant that James couldn't see him try to hide his smile.

"I understand what you were getting at now," James said. "I didn't understand at all, when you came the other night. Couldn't figure out why you'd agree to give up a viscountcy. But this makes sense of everything. We couldn't have a laborer as viscount. What if people found out?"

Edward wouldn't laugh. God, to be such a fool, imagining that *manual labor* was the worst a man could do. Running the metalworks was the most respectable thing Edward had managed in his years away. He had a sudden, wicked desire to show his brother his skills at forgery, just to see him choke. Instead, he filled his brother's glass with brandy and turned back.

"Here." But as he returned, he knocked his foot against the rubbish bin, tipping it over. "My pardon." He reached over and righted it, shifting the contents as he did. "How clumsy of me."

He caught a glimpse of Miss Marshall's masthead as he rearranged the papers. Just as he'd thought.

James waved this away. "I'm glad we had this chance to talk. I've been worried, to tell the truth. We were a bit at odds as children."

An understatement.

"But I see that won't persist. We've each found our place. You're happy, are you not?"

Happier than ever, now that he'd found his way into James's confidences. "I am," Edward said. "And I, too, am glad we spoke. But I must be getting on. I won't be in England much longer, and you've still work to do."

"Of course." A frown passed over James's face. "Do you mean to stay here for the night?"

"Don't be ridiculous. Of course not. The family can't risk my recognition, can we?"

Relief flickered over his brother's face.

Edward shrugged. "I've a room for the night in a place by the station. I'll be taking the train back to London first thing tomorrow. Speaking of which, is that today's *Gazette?*" He gestured to the rubbish bin.

"Yes."

"They still print the rail schedules, don't they? Mind if I take that copy from you and bring it along with me? It'll save me from having to look up the timetables tomorrow morning." Edward gestured toward the rubbish bin.

"Of course." James reached for it himself, but Edward beat him in bending down. He picked up the entire jumbled sheaf of newspapers, rummaging through them with a little more clumsiness than necessary until he found the proper one. "Ah. Here we are." He gave the newspaper a tug, rolled it up, and smiled at his brother. "Thank you. I'll be out of England soon enough—business will take me back to France, I'm afraid."

James made a face, as if *business* was a dirty word.

"But I'm glad we had a chance to speak."

"Of course," James said. "No matter what you've done, you're still my brother."

"How generous of you." Edward inclined his head. "You're too good."

And so saying, he slid the newspaper into the inner pocket of his coat—both the *Gazette* and Free's proof rolled into one. There. His primary object for the evening was accomplished. "Good night."

"Good night." But as Edward started to leave, his brother grimaced. "Wait."

Edward paused. "Yes?"

"Have you separated Shaughnessy from Miss Marshall yet?"

"No," Edward said slowly. "I haven't. He's stubborn." He'd not thought that his careful lies would bear fruit so soon. He stood in place, willing his brother to say more.

James sighed. "Can you keep a secret?"

"James." Edward shook his head slowly, patiently. "I *am* a secret. Who would I tell?"

"True, true. Well. In the interest of brotherly rapport, you might want to make sure that Shaughnessy is not at the press late tomorrow evening."

"Of course. Is there some reason?"

James hesitated, so Edward fed him another lie.

"No, no, don't tell me," he said. "I can see there is another reason. You've done something rather clever, haven't you?"

That was enough to push his brother over the edge. "Oh, not so clever," James demurred. "It's taken me ages to build up to this. It's just that tomorrow is when they're supposed to set the fire."

⌘　⌘　⌘

FREE HAD BEEN BURIED under a veritable onslaught of telegrams—seventy-three by four that afternoon—and the courier on his cycle brought more every hour.

That number didn't count the notices that would come in the mails. After the exposé that had been printed in the *London Review* this morning and echoed in papers around the country by noon, advertisers throughout England had been desperate to sever their ties with her. Subscribers would no doubt follow suit.

Free had left the headlined paper out on the front table, a reminder of what she needed to accomplish by the end of the day.

WOMEN'S FREE PRESS FOUND COPYING COLUMNS FROM OTHERS.

"Your response won't hold up." Amanda had come back from London that morning, and she was examining Free's hastily hand-scrawled defense. "This piece sounds like the thinnest of excuses. I wouldn't believe it myself if I hadn't watched you write those columns."

"Mr. Clark has proof," Free said.

Amanda snorted in response. "Mr. Clark is not here. Convenient for him, is it not? Here we are, asserting that someone—and while we suspect who it is, we cannot prove it, and so we dare not name him—has taken our work early, but we are not sure how. This unknown person has done this in order to discredit us for some unknown reason. The story is so thin that it would rouse the suspicions of even our most faithful adherents. We can't print this. We're better off printing nothing at all."

Free folded her arms and glared off into space. "So you think printing a bare denial is the best option." It had been her choice to wait until she had proof before proceeding; this debacle was what resulted.

"Yes," Amanda said.

"She's right," Alice said over her shoulder.

When those two agreed, they were almost certainly correct.

"Say simply," Amanda said, "that the *Women's Free Press* has reviewed its internal procedures and we are satisfied that the pieces we have printed were authored by our writers. We are looking into this matter."

"But—"

"Add that we will allow the reporter from the *London Review* to examine our internal archive of advance proofs, demonstrating that earlier versions of the columns were in our possession before the other newspapers went to press."

"But—"

"Don't defend yourself, Free, until you can do it well. You'll have one chance to build your defense in the public eye. Wait until your story is unassailable, or you'll lose."

Damn it. She wanted to do *something*. Free balled her hands into fists. The telegrams had come all day long, and every one she glanced at felt like a knife to her heart. Andrews' Tinned Goods—she'd worked with them for years. It wasn't right, wasn't *fair*, that they'd not even waited to hear her explanation before jumping to the conclusion of her guilt.

"We will win," Alice said behind her, setting her hand on her back.

She didn't want any of this. Even if she fended off these accusations, every hour she spent defending against them was an hour not spent on issues of substance. That bill of Rickard's, flawed as it was, was unlikely to even come under discussion unless she helped do her part to put it on everyone's lips. The very act of spending energy on this hopeless morass was a loss, no matter how it turned out.

She set her head in her hands.

The door opened. She turned, expecting the courier again.

But instead of the bespectacled boy from the telegram office in town, Mr. Clark stood in the doorway. He looked around the room—at her and Amanda and Alice at the table, arguing over that all-important response—and his eyes narrowed.

"Where are the men, Miss Marshall?" His voice was a low growl.

"What men?"

"The men I told you to hire." He took a step forward. "I know you don't trust me, but with what is at stake, I'd think you could at least bloody listen for a half minute."

"What men?" she echoed.

He looked at her—really looked at her, taking in the ink stains on her chin, the drifts of telegrams on the table beside her.

"Christ," he swore. "You haven't read my telegram."

"I've been busy." She glared at him accusingly. "Trying to piece together a response to this accusation without any of the evidence *you* claimed to have but took with you. I haven't had time to sort through all the messages. One more person canceling an advertisement or expressing their glee at my fall from grace—what would that have mattered? Things can't get much worse."

"Yes, they can," Mr. Clark growled. "I was wrong; I didn't have the full plan. This is not just about putting you in distress, Miss Marshall. You need to be seen to be in distress by the entire world. That way, when your press is burned to the ground, everyone will believe it arson. They'll think that faced with the certainty of financial ruin, you set fire to everything for the insurance money in a fit of desperation."

Free felt her hands go cold.

"He could be lying, Free." Amanda came to stand by her. "These so-called men he wants you to hire—who knows who they might be? Men under his control. And once introduced, they'll be here. Protecting us, so they say, but who knows what other master they'll serve? Do you really trust him?"

Mr. Clark's lips thinned, but he said nothing in his own defense. He simply folded his arms and glared at her, as if willing her to make up her mind—as if daring her to trust him now, when she had every reason not to.

But it wasn't his silence that decided her in his favor. It wasn't the memory of the last time she'd seen him—of the touch of his glove whispering along her jaw. It wasn't even the perilous thud of her heart, whispering madness in the back of her mind.

No. Her trust, such as it was, was won on a far more practical basis.

"On this," Free said, "I believe him."

He let out an exhalation, his arms dropping to his sides.

"But—" Amanda started.

Free turned grimly and went to the window. "I believe him," she said, "because I smell smoke."

Chapter Eight

THERE WERE NO MEN PRESENT, only the half-dozen or so female employees who had remained to run the printing off the press. Cambridge, with its fire engines, was a full half-mile distant. By the time Edward had made his way out of the door of the press, it was already too late. Smoke had begun to seep out of the door of the small house down the way in light wisps.

He opened it anyway. A wave of heat hit him, followed by an outpouring of choking, eye-stinging smoke. Gray clouds billowed in the front room; fire crackled. He looked up; flames were already eating into the beams of the ceiling overhead. There'd be no putting this out on time to save the structure. There was no sand and only a few buckets.

Free was right behind him. She squared her shoulders and shoved past him.

He grabbed hold of her wrist, yanking her back.

She pulled against his grip. "We can put it out."

"We can't," he told her. "I've seen more fires in my life than you could dream of. The smoke will kill you if you try." His throat was already irritated, and he'd only been standing on the threshold.

"But—"

"Is there anything in there that is worth your life? Because that is what it will mean if you go in now."

"My Aunt Freddy's letter." He could feel her whole arm trembling in his. "She left it for me when she died."

"Would your Aunt Freddy want you to risk your life for a piece of paper?"

"No," she whispered.

Her eyes were watering. If anyone ever asked him, he'd say it was the smoke irritating them. He didn't think that Miss Marshall would be willing to admit to tears.

He took off his cravat and handed it to her. "Wet this and wrap it around your mouth and nose. It'll help. We've work to do."

She'd not taken the time to put on a hat; her hair was coming out of its bun and trailed down her back like an angry braid of her own fire.

She took the cravat from his hands. "I thought there was nothing to be done."

"For your home? There isn't. But we need to set a firebreak to make sure the flames don't spread to the press."

It had been years since he'd been on the fire brigade; he'd thought the memory of those weeks had hazed together into nondescript forgetfulness, but it was all coming back to him now. That tree, there—they'd have to lop the branches back, and then dig a line in the turf.

Her shoulders heaved one last time. But by now, the flames were waist-high in the room beyond, and even she must have known it was hopeless. She turned away, marching back to where the women were coming out of the press.

"Melissa, we need shovels, or anything like shovels you can find. Caroline, you must go fetch help. Phoebe and Mary, start with the buckets."

Edward found a shovel himself and had started to mark off a perimeter when his brain finally caught up with his body. He looked up—at the women scattering in all directions, off to do battle against the blaze—and his mouth dried with a sudden realization.

This wasn't the fire that his brother had been talking about. *This* was the distraction.

He had no time to think. He left the shovel in place and ran back to the press building. The doors were open wide, but the press floor was empty. But the overpowering smell of paraffin oil assailed him. The floor underfoot gleamed in iridescent colors.

He looked around, saw nobody about.

There had to be someone here. The arsonist must be inside; the place needed nothing more than a match to go up. He crept forward, checking under a table, behind a chest of drawers. He came to the other side of the room—the wall where the glass window spilled light into Miss Marshall's office. Her door was ajar. And there, in the darkening shadows under her desk...

There was a boot tip poking out from the other side.

Emotion, he told himself, would be nothing but a burden now. He needed to act, and act quickly. And yet he could not dispel it. His stomach seemed full of rage.

He stalked into her office, grabbed hold of the man by the foot, and hauled with all his might. He was so angry he scarcely even felt the mass of the other man, even though the fellow must have weighed at least fifteen stone.

The man kicked out, knocking Edward's grip loose. Another kick targeted Edward's knees, and he crumpled to the floor. The arsonist scrambled to his feet, dashing to the door of Free's office.

Edward lunged for him, grabbing for his ankle. He had it—but the man stomped, and his boot found Edward's hand. Somewhere, pain registered. But in the moment, with the smell of smoke and paraffin overwhelming his senses, Edward felt nothing.

He reached up and grabbed the man by the collar with his other hand, twisting, cutting off air.

"You idiot," he said darkly.

The sound of wood striking against sandpaper—the brief smell of phosphorus—brought him back to himself. For a moment, he felt fear, and with it, every other sensation returned: the sharp pain in his hand, the burn of his lungs.

"Let me go," the other man said. "Let me go or I'll drop this now."

Edward's attention focused on the flare of the match, that perilous dancing flame. Hell, the fumes in this room were thick enough that they might ignite.

"Stop being an idiot and put that thing out," Edward growled. "You'll kill us both."

The man's hand trembled. Edward reached out—his hand didn't seem to be working properly—and crushed the flame with his glove.

His heart was beating like the wings of a flock of birds. The man kicked out once, twice—uselessly, now, because Edward had hold of him and was not letting go.

He could tell the moment the man gave up—when his limbs came to rest and he looked into Edward's eyes, his lips pulling into a resigned frown.

"Oh, yes," Edward said in a low growl. "You should be afraid. You are in a heap of trouble."

⌘　⌘　⌘

BY THE TIME NIGHT FELL, the last remnants of Free's home—charred and blackened embers, scarcely holding together in the shape of a building—had almost stopped smoldering.

It was gone. Her home, her place of safety… But that had been an illusion, too. Her hands were streaked with soot; her dress smelled of paraffin. But her press was still standing. Victory, of a sort.

Some victory.

She trudged back to her knot of tired, bedraggled employees. They'd all worked hard. She wished she could send them home. There was no time to be weary, though. There was too much to be done.

The most important of those things needed to be done quickly. "Amanda," Free said, "you'll need to leave now, if you wish to catch the night train to London."

"But—"

"We can't take even an instant to sit still and lick our wounds," Free said. "Every moment we spend combating this is a moment lost to a larger, more important fight. If something else happens, you need to be in London, where you can commission another press to print our paper."

More importantly, if something else was planned for tonight, if something happened to Free, she needed to make sure Amanda survived to carry things on. But she didn't say that; if she spoke it out loud, she might lose her nerve altogether.

She didn't have to. Amanda's chin quivered, but she nodded.

"Melissa, make sure Amanda gets safely to the station. While you're in town, let them know we have someone here that the constables will need to take into custody." That had to be done; if they had any chance of presenting this affair to the public, they'd have to be seen to play by civilized rules.

She didn't feel very civilized. She turned away, before she lost her nerve and begged her friend to stay. She didn't see Amanda off. There was too much to do, after all. She had a response to finish, a paper that needed to be out on the 4 a.m. train. There was no time to stop now.

"All right, everyone," she said in a carrying voice. "We have paraffin to clean up."

And while they were doing that, she had a story to uncover.

Mr. Clark had bound their captive at the wrists and feet and tied him to a chair. The man was stowed in the archive room. She needed to know who had sent him, what he'd been tasked with doing. And she needed to know it *now*—in time for her to write that story, before the constables came.

There was no time for anything but swift answers. And she had a scoundrel here, after all.

She took a deep breath and went to find Mr. Clark.

He was in the archive room. The space was small and dark. With an extra chair and the desk still in place, she and Mr. Clark were almost elbow-to-elbow, facing that bound man.

"What have you learned?" Her voice sounded shaky to her own ears. A bad sign, that. She struggled for control.

Mr. Clark turned to her. "His name: Edwin Bartlett. But unfortunately, he doesn't know who hired him. There was at least one intermediary, and I would guess more."

No. She refused to believe that. She had hoped that it would all be simple—that the arsonist would give up James Delacey at the first instant, that he'd be able to describe him perfectly.

It would have been some compensation for losing her home—to be able to place the blame publicly at his door.

Her voice shook when she spoke. "He's lying. He has to know more."

That was met with silence. She couldn't see Mr. Clark's face, and he didn't turn to her.

"He has to be lying," she said. She *needed* him to be lying. "Don't you have…" Her stomach turned at the thought of asking for more. The very idea made her feel ill.

"Don't I have what?"

"Some way." Her hands were shaking. "To encourage him."

"Encourage him." He made a rough noise in his throat, almost a growl. "Miss Marshall, I don't think you want me to say, 'Here, now, Edwin, there's a good chap.' Maybe you need to clarify what you mean by *encourage him.*"

No.

They didn't have time. The constable would likely be here in forty-five minutes, and in any event, with the deliveryman coming at half past two… She had little more than half an hour to get whatever else he knew, if she wanted to have this story in the next paper.

"He's scared as it is," Mr. Clark told her curtly. "Frankly, I doubt he's got the strength of mind to tell lies at the moment."

She breathed out. "Maybe we need to jostle his memory. Isn't there something you can do?"

"I don't know nothing," the arsonist put in, his voice a whine. "I've said it all, told all the details. It was a man from London who hired me, a big man. Bald head."

She felt sick.

She couldn't see much of Mr. Clark. But his silhouette straightened and he turned toward her. "You don't know what you're suggesting," he said. "You can't even say the word aloud. You want me to torture him."

Said out loud, that ugly word—*torture*—seemed to fill the room. She didn't want it. Every part of her rebelled at it. But there was that small corner of her that wondered. He'd burned down her house. He might know more. Wouldn't it be only fair if…?

Mr. Clark made a rude noise. "God. I forget, sometimes, how naïve you really are."

It felt like a slap in the face.

"I'm not naïve. Just because I can't say the word."

"Oh, you're naïve to even think of it." She'd heard him angry before, had heard him amused. She didn't know what this emotion he expressed now was. Something darker, something more real than she'd ever heard from him before. "You don't torture a man to get the truth, Miss Marshall. Didn't you read your history of the Spanish Inquisition?"

Free took a step back from that intensity. Her back met the wall of the room. "I don't understand."

"Of course you don't understand. You've read a story, no doubt, where a man had information. Someone wielded a well-placed knife to make him divulge his secret in time. Good prevailed, and they all lived happily ever after."

She felt sick.

"That was a tepid piece of fiction written by some man who sat at a comfortable fire, inventing a barely plausible tale for a gullible audience. You don't torture a man to find out the truth, Miss Marshall, no matter how the stories sound. Any *real* scoundrel will tell you as much. You torture a man to make him into someone else. True pain is like black ink. Enough of it can blot out a man's soul. If you're willing to use it, you can write whatever you wish in its place. Want him to swear to Catholicism? Hand him off to the inquisitors. Want him to believe the sun sets in the east, and the moon is made of green cheese? Ready the hot knives. But once you spill that ink on his soul, you'll never get it out. He'll say anything, be anything, *believe* anything—just so that you'll stop. You'll ask him about Delacey, and he'll invent any story you wish to hear, just to spare himself the pain. But it won't hold up under observation, because it won't be true."

She swallowed.

"So no, Miss Marshall. I won't give you your easy answer. It doesn't exist. Go write the messy, difficult story. Write the tale without a happy ending. We'll not get any other sort tonight."

It was a good thing it was dark; she didn't think she could look him in the eye.

She turned on her heel and stalked out of the room. The light in the main pressroom was blinding after the darkness of the archive room. The women—*her* women, women whose children she knew, whose hopes she'd listened to—were bustling about. Spreading sand to soak up the oil, shoveling that into buckets, and then scrubbing tables with soap and washing away the last of the residue with vinegar. Already the smell was beginning to dissipate.

Her hands were shaking. She'd never heard Mr. Clark talk like this before. That had been something close to a black rage—and over torture, of all things.

What kind of scoundrel *was* he?

She took a deep breath. He was the kind of scoundrel that was right.

She had to hone her anger to a fine edge. That poor, miserable creature in her back room was only a tool.

She needed a plan.

And for tonight, she needed a story. Maybe it would be an ugly, bare story, one with no simple endings or clear explanations. But it would be a story nonetheless.

⌘ ⌘ ⌘

BY THE TIME THE CONSTABLES ARRIVED, solemn in their blue uniforms, and took Mr. Bartlett into custody, Free's press was running, spitting out pages.

She'd stuck to the bare basics: that denial that she'd crafted before Amanda left, and then the story of the fire and the man captured.

Around midnight, Alice delivered an armload of blankets. Free busied herself setting up a pallet in her office. She was arranging the makeshift bedding when Mr. Clark came in.

"What are you doing?" he shouted over the sound of the press.

She hadn't been able to look at him since the archive room. She still couldn't do it now. She stared at the gray wool blankets in her hands instead. "I'm preparing to sleep here."

He folded his arms and glared at her.

"My house is gone." She had to yell to be heard above the noise, and it felt good to vent her anger. "Someone must stay here overnight to be certain nothing else will happen. Alice and her husband are bedding down in the archive room, and since I have nowhere else to go—"

"If you're staying," he said, leaning down to her, "I'm staying."

"Mr. Clark, don't be ridiculous."

"I'm not being ridiculous."

She made the mistake of looking up as he said that. His eyes were dark. She'd expected him to be smoldering with anger after their argument. Instead, he seemed cold—ice cold. As if he didn't care about her, didn't care about anything.

He cast her another dark look, and then shook his head and turned away.

Chapter Nine

THE PRESS FINISHED ITS RUN after one in the morning. They packaged the papers in weary silence, readying them to be taken down to the station. A little water and soap, and a nightrail borrowed from Alice, readied Free for bed, such as it would be tonight. But after Alice and her husband had retired, Free found herself unable to close her eyes. She stared instead at the darkened ceiling and realized she had one more task to do tonight.

She stood and went to her door.

Mr. Clark was out on the main floor. He'd shed his coat; Alice had apparently brought him his share of blankets as well, and he was sitting on these. His feet were bare and he was examining his hand in the moonlight. He looked up as she opened the door, reached over, and pulled on a glove. He didn't stand as she approached. He didn't speak. He simply watched her come closer.

God, he still radiated cold.

She was not wearing as much as she normally would have. Oh, she knew the nightrail covered everything that needed to be covered. Still, it left her feeling…naked. And she already felt more than a little exposed to this man.

She knelt beside him. He didn't move, not so much as an inch.

"Thank you," she told him.

His expression didn't change, not in the slightest, but he looked over at her as if he could freeze her heart.

She didn't stop. "Thank you for your help. For stopping the fire. For stopping *both* the fires." Her voice dropped. "Thank you for stopping me from doing something I would have regretted. I hadn't said thank you yet—and I owe you that."

"It was nothing."

"And thank you for staying now—"

He cut her off with a shake of his head. "You're making me out to be quite the hero, Miss Marshall. Tell yourself whatever lies you wish, but leave me out of them. I'm here tonight because I don't want to be alone. No other reason."

It took him a moment to realize that he was telling the simple truth. That she was sitting near him on the floor. Not *next* to him; not quite. Two feet separated them. Distance enough…and yet not enough distance.

He cast a glance in her direction.

"So, Mr. Clark," she said. "When have you ever seen a man tortured?"

"Elsewhere." He bit the word off. "It was far worse than you can imagine, Miss Marshall. I don't have the stomach to talk about it, and I certainly don't have the desire."

"Very well, then."

He pressed his hand to his forehead, shaking his head. "I don't know why I bother. There's no point to any of this."

Free traced a drawing on the floor with her finger. "My opinion? I think you bother because you're not quite as bad a man as you make yourself out to be."

"Yes, tell yourself that, Miss Marshall." There was a mocking tone in his voice. "Tell yourself that I'm your knight in shining armor, here to save you from fires and foes. That's a lie, but some people need lies to sleep at night. I'm here for my own reasons. I admire you. I *like* you." His smile grew darker. "I'll take you to bed, if you wish. But don't ask me to pretend that this"—he waved his hand about —"that any of this matters a damn. It doesn't."

"You don't really believe that."

He moved an inch toward her. "You're the loveliest woman ever to bash her head against a wall, but the wall you're battering is higher and thicker than the Great Wall of China, and there's only one of you. It's not the stones that will give way to you, my dear."

Free swallowed. "You've got it wrong."

"Ah, the wall is made of paper, then, and you'll burst through it at any second." He laughed at her, and she could hear that ice in his voice. "Give yourself another ten years, and maybe you'll understand what you're facing. Until then, go ahead. Keep fighting."

Free contemplated him in the darkness. "After tonight, do you still think that I'm naïve? That I don't understand how the world works?"

"There's no proof you *do* understand it. After everything you saw today, you still stayed up to send out your next issue. What do you imagine your little paper will change? Do you think that suddenly, Delacey will read one of your essays and say, 'Good God, I've got it all wrong. Women deserve to be treated fairly after all'?"

"No," Free looked away. "Of course I don't think that. I'll never convince him."

"Or do you imagine that there is a group of men somewhere who haven't yet made up their minds on the question of female suffrage? Men who are thinking, 'Well, I suppose women might be actual human beings, just like men. Maybe I had better look out for them.'"

Free felt her face flush. "Don't be ridiculous."

"Because I can tell you what will happen," Mr. Clark said in his dark, dangerous voice. "You women will squawk amongst yourselves about injustice and fairness. Maybe if you do it loudly enough, someday a handful of you will be allowed to vote, and it will be accounted a great victory. Maybe in fifty years, women will achieve a distinct minority in the professional classes. We might have a woman doctor, a woman barrister, and then five or ten of you might form an organization together and shake hands because something has been accomplished."

Free let out a breath.

"Maybe in a hundred years of women voting, you might manage a single female Prime Minister." He gave her a rough smile. "But just the one, and even so, people will never take her seriously. If she's stern, they'll blame her menstrual cycle. If she smiles, it will be proof that women are not strong enough to lead. That's what you're setting yourself up for, Miss Marshall. A lifetime of small wins, of victories that land like lead in your stomach. Your cause may be just. But you're delusional if you think you can accomplish anything. You're pitting yourself against an institution that is older than our country, Miss Marshall. It's so old that we rarely even need speak of it. Rage all you want, Miss Marshall, but you'll have more success emptying the Thames with a thimble."

He touched a finger to his forehead in mock salute, as if tipping a hat. As if she'd just departed the land of reality, and he'd wished her a pleasant journey. His words didn't match his actions, though. He came even closer to her as he spoke, leaning in with every sentence, until he seemed almost on the verge of kissing her.

"You're right," Free said, shutting her eyes.

He blinked and sat back, cocking his head. "What did you say?"

"I said you were right," Free repeated. "You're right about all of that. If history is any guide, it will take years—decades, perhaps—before women get the vote. As for the rest of it, I imagine that any woman who manages to stand out will be a target for abuse. She always is."

His eyes crinkled in confusion.

"What I don't understand is why you think you need to lecture me about this all. I run a newspaper for women. Do you imagine that nobody has ever written to me to explain precisely what you just said?"

He frowned. "Well."

"Do you suppose I've never been told that I'm upset because I am menstruating? That I would calm down if only some man would put a child in my belly? Usually, the person writing offers to help out with that very task." She swallowed bile in memory. "Shall I tell you what someone painted on my door one midnight? Or do you want to read the letters I receive?" Free wrapped her arms around herself. "I am here, on the floor of my press, because I told a man I wouldn't bed him, and so he burned my house down. So, yes, Edward. I know the obstacles women face. I know them better than you ever will."

He exhaled harshly. "God, Free."

"Do you think I don't know that the only tool I have is my thimble? I'm the one wielding it. I *know*. There are days I stare out at the Thames and wish I could stop bailing." Her voice dropped. "My arms are tired, and there's so much water that I'm afraid it'll pull me under. But do you know why I keep going?"

He reached out and touched her chin. "That's the one thing I can't figure out. You don't seem stupid; why do you persist?"

She lifted her face to his. "Because I'm not trying to empty the Thames."

Silence met this.

"Look at the tasks you listed, the ones you think are impossible. You want men to give women the right to vote. You want men to think of women as equals, rather than as lesser animals who go around spewing illogic between our menstrual cycles."

He still wasn't saying anything.

"All your tasks are about men," she told him. "And if you haven't noticed, this is a newspaper for *women*."

"But—if—"

"I had myself committed to a government lock hospital," Free said. "I was locked up with three hundred prostitutes suspected of being infected with syphilis, so I could report accurately on the cruelty of the attendants, the pain of the examinations." She still couldn't bring herself to recall those in any detail—the feel of being held down, the invasive metal tools wielded without an ounce of gentleness had all hazed to thankful forgetfulness. "I told everyone that there were women dying in pain with no comfort but to be tied to their beds writhing in agony. I reported that there were women who had shown no signs of disease in two years who were still kept like prisoners."

"And yet the government is *still* locking up women with syphilis. The Thames rushes on, Miss Marshall."

"But the two women I learned were free of symptoms are now free. And every time Josephine Butler speaks to a crowd of men, she sketches a picture with her words of what those thousands of women endure. Grown men weep to hear it, and we chip away at that wall, day by day. It *will* come down someday." She raised her chin and looked him in the eye. "You see a river rushing by without end. You see a sad collection of women with thimbles, all dipping out an inconsequential amount."

He didn't say anything.

"But we're not trying to empty the Thames," she told him. "Look at what we're doing with the water we remove. It doesn't go to waste. We're using it to water our gardens, sprout by sprout. We're growing bluebells and clovers where once there was a desert. All you see is the river, but *I* care about the roses."

His eyes were dark and the light was dim enough that she could see scarcely make him out. But his whole body was turned to her.

"Everything about you matters to me." He leaned in. "It shouldn't. I keep telling myself it shouldn't, that it's only the lust talking. But every time we talk, you turn my world upside down." His smile was tight and weary.

"You're wrong again. The world started out upside down. I'm just trying to set it right side up."

"Either way gives me the most astonishing vertigo."

He reached out. But he didn't touch her—his hand was gloved, and he held it, poised, a hair's breadth from her cheek. She could feel the warmth of him. But he pulled it back with a shake of his head.

"Good night, Miss Marshall," he said.

❃ ❃ ❃

EDWARD WASN'T SURE what roused him in the middle of the night. A sound, high-pitched; a rustle perhaps.

He came instantly awake. His heart rate accelerated; he jumped soundlessly to his feet. But there were no footsteps, no sounds of anyone shuffling about outside. And then that noise sounded again—a soft, muffled moan coming from Miss Marshall's office.

He went to the window that looked in on that space.

The only illumination was the moon, and that came in only indirectly through a single high window. Her form twitched; her hand reached up, as if to push someone away.

He should have let her sleep.

But he was so far beyond *should* when it came to her that he knew he wouldn't. Dangerous to enter her office. He was in his shirtsleeves, and she... He could see her ankle poking out from under a blanket, the flash of her wrist. Miss Marshall was far too undressed for his peace of mind.

He opened the door anyway, kneeling beside her. He set his hand on her shoulder.

"Miss Marshall," he murmured.

She turned again, unwaking. He brushed her forehead. A clammy, cold sweat met his fingers.

"Free." He ran his hand down her cheek.

Still she didn't wake.

"Darling," he whispered.

Her eyes opened on that. She blinked, hazily, up at him. God, he was in so far over his head. With her hair spread out around her, her eyes not quite focused on him, she was the most beautiful thing he had ever seen. He could not have captured her, not with pencil or paint. He couldn't have tried. After all, a man could only draw what he could comprehend.

"Shh, darling," he whispered. The endearment, once used, came too easily to his tongue a second time. "You were having a nightmare."

She exhaled, pressing her lips together. Then, very slowly, she sat up. "I know that," she said tartly. "It was my nightmare."

He wished he could whisper sweet nothings in her ear. *It will all be right. Sleep again; I'll not let anything harm you.*

But he wasn't a sweet nothing sort of man. She dragged her hand over her face and sighed.

"I'm sorry," she told him. "I shouldn't have snapped at you. It's just that I know I shouldn't have nightmares. It's ridiculous."

"Shouldn't you?" he asked gravely.

"It feels foolish to admit it. Like I'm admitting to fear."

He cast another glance at her. "And you're not afraid?"

She didn't answer.

"Of course you're afraid, Miss Marshall. Fear is only foolish when it's irrational. You have men painting threats on your door, burning your house down. If they're writing you letters suggesting that you need a child in your belly, I doubt they're offering to put it there only if you're willing."

She let out a shaky breath. "I still have nightmares about being in the lock hospital." She took hold of a curl of her hair, wrapping it around her finger. "And that makes no sense. I was there only for a few weeks, and there's no danger of my being sent back."

He fell to silence.

"I knew my brother would get me out. And still I remember the baths—ice water in winter. Brown ice water. They didn't change it between women."

He shuddered.

"And the medical exams. It wasn't like having a doctor listen to your pulse. They had to examine you visually." She let out another breath. "Everywhere. I tell myself I'm strong and brave, but I had been going to spend two months there. I broke after two exams."

He took her hand in his. He was still wearing his gloves—he'd been feeling too self-conscious to take them off. He didn't say anything. He wasn't sure if he was holding her hand to give her strength, or to drive away his own plague of memories.

She sighed. "But then, what would you know of it? You're not afraid of anything."

He ought to have laughed. He should have told her that fear was for other men, because *he* was the thing that they feared.

Tonight, he couldn't make himself tell her that lie. Instead, Edward let out a long breath. "Percussion fuses are the very devil."

She didn't say anything, and for a long while, he didn't either. Their hands tangled, warmth meeting warmth.

"I was in Strasbourg," he finally said. "Seven years ago, during the siege. I was on the fire brigade. The Prussians had these rifle-bored cannons that could shoot shells an impossible distance—right into the center of the city itself. All those shells had percussion fuses so they exploded on impact. There was no place safe. Cellars, if you lined them with bags of sand—but then the danger was that the house would collapse on top of you. Later, I heard that in the first days of the siege, the Prussians had sent through a shell every twenty seconds. You can't imagine it, Miss Marshall. Everything burned, and what didn't burn, splintered. Have you ever seen plaster dust ignite in the air? I have. And we've not begun to talk about the machine guns—capable of sending out bullets at the speed of a hand-crank."

She turned her head to look at him. Her fingers played in his.

"The worst were the shells that didn't explode on impact. They could go at any time. I saw a man ripped to shreds by one in front of my eyes."

For a long moment, he didn't say anything. He couldn't.

"I don't believe in lying to myself," he said. "I'm afraid. To this day, I can't hear a loud noise without jumping. And I never do like sleeping in small spaces. I'm always afraid the walls will come down on me. Fear is a natural response."

Somehow, his arm came around her.

"It's what you do with your fear that matters. And that's what I can't make out about you."

She turned to look in his eyes.

"Lightning always strikes the highest tree on the plain," he told her.

Her eyes were wide, glinting in the dim moonlight.

"Most people who are struck by lightning learn to keep their heads down. It's only people like you who grit your teeth and then come out again, refusing to cower. That's what I can't understand about you. You've been struck by lightning, again and again, and still you stand up. I don't see how you are possible."

God, it was so easy to hold her. To pull her closer to him, to feel her body against his. The curve of her breast pressed against him, the line of her leg.

She didn't answer. Instead, she tilted her head up to him. His arm came around her; his lips came down on hers, and the rest of the world—the dark room surrounding them, the uncomfortable feel of hard boards beneath too-thin blankets—seemed to slip away. There was nothing but her shoulder under his hand, her lips soft under his.

Kisses were dangerous things, when a man wanted a woman.

They made him want to toss his heart in her lap. They weren't just an exchange of pleasantries; they offered a glimpse into the future. A kiss hinted at the pleasure that might come from a night in bed, at the deliciousness that a heady, week-long affair might bring.

But when Edward kissed Frederica Marshall, something terrible happened—something that had never happened in a lifetime of kisses.

He didn't see an end.

He wasn't going to want a sweet farewell in a few weeks' time. He wouldn't walk away with a light heart. He was going to want more and more—more kisses, more of her, again and again.

He was going to want the sweet taste of her, the feel of her fingers resting in his until the end of his days. The arsonist had stomped on his hand; it was badly bruised. Perhaps that was why he squeezed her hand in his, welcoming the sharp pain as a reminder.

He pulled away. Her eyes shone up at him, bright and hazed with desire.

Oh, he had known this was happening from the first moment he'd met her. He'd *known,* and he'd lied to himself, calling it desire, want, revenge—anything but what it was: He was falling in love with her.

He hadn't thought there was anything left to him that could fall in love.

He pulled away. But he couldn't make himself be abrupt with her. Not even now. "Free. Darling." His hand slid in her hair, stroking it gently. "Get some sleep."

He stood.

It was only when he was at the door of her office that she spoke.

"Was it in Strasbourg that you were tortured?"

A sick, black pit opened around him. This time, she had not said *that you watched a man be tortured.* She'd figured that out as well. He stood in place for a moment, simply forcing his lungs to work.

When he had control of himself, he turned back to her. He made himself smile, even though the smile was a lie. He made sure his voice was easy, even though nothing about him would ever be easy again.

"No," he said. Casual—that was what he wanted. Casual, so that she'd not suspect the truth. A casual man would not have lost himself completely.

He shrugged negligently, and even though she could not see it, he found a negligent smile. "That came after."

⌘　⌘　⌘

FREE AWOKE THE NEXT MORNING to the sound of someone moving about her press. She jerked to her feet, brushing her unruly hair into some semblance of order with her fingers.

But the only person she saw through the window was Clarice, the woman whose morning duties required her to get everything in readiness for the day. Clarice was folding up the blankets where Edward had slept that night.

He wasn't anywhere in sight.

Free dressed swiftly and came out into the main room. "Good morning." She wondered if Clarice knew why she'd slept in her office—but by the sympathetic look on her face, she'd been told everything.

At least, everything that had happened until midnight.

"Here," Clarice said, handing her a piece of paper. "Mr. Clark gave me this a half hour ago, as he was leaving."

Leaving.

She took the paper.

Miss Marshall—

Business takes me elsewhere for the moment. I'll be back this afternoon.

—E.

Nothing more. Last night, everything had changed between them, and it wasn't just the kiss. There was something about sitting with a man in the dark, sharing secrets well past midnight, that altered the course of what was to come.

Two days ago, she'd have said she didn't trust him.

This morning?

It felt as if he were still here, still holding her hand. Still telling her that he couldn't comprehend how she continued. She felt all of that even though he wasn't here.

And yet he had the right of it. There was business to take care of—more than she could possibly comprehend. Reality landed on her shoulders like sacks of heavy flour.

She had men to hire to secure the place at night. She had to see to the details of her burned-out home, and incidentally, she ought to find another place to stay until she could build a new one. She needed clothing, a comb, tooth powder—too many items to list. There were advertisers to appease, a story to discover, and James Delacey to destroy. And on top of that all, the paper would have to go out yet again tomorrow.

Better to begin early. Free raised her chin. "Well, let's get started."

Chapter Ten

THE STABLES WERE QUIET and peaceful, pleasantly dark after the midmorning sun. Edward felt totally at odds as he stepped inside. His right hand had hurt last night; it ached now. His palm was dark red with a forming bruise—but nothing was broken, and pain was the least of his worries.

Patrick Shaughnessy stood at the far end of the stables, examining a mare's hind leg. He glanced up as Edward came in, but kept on with his work with no more than a nod of acknowledgment. Patrick's father had been like that, too—not one to interrupt his work unless there was blood or a broken limb.

After a moment, Edward mounted the ladder to the hayloft and found a pitchfork. Pitching hay with his bruised hand was a difficult prospect. At first, the pain was just a twinge, but it grew to a sharp throb. Every forkful hurt a little more. It was as good a reminder as any. Deep down, there was nothing but pain.

It took some ten minutes for his muscles to remember the proper rhythm for the work. The pain concentrated in the palm of his hand, pulsing in time to each thrust.

All you see is the river, but I care about the roses.

Hard to remember there was more than the river, when it had once overflowed its banks and swept him away. He'd almost drowned. He'd learned his lesson: Don't go near rivers. Don't go anywhere near rivers.

Miss Marshall spent her life daring those more powerful than her to swat her down. The hell of it was, her determination was some kind of contagion. He could feel it infecting him, making him *believe*. Making him tell himself lies like *I could do some good* and *I want her forever*.

He gritted his teeth and pitched hay, picking up a heavy forkful and letting it slide to the box in the stall below.

No, he had to remember that she was wrong. You had to keep your eye on the river, no matter what she said. If you let your control slip, rivers would pull you under. In your desperation, you'd claw at anyone around just to get a gasp of air. You wouldn't even realize the harm you'd done until it was too late.

"I think," Patrick's voice said behind him, "that Buttercup has had enough now."

Edward stopped, breathing heavily, coming back to himself. He set the pitchfork down, looking out over the stables beneath him. Horses munched peacefully on oats and hay, tails swishing in idyllic rest. A stallion stamped restively and shook its head.

It was peaceful here, and part of him wanted to take up residence in this stable. But there was no way he could crawl back into his childhood.

Instead, he looked back at Patrick. "You have always been my greatest liability," he said solemnly.

Another man might have taken offense at those words, but Patrick understood him.

"It never mattered where in Europe I went," he said, "or how much time elapsed. You never stopped mattering to me—you and Stephen. I wished I could be the hardened fellow who never cared. But I saw Stephen the other day…"

Edward shrugged.

"You never wished for any such thing," Patrick said stoutly.

Edward contemplated this. "Yes. You're right." He sat down, dangling his legs over the edge of the hayloft. "After all these years, after everything I've done. You're still more my brother than the man who shares my blood. The surprise isn't that I'm still hanging around you. It's that you've not recognized me yet for what I am."

He had tried. God, he had tried to drive Patrick away. He'd told him every vile thing he'd done—as if he, like his friend, were Catholic, and Patrick his confessor. Every forged letter. Every piece of blackmail. Every wrong act, he'd relayed to his friend by letter. Every time he'd been certain that this brazen theft, this false story, would set his friend against him.

"Oh, I know what you are," Patrick said quietly. "I'm just waiting."

Edward flexed his hand. "Love is hell," he said shortly. "It makes me realize I still have something to lose. It was bad enough when it was just you and Stephen."

"Oh?"

Edward kicked his legs angrily into space. "Oh." He let that syllable hang for a few seconds before continuing on. "You were right, you know. Miss Marshall is very clever." That was all he needed to say.

"And what are you going to do about it?" Patrick asked.

There was part of him—a foolish, damnable part of him—that wanted to give the answer that would make his friend smile. *I'm going to stay in England and woo her.*

He had but to hear the thought to recognize its impossibility. If James discovered Edward hanging about England for good, he'd never rest for fear that he'd lose the title and his estates. And if Edward was found in the company of Frederica Marshall, James's sworn enemy? James might finally muster the nerve to do more than burn down a few buildings.

Edward could take over the title. Announce himself as Edward Delacey. He prodded the idea gently in his mind; it felt as sore and tender as his bruised hand. The water he'd landed himself in was deep indeed, if he'd even consider the possibility.

Edward shook his head. "I'm going to do the same thing with Miss Marshall that I do to everyone I love. I'm going to leave before I can do her harm."

Patrick looked at him, his mouth quirking skeptically.

"I will," Edward said. "Just as soon as I can get everyone else to leave her alone."

⌘ ⌘ ⌘

EDWARD RETURNED TO CAMBRIDGE in the afternoon, but when he arrived at the press and opened the door, he almost turned on his heel and walked away. Stephen Shaughnessy stood two feet away.

The other man didn't look around as Edward stood in the doorway. His back was turned to Edward, and he was gesticulating in exaggerated motions, arguing in excited tones. He was almost Edward's height. A massive change since Stephen had followed him around all those years ago.

Here he was, still following him around. Inconvenient as ever. Edward found himself smiling.

Stephen and Free—no, he'd best keep his distance as much as possible—Mr. Shaughnessy and Miss Marshall had their heads bent over a table.

"No." Miss Marshall brandished a blue pencil. "You can't say *Dukes get all the attention.* That sounds bitter, and you mustn't sound bitter." She crossed off a line as she spoke.

Edward could turn around and return in half an hour. By then, Stephen would no doubt have departed. No matter what, he couldn't risk being recognized.

Miss Marshall was wearing a ghastly green gown, one that had no doubt been lent to her by a friend. It fit rather poorly, gaping at the bosom and stretching at the hips. The color dimmed the fire of her hair—which, without her normal pins, refused to stay in place. Little strands made an auburn halo around her head.

He'd never seen anything quite so lovely.

Miss Marshall nodded to Stephen. "This part is good here, but this introduction strikes me as too serious. It won't do."

"Aw, Free."

God, Edward knew that phrase. How many times had they heard *Aw, Edward* or *Aw, Patrick* when they were younger?

Stephen turned wide, begging eyes on her. "Can't I—"

"No," she said severely. "You can't. Stop whining and do it right. Now do I have to glower at you for the next ten minutes, or can you produce a creditable paragraph on your own?"

Edward should leave now, while Stephen was still occupied. Before he was recognized. And yet now that he stood this close, he didn't want to go.

Besides, what was the likelihood that Stephen would recognize him? Edward's own brother hadn't. Stephen still thought him dead, and Edward's mirror told him how much his looks had altered. Even his accent had shifted. Nine years living on the Continent, scarcely speaking English at all, had changed the natural cadences of his speech.

Miss Marshall looked up at that moment and made his decision for him. She looked at him and then her whole face lit up. He almost staggered back under the force of her smile. It made him feel…reckless. A man couldn't disappoint a smile like that.

"Mr. Clark. You've returned."

She sounded almost surprised. As if he were the sort to assist her in her predicament, kiss her, and then walk away.

He was. That was precisely the sort of man he was, and there was no losing sight of it.

He smiled at her nonetheless. "I have. This time. It turns out there's something we forgot last night—"

At that moment, Stephen looked up from his paper. Every muscle Edward possessed tensed involuntarily, waiting.

"Wait, Miss Marshall," Stephen said. "I don't need ten minutes. I have it…" His eye fell on Edward, and he trailed off, frowning.

Only one way to handle this. Tell the lie before the other man had a chance to recognize it for falsehood.

Edward stepped forward. "I'm Clark," he said casually. "I'm an admirer of your column."

Stephen blinked at him quizzically, as if trying to figure out why he seemed familiar.

"Shaughnessy," he said faintly, by way of introduction. "So *you're* the Edward Clark that I've been hearing so much about."

Miss Marshall colored faintly at that, and Edward felt gratified despite himself.

"I'm assisting Miss Marshall with a delicate matter," Edward said. "Now, if you'll excuse us—"

Stephen simply smiled. "No, not yet. I have to run this by Free."

Stephen used her pet name far too readily for Edward's comfort. It gave him a sense of domestic tranquility, as if the three of them might become friends. As if they might spend evenings together, laughing and telling stories.

"By all means," Edward said disparagingly. "If you can't pen a simple paragraph without Miss Marshall's supervision, far be it from me to hinder you."

Stephen cast him an amused look, but he turned back to Miss Marshall.

"It goes like this." Stephen cleared this throat. "Miss Muddled, your mistake lies in thinking that your voice deserves to be heard. You should first think of things from a lord's point of view. Who, in all of England, is more powerless than a duke?"

Edward's eyebrows rose.

"Technically," Stephen continued, "we all know the answer to that question: Everybody is. But everyone below a duke is also, from said duke's perspective, a nobody. That makes the duke the most powerless man in England. The nobility controls the House of Lords, commands the highest social respect, and yet they control a mere ninety-five percent of the wealth. If people like you continue to demand living wages, how will a duke hire the hundreds of servants to which he is entitled? The very fabric of our society unravels in horror at such a thought."

"Better." Miss Marshall nodded. "I still don't like the last sentence. It's too overblown. Continue more in the same vein as the first part—perhaps something like, 'Won't someone think of the dukes?'"

Stephen made a note on his paper. "Right."

"Do the nobility really control ninety-five percent of the wealth? That figure seems high. One would think that the industrialists' holdings—"

"Oh, no," Stephen said with an easy smile. "I just made that up right now."

Miss Marshall set a hand on her hip. "Stephen Shaughnessy," she threatened. "You may write a satire column, but by God, you will write an *accurate* satire while you're working with me."

"I was standing here the whole time!" Stephen said. "You saw me. I didn't have a chance to go and look up facts. Besides, it's much more fun just making things up about lords. That's what they do in Parliament; why shouldn't I have the opportunity to return the favor?"

"Stephen." She glared at him, doing her best to look annoyed, and Edward wanted to laugh out loud.

Thus had all his interactions with Stephen played out—trying not to laugh when Stephen said the things he did. He was impossible to reprimand. But…

"By the by," Stephen said, "what is the difference between a viscount and a stallion?"

Miss Marshall shook her head. "What is it?"

Stephen gave her a broad smile. "The first is a horse's arse. The second is an entire horse."

She buried her head in her hands. "No. You cannot distract me with terrible jokes. You are supposed to be looking up facts. Shoo!"

But Stephen didn't stop. "What's the difference between a marquess and a paperweight?"

"I'm sure you'll tell me."

"One of them can't do anything unless a servant helps it along. The other one holds down papers."

Miss Marshall simply looked at him and shook her head. "They're getting worse."

"Is there an entire series of these uncivil jokes?" Edward put in. "And if so, can I hear more of them?"

"Uncivil?" Miss Marshall looked about the room and then leaned in. "Oh, Stephen is being very civil, Mr. Clark. Very welcoming to you. Stephen and I don't tell lord jokes around just anyone."

Stephen leaned in. "As a fine point," he pretended to whisper, "I don't tell lord jokes around Lady Amanda. She's a halfway decent sort. It's not *her* fault her father's a marquess."

"Yes," Miss Marshall put in darkly. "It was her mother's. Marrying a lord. Hmph."

Edward blinked at that. "Miss Marshall, are you trying to tell me that you didn't dream of marrying a lord when you were young? That you didn't play at being a lady, imagining what it would be like to be waited on hand and foot? I thought every little girl with any inclination at all to marry dreamed of catching the eye of a lord."

"God, no." She looked horrified. "Farm girls who catch the eye of a lord don't end up *married*. If we're lucky, we don't end up pregnant. No. When I was a girl, I wanted to be a pirate."

That brought up an all-too-pleasant image—Miss Marshall, the rich, dark red of her hair unbound and flying defiantly in the wind aboard a ship's deck. She'd wear a loose white shirt and pantaloons. He would definitely surrender.

"I am less shocked than you might imagine," Edward heard himself say. "Entirely unshocked."

She smiled in pleasure.

"A bloodthirsty cutthroat profession? Good thing you gave that up. It would never have suited you."

Her expression of pleasure dimmed.

"You'd have succeeded too easily," Edward continued, "and now you'd be sitting, bored as sin, atop a heap of gold too large to spend in one lifetime. Still, though, wouldn't it solve ever so many problems if you married a lord? James Delacey could never touch you again if you did."

Stephen's eyes narrowed at that. Miss Marshall's expression changed from amused to serious.

Edward didn't know what he was thinking, asking her about marriage. He wasn't a damned viscount. He refused to be one. And whatever odd flutterings he may have felt in her presence, whatever odd imaginings he had harbored, he wasn't going to marry her.

And yet... It was tempting, too. While he hadn't been paying attention, his mind had constructed a might-have-been, a world where he'd never been cast out, where he'd never had to make his heart as black and hard as coal. If he'd been Edward Delacey, he might have courted her in his own right. Edward Delacey, dead fool that he was, could have had the one thing that Edward Clark never would.

Miss Marshall snorted. "God, no," she said with a roll of her eyes. "I'd rather carry a cutlass."

"Ah, but think of the advantages."

"What advantages?" She looked around her. "I've built something here. It's a business that is not just for women, but for *all* women. We print essays from women who work fourteen hours a day in the mines, from prostitutes, from millworkers demanding a woman's union. Do you think I'd give this up to plan *dinner parties?*"

Like this—intense and serious—she was even more beautiful than before. She tossed her head, and he wanted to grab hold of her and kiss her.

It wasn't as if he wanted to marry her; God forbid that he contemplate anything so permanent. But he'd entertained the idea. Viscount Claridge, he was sure, would have been able to woo her. It had been a strange sort of comfort—that even though he couldn't have her as himself, some other version of himself might have accomplished it.

But there they were. Edward Clark, liar and blackmailer extraordinaire, had a better shot at Frederica Marshall than Viscount Claridge. It was the worst of his damned luck that they happened to be the same person.

He was saved from having to come up with an answer by Stephen.

"Hold on one moment," Stephen said, setting a hand on Free's arm. "Do you mean to tell me that *James Delacey* is causing you difficulties?"

Miss Marshall glanced over at Edward, and then sighed and looked back. "We believe he was behind the fire." She sounded tired once again. "We think he's behind the charge of copying, too. And that ugliness with you the other day."

"I know James Delacey." Stephen's lips thinned. "He used to delight in tormenting me as a child. I would follow my brother around all the time, just so I wouldn't find myself alone with him."

Stephen had never said a word of that as a child.

"He whipped a skittish mare that he shouldn't have been riding. It reared and kicked my father in the chest, and then he told everyone that my father had mishandled it. No surprise that he's still an ass." Stephen glowered bitterly. "I do wish..." He trailed off, giving his head a shake.

"What do you wish?" Miss Marshall asked.

Stephen looked up, past Miss Marshall. Right past her, straight into Edward's eyes. "I wish his elder brother was still alive."

Stephen could have just been addressing Edward out of politeness. They were part of the same conversation; people conversing with one another looked at each other. Still, Edward felt a cold chill run down the back of his neck.

Stephen continued. "He was a much better sort. Just goes to show that life isn't fair. People like Ned Delacey perish, while his brother gets the title. That right there is everything that is wrong with the House of Lords. In any event, I didn't mean to interrupt. If the two of you are talking about how best to deal with Delacey, I'll let you get on with it."

"Do you think you'd have anything to add to the conversation about him?" Miss Marshall asked.

Stephen looked straight at Edward. "Clark," he said, "have you had a recent conversation with Delacey?"

"I have," Edward said solemnly.

Stephen waved them off. "Then I trust you to deal with him. My knowledge of the man is far in the past. Clark's your man, Free."

Miss Marshall simply accepted this with a nod and gestured to her office. "Mr. Clark. If you will."

Edward brushed past Stephen. But he'd gone only three steps when Stephen spoke again. "Oh, Mr. Clark."

Edward turned.

Stephen was smiling—that sure smile he employed when he was certain he was about to say something very clever.

Edward felt a dreadful sense of foreboding. "Yes?"

"Ask Miss Marshall who her father is." And then, while Edward was frowning in confusion, Stephen winked.

Chapter Eleven

FREE FOUND HERSELF BLUSHING as she entered her office. It was the same room as always: desk, chair, papers kept in careful stacks. But the last time they'd been in this office together, she'd kissed him. Even though everything had changed—it was broad daylight, instead of dark night; she was fully clothed instead of dressed for sleep—somehow, the echo of that kiss still connected them, a solid, visceral thing.

Apparently, she'd let enough of her interest show when greeting Mr. Clark that Stephen had noticed, if that last cryptic comment meant anything.

Mr. Clark came in behind her. She seated herself safely behind the desk, smoothing her skirts into place.

He stood on the other side of the desk and watched her intently. "Who is your father, Miss Marshall?"

"Don't listen to Stephen," she huffed. "He's a bit of a jokester. It doesn't mean anything."

"No?"

She sighed. "My father was once a pugilist. I told you he used to take me to matches when I was younger."

His face went completely blank.

"Stephen was teasing me," she explained to him. "Implying that I needed to let you know that my honor would be protected. Which is ridiculous, frankly. If you intended to force me, you've already had the chance, several times over. As for what happened…" She was blushing again, and she hated blushing. Blushing implied shyness; shyness meant that whatever she felt could be used against her.

He was looking at her lips. "As for that?" he asked quietly.

"*That* is not any of my father's business." And she wouldn't have minded repeating that kiss.

Mr. Clark didn't seem to agree. He lowered himself gingerly into the chair, but kept his eyes on her desk. His expression had gone grim.

"Marshall." He shook his head. "I should have thought. I don't suppose your father is Hugo Marshall, then."

"Oh, do you know of him?" That was unusual. "He only fought for a few years, and as he was never in the heavyweight class, he's not much remembered."

Mr. Clark sighed and rubbed his chin. "There's an account of his fight with Byron the Bear in *Prize-Fighting Through the Ages.*" At that, he finally looked up at her—but his glare seemed almost accusatory. "My childhood friend and I used to reenact that one. That fight was the subject of one of my first decent oil paintings." The glint in his eyes brightened. "I named my first horse *Wolf* after him."

Free huffed. "It's hardly my fault you made a hero of my father."

"No," he said softly. "But every bloody time I convince myself I ought to walk away from you…"

"Well," she said simply, "you wouldn't have that problem if you stopped convincing yourself of stupid things."

He blinked at that, his mouth working, but there was no point leaving him time to protest. Free moved on briskly. "Now, I've been thinking about our next move. We must connect this fire and the copying to James Delacey. Somehow."

He took a breath, looked in her eyes. There was a beat, as if he were considering repeating his complaint, and then he shrugged.

"As to that, I have an idea. I'd have told you last night, but we were…busy." He smiled, a languid, suggestive smile that sent a little shiver down her spine. "And then we were…busier. Between all our busyness, it completely slipped my mind."

"What slipped your mind?"

His fingers went to the buttons of his jacket, and her mouth dried. His buttons were simple cloth and metal affairs, scarcely worth a second thought. And yet as he undid them, she had second thoughts and third thoughts, none of them proper. His gloved fingers were long and graceful, and every button he undid revealed another inch of creamy linen, one that hinted at broad shoulders and strong muscles.

He'd not shown her the slightest bit of skin, but the act of unbuttoning his coat sparked indecent thoughts—memories of his arm coming around her, his mouth on hers…

He stopped undoing buttons, and she realized he'd only wanted to reach the inside pocket. She sat back in disappointment.

"I stole this from Delacey the other night," he told her, "before I became distracted by thoughts of fire and other perfidy on his part. We made those advance proofs, as you may recall, so that we could tell how they were going astray. Tell me, Miss Marshall." He handed her the paper. "Who did you send this one to?"

She took the page from him, spreading it out on her desk.

She could see him doing up his buttons out of the corner of her eye. Terrible, terrible man. Teasing her with the prospect of more. But if he could pretend it was nothing, she could, too. There—this was the one with the transposed lines.

"This is the one I sent to my brother."

He nodded as he did back the last of his buttons. Alas.

"Do you think there is any chance your brother is personally sending them on? Perhaps he wishes to bring you in line."

"No," she said automatically. "Oliver would never do that."

"Can you be absolutely sure of it? He's not your full brother, is he? Only half, and from what I understand, the other half-brother is a duke. He doesn't sound trustworthy to me."

She rolled her eyes. "I'd as soon mistrust you." It took her a moment to understand how she'd meant that: She'd talked about mistrusting *him* the same way she might have talked of pigs taking flight, or hell acquiring icicles—as if it were such an obvious impossibility that anyone would scoff at it.

But he didn't take it that way. He smiled brightly at her, as if he didn't expect trust, as if last night hadn't happened at all. "You're right. I waited with the mails. Easy enough for me to filch out one copy and return with it just now."

An untrustworthy man would have protested his innocence. But surely a trustworthy man would have been annoyed at being doubted. He was the oddest enigma: a man who neither expected nor wanted her trust. A man who kissed her, told her he wanted more, and made no move to secure it.

"If you really want to know for sure," he said, "you can send a telegram and ask. That way you can make sure it arrived at least."

She looked him in the eyes. "Mr. Clark," she said, "there are six people I am sure are not at fault here. My brother. His wife. Amanda. Alice. Myself." She swallowed. "You."

He smiled faintly in response. "But we already know you're too trusting. My list is one entry long: you. Are you certain about your brother? He's an MP, is he not? How much of an embarrassment are you to him?"

"Oh, not much," Free said. "He always bails me out of gaol. If he wanted to stop me, he would have just left me in the lock hospital. He always says that I'm extremely useful politically because I make him look like the *reasonable* Marshall."

"That's ridiculous!" Mr. Clark growled. "You're extremely reasonable."

"Mr. Clark, did you just use an exclamation point? I could have sworn I heard one."

He didn't even blink. "Of course not," he scoffed. "I borrowed one of yours. It's allowed, when I'm talking of you.

But this is neither here nor there. You see, Miss Marshall, we know something now, and Delacey doesn't know we know it. If your brother is not the culprit, it's one of his staff. It's likely someone who works closely with him."

"That would make sense," she said slowly.

"And while Delacey would never talk directly with an arsonist, my guess is that he might make himself known to a secretary or a man of business. And that…" He smiled, charmingly. "That, Miss Marshall, is where we can get the proof we need to publicly hold him responsible."

"Do you have any suggestions as to how we will manage that?"

"As it happens, I do." His smile spread, and his eyes glittered wolfishly. "It's simple. Blackmail first, followed by a public accusation." He glanced over at her. "That is, assuming that you don't mind bending the rules a little?"

Odd, what a strange thing trust was. A week or so ago, she'd never have trusted Mr. Clark, not for the slightest instant. In that time, little had changed. He was still a blackmailer, still a forger. He was likely even still a liar.

But he'd saved her last night, and now they knew things of each other—things that seemed more important than such details as the name he'd been born with, or the nature of his revenge. He knew she had nightmares about the lock hospital; she knew he'd been in a fire brigade in Strasbourg.

He sketched out a plan; she pointed out where her brother would comply and where he might not. At the end, Edward took his leave. There was, after all, much more work to do. But she felt as if she'd been carrying a great burden a long distance, and the end was finally visible.

She watched him leave. Still, there was one last thing niggling at her.

She waited until he'd left the press before standing up. Stephen Shaughnessy was still on the floor, giving his column a final look-over. She gestured him over.

He came in. "Yes, Miss Marshall?"

He looked…so innocent. Stephen was *good* at looking innocent; a necessary skill for a man who had a dreadfully mischievous sense of humor. Most of the time, his humor served her. But now…

"Do you have some passing prior acquaintance with Mr. Clark?"

He glanced behind him, toward the front door where the man had disappeared. "No," he said thoughtfully. "I *don't* have a passing acquaintance with him. Why do you ask?"

"Just a thought." And yet now that it had occurred to her, she realized it made a strange sense of things. The first time she'd met Mr. Clark, he'd asked her about Stephen. They'd formed their partnership when Delacey had put Stephen in imminent danger of arrest.

It could have been a coincidence.

"You know how terrible I am at recalling names and faces." He spread his hands before him. "I could have met him a thousand times and not recognized him."

Both Stephen and Mr. Clark had dealt with James Delacey in the past. And Stephen had suggested that Mr. Clark ask about Free's father—and while she'd assumed that Stephen had been twitting her about blushing on Mr. Clark's arrival, it would also have fit if he knew Mr. Clark idolized the man, and was teasing him about it.

"Are you absolutely certain?" she asked.

Stephen shrugged. "I'm never certain about something like this. But it wouldn't make any sense. How would I have met him? How old would you say he is?"

"Maybe the tail end of his thirties?" It was impossible to guess, really. That white in his hair, she suspected, was deceptive. He didn't act like an older man.

She'd felt him lift her, too—and he'd seemed young enough then.

"There you are," Stephen said. "The only men I know who are above thirty-five are friends of my father and tutors at school. And while I know very little about Mr. Clark, I don't think he's a tutor."

"Right." She sighed. "Well, let me see your column again, and we'll see if it's up to snuff."

❀ ❀ ❀

EDWARD WAITED HALFWAY DOWN the path to the university, pacing up and down. It took Stephen twenty minutes to appear. He had his hands in his pockets and he was whistling some complicated ditty.

He caught sight of Edward as he drew nearer. But instead of frowning or jumping in surprise, Stephen gave him a brilliant smile. "Edward," he called out. "Good to see you. I'm glad you're not dead."

That little… Edward shook his head in mock anger. Stephen had known it was him the entire time, and he'd given scarcely a hint.

"Delacey, eh?" Stephen came up to him. "You're taking on James Delacey?"

Edward huffed. "Shut up, clod." And then, because that seemed unduly harsh, he reached over, removed Stephen's hat, and ground his knuckles in Stephen's hair. Or at least he tried to. The angle was no longer quite so convenient; he scarcely managed to apply his knuckles to his head.

Stephen simply looked over at him with raised eyebrows. "Unimpressive, Edward. That doesn't work so well when I'm no longer waist-high."

"Why didn't you say anything back there, if you knew?"

"Huh." Stephen rolled his eyes. "Look at me. I'm just a nobody, with neither sense nor discretion. Why would I keep my mouth shut? It's not as if my brother corresponds regularly with a man named Clark, a man I've never heard of and who he refuses to answer questions about. But, no, there's nothing suspicious about that."

Edward glared at him.

"I was certainly not suspicious when I heard there was a mysterious Mr. Edward Clark hanging about the press. Said Clark appeared just in time to foil a plot to have me tossed out of school, if not worse. But do I know an Edward Clark? No, of course I don't. I only know an Edward Delacey. That's the man who saved my life when I jumped out of a tree into sucking mud."

Edward frowned. "No, I didn't. That was Patrick."

"I would remember. It was definitely you."

"It wasn't."

"In any event, if my brother says that Edward Delacey is dead, who am I to contradict him?" Stephen rolled his eyes. "Really, Edward, after all these years, do you have to ask where my loyalties lie?"

Edward didn't even believe in loyalty any longer. "You haven't seen me in God knows how long."

Stephen shrugged. "Yes, and while we're at it, thanks for paying my school fees."

Edward put his hands on his hips. "How the devil did you know about that? Did Patrick tell you? I'd thought more of his discretion than that."

"No, but it was either you or Baron Lowery, and Patrick is very insistent on not accepting presents from Lowery." Stephen shrugged. "I'm glad you're alive. Even without that."

When Edward had appeared to James, James had said almost exactly the opposite. It made Edward feel almost sentimental.

Instead of showing it, he simply raised an eyebrow. "*You're* glad I'm alive? Imagine how I must feel."

Stephen laughed. "Miss Marshall asked if I knew you."

Edward stiffened. "And you said?"

"Do you remember that game we used to play, the one that annoyed Patrick? Where he'd ask questions, and we'd do our best to tell him falsehoods without actually uttering an untruth?"

Edward gave a crack of laughter. He had memories of lying in a field watching clouds go by, trying to make Patrick go mad by telling not-quite-lies. God, he'd almost forgotten that.

"Well, I can still do that. 'A passing acquaintance, Miss Marshall? No, I don't have a passing acquaintance with Mr. Clark.'" Stephen smiled. "No need to mention that he's my long-lost friend."

Of all the things that Stephen could have said, that was the one that almost brought Edward to his knees. He felt the weight of a sudden, choking emotion. The other man's casual smile seemed a heavy burden.

"I've been wishing I could introduce you to Miss Marshall ever since I found out about her father. Just to see your face when you found out."

That fantasy played out again—the one where Edward Delacey, whole, and unblackened, met a fiery Miss Marshall.

She'd have laughed in his face. And truth to tell, his old self wouldn't have had the strength to deal with her. She would have utterly overwhelmed him.

"Play your hand right," Stephen said, "and maybe you can beg an introduction."

He could have friends, family...and Free.

But then it never worked out that way.

Edward shook his head. "Play your hand right, and maybe she'll never discover you lied to her. I'd hate to incur her wrath, if I were you. She seems rather fierce."

⌘   ⌘   ⌘

THE TELEGRAM HAD ARRIVED late last evening, and Amanda had tossed and turned all night, dreading what she needed to do.

It was ridiculous to hold a grudge against Free for asking her to deliver this message—and she didn't really feel grumpy about it. Not truly. But no matter how she tried to tell herself she need only address herself to Mrs. Jane Marshall, every time she looked up from her comfortable, cushioned chair, it wasn't Mrs. Marshall, garbed in a flowing pink gown that emphasized her plump curves, that her gaze fixed upon.

It was Miss Johnson. Miss Johnson wore a demure pastel purple that should have seemed washed out next to her friend's exuberantly-colored silk. But she glowed in it, the picture of beauty, good health, and perfection.

The women were looking at Amanda in something like horror. No surprise there—she'd just told them about the fire, the threat to Free's newspaper, and Free's plan, which would require them to host a massive soirée on not even a week's notice.

"Of course we'll help," Mrs. Marshall said stoutly. "Any way we can."

Of course they would. It was, after all, Free that they cared about. The thought of helping Free had Miss Johnson glowing in excitement.

"We shall be extremely busy," Mrs. Marshall said.

Miss Johnson smiled. "I don't mind. And there's an added benefit." She turned to Amanda. "Lady Amanda, I shall finally have you at one of my parties. After all this time! What a triumph that will be for me."

Amanda felt almost dizzy. "Oh, no," she said. "No. Of course I'm honored, but no, I couldn't. It's imposition enough to ask you to do such a thing in so short a time. I could not expect an invitation."

"Don't be silly." Mrs. Marshall frowned at her. "You're asking us to invite hundreds. One more could hardly signify. And you're a friend of the family twice over—once through Free, and again through your Aunt Violet."

"I couldn't," Amanda said again.

But Mrs. Marshall shook her head. "Of course you could."

"I *couldn't,*" Amanda repeated.

"But—"

"Jane." Miss Johnson set a hand on her employer's shoulder. "Why don't you go speak to the staff and inform them of what is to come? *I'll* talk with Lady Amanda."

No. Amanda felt her eyes widen in panic, but she could hardly cling to Mrs. Marshall and beg her to stay. What was she to say? *I'm afraid of your secretary. She's too pretty.*

"But—" Mrs. Marshall started.

Miss Johnson looked over at her and pursed her lips. Something must have passed between them, because Mrs. Marshall sighed.

"Yes," she said, "of course, Genevieve."

The door closed on her. It did not make an ominous, resounding thud; it shut with an almost inaudible snick.

Miss Johnson turned to Amanda. "I didn't think when I insisted earlier. Do you have anything to wear? All your things must have been burned in the fire."

Amanda wished she had that excuse. But no, Genevieve would volunteer to find something for her, and being fitted for clothing with the impeccable Miss Johnson watching would be altogether too much for Amanda's composure. "I have a suitable frock," she choked out. "At my aunt's house."

Miss Johnson's face grew more sober. "Then is it me?" She looked down. "I hope I've done nothing to make you feel unwelcome. You must know I think highly of you. Very highly."

Oh, that was not helping matters. Amanda gulped in air. "It's not you." And that was only a little bit of a lie; after all, it wasn't Genevieve herself who posed the problem. It was simply everything she represented. "I just don't go out in society any longer."

"No?" Miss Johnson frowned. "Why not?"

Amanda looked away. "The last time I did was years ago. I arrived at an event with my aunt. My sister was there." Amanda's hands balled into fists of their own accord. "My parents had tossed me out two years before, when I refused to marry. They thought I would bend to their will eventually. I didn't." She swallowed. "I hadn't seen my sister since then."

She hadn't seen anyone in her family in years, and she'd missed them terribly.

"I caught a glimpse of her across the room. I had known she was out, had hoped to be able to speak with her. I started toward her. And she looked the other way and walked away from me."

Miss Johnson inhaled.

Amanda looked down. "At first, I assumed it was an accident—a coincidence, that she'd just not seen me. So I found her in the cloakroom at the end. And she told me…"

She could still hear Maria's words, as plain as if they'd just been spoken.

You ruined my life, Amanda. You're ruining it just being here, making everyone whisper about you and what you've chosen. You walked away from the family once. I wish you'd do it again, and this time for good.

"She told me she never wanted to see me. That my very presence was a cause for gossip." Amanda couldn't look at Miss Johnson. "After that, it all began to crumble. Every time I went out in society, every time I spoke, I could just hear her words. I could feel myself ruining everything for her. Just by speaking, by sitting in the wrong room. By breathing."

It sounded so foolish when she said it.

"So it's that simple. Every time I'm in polite company now, I feel unwanted. And I know that sounds as if I'm asking for sympathy. I'm not. I made a choice, and I don't regret it. I just wish…"

Miss Johnson leaned across the table. That didn't help either—her physical presence set Amanda on edge, her entire body lighting up in response. Her lungs hurt with the effort of taking in air.

Amanda wouldn't have moved away for the world.

"I'm so sorry that happened to you," Miss Johnson said. "I can't imagine it. When I made my own decision—similar, and yet not the same—my sister never once questioned it. She told me that no matter what I chose, no matter how I felt, she would always love me. Without her, I doubt I could have chosen as I did. I don't know what I would do if she ever said such things."

Amanda swallowed bitter jealousy at those words. "Well. Now you have it. It isn't you, Miss Johnson. I don't think I can go out in society any longer. My own sister couldn't forgive me for walking away from a society marriage and attending university. How could anyone else?"

Miss Johnson considered this. "How long has it been since you saw your sister?"

"Since I was twenty." She frowned. Her memory was as sharp as if Maria had walked away from her yesterday, and yet... "That's about seven years now."

Miss Johnson pulled back at that. "You're only twenty-seven? I had always imagined you older."

Amanda felt her cheeks heat. She was fairly certain that Genevieve Johnson was older than she was. But one couldn't tell by looking at her. She still looked fresh-faced and young; by comparison, Amanda was painfully ancient, her hands stained with ink that would not scrub out, her first wrinkles appearing around her eyes.

Amanda didn't care about her appearance—truly she didn't—but...

"It's just," Miss Johnson was saying, "your columns, when I read them, I don't feel like I'm listening to someone my age. You always sound so sure of yourself, and you're so clever. I suppose I should have realized."

"You don't need to be nice to me," Amanda said in misery.

"I'm not being nice. I'm jealous of you, if I must admit it. After all, you're a lovely woman who has found her own place in the world. People respect your words. They know who you are. They talk about you as someone other than your parents' child."

Amanda looked up. "Now I *know* you're being nice to me. Everyone adores you. Who couldn't? You've managed to make your own life where you're accepted by everyone, without marrying or...or..." She stopped.

"It's true," Miss Johnson said with a smile. "I have an excellent life. But I'm always aware that if something were to happen to Jane, I would have nothing to do. You have your own life."

Butterflies descended into Amanda's stomach again, hammering at her with their wings.

"That column you wrote," Miss Johnson said, "that one from six months ago, about the life a woman could have without a man. The one you wrote in response to Lord Hasslemire? I felt that one." She set her hand on her belly. "I felt it here, when you wrote about how Hasslemire talked about a lady's life as a collection of things that women did for men. When you said that a woman could exist for herself, without needing to serve someone else's needs…" Miss Johnson smiled. "Do you know how many women clipped that column and sent it to me? *Seven.* I don't know what you think you're going to see on that ballroom floor, Lady Amanda. I'm sure you're right. There will be a great many women who frown at you. But there will also be women who know you through your words, who will want to take your hand and squeeze it just so that a little of your strength will come to them."

"But I walked away from them," Amanda said stupidly.

"Maybe," Miss Johnson said quietly. "But here we are, walking back to you." She took hold of Amanda's hand and gave it a quick squeeze. So simple a gesture, to send such a shock through her. Amanda felt bewildered for a second, completely unable to respond. Her fingers lay like dumb, dazed caterpillars, unresponsive, incapable of returning that tight grip. Miss Johnson stole her hand away before Amanda had a chance to marshal her nerve.

"Trust me on this, my dear," Genevieve said. "There are a great many women out there tonight who want the honor of your acquaintance."

"And you?" Amanda's voice sounded rusty; her words scraped in her throat.

"I already have the honor of your acquaintance." This was said with a little smile, but that faded, and Miss Johnson looked away. For a moment, she looked almost vulnerable.

"Do you think…" Amanda had not felt brave in company in a long time. She tried it on tentatively now. It slipped from her fingers, but she went on anyway. "Miss Johnson, do you suppose you could consider friendship?"

Miss Johnson turned to her. There was a wry look in her eyes. She shook her head a little.

Of course. It was one thing to claim acquaintance; it was quite another to be a friend, to be someone who would be seen with Amanda in public. Amanda drew back.

"Oh," Miss Johnson said. "*No*. That's not at all what I meant. Don't mind me; I'm just a little foolish sometimes. Yes, Amanda. I'd be honored if you were my friend. But you'll have to start calling me Genevieve."

Maybe she was lying; maybe she was just being kind. But when she smiled, it was impossible to doubt her. And when Miss Johnson reached out and took Amanda's hand in hers, she felt her own smile creep foolishly across her face.

"Very well, Genevieve," Amanda said. She squeezed the other woman's hand. "Very well."

Chapter Twelve

"So." The man across the desk from Edward folded his hands and frowned. "These are rather unusual circumstances, Mr. Clark. I find myself curious to see how you will explain them."

It had been a mere twenty-four hours since Edward and Free had hashed out a plan—twenty-four hours during which he'd scarcely slept, after running back and forth between Cambridge and his brother's estate. He'd finally ended up here in London. That was no reason to admit exhaustion. Edward leaned back casually, resting his hand against the brocaded arm of the chair. The man across from him didn't look as much like Free as Edward had expected. His hair was brighter: almost orange. He was a great deal taller, his features less delicate. But his arms were crossed, and his suspicious glower could have been a twin for Free's.

Marshall frowned, and Edward changed his mind. Free was much prettier when she glared at him.

Her brother sniffed and shuffled through the papers Edward had handed him. "So, you're an Englishman who has spent some time in France."

"Yes," Edward said lazily.

"You're doing some work with James Delacey." Marshall grimaced at that.

"If you call it that," Edward said.

"And you've come to see me."

"You *do* appear to have basic literacy," Edward said mockingly. "Well done, Marshall. You read your sister's letter. Not everyone who has gone to Cambridge could manage so much."

Mr. Marshall's eyes narrowed further and he set down the papers. "My sister has never before mentioned you, does not live in France, and works mostly with women on women's issues. Would you care to explain your acquaintance with her?"

Edward considered this carefully. "No. I wouldn't."

Free's older brother made an annoyed noise in his throat. The silence stretched. Edward supposed it would have been uncomfortable to another man. Every tick of the clock no doubt was intended to make him feel more and more awkward. But he was tired enough that a rest—any sort of rest—was welcome.

He simply put on a pleasant smile, and when Marshall's expression darkened, looked about the room and began to hum.

Marshall glared at him more fiercely.

"That tactic won't work," Edward said after a minute. "I'm not going to volunteer any more information than you have in front of you. I'm not scared of your glowers. I can sit here as long as I please without saying a thing. It's your time, if you wish to waste it. If it makes you feel any better, your sister said to tell you that it's none of your business who I am to her, and that she won't have you barbarically assuming that she's in need of protection from me."

"Yes, well," the other man said shortly. "Barbaric or not, I have some small idea what my sister endures, being what she is. If I can stop it in some small way, I will."

"That's good to hear," Edward said. "But so far as I can tell, you haven't stopped anything. *I* have. So set aside your masculine trumpeting. I haven't come to pass whatever test of loyalty you want to mete out to me. You're here to pass mine."

Oliver Marshall was a Member of Parliament, well respected, liked by many. Even his enemies spoke highly of him. Mostly.

That likely meant that he played fairly—again, *mostly*. He probably told the truth, respected others, and gave his word and meant it. As such, Edward held a natural advantage over him.

"I beg your pardon," Marshall was saying in faint outrage. "Are you questioning my devotion to my sister?"

Edward undid the twine holding another clump of papers together. "It's not my pardon you'll need. It's hers. Has she told you about the duplications of her columns?"

"Yes. Of course. That's the whole point of this whirlwind affair coming up, the one that's driving my wife to distraction. I don't know what you're driving at, but—"

Edward snapped a sheet of newsprint out flat and held it up. "Do you recognize this?"

"Of course. That's my sister's paper. The edition that came out a few days past."

"No," Edward told him. "That's the advance proof she sent to you. The precise page, mind you—there's a note you scrawled in the corner, right there. Now, did you give this to Delacey yourself?"

"Delacey? That ass? Why would I give him this? Why would he...ah." Free's elder brother stopped talking and frowned, reaching for the paper. "Ah," he repeated. His eyes grew darker. "Someone in my household is passing things on." He shut his eyes and grimaced. "That's extremely unfortunate."

It was almost sweet how good-natured the man was. That all he could see was inconvenience in such a thing, instead of opportunity.

Edward smiled. "No. It's going to be extremely useful, as soon as we can figure out who it is. If it isn't you—and Miss Marshall believes it is not—then the number of people it could be is small. And we can use them."

Mr. Marshall nodded. And then he frowned. "I still don't understand. Why did my sister send you to tell me all this? Who *are* you?"

"She's busy," Edward said shortly. "As for me? I'm the one who is going to figure everything out. Let me tell you how."

⌘   ⌘   ⌘

MISS MARSHALL'S BROTHER had the most comfortable wardrobe that Edward had ever hidden inside. It was spacious enough to fit two people, and, as it was apparently used as extra storage space for Mrs. Marshall's gowns, was filled with colors so bright that the space seemed welcoming even in the dim light filtering in through the doors.

Not so the man who crouched next to him. He'd known her brother was a Member of Parliament, which was already one strike against him. From what Free had said, he'd expected a stodgy stick-in-the-mud who constantly frowned at his exuberant sister.

Instead, he'd seemed genuinely concerned for her welfare. He'd absorbed the details of the fire, and Edward's role in it, with a darkening expression. When Edward had told him about Delacey, he'd growled and offered to beat the man into a pulp.

No; he wasn't feigning that deep protectiveness for his sister. It was all the more obvious because he clearly treated Edward with suspicion. Which meant he was in possession of a working mind, something Edward could hardly begrudge him. He had volunteered to watch the study in secret with Edward when they'd left it empty—tantalizingly empty. They'd left the next advance proof that Free had sent along from Cambridge resting on his desk as bait.

That was how Edward found himself in a small, enclosed space with Oliver Marshall. Small, enclosed spaces still made him uneasy, but this one didn't smell of smoke, and no choking plaster dust hung in the air. The door to the wardrobe was cracked open, letting in fresh air and light.

For the first few minutes, they sat in silence.

Then Marshall leaned forward and whispered. "If you hurt my sister, you'll know pain like you've never known pain before."

Edward glanced back at the man, amused. Marshall was soft. He probably thought that a few cross words and a fist in the face were the worst that humanity had to offer.

"I sincerely doubt that," he answered in a low voice. "I've known a lot of pain."

And yet he suspected that what the other man had said was true on some level. He wasn't sure when all of this rigmarole had stopped being about revenge and started being about her. Hurting Free would be its own peculiar sort of pain.

Marshall growled.

"Really," Edward responded, "you ought to save your breath. There's no point threatening me. You'll never be as good at it as your sister, and threats only work on men who fear. I don't."

"You have no idea what I'm capable of doing."

Edward smiled, and reached over and patted Mr. Marshall on the knee, being sure to turn his face so that the light caught the condescending edge of his smile. "There, there," he said comfortingly. "You're very frightening, I'm sure. But I've met your sister, and trust me, if *Free* doesn't scare me, you can't."

He deliberately used her pet name to provoke the other man. He wasn't sure why. He could have charmed the other man, smoothed his ruffled, outraged feathers. Instead, he was doing his best to avoid any sense of camaraderie. The last thing he needed was to earn the approval of Free's brother. Once he had that, well… It was a short road to thinking that he could be a part of the family. Best to keep things at arm's length.

Edward looked off through the crack in the wardrobe. "Free does many things well."

There was a long pause. "Are you *trying* to provoke me?"

Edward didn't answer.

"You are. I swear to God, I will never understand my sister."

"Hardly surprising, as her understanding is superior to yours."

Instead of taking offense at that blatant insult, Mr. Marshall looked greatly amused. He shook his head and looked away. "Of course. I should have realized what was happening the first time you attempted to insult me by complimenting my sister. She got to you." It was Marshall's turn to give Edward a condescending clap on the shoulder. "Don't feel badly; she does that often."

Edward managed to keep his face devoid of all expression.

"This may be the first time she's had one of Delacey's thugs following her about like a baby duckling, though. I take it all back, Mr. Clark. No pain for you. You've given me material to tease her with for years to come."

One of Delacey's thugs. That's how he'd introduced himself to this man. Better that than telling him the truth.

"I object to being called a duckling," Edward replied smoothly. "I consider myself a full-grown mallard."

Marshall smirked. "How long did it take her? People usually react to her fairly swiftly—either love or hate, there's rarely an emotion between. A day? A week?"

He thought of Free the way he'd first seen her: standing on the bank of the Thames, leaning forward.

"Two to five," Edward muttered.

"Days?"

"Minutes."

Marshall let out a crack of laughter.

"Hush, you," Edward growled. "We're being clandestine here."

"So we are." The other man dropped his voice back to a low whisper. "It's almost sweet. Here you are, sitting in a closet, trapped with a man you dislike, stricken by adoration for my little sister."

Edward supposed he deserved that after needling the man earlier. Marshall was trying to provoke him right back.

"Yes." Edward rolled his eyes. "It's a terrible secret, that. I am trying dreadfully to conceal it. I openly altered my life for weeks on end for your sister. I single-handedly stopped an arsonist from setting fire to her business. When confronted with that evidence, it took you a mere three hours to determine that I harbored an affection for her. Truly, you have a massive intellect."

This was met with a long pause. "Are you really left-handed?" Mr. Marshall asked.

"No. I've just been pretending to use my left hand my entire life because I enjoy never being able to work scissors properly." Edward rolled his eyes. "What do you think? My father tried to encourage me to use my right more but it never did take." Thankfully. He'd hate to rely on his right hand now.

"I was just wondering if it was an attempt to worm your way into the Brothers Sinister. It won't work; you had to be at Cambridge with us to be a member. Or be Violet."

Edward looked at the other man. "Marshall," he said levelly, "I don't know what you're talking about, but any organization that claims you for a member doesn't get to call itself sinister, whether you're left-handed or not. I would be insulted to be offered membership in such a namby-pamby organization. It would be like the Archbishop of Canterbury calling a select club of his compatriots 'Bad, Bad Bishops'."

Marshall sniggered.

"Watch out for the clergy," Edward said. "They're absolutely wild. Sometimes they have an extra biscuit at tea."

Marshall gave him a look that seemed faintly like approval. "You're awful," he said. "I finally begin to understand my sister's interest."

That was when Edward heard a faint noise from outside the closet. He reached over and clapped his hand over the other man's mouth. Marshall went still. The door opened on a soft sigh, and then closed with quiet deliberation. Footsteps padded across the room. Edward smiled to himself. Whoever they were dealing with was a complete amateur. Sneaking about in a surreptitious manner drew far more suspicions.

Edward took his hand away from the other man's mouth and held a finger up to his own lips.

A man crept into view, and beside him Marshall gave a low growl in his throat. Well he should; Edward had seen the man in the halls earlier. He'd been on the list of suspects that he'd drawn up with Free. It was Mark Andrews, Mr. Marshall's undersecretary.

Andrews crept to the desk, looking from side to side as if he were a spy in a stupid novel. The little secretary reached out and took hold of the advance proof on the desk. This he folded, and then slid in his pocket.

"You'd better go," Edward muttered.

Mr. Marshall swung the wardrobe door open. "I say, Andrews." He stepped out as if he removed himself from wardrobes on a regular basis.

Andrews jumped at his appearance and emitted a high-pitched yelp.

Marshall straightened, patting his jacket into place. "What are you doing?"

"Sir!" Andrews scrambled a pace back from the desk. "I was just—straightening? Yes, I was straightening. Your desk. Because it was…not straight."

"You were taking the advance proof my sister sent this morning," Mr. Marshall said with a shake of his head.

"I—uh—no, see, the corner had ripped, and I intended to mend it."

Marshall clucked sadly. "It's no good, Andrews. We know you've done it before. You've been working with Delacey for months, and we can prove it."

There was a long pause. Edward watched, curious to see if Andrews would manage to be more competent than he'd thus far observed. But no. The man sank into a chair and set his head in his hands. "Oh. That's bad," he muttered.

"I won't press charges," Mr. Marshall said gently, "so long as—"

Edward had—quite deliberately—not talked strategy beyond apprehension with Mr. Marshall. It was best to nip this in the bud. Edward stepped out of the wardrobe, interrupting this benevolence. "So long as you do as I say," he said smoothly.

Mr. Marshall turned to him, scowling. "Wait. What are you doing?"

Edward waved his hand. "Free and I didn't tell you the full plan. You'd have objected."

"I'm objecting now."

Edward ignored him. Instead, he walked up to his quarry.

"Here's what you're going to do to avoid a prison sentence, Andrews." He let his voice drop to a deceptively gentle register. "First, you're going to take this advance proof." He tapped Andrew's pocket. "And you're going to deliver it to…who is it that you normally deliver these to?"

"Alvahurst," Andrews said. "Delacey's secretary."

"Good. You're going to give it to him, just as you always do."

Andrews looked puzzled.

"But you'll tell him that you've heard plans that might interest Delacey. Mr. Marshall, see, is holding a soireé in a few days—one for his sister, who as we all know, is terribly beleaguered. You've heard that she's desperate, and you think that Delacey would find the gathering amusing. When Alvahurst asks you to see if you can obtain an invitation, give him this." Edward handed over a thick card.

"I say. Where did you get that?" Mr. Marshall asked. Edward ignored him again.

"You'll have more duties on the night of the gathering," Edward told him. "But we'll discuss those later. Now, are we clear on what you're to do?"

Andrews winced. "But—sir." His hands shook. "I don't think I've the nerve for it."

"Of course you have the nerve for it," Edward said, pitching his tone to warm comfort. "You have the nerve right now to be contemplating telling Alvahurst that you've been discovered. If you have the nerve to lie to *my* face, you can lie to his."

Andrews went green.

"But then, you're a clever fellow. What can Alvahurst do for you, aside from offer you a few extra coins? I can do much,

much more. You see, stealing from an employer is a bad business. I doubt the magistrates will show you an ounce of pity. Mr. Marshall's sister here runs a newspaper. Your reputation will be ruined. Even if you escape imprisonment, you'll never work again."

"Wait," Mr. Marshall said. "Are you blackmailing him? That's illegal." He looked frustrated. "I'm an MP now. I can't support that."

"No, you draw your ethical line at two biscuits with tea," Edward said with a scoff. "I know you won't support this. That's why we didn't tell you. Your condemnation, irrelevant as it is, is noted."

Marshall took a step forward. "Don't listen to him, Andrews."

"Don't listen to *him,*" Edward responded smoothly. "He's no threat to you. He was willing to let you off at the first opportunity, that's how understanding he is. The person you should be afraid of is *me*. I'm the one who knows where your banking records are kept. I can ferret out every payment that Delacey has made to you, match it up with the corresponding draft from his accounts."

Andrews swallowed.

"I know all about your mother," Edward said. "And your wife. Claudette, is it?"

Andrews paled.

"Marshall here is vaguely upset. He might talk sternly to you. I, on the other hand, am a *very bad* enemy to have, and a lovely friend. So tell me, what are you going to do?" Edward held out the invitation once more.

Andrews flinched back. His breath cycled. He stared at it and then slowly lifted his eyes to Mr. Marshall.

"Sorry, Mr. Marshall," he said quietly. "But—but—"

Mr. Marshall folded his arms in disapproval.

"Here. Repeat after me what you must do," Edward said, and when Andrews got it wrong, as Edward had suspected he would, he coached him once, twice, three times.

"There," he said at the end. "You'll do very well."

"Do you think so?" Andrews smiled hopefully.

Of course he didn't. Edward would have to introduce himself to Alvahurst to make sure everything went off as anticipated.

"Of course you'll do well." Edward clapped the man on the back. "I know you'll do well, because I'll know the instant you set one foot wrong."

He could feel Marshall's eyes digging into his back, but he escorted Andrews from the room and called a footman to take him out of the house.

He turned back. "There. Now was that so bad?"

Marshall was shaking his head in disapproval. "You knew it was him," Marshall said.

"He was one possibility." Edward shrugged.

"But you said you had proof. And you mentioned his mother and his wife. If you didn't know…"

"I knew something about every possible subject." Edward looked over at Marshall and frowned. "I just mentioned his mother and his wife. He filled in the rest himself. Come, Marshall. These are standard intimidation tactics—threaten small, and let the target's imagination cast the necessary shadows."

"Standard intimidation tactics?" Marshall asked. "What *are* you? And what are you doing with my sister?"

Edward smiled at him. "One of these days, you're going to realize that your sister doesn't need a man who follows the rules. There are too many rules and only one of her. Keep your brotherhood of left-handed do-gooders, Marshall. Your sister needs a man who is *actually* sinister. Now if you'll excuse me…"

"Where are you going?"

Edward simply smiled. "Someone has to make sure that Andrews performs—and that Delacey takes the bait."

"But—"

"Complain to your sister," Edward said. He felt only the slightest twinge of his conscience as he said it. "She'll take care of everything."

Chapter Thirteen

THE EVENING OF THE SOIRÉE did not start out as ghastly as Free had feared. She'd expected whispers about her paper, and numerous sidelong glances. Those were certainly in evidence.

But Amanda joined her, looking stately in cream and pearls. Several of the women here had come because they enjoyed the newspaper, and she and Amanda were swarmed. They were bombarded with questions about what it had been like to have a university education. Still others asked her surreptitiously whether she thought that a lady—no, not the speaker *herself*, of course; they were all only asking for friends—might perhaps choose to take on duties that until this point had been seen as strictly within the male purview.

Yes, yes, it was all possible, Free told them. Hard as well, but then difficulty was the seasoning of life.

She even joked about men trying to discredit her, and received laughter in response.

All things considered, it was not the worst evening she had ever had. She was even almost enjoying herself. And then, halfway through the night, she thought she saw someone.

It was a trick of the light, an impossible, unbelievable thing. But there, between the column and the terrarium, she thought that she saw Edward Clark in the room. The shape of his nose; the way he held his glass. The light glinted off his hair.

She'd not seen him this last week except in passing—a few minutes here, a few minutes there, scarcely enough time to tell each other what they'd done, and for him to take her hand.

That touch of glove on glove, hand in hand, had brought her back to the floor of her office and the dark velvet of that night when he'd kissed her. But he'd let go and left every time.

Edward wasn't supposed to be in the ballroom. Not that he would let a thing like what he was supposed to do stop him. Not that she cared that he was upsetting the plan.

In that bare, shining moment when she beheld him, Free felt herself light from within. She couldn't help herself—she smiled, bright and welcoming, and that was nothing to the sheer pleasure that flooded through her. Finally, someone she could have a proper conversation with, someone who would make her laugh, who... who...

He turned toward her, and all that incandescent joy became ice-cold inside her. The man wasn't Edward. How could she have thought it? At that angle, with those shadows on his face and the light in his hair—but she'd been so, so wrong. This man was softer, rounder, completely dark-haired instead of having threads of white scattered through his hair.

He looked nothing like Edward, nothing at all. How could she have made such a mistake? And this was not just a mistake; it was a horrifying one. The man she'd mistaken for her Mr. Clark was precisely his opposite. He was, in fact, James Delacey, the soon-to-be-seated Viscount Claridge, and the author of her current misery. What a dastardly illusion. It was like biting into a strawberry expecting sweetness and getting a mouthful of dirt instead. Free took a step back.

But he'd seen her. He'd caught her looking at him in that instant, caught that initial flush of happiness on her. He frowned, and then slowly, he started toward her.

She wasn't going to flee from his presence as if she were a partridge. She'd come here tonight to defeat him; he'd learn that soon enough. Free folded her arms and watched him approach.

He stopped a few feet from her. "Miss Marshall."

She inclined her head, refusing to pay him more than that bare courtesy.

He tilted his head and smiled, as if remembering a private joke. "Your brother has a lovely house," he said. "When your newspaper fails, as I suspect it soon will, I know you'll be well taken care of."

"Fail?" Free said. "How odd. I don't even know what that word means, except when I use it to describe you. No doubt you are more intimately familiar with the implications."

His face grew dark. "Careful, Miss Marshall," he said in low tones. "I will *love* it when you're forced to depend on your brother. How badly will it rankle you to rely on a man, when you once had your own independence? Just think, my dear. You could have relied on me instead."

An angry flush rose in her cheeks. "Is that why you wish me harm?"

"Miss Marshall, harm comes to you because of who you are." He shrugged. "Not because of me. A woman in your circumstances should *expect* to be hated."

"And what circumstances are those?" she asked. "So far as I am aware, the only circumstance of note is that you made me an offensive proposition and I refused. From that, we come to all of this?"

His hands clenched at his sides. "I've already forgotten that," he said coldly. "I do not wish to think of it."

"Of course you don't want to think of it," Free told him. "It's obvious that you don't want to think at all. But despite your carefully cultivated ignorance, you'll have to comprehend that a woman has a right to say no."

He bristled further. "That's precisely it. You said no, so that is what I wish for you. No newspaper, no voice, no reputation, no independence." He looked away. "*No* is apparently all you understand, and so I've made sure that when I talk to you, I use language that you can interpret."

"I see." Free glared at him. "You're as sordid and despicable as I thought."

He held up a hand. "It would be sordid, Miss Marshall, if I threatened to do those things to have you in my bed. As it is, I don't want anything from you. I just want you to understand what it's like to be humiliated. Tit for tat."

It was hardly that. She'd told him no in private, and had only wrenched his arm when he tried to kiss her as a form of persuasion. He'd set fire to her dwelling and had tried to do the same to her business. He could have killed someone. Only the most self-centered fool would equate those two things.

Someday, she told herself grimly, someday, she'd look back at this moment and she'd turn it into a damned good joke about lords. Something like…

"So sorry to intrude," said another man, coming up to them. "But Miss Marshall, you did tell me earlier that you wanted to be introduced to Mrs. Blackavar, and she is just over here. She mentioned she had a headache, but I told her she couldn't possibly leave before you'd met."

Free looked up to see the Duke of Clermont smiling at her.

Clermont was…

A lord, yes. But he was also an acquaintance. She scarcely knew him herself, although their paths had crossed quite a bit. He was her brother's brother, and that made them…absolutely nothing. She had no idea who Mrs. Blackavar was; she hadn't talked to Clermont in months, and then only in passing. On the other hand, she wanted to stay with Delacey about as much as she wanted to stab herself repeatedly in the eye with an ice pick.

"My apologies, Delacey," Clermont said with a little bow, "but if you'll excuse us…"

"Of course." Free took Clermont's arm. "Thank you." She allowed him to conduct her away.

When they'd gone a short distance, he leaned down to her. "I'll take you back, if you like," he whispered. "But you had gone bright red here." He indicated a semi-circle on his cheek. "When Oliver looks like that, it usually means he's on the verge of punching someone in the face." He glanced at her. "I… Maybe I presumed a little, but…"

They were a little more than nothing to each other. She found it difficult to believe in the other half of Oliver's life—but here was proof that it existed anyway.

It was odd, sharing her brother with this man. He knew Oliver as well as she did. Perhaps, she admitted to herself, *better* than she did. It was so strange, her brother having a brother, one whom she scarcely knew.

"No," she told him. "You were perfectly right. If I'd had to stay one more minute in his company, I would have clawed his eyes out. Which isn't a problem, but there would have been witnesses." She glanced over at him. "It was good of you to intervene, Your Grace, especially when you have no obligation to me."

He smiled oddly at that. "Oliver had to leave the room momentarily," he told her. "If he'd been here, he'd have walked over himself and done the same thing. I was just acting in his stead."

Maybe the Duke of Clermont felt that same strangeness that she did, that they ought to mean something to one another, because he cleared his throat and looked away. "I'm not your brother, but I'm still an interested party. And if there's ever anything you need, anything I can do for you, please ask."

"I should hate to put you out, Your Grace." She smiled. "Besides, while I was listening to Delacey, I was developing a theory that all lords were self-centered. You're smashing that to bits, and it was my only comfort."

"No, no," he told her, taking her hand and threading it through his arm. "Keep your comforts. We are all self-centered, Miss Marshall. It's only that some of us are better at hiding it. Now, let me introduce you to Mrs. Blackavar. You'll like her."

Free glanced behind her.

James Delacey glared at her still. But it was the grandfather clock behind him that she noted, its face showing twelve minutes to nine.

Delacey could glare all he wanted. But in twenty minutes, the show would start—and after that, he'd regret everything.

⌘ ⌘ ⌘

IN THE END, it was even more glorious than they had planned.

Oliver's undersecretary, looking pale and frightened, came into the ballroom. Free had been watching for him; he stole through a servants' door, sweating profusely. His forehead shone in all that crystal light. He plastered himself against the wall, looking about the room until his eye fell on Delacey.

He inhaled, straightened his spine, and then did his best to slink to the man through the crowd.

That was Free's cue. She signaled, and a servant brought her a sheaf of papers.

Andrews, meanwhile, bumped into everyone as he moved. He ducked his head in apology every time he did, jumping away and inevitably jostling someone else as he did it, necessitating yet another apology. Free would almost have felt sorry for him had he not been part of the plot to destroy her. As it was, her sympathies were low.

"Pardon," she heard him mutter as he moved by her. "Pardon. So sorry. Argh." That last happened as he knocked a wineglass out of a woman's hand.

By the time Andrews found Delacey, half the room was pretending not to watch him. Free had situated herself a strategic ten yards away, with a perfect view of the coming storm.

"Sir." At least, that's what she assumed Andrews said; from here, she could see only the movement of his lips.

Delacey turned to Andrews and then turned a little pale. But he harrumphed creditably and narrowed his eyes. "Do I know you?"

"Sir." This, she could hear. Andrews spoke a little louder, but just as importantly, those around him had stopped talking, the better to overhear. "Yes, sir. Of course. We've *never spoken before.*" He said that with a little flourish, as if he were winking at the man. "But the thing we've never spoken about…"

Delacey took a step back. "What part of *I don't know you* escapes your understanding?"

"Yes, I know, that's what we say, but—"

Delacey scowled. "I do not know you, you idiot."

"But things have changed. I'm suspected, and I must give you this because—" Andrews leaned in close, whispering.

"What did he say?" someone nearby asked. Those closest murmured to their neighbors, and they to theirs.

"He said…there's a horse in the grain?" someone near Free said in confusion.

"No," another man contradicted. "He said he's being called out."

But by that time, the poorly understood whispers were irrelevant. The little undersecretary removed a sheaf of papers all bound up in twine from his jacket.

It was Delacey's own file. Mr. Clark had stolen it that very morning. Delacey must have recognized the contents, because he took a step back, his eyes growing wide. "How did you get that?"

Andrews held it out helpfully. "You gave it to me?"

"I didn't! I never!"

One of the few protests Delacey had made that was actually true, Free mused. Poor man. He had no idea what was happening to him.

"Take it," Andrews gestured. "Here, before they find me—"

Delacey stepped back just as Andrews lunged forward. The papers slipped from the secretary's grasp, scattering widely over the floor.

"Here," a nearby man said. "Let me help you gather those."

"No!" Delacey said, leaping on the pile. "Nobody look at them!"

Naturally, of course, everyone did.

"I say," a man near the papers said, "Delacey—this is a draft of a letter to the *Portsmouth Herald,* asking them to print a column."

"By God," another voice said. "There's a statement of account here—according to this, he's…" The rest of that sentence was caught up in a swelling murmur.

Free didn't ask questions. She didn't ask how Edward had stolen a file that had notations in Delacey's own hand. The details of his plan, while not spelled out, were hinted at in such detail that it became clear what Delacey had been doing—that he'd filched early copies of her columns and paid others to reprint them to discredit her, that he'd hired the man who had set fire to her home.

It was *possible* that Delacey was such an inveterate record-keeper that he'd kept written notations on the arsonist he'd hired. And if he wasn't? Well. He was now, and she wasn't going to feel sorry about it. If he kept this up, next time, he might actually kill someone. Sometimes there was no point in playing fair.

Right now, she only watched, making mental notes about the changes she would have to telegraph back to her office for the column she'd already written, waiting to go to press as soon as the events of the evening came to an end.

To her side, she noticed her old colleagues—Chandley from the *Manchester Star,* Peters from the *Edinburgh Review*—taking note of this all. She'd asked Jane to invite them particularly. Usually, she'd be delighted to have an exclusive story on a matter of this magnitude. But this time, she wanted every paper in England to know what was in that file that had spilled. Chandley and Peters would write their own pieces, to be published in the next few days, explaining how they'd been hired to print duplicates of her columns.

The details of his entire plan would be discussed and made public.

Delacey had given up trying to gather his papers; now, he was simply trying to escape the room.

Free crossed over to him, caught his coat sleeve before he managed to exit. "No business." She was trying not to gloat. "No reputation. That is what you promised me, is it not? Remember this, Delacey. Everything you try to bring down on my head, I will bring back to you a thousandfold."

He glared at her. "How did you do it? How did you get that file?"

If she'd truly wanted to taunt him, she'd have told him that one of the men he'd hired had turned on him. But she didn't know what Edward was to him, and she didn't want to put Edward in danger.

She simply smiled and handed him the papers she'd been carrying ever since Andrews entered the room.

"James Delacey," she said solemnly, "you are hereby served with notice of a suit against you. I'm asking for compensation for the fire you started."

He stared at these papers, his lip curling in distaste. "You think you'll win this way? With papers and a suit at law, perhaps a fine of a few hundred pounds?"

"I don't care if I prevail on the suit. I care that everyone will hear the evidence, will discover how foul you are. That's how I will win."

He let out a long, slow breath. "You stupid girl," he said softly. "I've already won. No matter what you say publicly, no matter how you stain my reputation, it doesn't matter. You see, *I* can vote." He spat on the floor next to him. "And the last I checked, the only bill supporting any form of female suffrage that was even remotely mentioned this term was Rickard's, and *that* was just a showpiece. Celebrate your victory, Miss Marshall. It doesn't mean anything. It never will."

"You don't believe that. If I am already defeated, why did you even waste time bringing me down?"

His lip curled and he gave her an ugly look. "For the same reason I kill mice. Rodents will never rule the world, but even hiding in the walls they're still vermin." He hefted the papers she'd given him. "Congratulations, Miss Marshall. You survived to hide in the walls for a little longer."

Chapter Fourteen

"Free," Oliver said later that night. "We haven't had much time to talk, but—"

Free yawned. It was not quite by design, that yawn. She *was* tired. After the guests had left, she'd stayed up even later composing changes to her article the next day. Oliver had sent one of his servants off to the telegraph office, and then had brought her up to the room he'd set aside for her for the evening.

He smiled at her. "And I know you're tired. But that fellow you're working with, that Mr. Clark..." He paused, looked away. "I'm not sure he's proper."

Free blinked at her brother. Oliver had paid her bail four times, had been the one to retrieve her from the lock hospital. He'd read every column she'd written in her paper. He knew how she spent her time. *Propriety* was not a word that had often been associated with her. That was a word that belonged to misses on the marriage mart.

"Oliver, are you worried about my *reputation?* That's sweet. Stupid, yes. But sweet."

He flushed. "No. That's not it. I'm not sure he's, um." He cleared his throat. "Law-abiding. You know, he blackmailed Mark Andrews."

Was she supposed to feel *sorry* for the man who'd done his best to ruin her paper? Who had stolen and lied and betrayed her brother's trust? Oliver really had been in Parliament too long. "And Andrews gave in? Pfft. Weakling."

When Edward had tried to blackmail her, she'd not so much as budged.

Oliver shook his head, sighing. "I can see you're not much swayed."

"I know he's a scoundrel," Free said. "He told me so himself. And you know me. If I was the sort to fall in with the first scoundrel who presented himself, I'd never have made it so far."

"Well, there is that." Her brother looked faintly relieved.

He shouldn't have. She'd just called to mind Edward's first blackmail attempt with great fondness. She could see herself with Mr. Clark at some point in the future—an old married couple sitting on a porch in summer, holding hands and reminiscing over past times.

Do you remember the time you blackmailed me?

Yes, dear. You blackmailed me right back. It was the sweetest thing. I knew then that we were meant for each other.

She wasn't thinking about how dreadful he was any longer. She'd been thinking that her first investigations would have been so much easier with Edward to forge her references.

"I'm tired," Free told her brother. "Thank you for everything. I'd never have been able to rid myself of Delacey without you." She leaned up and kissed his cheek. "You're my favorite brother."

"I'm your only brother," he said in dark amusement.

"You see?" Free spread her arms. "I can't count on any of the others to even exist when I need them."

"Go to sleep, silly." But Oliver was smiling as he extinguished the lamp and left.

Free's mind didn't calm when she put her head on the pillow. Instead, it raced ahead—to the last rendezvous she had planned for the evening. One that she had not-so-coincidentally neglected to mention to her brother, on the theory that what brothers didn't know couldn't keep them awake at night.

The noises of the household died away. The servants' footsteps retreated belowstairs, then their voices ceased altogether. When the house had been quiet ten minutes, Free slipped on a robe and slippers and tiptoed out, down the wide stairs, back through the pantry, out the servants' door. The moon lit the mews in silver. She looked around, waiting…

"Free."

When had he begun to call her that? She turned to the sound of his voice.

"Frederica," he repeated, in that low, dark voice.

Edward came out of the shadows of the stables, and she put her arms around herself. She hadn't *precisely* lied to her brother a half-hour past. Edward wasn't the *first* scoundrel she'd met, just the best one. Amazing, how the world around her seemed to alter simply because he was present. She might have said his voice was like velvet, that the air was warm and welcoming. But his voice was far more like gravel with that hint of abrasion to it. The night was cooling off, and while a breath of warm air carried the sweet scent of newly cut grass in the square, it warred with the more mundane odor of the stables.

She looked up as Edward drew near, but could see only shadows on his face. "I take it you served Delacey successfully?" he asked.

Rodents will never rule the world. Even invoking that man gave her a shiver. She might never rule the world, but she could still gnaw a mighty hole in his plaster. "I did."

"How does it feel to vanquish your enemy?" he asked.

How odd it was, this doubled view of the world. Everyone had seen Delacey's papers. The account in her newspaper, speeding off the press as they spoke, would not be the only one. All of London would know that Delacey had arranged for the copies to be made, had burned down her house.

Yes, she might be vermin, but there were a lot of mice gnawing in concert, and together they might take him down.

She didn't answer. Instead, she turned to him. "How does it feel to have your revenge?"

Because he had it now. This was all he had wanted: to foil Delacey's plans and humiliate him. He'd no reason to stay around, now that was finished.

So why did everything still feel so unsettled?

He took a step toward her. "Strange you should say that." His voice was whisper-soft. His hand stole up to brush her cheek. "I don't know. Over the last days, I've scarcely thought of revenge at all."

His fingers scarcely grazed her skin, but even that light touch sent a cascade of electricity through her.

"I should like to know something," she said. "I need to know why you started our conversation all those weeks ago by blackmailing me."

There was a pause. He pulled away from her, straightening so that he was a great, dark tower of height. "I should think that was obvious. I wanted you to do something; I had the means to make you do it. So—"

"But you didn't have to. You said it yourself—you could have charmed me. You could have written yourself any sort of reference. But you've never tried to win my trust. Not once. Instead, from the very beginning, you told me repeatedly that you were a scoundrel and I shouldn't trust you. Why did you do that?"

She couldn't hear him breathe. She listened, straining, through the sound of crickets. But his silhouette remained utterly still.

"I suppose I did," he said softly. "How curious. I hadn't precisely realized."

Now Free couldn't breathe, waiting to hear his response.

"That first time we met on the bank of the Thames." He spoke slowly, as if he were choosing his words with precision. "You bowled me over. I remember watching you leave, feeling as if I was in need of an exclamation point. But I didn't have room for anything except full stops." He shrugged. "You have to set boundaries before you get in the thick of things, because once you're caught up in the act, you lose your head. You need to decide when to walk away: from cards, from a confidence game." He glanced over at her. "From you. Maybe that's what

I was doing. Making sure that I would walk away before I lost my head. I had to make sure you would never trust me, because otherwise…"

She had no idea what words to interpose in that pause. She knew he'd admired her. *That* much had been obvious, even that first day by the river, and it had only become more pronounced as time passed.

"It doesn't matter now. I know you well enough to know you'd never have implemented your threats."

She heard his sharp inhalation, saw his hand jerk toward her and then slip away. "I would like to think I wouldn't." His voice was low. "But long experience tells me that I can't make that promise. Don't tell yourself otherwise. I don't trust myself, Free, and you shouldn't either."

Oh, she didn't trust him—at least not to tell her the truth about himself any longer. "Do continue," she said politely. "Suppose that I went and told Delacey about your involvement. That would surely ruin *some* of your other plans. How would you stop me? Would you pen a letter I wrote to a lover, filled with sordid imaginings? Or would you aim for the purely financial? I can give you my banking arrangements; if you wish to make a hash of them, I can provide you with all the necessary details."

"Free." His voice was dark and forbidding. "Don't."

"Or maybe you'll attack my parents. My sisters. I'll make a list of all the people I love. I can hand over a complete dossier tomorrow, if that's convenient. Of course, if I am allowed to register a preference…" She took a step toward him and set her hand on his chest. "I would prefer to be ruined by you. In the flesh."

He growled deep in his throat, and his hand came up to cover hers. "What are you doing, Free?"

"Tell me, Edward. Tell me truly. What is this awful thing you'll do to hurt me?"

He didn't speak.

"I won't even try and evade it. I'll make it simple for you. All you have to do is look me in the eye and tell me that you could willingly ruin my life if I threatened yours. Go ahead."

He let go of her hand and turned away from her.

"I knew it," she said. "You stupid, stupid man. I knew it. You with your 'of course you don't trust me's and your fake blackmail. You're so clever, you almost fooled me." She felt her throat catch. "You almost made me believe that I *couldn't* trust you. But you failed, do you hear me? You failed utterly. I could put everything in your hands, and you'd never betray me. I could shut my eyes and throw myself to the ground, and you'd catch me before I had a single scratch."

He blew out his breath.

"I knew it when I first saw Delacey in there," she said. "For the tiniest instant, I thought he was you. Don't be offended; it was a trick of the light. It was a trick of my heart, looking for you even when I knew I wouldn't find you. For just one moment—that moment when I thought that I'd seen you—I smiled. And I felt the whole world come alight."

He was stock-still, completely unmoving.

"And then he turned, and I realized who it was." She gave a little laugh. "Once, many years ago, I had this dream. It was rather racy, if you must know. There was a young man I fancied, and in my dream..." She cleared her throat delicately. "In any event, I shut my eyes in my dream, focusing on the sensation. And then I opened them, and as things are in dreams, that handsome, charming young man had turned into the aging vicar. All my want washed away in a cold flush of revulsion. That's what it felt like tonight. He came and spoke to me, and all I could think was, *Free, you idiot, this is what it's like not to trust a man.* I don't care what you say. You would never, ever hurt me."

"I would," he growled.

"You're so arrogant that it never occurred to me that you doubted yourself so. But you do, don't you?"

He made a surprised noise. And then he turned back to her. "I doubt every inch of happiness that comes my way."

She set her hand on his wrist. "Don't."

"I can't ask you to trust me," he said. But he didn't draw away. Instead, he turned his hand in hers, so that his gloved fingers faced hers, interlacing.

"You don't have to ask." She ran her thumb along his palm. "That's the beauty of it. You don't have to ask me to trust you. I already do."

"You shouldn't." He wrapped his other arm about her waist, pulling her to him abruptly. "A trustworthy man would never do this." And before she had a chance to say anything— before she could even contemplate the heat of his body pressed against hers or the hard muscle of his chest—his lips found hers. No preamble; no light brushes. There was no need for it; the memory of their last kiss was on both their lips already. His mouth was hard and desperate, lips opening to hers. The unshaven stubble on his cheeks brushed her. It made the kiss all that more complex—so sweet, so lovely. She'd wanted this—wanted him—and now she didn't need to hold back.

Still, she set one hand on his chest and gave him a light push. "Wait."

He stopped instantly, pulling away. "What is it?"

She laughed and dropped her voice to mimic his. "'A trustworthy man would never do this.' Oh, yes, Mr. Clark. Look how untrustworthy you are. You stopped kissing me the instant I asked you to do it."

"Damn you, Free." But there was a note of dark amusement in his voice.

She twined her arms about his neck. She had to stretch up to do it, her body lengthening along his. She leaned forward and set her lips against his neck. "Damn us both."

He tasted of salt, and he let out a breath as she touched her tongue to the hollow of his neck, following it up his jawbone.

"You'll pay for that." His voice was a low rumble in his chest. His fingers slid up her ribs; his left hand cupped her breast. And then he kissed her again. This time, his kiss was slow and gentle. His fingers against her breast warmed her, making slow circles that matched the stroke of his tongue. She'd been right: He was the absolute best scoundrel she'd ever known.

She'd heard another girl talking about how a man's kisses had made her insensible, unable to think. It seemed so odd now. Why would anyone want to *stop* sensing at a time like this, stop thinking about how lovely it all felt? The entire world felt *more*—sweeter, more solid, more real, as if his mouth on hers grounded her to earth. As if that careful caress, the fingers of his left hand sliding under the neckline of her gown, were sketching the details of the night sky for her, putting in moon and stars over the dark cloud of London's soot.

He'd backed her against the wall of the mews. She felt the rough planks against her spine. But she simply leaned back and took the opportunity to explore him—to run her hands down his chest, feeling every curve of muscle go taut beneath the linen of his shirt. He stepped into her, leaning against her until they were hip to hip, until she could feel the hardness of his erection pressing into her. Her whole body sang in response.

He pulled back just long enough to lean his forehead against hers. "Lovely Free," he whispered. "God, I should not be doing this."

"Too true. You should be doing more. Much more."

He shook his head, but leaned in to kiss her again. And this time, it was a whole different world of a kiss—a kiss that said it was coming before, a kiss that promised a night after this one, and a night after that. It was a kiss that said that all those weeks they'd known one another had been only a prelude to this moment. This was only the second act of the play, but the climax was not out of sight. It was a kiss of bodies, of hips and hands, of breasts and tongues. His hands tangled briefly in her laces, loosening her bodice; she helped him undo it, just enough so that he could lean down and set his mouth there, right on her nipple.

"Stop," Free said. And he did, pulling away when she least wanted him to, even though his body vibrated with want and his hands clenched on her hips.

"I'm sorry," he said hoarsely. "Sorry—I shouldn't have—"

She laughed. "You stopped again. Edward, if you don't want me to trust you, you shouldn't be so trustworthy."

He let out a breath. "Ah, you're teasing me."

"I'm proving something to you," she said. "Because you seem to think that you don't deserve to be trusted."

He didn't say anything. Instead, he leaned down and took her nipple in his mouth. She could feel his tongue, swirling in a long, lazy circle. He set her aflame, caressing her. It wasn't an answer, and yet it was.

Please, he said.

Yes, she said.

Trust me. Trust this.

She'd talked to enough ladies of the night that she knew the lack of a bed was no impediment. But he made no effort to take it further than the press of their bodies, the touch of fingers against willing flesh. He did nothing more than stoke their heady, insistent desire. He kissed her, touched her, brought her to small, silent gasps as her body came to life. Another five minutes, and a little less clothing, and he could have brought her all the way to ecstasy. He didn't though. He held her until the last dim light in the garret across the way winked out, until the streetlamp twenty yards down began to flicker. Until her head spun with lack of sleep and kissing, and her body ached for what was to come.

"Come to me," she whispered to him. "Come to me tomorrow night."

His hands tightened on her body and he shuddered. He didn't let go of her, but he drew his head back.

"Frederica," he said in a low voice. His hand slid up her nightrail, sliding the sleeve back onto her shoulder, covering her up. "If I take one night from you, I'll want all the rest of your nights. And even I'm not so selfish as to demand them from you."

She put her hand over his. "What happened to the man who told me he was maddeningly brilliant? To the scoundrel who asked me to think about how attractive I found his muscles?"

"Bluster will last me a night. Swagger, a week." His hand brushed her face. "Beyond that? I can't promise you anything more."

The night seemed absolutely still around them—soundless and empty, without even the rustle of wind to disturb them.

He took her hand in his and kissed her fingertips. "Pain is a black ink," he told her. "Once it's spilled on a man's soul, it'll never scrub out. Deep down, Miss Marshall, there's nothing to me but blackness." He leaned in. "And Free, darling—I think you know that."

"You're an idiot." Her voice trembled.

"That's what I just said. I never did have any sense." But he didn't leave. Instead, his arm crept around her. His body warmed hers. He wouldn't leave; she was sure of it. Sure of him, when he leaned down and pressed his lips to hers again.

"Sweetheart," he murmured.

"My darling scoundrel."

He let out a little laugh. "Precisely. I'd rather leave you wanting than stay and earn your hatred."

And then he did pull away. The air was cold in his sudden absence; the night was dark. He gave her one last smile—as cocksure and arrogant as any he'd ever given her—and then he began to walk away. Really walk away, as if this were all over.

"Edward," Free called before he'd made it six paces.

He paused, straightening, and then half-turned, looking back at her.

"We both know you'll return," she told him.

For a long while he stood, not saying anything. Then he shook his head.

"I know," he said. "I never did have any sense."

Chapter Fifteen

"ALL I WANT," EDWARD SAID, "is to know if he dictates a letter with her name in it."

His brother's secretary sat across the table from him, a glass of ale in front of him. Peter Alvahurst frowned primly, as if he were pretending to have morals.

"I don't know," he demurred.

Alvahurst had been the one to bribe Mr. Marshall's undersecretary in the first place. Edward knew precisely what sort of man he was, even if Alvahurst would not admit it.

Edward took a second banknote out and set it on the table between them. The surface was sticky with layers of spilled ale.

"I understand your concern," Edward said smoothly. "I don't want you to reveal the contents—that would be wrong, of course, and you aren't the sort of man who would betray his employer for money."

"Too right." This was said with a self-righteous nod.

Mr. Alvahurst was precisely the kind of man who'd meet a shady character in a darkened pub and let that man dangle money in front of him. But Edward had always found that preserving a man's illusion of himself was more important than simply offering money. Let someone think himself upright and honorable, and he'd slit a man's throat for a halfpenny.

"You know how much difficulty your employer's last encounter with Frederica Marshall caused him," Edward said. "And I know how loyal you are to him. We're much alike, you and I. We're looking out for his interests."

"That's true." Mr. Alvahurst licked his lips and glanced at the ten pounds on the table. There was no evidence at all that Edward was looking out for Delacey's interest—no evidence but Edward's word and ten pounds. Edward took out a third note, but he didn't slide this one any closer. He held it lightly, letting Alvahurst know of its existence.

It had been three days since he'd left Free in the mews. Three days, in which he'd tried to convince himself to walk away as he should. Three days, during which he'd heard her words ringing in his ears. *You'll return.*

No.

He knew what he did, and what he did well. If he came back to her—really came back—he'd start telling himself lies, just like Alvahurst here. He'd tell himself he was noble, that he was doing things for her.

He could feel the tug of all his old dreams.

Free wasn't naïve and she wasn't stupid. But she believed in a future—believed in it so hard that she made him want to believe, too. He could almost see that garden she'd talked about, blossoming with every step she took.

And he'd told her the truth of himself: There was nothing left to him but a scoundrel.

And so the scoundrel in him smiled at Mr. Alvahurst. "So just send a message, a short one, if he mentions Miss Marshall. We both know he'll do it, so you won't be telling me anything I don't already know."

Only now, when Alvahurst was most vulnerable, did Edward add that third banknote. That made the stack on the table worth half a year's wages to the man. Alvahurst shut his eyes. And then slowly, as if savoring the moment, he reached out and pulled the notes to him.

Edward simply smiled. He might not be able to keep Frederica Marshall, but at least he could keep her safe.

And maybe, just maybe, he could give her one last thing before he walked away from her for good.

⌘ ⌘ ⌘

FREE HAD NEVER QUITE believed that Edward would disappear entirely, but days passed with no word from him.

So when he appeared late one afternoon, she felt a frothy, bubbly joy, one that could scarcely be contained.

He stood in the doorway of her office. He was, as always, the consummate scoundrel. He leaned against the doorframe, smiling—almost smirking—at her, as if he knew how rapidly her heart had started beating.

If that was how they were going to do this…

She simply raised an eyebrow in his direction. "Oh," she said with a sniff. "It's you."

"You're not fooling anyone," he said.

She could feel the corner of her mouth twitch up. Last time she'd seen him, he'd kissed her so thoroughly she had not yet recovered.

"I'm not?"

"I heard it most distinctly," he told her. "You might have said 'It's you,' but there was a distinct exclamation mark at the end. In fact, I think there were two."

"Oh, dear." Free looked down, fluttering her eyelashes demurely. "Is my punctuation showing once more?"

His eyes darkened and he took a step into her office. "Don't hide it on my account," he growled. "You have the most damnably beautiful punctuation that I have ever seen. You make a man feel greedy."

She couldn't keep the smile off her face.

"It's a shame," he continued, "that I'm not here to be greedy. I'm here to say farewell and to leave you a memento."

All that bubbly, incandescent joy turned to sharp crystal. She inhaled slowly, looking up at him. He was smiling still, but there was a sadness to that smile.

"Shall we go for a walk?"

"You mean," he said pitching his voice low, "should we escape the view of your employees and find a nice, empty field hereabouts where I can kiss you senseless?"

"Yes." She would not blush. "That is what I mean."

That flare of want, the way his hand clenched at his side before flattening against his trousers... She could almost feel him on the verge of acquiescing. But instead, he shook his head. "We'd better not. It was painful enough stopping the first time. As I said, I'm here to give you a present."

"How exciting." It wasn't. She didn't want a present. "So you brought me a present. Is it a *nice* present? Will I like it?"

"Not particularly," he responded. "And I don't know."

She laid her hands on her desk and sighed. "Drat. I was so hoping that you'd somehow procured the right to vote for women. That would have been lovely."

That won her another smile. And oh, what a lovely smile it was, lighting his entire face, lighting the entire room. But he simply shook his head again. "Miss Marshall, you had better learn to be more acquisitive and less political. Until then, I suspect any presents you receive will always disappoint you. Do you wish to be the sort of curmudgeon who hates Christmas?"

Even now, she couldn't work up a proper outrage against him. "Oh, very well. You've convinced me. I don't wish to hate Christmas." She gestured; he entered her office, shut her door, and then seated himself. This was as far as they'd come since their first meeting weeks ago: They were still on opposite sides of this desk.

She looked away from him, lining up her inkwell with her pens and pencils. "I knew you would come back."

He leaned over and deliberately turned one of her pens at an angle askew with all the other implements. "When we finish this conversation, I'm going to stand up and walk out of this room. I won't stop until I reach the train station. I'll be across the Channel by tonight."

Her chest squeezed. She let out a long, slow breath. But he returned her pen to a straight line and leaned back in his chair.

"There are too many things I haven't told you." He looked her in the eyes. "But the first thing you should know is that I don't just want you in my bed for a week or two. I want you forever."

She felt as if she'd been thrown back against the wall. Her lungs did not seem to be functioning properly. But he'd said it so smoothly that she wasn't sure she'd heard him right.

"I don't *always* take everything I want." For an instant, a glimmer of a smile passed over his face. "No doubt this attack of morals is temporary on my part. Suffice to say that if I stay much longer, I'll begin to forget all the reasons I'm terrible for you. Selfishness makes a man lie to himself, and while I have no problem being selfish, you make me want to tell myself the sweetest lies. And while I'll lie to the entire world, I don't choose to lie to myself."

"What sort of lies?" she asked.

His lip curled sardonically. "The worst sort, Miss Marshall. You make me think I could be someone."

"Aren't you?"

"No."

She frowned at him.

"Nobody good. But I believed I was. Once." His hand shifted to cover his jacket pocket as he spoke. "My family was wealthy. Not so socially exalted that we could do whatever we wished; we stood just high enough to be hampered by every last expectation."

He'd rarely spoken of his past. Free sat, waiting for him to continue, afraid that if she so much as breathed too loudly, he wouldn't go on.

But he did. "I was friends with the son of one of my father's servants. Good friends." He set his hands—still gloved, she noticed; she'd never seen him take off more than the one glove. "A little unusual, I suppose, but there weren't many other boys my age about. Normally, such friendships vanish when a boy goes to school." Edward shrugged. "This one didn't. When I was seventeen, his father was kicked by a horse in the course of his employment. He fractured four ribs and broke a leg in three places. He wouldn't have been able to work for months. Rather than granting the man time to recover, my father hired someone new in his place. After twelve years of service."

Free sucked in a breath.

"Of course I spoke up. It was unjust, and this was my friend being cast out, with an injured father who would have no way to make a living."

"That was good of you."

He shook his head. "That was foolish of me. There's nothing more stupid than telling dangerous truths to a man who controls your life. By that time, I had some fairly unusual political notions." He smiled vaguely at that. "Reading is dangerous. I thought we could organize a mass response among the tenants, demanding—ah, well. Never mind that. It didn't go well. The tenants balked, and instead of revolting, they told my father. The end result was that my father realized, after years of ignoring me, that I had developed dangerously plebeian sympathies. So he didn't just toss my friend and his family out on their collective ear. He had my friend and his brother whipped for attempted rabble rousing. In front of me." He let out a long breath. "And then he banished me. He had it put about that he was sending me to France to work with the masters. For my art.

"He did send me to France. But he sent me to live with a blacksmith in Strasbourg, not some painter in Paris. He thought I'd get a taste of manual labor, of the life of a regular man, and I'd recant all my beliefs in exchange for a taste of white bread and the comfort of a valet." That smile twitched up even more. "It didn't work. For two years, it didn't work. And then war was declared with Prussia. I asked my father to send a letter of credit so I could return home; he refused. I went to the consulate in Strasbourg before the army arrived, only to find that my family had told them there was an impostor pretending to be me in the environs. I was ejected without assistance."

Free made an involuntary noise of protest. He had already told her what had followed—*have you ever seen plaster dust ignite in the air?* He'd hinted at far more.

"So I vowed I'd never go back to them. I had my art, and what is art but the second cousin of forgery? It's odd—lie about the world long enough, and everything in it stops feeling real. As if I'm nothing but a figment of someone else's imagination. I don't dare lie to myself, or I'll lose touch completely."

There was a great deal he hadn't told her. She could tell it from the uneasy shift in his shoulders. "I imagine it wasn't as easy as knocking off a forgery right away."

He tensed. "Nothing is ever easy."

"Nonetheless."

He didn't say anything for a long time. Then he finally spoke. "My father thought he could change my character with a little discomfort. He was wrong. It took pain." He looked away. "Someday, try forging a letter of credit and delivering it to a man who is worse than you."

That night after the fire seemed so distant—even though it was scarcely a week past. But Free could recall the words he'd given her late at night. *Pain is a black ink. Enough of it and you can blot out a man's soul.*

"On second thought." He gave her a brilliant smile, one that almost broke her heart. "Don't try it. You don't want to know what will happen."

"Was it very painful, then?"

His lip quirked in disgust. "Just enough to prove I wasn't the resilient white knight I believed myself to be. I was a liar and a fraud and a cheat, just like everyone else. I needed to learn that lesson." He took a deep breath, and then he looked up at her. His eyes met hers. They sparkled with that look she knew so well, that black humor that she'd come to care for. "I didn't much mind until now."

Her heart thudded in her chest.

"I don't think I can stop being a liar and a fraud," he said. "But, for the first time in a very long while, I'm beginning to believe in something." His voice dropped. "In someone. I'm sorry, Miss Marshall, but I can't let myself do that."

She could scarcely breathe. She didn't know what to say. She only knew she couldn't look away from him, couldn't have told him to leave no matter what he revealed at the moment.

"There." He brushed his hands together. "That's said. It's a pack of lies." He shrugged. "It's as honest as I know how to be at this point. That's why I'm leaving, Free." He looked over at her. "I brought you something."

He reached into his jacket pocket. His hand closed on something—something large enough that he had to turn his wrist to get it from his pocket. She caught a flash of gray metal.

"Here." He reached out and set the piece on her desk. "It's a paperweight. You have papers; I thought you might put this to use."

Free leaned forward and picked up the piece he'd placed before her. It was heavy and yet intricate. The paperweights she had seen before were fussy blown-glass balls encasing pleasant flowers. This bore no relation to those things. It was a single strip of iron, worked into a curlicued ball. The metal doubled and tripled back on itself. It was warm from resting in his pocket; the edges were rough against her skin. And yet it seemed surprisingly delicate.

"What is it?"

He shrugged. "I don't know. Nothing but a big wad of metal."

"This is beautiful," Free said slowly. "Beautiful and somehow, sad. And harsh. All at the same time. I've never seen its like. Where did you find it?"

He shrugged indifferently. "Just outside Strasbourg. Some six years ago."

"Did you commission it yourself or did the artist have a regular stock of these paperweights?"

Edward snorted. "I commissioned it," he told her. "It's just a *trifle*."

She didn't think it was a *trifle*. She turned the piece around, catching hints of half patterns hidden in every twist of metal. "Was this to commemorate some occasion? The artist that made this was an incredible genius. The loops look random at first, but they're not. When I look at it from this angle, I almost see…a rose? There are thorns on that part, I think, and these loops from this angle form petals." She gave it a quarter turn. "But this looks like a hawk. I could stare at this for hours." She looked up at him and suddenly frowned. "Edward, are you well?"

"Perfectly so." The smile he gave her was just like every smile he'd ever delivered—easy, untinged by emotion and, Free realized, utterly false. His left hand gripped the arm of his chair so tightly that his glove bunched. His other arm was ramrod straight, braced against his leg as if it were the only thing that held him upright.

He was lying to her. Of *course* he was; he hadn't given her this piece because it was an inconsequential paperweight that he'd commissioned on a whim. It was because it meant something to him.

"Don't be such a man." Free stood, rolling her eyes. "You've gone pale. Here. Let me get you a glass of water."

"I am not pale," he said brusquely. "I don't need a glass of water."

She came around the desk and she set her hand on his wrist. "Your pulse is racing."

"It is not," he said in contradiction of reality. He had begun to breathe fast, and his skin was turning paper white.

Free rolled her eyes again. "Stop being ridiculous. Now are you going to stay here while I fetch you something to drink?"

"Hmph."

"That wasn't definitive agreement, Mr. Clark. Let's try this again: If you get up now, I'm kicking you in the shins. Your shins won't like it, and my toes will like it less." She gave him a tight smile and ducked away.

But as she found the pitcher of water, she considered. He'd said he needed to tell her a great deal the other night, but that he wouldn't. She'd thought he didn't *wish* to. She of all people should have realized that the memories he held were so painful that he *couldn't*. After everything he'd told her, she should have understood that much.

He was still in her office when she returned. Instead of seating herself in the chair on the opposite side of her desk, she leaned against the edge of the table, a few feet from him. "Better, Edward?"

He took a sip of water. "I thought you wouldn't do this caretaking stuff. You know, too feminine. Too motherly."

She simply smiled. "I believe that women are human beings. That belief is not diametrically opposed to thinking that men are human beings, and that if one human being has the opportunity to be kind to another, she should do so." She looked at him. "And I knew you would say that. That you'd say something to provoke me to avoid talking about yourself. You're always deflecting my questions."

"Only because you ask impertinent questions. I'd have no need to deflect anything, if you stopped snooping."

She pushed to her feet, walked to her door. But she didn't leave. Instead, she made sure it was firmly shut. "Mr. Clark," she said softly. "Edward. I don't think you gave me a lump of metal that you'd been carting around for six years for no particular reason. Talking about this particular lump of metal is difficult for you. You don't have to tell me anything."

He took a breath. "I lied when I said I commissioned it." He didn't look at her. "Or, rather, it was a mangling of the truth. I commissioned it, but the artist was myself."

She blinked and looked at it again. "Oh. My."

"Don't look so surprised. You've seen my sketches. You know I have some capabilities as an artist."

"Some, of course. But sketches are one thing. Any number of people can manage a creditable sketch. This is something else entirely."

"I spent two years with a blacksmith." He shrugged. "I learned a few tricks. And I had to decide who I was. I couldn't be the useless little rich boy I had been all that time. I felt as if I were trapped in a labyrinth with no way out, traveling tangled paths that could not lead me to the surface. I made that"—he nodded at the paperweight—"trying to find myself in the man I became."

Free looked at the piece again.

"No," he told her. "You won't find me in there. That's the whole point. I only ever found a collection of twisted passages leading nowhere. I never found a place to go, a person to be. I learned to believe in nothing, because that way I would never be disappointed."

"So." She picked up his paperweight and turned it over. "This was your search for a heart?"

"No." His voice was ever so quiet. "I made that when I gave up on having one altogether. I didn't think there was any point in looking for such a ridiculous object until I met you. At some point in the weeks of our acquaintance, I realized I *did* have one buried somewhere." He looked over at her. "There's no point in searching it out now. By the time I realized it existed, it was already yours."

Oh. Her chest felt too tight. She could almost feel her eyes stinging in response. "And still you're leaving."

"I am."

Free knew that she was the sort to push others. She knew because she'd been told it, time and time again, and because…well, frankly, it was true. Other people were often wrong, and she had no qualms about letting them know.

But if she had one regret in her life, it was pushing too much at the wrong time. When she was younger, she had pushed her Aunt Freddy. Freddy had been beset by a complex mix of fears, ones that Free still didn't understand. Still she'd pushed, as if she somehow knew better than her own aunt what Freddy needed.

And what had she accomplished by that? They'd both been miserable, and in her aunt's final days, she'd made Freddy feel as if she were not good enough.

Sometimes, she'd learned, the only way to move forward was to stop pushing.

"Very well," she heard herself say calmly.

It was rather like his gloves; there were some things a man needed to speak about when he was ready. A man like Edward didn't give her a piece crafted by his own hands because he wanted to walk away and forget her. He did it because he wanted her to remember. Maybe he needed to leave for now. But deep down, he expected to come back when he'd sorted himself out.

All she had to do was leave the door open.

"I suppose I should send you a memento in return," she said casually. "If you'll give me your address, I'll send you issues of the paper."

It was as obvious a falsehood as the one he'd delivered about the paperweight itself.

He snorted. "Are you lying to me, Miss Marshall?"

"Of course I am." She smiled at him. "I thought it would put you at ease."

He laughed, that dark, appreciative laugh she'd come to adore. "Touché, my dear."

For a second, they stared at one another, her will matching his.

"Just the paper, now," he warned. "No letters."

It was a victory of a sort, that she'd made him tell that lie. He clearly knew it was a lie; he gave his head an annoyed shake.

And then he rubbed a hand through his hair and looked away. "I own a metalworks in Toulouse," he mumbled.

"Why, Mr. Clark, that sounds surprisingly respectable."

He raised an eyebrow at her. "Don't make too much of it. I've only had it a few years. And you'd best not ask how I got the money to start it." He smiled tightly. "For that matter, don't ask how I got the first references I needed so that business would start coming in."

"Does this metalworks have an address?"

He wrinkled his nose at her. She smiled calmly in return while her heart raced. Then slowly, ever so slowly, he took a sheet of her paper and scrawled a few lines.

"I won't write back," he told her.

He was such a dreadful liar. Let him lie, if that's what he needed for the moment.

He didn't take hold of her, didn't even touch her. He simply stood and strode to the door. "You have my best wishes, Free. Now and always."

And then he turned and left.

Chapter Sixteen

EDWARD HAD KNOWN WHEN he gave Free his address that he might as well have given up right then. The last thing he could withstand was a sustained correspondence. He managed to let the first of her letters pass without a reply. The second was harder. She told him about construction on a new home, about how her suit against his brother was prospering—well—and the public response to the revelations they'd jointly engineered at that soireé—even better. Her advertisers were returning, her subscribers were more loyal than ever, and her subscription numbers were up ten percent and still growing. Everything was looking up, she told him.

Everything, she said, but one little thing. She didn't specify what that was, but he didn't need to ask.

It took all his willpower to keep his silence.

But then two weeks passed—two weeks in which her newspapers arrived without any personal notes at all. That circumstance should not have had him grumbling in complaint.

Still, when he saw a scrap of paper attached to his paper one morning, he grabbed for it.

Apologies for the silence, she wrote. *I've been busy. See attached.*

He read through her piece. His heart beat faster as he read; his fists clenched on the paper. And when he reached the end of it, he didn't just give up on the notion of chivalrously ignoring her; he grabbed for his own paper and scrawled a response.

May 14, 1877

Good God. Are you trying to stop my heart? Nothing from you for all that time—and then only one brief note. I had thought you'd given up doing investigative work personally. You understand that when you go into a very dangerous mine that you are putting yourself in danger?

You could have died. You almost did.

I won't stand for—

Edward stopped, and imagined himself saying that to Free in person. She'd make a rude noise—and all too well-deserved. He crossed that off, too, and stared at the paper a long while before trying again.

Even if you think nothing of your own safety, think of—

That wasn't any better, to imply that she hadn't thought about the consequences of her actions. He scratched that through.

Tell me, do you imagine yourself invulnerable, or—

He took a deep breath. It was almost as if he could hear her responding, taunting him. He scratched dark lines through this, too. After a long while, he wrote again.

I have sat in one place crossing lines off this letter for far longer than I should. It's almost as if you are sitting over my shoulder, offering your sarcastic thoughts in response to my most protective impulses. You're obviously intelligent enough to understand the risks you're taking, and you've decided they're worthwhile. I know better than to argue with you on that score.

So I will swallow all my other worries and end with this: I have sat with you at night and felt your fear. I do not know how you face it again and again. It is more than I could do.

You bewilder me.

Edward

It would be foolish to send the letter. It sat on his desk for days while he argued with himself. Finally, he slipped it into the mails, and was even more annoyed when that did not feel like an act of weakness.

It was a matter of days before he heard from her again.

May 20, 1877

    Dear Edward,

    It was nothing. All in the name of reporting, really. It was rather fortuitous, in fact, that I experienced a cave-in. Under such circumstances, I could…

    Oh, very well. I can see you tapping your foot impatiently at me. I'm not fooling you, am I?

    I always write my articles so that I disappear. The words are about the hospitals and the inmates, the streets and the streetwalkers. If I reference myself at all, I talk about the false persona I invented to do the investigations. To everyone in the world, I can pretend that all those things happened to someone else.

    Everyone but you. I may give false names and false backgrounds, but the things I've reported have always happened to me. *You may find it bewildering that I'm still willing to take it on.*

    But to me, knowing that you know, that there's one person who knows I'm not truly fearless…well, that makes it bearable.

    Just don't tell my brother.

    Yours,

    Free

Edward thought a long while before responding.

May 28, 1877

    As I don't believe in sending letters filled with treacle-like sentiment, I feel as if I should…send you a puppy or something.

    Alas. I don't know if puppies keep when sent through the mails—and I doubt they'd pass through customs these days.

    It's too bad you aren't a pirate, as you'd once planned. That would make puppy delivery far more efficient. I'd bring up my own ship next to you and send you an entire broadside of puppies. You'd be buried in very small dogs. You'd be far too busy with puppy care to worry about anything else. This is now sounding more and more invasive, and less and less cheering—and nonetheless I have yet to meet anyone who was not delighted by a wriggling mass of puppies. If I ever did meet such a person, he would deserve misery.

    Do not doubt the power of the puppy-cannon.

Edward

P.S. If there is no puppy attached to this message, it is because it was confiscated by customs. Bah. Customs is terrible.

After that, it was impossible to pretend he was not corresponding with her.

June 3, 1877

Free—

I don't know what you mean. I do not resort to the ridiculous to avoid talking about feelings.

My God! Look behind you. It's a three-headed monkey!

Now, what were we talking about? Ah, yes. You were telling me that Rickard was circulating a modified bill. Let me play devil's advocate to your outrage: Even if only some women vote, it will prove that the sky can still remain firmly attached to the heavens and will forestall the worst doomsayers of the lot…

There was no point lying to himself now about what was happening. He'd done a terrible job of walking away from her, and look what had happened. Now he was no better off at all. There was no future in this though. What was he to do, tell her the truth of who he was? Let her know that his brother had been the one who caused all her problems, and then ask her to be his viscountess? She'd hate the prospect.

It was the chance that she might not say *no* that most shook him.

He was disgusted with himself when he began to look for a buyer for his metalworks.

June 10, 1877

Free,

I don't feel qualified to advise you on answering your brother's worries. I understand his concern, but you don't have to listen to him. You only pay attention to him because you love him. This is what happens when people love you: They start annoying you.

Next time, if you wish to avoid this, try to poison your sibling relationships at a much younger age. It works wonders, I've found.

Yours,
Edward

June 21, 1877

Free,

Yes, I did manage to wrap up that bit of business I had mentioned before. As for the other thing—yes, I do have a younger brother. He's my only living family. If you must know, he's the one who told the British Consul in Strasbourg that I was an impostor. Suffice to say, I don't think you would like him.

The only reason you are writing to me about my brother is because yours has gone on that elaborate trip. Tell me more next time you write. Is he in Malta yet? And when was he supposed to be back— August?

Edward

P.S. You are only proving me right. Love. Aggravation. Once again, they go hand in hand.

Edward sighed and looked up from the letter. He was dillydallying. But what was he to write instead? *I was born Edward Delacey, and my brother burned your house down. I was born Edward Delacey, and I could be Viscount Claridge if I mentioned that fact in England.*

He couldn't bring himself to tell her. He couldn't walk away. He didn't want to claim her under false pretenses. But if he ever told her the truth...

I was born Edward Delacey. Marry me anyway?

Ha. There was no point even thinking about the matter.

Instead, as he had so often in the months since he'd met her, he tried to sketch her. His memory of her seemed as sharp as ever. Her eyes, mobile and intelligent. Her lips, sweet and smiling. He'd tried to draw all his memories: Free crouching next to him on the bank of the River Cam, opera glasses raised to her eyes. He'd attempted to capture her standing in the mews, the moonlight shifting across her skin.

His sketches never came out right. No matter what he did, how he tried, they were always missing some unknown element. He still didn't know what it was. He put his notebook away in disgust.

But the letter that arrived from England early one July morning was not from Miss Marshall. Edward opened it curiously and then froze.

Mr. Clark,

This last week, the Honorable James Delacey sent not one letter mentioning Miss Marshall, but seven.

Sincerely,

A.

In the end, Edward didn't even take time to answer any questions. The first letter he sent was in French.

July 6, 1877

M. Dubuque—

I'll take thirty thousand francs for the metalworks after all. Five thousand in earnest money will do; we can arrange the rest at some later date. Correspond with my solicitor in London, please; the direction is below.

Clark

On his way out of town, he sent one last telegram.

FREE
WILL BE THERE IN THREE DAYS
EDWARD

⌘ ⌘ ⌘

"WHAT ARE YOU DOING?" Alvahurst hissed.

Edward shouldered past his brother's secretary into the dark room beyond.

He had spent the last two days traversing France by rail, arranging passage across the Channel, and racing to London.

Every hour that passed was an hour in which his brother could cause Free harm.

"You can't come in here," Alvahurst was saying. "We'll wake my wife."

"We'll whisper," Edward told him. "Or we could stand outside. It's quite simple, Alvahurst. I need to know what Delacey wrote about Miss Marshall."

Alvahurst rubbed bleary eyes and looked around the front room of the flat. There were, Edward noted, dozens of items that could be used as weapons. Alvahurst, however, didn't reach for a one of them. Instead, he gestured to a chair next to the fireplace.

Edward sat next to the poker.

"You told me you'd never ask after the contents of the letters." Alvahurst looked ridiculous, his limbs sticking out from a nightshirt and cap. He sounded even worse.

Edward had neither the time nor the patience to indulge him.

"I lied," Edward said. "If you don't tell me everything, I will go to James Delacey and tell him the truth. I have a letter in your own hand, in which you violate his confidences. How long will your employment last if Delacey discovers what you've done?"

Alvahurst winced. "But—"

"I have no time to be gentle," Edward told him. "You knew the instant you took my money that you'd agreed to be my creature. We might have told some lies to each other during the negotiations, but we both knew what was happening. Now start acting like it."

Alvahurst sighed, and then slowly, revealed what he knew.

When he'd finished, Edward frowned. "That makes no sense," he said. "Even James is not so stupid. She's been to gaol before. Another arrest will hardly make a difference, and she'll be released—"

"Ah, that's it," the secretary said. "It's not the imprisonment itself that he cares about, but what will happen once she's held. The station has instructions not to release her.

Her brother—the only one she knows who could raise a fuss—is abroad on some kind of a trip. When the sergeant there is finished with her, she'll know how to keep her mouth shut. Do you know what can be done to someone in custody?"

A pool of dark fury rose up, threatening to choke Edward.

Oh, he knew. He definitely knew. The room receded around him. He held on to the arms of his chair, gripping them as he felt himself enveloped in dark, clammy fog.

Do you know what can be done to someone in custody?

Black water, thick and choking, so he could scarcely breathe. Pain that happened to someone else, someone who would believe anything to make it stop. He took a deep breath, shoving the memory away. All that had happened to Edward Delacey, and Edward Delacey scarcely existed any longer.

"So if that's all you need to know," Alvahurst was saying, "you might consider leaving before my wife wakes and asks what I'm doing."

He was sitting in a darkened room, not in a black cellar. Still, Edward surreptitiously rubbed his right hand. "You've told me all I need."

All that he needed, and yet still it was not enough. All he could do as Edward Clark was thwart his brother, plan by plan. He could spend the rest of his life bribing secretaries and blackmailing servants, and he'd only ever stay in one place.

Edward Delacey, on the other hand…

The thought made him feel almost feverish—that he could put on those old ideals, that old identity. Now *there* was an ill-fitting skin.

But if he didn't…

You could do some good, he heard Patrick saying.

Edward didn't do good. He had to remember that, no matter how he might try to fool himself. He left the home of his brother's secretary, feeling dizzy and nauseated. No matter how hard he tried, one day James would succeed in hurting Free.

Do you know what can be done to someone in custody?

Maybe his brother didn't intend anything more than a talking-to. But after everything Edward had seen James do? He wasn't willing to wager on it. He had to stop this now. Any way he could.

All this time, he'd kept himself away from her by reminding himself what he was. There was no future in being with him, and he refused to let himself lie and believe otherwise. Now, for the first time, it all became clear.

He could have her. He could keep her safe. And—best of all—once she discovered what he'd done, what he hadn't told her...

He wouldn't have to tell himself lies about the future they wouldn't have. She'd get rid of him herself.

⌘   ⌘   ⌘

HE ROUSED HIS SOLICITORS at four.

At eight in the morning, Edward presented himself at Baron Lowery's London home.

The man he was about to become should have knocked on the front door. But he had enough of his old self to him that he went back to the mews. He roused a groom, who went into the house. Ten minutes later, Patrick came out.

"Edward." Patrick came forward, grabbing hold of his arms. "You didn't tell me you were in England. How did you know I was in London?"

"I surmised as much from the newspaper," Edward said, his voice low. "You see, Baron Lowery is on the Committee for Privileges, and they're meeting in two days."

Patrick looked at him. They both knew why the Committee was meeting. The Committee always met when a man made a request to join the House of Lords. They did the boring work of listening to the evidence detailing a man's right to take his seat.

Three days ago was the seventh anniversary of Edward's last official correspondence with his family. James had been waiting for precisely this moment.

"Are you…" Patrick's eyes widened.

"I am," Edward said. He felt sick to his stomach. "I won't do any good—don't give me that look—but at least I can stop him from doing harm."

Patrick let out a long sigh. "I'll get George," he said.

It took fifteen minutes before Patrick came down again, accompanied by a man in robe and slippers. Baron Lowery took one look at Edward. His nose wrinkled.

"You." That might have been disgust in Lowery's voice. It might have been curiosity.

"Me." Edward came forward. His heart was pounding. He thought back to his childhood—to the Harrow-educated accent he had once had, one that he'd done his best to lose over the years.

He recalled years of privilege that he'd shed over the course of a fortnight. He made himself stand straighter.

"We were not properly introduced when last we met," Edward said. He sounded like a caricature of himself, a stuffy, upright little snob, someone who deserved to have the stuffing beat out of him.

But he held out his gloved hand expectantly to Baron Lowery.

"I told you that I was Edward Clark. But I was born Edward Delacey," he said. "I'm not dead. And I'm the current Viscount Claridge."

Chapter Seventeen

FREE HAD KEPT EDWARD'S confusing telegram—both so straightforward and so utterly baffling—in her pocket for the last few days, pulling it out at odd hours, until the cheap paper had begun to fray at the edges.

He was coming back. She'd always known he would return in his own time, and yet now that it was happening, she couldn't quite bring herself to believe it.

She was standing out of doors now, with Amanda by her side. Together, they contemplated the replacement cottage some fifty feet distant. It had been completed a mere two weeks ago.

The last months had erased all evidence of the fire she had fought with Edward. Grass had grown over charred marks; trees had been replanted, flowers put back in boxes. Her memories of that night were rather more permanent.

Edward was coming back. She smiled.

"We should paint the cottage white," Amanda said. "One can never argue with white."

Free frowned. "What's the point of doing something that nobody can argue with? Don't you think yellow would be nice?"

"You would say that." Amanda smiled faintly. "Well, I'm with Aunt Violet half the time now. Maybe we can compromise on a stately gray."

"Gray! No, anything but gray. Gray is nothing but a white that can't make up its mind."

To anyone else, it would have sounded like an argument. But Free understood it for what it truly was—a distraction. She'd shown Amanda the telegram, and Amanda must have known how nervous she was.

Behind them, the sun was high in the sky, and the press was running, a comforting clatter at this distance.

That was when she saw a man coming up the track from the university. He was walking in that swift, direct way of his, long strides, arms swinging. It took less than a second for Free to recognize Edward. She didn't need to see his face; she knew him deep in her bones, as if something resonated between them across even this distance.

She had a brief moment of panic—what was she to do?—and then she remembered that she didn't panic. Good to know that; her heart must be racing for some other reason.

"Free," Amanda asked, "why have you turned bright red?"

"No reason," she said rather stupidly, as he would arrive in the next few minutes, and her lie would be obvious.

Amanda, no fool herself, peered down the road. "Ah," she said sagely. "There's your Mr. Clark after all. Right on time."

Free had only that one too-brief telegram to guide her expectations. She didn't know why he'd come back, what he intended with her, or if he'd walk away again. She didn't know if she should hope or despair.

She looked back in his direction. "Ha, is it? No. It can't be. He's seen me, and he hasn't so much as lifted a hand in greeting. But then, I've seen him, and I haven't..." That logic would get her nowhere.

She lifted her hand, gave a little wave. A moment later, he saluted her in return.

"Free," Amanda said. "I'd never thought I'd say this to you of all people, but are your nerves overwrought?"

"No," Free wrung her hands together. "My nerves are neither over- nor underwrought. They are wrought to the precise degree demanded by this situation."

Amanda snorted in disbelief.

"The situation," Free admitted, "is one of both dreadful confusion and enormous anticipation."

He'd turned off the main track, starting up the path that led to her press. Her heart pounded. Her palms prickled.

"That's it, then," Amanda said with a smile. "I'm going in."

"Wait…" But her protest was halfhearted. He was coming up to her now. His jacket was rumpled from travel and he was in desperate need of a shave. Free didn't care— not one bit. She drifted down the path to him, holding out her hands.

Distance vanished. Time vanished.

"Mr. Clark." Behind her, the press still thundered on. She could scarcely hear it for the ringing in her own ears.

He didn't hesitate. He twined his fingers with hers, pulling her…not close, not really. Not when she'd imagined him so much closer for many months now. They were no closer than two people would be if dancing a country reel. But her pulse beat as if she'd just danced two sets with him, and she'd done nothing more than take a few steps down the path.

"Mr. Clark," she repeated, looking up at him. "You are *very* tall."

"And you," he said in a low voice, "you, my most maddeningly beautiful, brilliant, Free. You are perfectly sized. If you *Mr. Clark* me once more, I shall be forced to do something dreadful, something like kiss you in public."

Even her wildest fantasies had not had him saying something like that on arrival. She squeezed his hands and then looked up into his dark eyes.

"I'm sorry, Mr. Clark," she said. "What did you say, Mr. Clark? Mr. Clark, I fear that I have become rather hard of hearing. The noise of the press is terribly distracting. What was that you said you'd do if I called you Mr. Clark?"

His hands tightened on hers and he inhaled, leaning in. But despite the hungry look in his eye, he didn't make good on his promise.

"Alas," he said. "Business comes before pleasure. There's something you must know."

Business. She could hardly care about business when he'd called her *maddeningly beautiful*, when he'd taken her hands and threatened to kiss her.

He eyed her. "James Delacey is targeting you again."

Of all the things she thought he might have come to tell her…

Free frowned in confusion. "And you heard this all the way in Toulouse?"

"I hear everything." He said this with a small smile. "There are some things you ought to realize. First, they've quashed the permit for your demonstration tomorrow. You should have received notice of that, but he managed to quash that, too."

"That's an annoyance." Free frowned. It was too late to call matters off. They had no way to contact the participants, not at this late a date. The last call had gone out in their papers two days before. And she couldn't leave the women to face the consequences alone.

"It's more than an annoyance."

"Yes, it's a crying shame. We had planned such a nice demonstration, too. For every four women wearing white, we'll have ninety-six in black wearing gags, to represent the proportion of women who would be able to vote under the proposed bill. It's going to make such a striking display. We'll have photographs of it all." She sighed, but then brightened. "And the only thing that could make it better would be if they arrested the lot of us. Then *all* the newspapers will cover the story."

He didn't smile. "This is different. The constables have orders not to release you. And Delacey has plans for what will happen afterward."

She shrugged. "My brother will raise the biggest… Ah. Well. I suppose he won't." He couldn't, at least not immediately. He was out of the country with his family. "My father?"

"A fine pugilist, but he hasn't the political clout necessary to effect your release. Free, I don't think you're taking this seriously. You don't know what Delacey will do to you, and—"

She couldn't think about that, not without a shiver of fear. Free shook her head. "What about the Duke of Clermont? He's in town. He's my brother's brother. It's complicated, and I'd hate to lean on him, but in a pinch, he'd do."

He looked faintly annoyed. "I wasn't thinking of Clermont," he grumbled. "You're making this difficult. You see, I had rather hoped that you might ask your husband to release you."

Free's mouth went dry. Her mind ceased to function.

"I haven't got a husband." But she could not look away from him, from his dark eyes resting on her. His hands still held hers. "And even if I did, he hasn't any political clout."

"Ah, but here's the thing," he said. "If you *did* have a husband, he might come up with any sort of political clout he wished. A signed, sworn statement of release from dead Prince Albert, if that would do the trick."

Free choked. "Please don't do that."

"Of all the things that James might threaten, holding you in custody and doing you harm… I can't bear thinking of the harm he might do." His voice was low. "I'd learn necromancy and raise the dead myself, just to get you out."

He was driving all possibility of thought from her. All thoughts of permits and arrest had been driven from her mind. She swallowed and looked up into his eyes. "Luckily, you don't need to learn necromancy."

"Luckily," he agreed, "I don't."

"Even more luckily," she heard herself say, "I don't need a husband for that. I have you, and you could forge me false release papers without marrying me. Even if that were our only prospect. Which it isn't."

"Unluckily," he said, without breaking into a smile, "you are right. There are several sad, gaping holes in my logic. I don't suppose you're interested in marrying a failed logician with necromantic tendencies, by any chance?"

Free took a deep breath. It didn't seem to calm the whirl of her head. "That's…a proposal of marriage? I just want to clarify matters. You see, it could also be a madman's babble, and I want to be certain."

"It's a proposal." His hands squeezed hers. "Of marriage. And this"—he reached into his pocket—"is a special license. Did you know the vicar will be around today until six?"

"Oh my God." She dropped his hands. "Are you asking me to marry you *today?* Before you've had a chance to meet my parents? With nobody around to witness but Amanda and Alice?"

"I'm asking you to marry me within the next hour." He simply looked at her. "I can't think of a reason why you should. I have no moral sense to speak of. I lie, I cheat, I steal, and I'll probably drive you away screaming within the week. But if you marry me, I'll only do those things on your behalf."

She shook her head reprovingly. "Edward."

"Was that not any better as proposals go?"

"No. Not particularly. I can't even tell if you mean it seriously."

"Then try this one. I've spent all the last years of my life wandering around thinking, 'This world is a terrible place; how can I take advantage of it?' And then I met you." He fell silent, but his eyes met hers.

Dark, deep pools. She'd only dreamed of him looking like that, looking at her as if she were everything to him. She felt her toes curl.

"I met you," he continued, "and you said, 'This world is a terrible place; how can I make it better?' You kicked the foundation out from under me. You changed everything. You made me think that there might be more to my life than unending betrayal. So yes, Free. I want you. I want you to sit with me at breakfast and make me smile. I want you to lie with me at night and kiss me. I want you underneath me. I want everything about you."

"Better." Free squeezed his hands. "Keep going. I think that you can reduce me to a little puddle in another two minutes, if you keep at it. I'm halfway to liquid as it is."

"Ah," he said, leaning down to her. "Then I'd better stop. I love you with steel in your spine."

She could not bring herself to let go of him. He was right. There were a thousand reasons she shouldn't marry him. She didn't even know the name he'd been born with. That hardly mattered; the family that had rejected him was nothing to her. Still…

"I have a handful of questions."

"Only a handful?" His tone was light, but his hands tensed in hers.

"I'll restrain myself for now," she said, "and delay the other million for some later time. First, what of your business in Toulouse? Will we live here, and if so, what do you plan to do?"

He met her eyes. "I sold my business three days ago; I knew I was returning to England. As for what I am planning to do…" He let out a sigh. "There's no hope for it, but I am going to pretend to be respectable. If I had my way, I'd start a metalworks here. I'd never interfere with your paper unless you wanted, and alas, I fear that general illicit activities would cause you problems. So I'll abstain as best I can."

She nodded. "Only one more question."

She could feel the tension in him, every muscle from his shoulders on down going rigid.

"And that is: Do you love me?"

"*That* is a waste of a question." He let go of her hands, but only to put his arm around her waist and draw her to him. "You know I do. I promised that if you *Mr. Clarked* me one last time, I'd take my retribution. And while I'm hardly the sort to keep inconvenient promises, this one…"

He leaned into her. His forehead touched hers; her lips warmed with the flow of his breath.

"This promise," he whispered to her, "is the opposite of inconvenient."

Free let out a soft sigh and brought her face up that last half inch, touching their lips together. He tasted so sweet that she could scarcely believe that she was kissing him again after all this time. But she set her hands on his shoulders, and he was real and solid. Her body pressed against his. Her mouth opened to him. Kissing him felt like sipping lamplight; she became more radiant with every touch of their tongues.

"Free, darling."

"Edward," she breathed.

"I still don't have a good reason for you to marry me, but I have a multitude of bad ones. It's impulsive. It's foolish. I'm a scoundrel. There's too much I haven't told you, and no time for me to explain everything. You'll hate me at least three times after this, before I convince you to love me." His arm slipped down her body, pulling her even closer.

"But will you?" she asked. "Convince me?"

"Probably not," he said huskily. For all the carefree tone of his voice, his eyes told a different story. He kissed her again, a long lingering kiss.

She couldn't quite believe this was happening. Months of correspondence—some of it warm enough to heat her for nights—still hadn't prepared her for this. He'd sold his business, come to London, and obtained a special license?

It all seemed to be happening so swiftly. Almost too swiftly.

"That special license you claim to have." She swallowed. "Is that a *real* special license, or is it the *Edward* sort of special license?"

He leaned down and kissed her again. "You think I'd procure a false license? For God's sake, Free. I'm trying to rush you *into* marriage. I have no desire to end that state any time soon. The only thing I forged was proof of my residency, and my solicitor assures me that can't be used to invalidate a duly issued license. I asked."

"Oh," she said. She wanted to laugh. "Very well, then. I'm convinced."

His hand tightened on hers. "Is that an *I'm convinced it's a real license,* or…"

From the moment she'd received his telegram, they'd been coming to this. No, from before. Every instant since she'd met him had been leading to this pinnacle.

She smiled up at him. "Neither. It's more like this: You idiot, why did it take you so long?"

Chapter Eighteen

AFTER THE WHIRL OF THE NEXT FEW HOURS, Edward couldn't quite believe that it had really happened.

Frederica Marshall had married him. With scarcely a thought, without a moment's hesitation. Tomorrow, she'd find out who he was and what he had planned. But tonight...

The sun had not yet set. They stood on the doorstep of her home, so newly completed that he could still smell the clean scent of sawn boards. He had his arm around her, refusing to let go for fear that she might come to her senses and leave at any moment.

"I'm off to London," Lady Amanda was saying to Free. She had been one of their witnesses. "I had planned to go down early for the demonstration, and, well..." She glanced at Edward, and shrugged her shoulders. "All the more reason for me not to change my plans. I'm just here to get my bag."

"Are you still speaking to Genevieve tomorrow?" Free asked.

Lady Amanda flushed faintly. "Yes." She glanced over at Edward again, and then looked away. But even though the glance she cast him was suspicious, she didn't say a word.

He appreciated Lady Amanda's silence, even though he didn't deserve any circumspection. There would be time enough for Amanda to tell Free what he was.

God, it was sweet to hold Free, to think of her as his wife. The brilliant smile she angled up at him was the sweetest yet. It was a shame it wouldn't last the week.

"Shall I carry you over the threshold?" he asked, once Amanda had retrieved a valise by the doorway and taken her leave.

She smiled. "It's my house. Maybe *I* should carry *you.*"

"Don't." He touched his gloved hand to her cheek. "I'd hate to break you this early in the evening. I have plans for you."

She tilted her head to look up at him, and he reached out to her.

It seemed impossible that he should have her. But he did, temporary though the state was. She rested her cheek against his hand and smiled up at him, her eyes glowing.

"One of these days," she said, "you'll learn that I don't break."

"I already knew that." He slid his arm around her, brought her close. "Now, my most lovely Free."

He could tell her now. Tell her that he'd lied to her all this time, that the man she'd married was both Edward Clark and some other long-gone fellow by the name of Edward Delacey. He could tell her that on the morrow, he was going to change everything.

But that light in her eyes shone for him. She stood on tiptoes, her hands resting on his shoulders, her lips breathing warmth against his jawbone.

"Now, Edward," she said, and he was lost.

He wrapped his arms around her, picking her up and taking her into her house. He shut the door behind him with a final thump.

Tell her now.

That was his conscience speaking. He would have thought the fool thing would have learned its lesson by now. He kissed her instead, taking her head between his hands as if he could pin her in place beside him not just for the moment, but for every instant that followed, and every one after that.

"Yes," she said against his mouth, her hands on his chest. "I can tell you're no gentleman. You're far too well put together."

"The better to hold you against a wall with, my dear." He leaned down and kissed her again, as if he could steal her breath away.

But he didn't need to steal it; she gave it to him willingly, her arms wrapping around him, her lips melding with his, her body pressing to his without any hint of shyness.

No, Free didn't need to be coaxed into marital relations. Her hands explored him, undoing the buttons of his waistcoat, untucking the tails of his shirt. Her fingers were cool at first against the muscles of his abdomen—but he still hissed, and a jolt of lust went through him at her touch.

The way he felt about her, she should have fit perfectly against him. But she was too short by inches to kiss in comfort. That discomfort made it impossible for him to forget himself, as if the strain in his neck, the tension in his lower back as he bent down to her, was recompense for every last lie he'd given her. Kissing her was both punishment and pleasure.

"I've wanted you in bed for far too long," Free said against his lips.

"Ah, God." It ached everywhere to pull her close, to feel the curve of her waist in his hands. Not just in his tightening muscles, not only in the throb of his erection, but somewhere deep inside him.

Her lips were soft, her breath was sweet, and at least for tonight, she was his.

She took his hand in hers. Her fingers curled around his. For a moment, he felt like an innocent youth. There was nothing between them but shy, sweet desire. Nothing but want, distilled by months of aching. It was easy to follow her down the corridor, easy to open the door to her bedchamber. The curtains were open, and the sunset spilled red over the floor. Enough illumination that he could see her expression, the lovely line of her chin, the color of her hair warring with the sunset.

He slid his finger under her chin and tilted her face up to his. "I want your hair down."

She let out a shaky breath. A small smile grew on her mouth, and she shut her eyes as if she were savoring the sound of him. But when she spoke, her voice was steady.

"I have nineteen pins in my hair. You have hands. You seem perfectly capable of finding them yourself."

"So I am." He took off his left glove and set it on a chest of drawers. "So I am."

The first was easy to discover; just a little bit of metal glinting above her ear. Knowing that one was there, he looked for its mate on the other side. He found it hidden behind a curl. Number three was thrust through the braided knot of hair at the back of her neck; he slid it out, leaning down so that he could place a kiss against her neck. She shivered in response. He didn't want to let her think, and so he nibbled at her ear as his hands found numbers four through twelve. She sighed as he kissed her, leaning into him. He held her braid in place as he took out the pins. It was almost a game, to make sure never to tug on her hair, never to cause her the slightest bit of pain.

Number thirteen was tangled with a bit of soft yarn that she'd used to tie her braid in place. He removed this and pulled away from her, holding it up in front of her nose. "You said nineteen pins. You said nothing of this, my dear."

"You're right," she told him with an eyebrow arched to naughtiness. "I didn't mention any yarn at all. Now what are you going to do about it?"

"You'll have to owe me for it."

"How?"

"Let's just put it on your account." He smiled at her and went back to removing the pins. To remove the remaining ones, he had to undo her braid, run his hands through her hair. He turned her head toward him as he did and took her mouth. Their tongues met, and he lost himself in the simple act of kissing her. There should have been an urgency to it, a rush to complete the act he'd wanted for so long. But despite the throbbing pound of lust in his body, the rising tide of his desire, he felt…calm. He was soothed by her.

He found the last pin and slid his hand down her face, down the column of her neck, resting his fingers in the hollow of her throat. He could feel the beat of her pulse, hungry and insistent.

"You haven't even taken off your other glove," she told him, "let alone any of the good bits."

"Ah, but there was that thread," he told her. "That undisclosed yarn. I'm not taking anything else off, not until you're completely bare."

Her pulse jumped under his fingers. "Oh?" she said. "Oh."

"That *is* a punishment," she said. "I had been hoping to see rather more of you."

He almost growled. "You will. Your wish is delayed, not denied."

She smiled at him. "Then I suppose I should take off everything."

He hadn't been sure what to expect—really, he didn't care what path they traveled on, so long as they were intent on the same destination. But this… oh, *this*. She smiled at him, and he thought his heart might stop. Then she undid the buttons of her cuffs, and then her coat. She removed it, revealing a gown of dark gray. God, he was going to go mad with want. She unfastened the sash, reached behind, and loosened her laces. And then she pulled off the fabric in one swift motion, revealing corset and petticoats, and another two inches of her bosom. Her corset was cut so close to her nipples that if he'd slid his tongue along her neckline, he would have felt the pebbling, responsive edge of them.

Still she didn't hesitate. She unhooked her corset, loosening it enough to lift it off her frame. And then he *could* see her nipples through the thin fabric of her shift, pink and perfect and lovely. His breath was growing hoarse, but she didn't stop. She unbuttoned her petticoats, let them fall heavily to the floor. The last daylight shone through her chemise,

illuminating her legs. Bloomers came off next—then she
pulled off her chemise.

"There," she said. "Is that bare enough for you?"

It was. Her skin was smooth and naked, all curves of
breast and hip. Darker red curls between her legs beckoned
him to come closer. His whole body seemed wound tight.
There was just that hint of bravado in her voice, that upward
tilt of her chin. Those were the only signs that she felt any
nerves at all. She faced him, though, as if she were sure of
herself, sure of *him*. He never, ever wanted her to doubt.

And God, how she would.

"No," he said. "It's not bare enough for me. Not yet. Let
me show you how it's done." And so saying, he guided her to
the bed, pushed her to sit on the edge. "Spread your knees,
lovely one." She blinked at him, and after a moment, she did.

He knelt between her legs. "*This* is bare enough for me."
And so saying, he set his mouth to her sex. She was sweet and
wet, and she let out a shaky breath as his lips spread her open,
as his tongue darted out and claimed her.

"Edward." It was not quite a question, not quite a
response.

"Tell me if you like it," he said, and slid his tongue up to
find the nub of her nerves.

She let out a gasp. "Oh my God, I…do. Yes. Right
there."

He spread her knees wider and leaned in, finding the
rhythm of her body. The catch of her breath; the rise of her
chest. The pulse of her clitoris against his lips, the taste of her
desire. It matched the flow of blood to his own body, the want
that was swelling his cock. She was utterly bare to him, every
impulse, every desire impossible for her to hide. Her hips
flexed up to meet him; her hands tangled in the length of his
hair, urging him on. He could feel the flush of her pleasure as
it rose on her skin, that delicious warmth spreading
throughout her. He could taste the slickness of her sex,
growing wetter with every stroke of his tongue. He could
sense her orgasm, coming swiftly upon her, flowing over her
until her hands clenched and she cried aloud. Her thighs

pressed hard against him. He growled and took it all, every last bit.

And then—when her breath died down, when the last of her cries faded from the air—he took off his coat and kicked off his shoes. He undid his shirt, the buttons of his trousers. He felt impossibly eager. And yet he seemed to be moving slowly through treacle, as if there was a solemn deliberation to his actions. Her eyes opened and she watched him stepping out of his trousers, sliding down his smallclothes. He folded these, setting them atop everything else.

He was hard, so hard. He knelt on the ground before her, set his hands on her knees.

"Is this…" she said. "Is this how we're going to do this?"

"Like this," he told her, and fitted his cock against her sex. "Exactly like this. Slowly. Tell me if it hurts, and we'll give it time."

She nodded. "I had thought it would be different."

"This way, I can watch you," he said. "And if I'm on top of you, I can't use my hands."

"Oh."

"I very much want to use my hands."

"Oh." That was said in the back of her throat, at almost a purr. He felt it in the base of his cock.

So he used his hands, sliding his fingers between her legs, testing the slickness of her. She was ready and aroused; he rubbed the head of his cock in her juices, luxuriating in the feel of her. When she moaned and lifted her hips to him, he slid an inch into her. God, she was so tight around him. The feel of her body, warm and wet around his, pressing all around him, was the second sweetest thing he'd ever experienced. The look in her eyes—that starry, trusting look—was the sweetest.

"All right?" he asked.

"Better than all right." She smiled at him.

He slid in another inch. She felt good, so good. "Lovely weather we had today."

She laughed. "The weather? Are we really talking about the weather? Now?"

"I told you. I want to be in complete control. We can talk about the weather, or I could think about how amazing it feels to sink my cock into you." God, she felt so good. Better than anything he had imagined. "And then it will all be over too fast."

"So it would ruin everything if I talked about how this felt?" she asked. "About how delicious it is to run my hands along your shoulders. How much I want your thighs against mine. I could tell you that I'm still sensitive everywhere from what you did before, and that you're driving me mad, going as slowly as you are."

"Free." His cock pulsed in protest.

"You keep acting as if I will break." She smiled up at him. "Here's a secret."

He dropped his head to hers.

"I plan to do just that," she whispered. "To break in pieces, and I insist on having your help in getting there."

It was too much for him. He took hold of her hips and slid all the way in, seating himself deep inside her. She made a noise deep in her throat, and he was lost. Lost in the feel of her, lost in the certainty of her. He slid out and then in. He'd thought of claiming her, but it didn't feel that way at all. He was the one driving into her, but it was her touch on his face that undid him. He set the pace, but her muscles tightened around him, squeezing him, and he lost any control he'd had. He took her hard and unrelenting, no sweet words, no pauses to make certain that she was well.

But he didn't need her to tell him in words. He could hear it in her breath, feel it as he brought his hand between them, found that sensitive nub he'd worried earlier. She was gasping now. He brought up his right hand—still gloved— and found her breast. Her nipple was hard against his touch; she threw her head back.

More. More. She needed more, and he gave her all of him, every thrust, every breath, every last caress, until she convulsed around him again. And then he gave her everything in return, spilling into her, his mind turning to nothing but light, nothing but her.

Breath returned first as his body calmed. Then, slowly, his thoughts returned, one by one, like reluctant fowl returning to the hen house. He needed her. He adored her. And when she found out who he was, she was going to hate him.

He pulled away from her heavily. She swung her legs onto the bed, reached out, caught his hand. And before he knew it, she'd pulled her back to him. Her lips brushed his collarbone, his neck. His mouth. He had no choice in the matter. He had to kiss her.

The sun had set by now, and early moonlight spilled across her face, across that lovely, delicious smile that he'd won from her. She reached out and tangled the fingers of her right hand with his left.

"Edward."

He savored the caress in her voice, that lilting lovely tone of satisfaction. Maybe he'd have a chance after all—maybe, if he could make her smile like that again…

"Darling Free."

"I have a question."

He felt every muscle in his body come alert, his shoulders going rigid. No. Foolish. There was no chance. He stopped breathing. *God, Free. We could have waited until morning to destroy everything.*

"Yes?" he managed. The word came out roughly.

"You don't have to answer—not if you're not ready. But why do you always wear a glove on your right hand? You didn't even take it off tonight."

Not the question he'd feared. Thank God, not that one. He was so relieved, he was even willing to answer her. He didn't say anything at all; he simply removed his right glove and held out his hand to her. In the moonlight, it was all too obvious that his two smallest fingers had been cut off at the knuckle.

She inhaled sharply. And then she took his right hand in hers.

"What happened?"

"It was after Strasbourg had surrendered. I'd been sent back to occupied Colmar—that was the village where the blacksmith who had taken me in lived. At that pointed, I only wanted to return home, but now the path back to England led through a foreign army. With no funds and no access to official channels, my choices were limited. So I did the only thing that seemed reasonable at the time." So long as he said the words, and didn't think of what they meant, it would all turn out right. "I forged myself safe-conduct papers and a letter of credit."

Her fingers were warm against his.

"I tried to use the letter of credit first. But the banker— a man named Soames—realized it was a forgery."

She inhaled.

"But he didn't turn me in. You see, he was ambitious. He realized that it would be more useful to have his own personal forger than a worthless Englishman subject to martial law in the midst of an occupation. So instead, he used me."

"He blackmailed you?" But Free's voice was uncertain, and her fingers, gentle against his, suggested that she knew that wasn't the case.

Edward let out a long breath. "The first man he wanted me to betray? Blackmail wouldn't have worked. I didn't lose my fingers in an accident, sweetheart. I lost them slowly, over the course of two weeks. The fingers weren't even the worst part. He only started on those after he'd near-drowned me a half-dozen times."

Her hand twitched against his.

"Pain rewrites everything. You don't just *do* things to make pain stop. You believe them. Even as you're sitting, forging a false letter purporting to establish that a man is part of an armed resistance in occupied territory. Even while you're perpetrating the fraud, you can convince yourself that it is the truth. I can still remember some of the events I invented for Soames as if they really happened. As if I had been standing there. I forged mortgages and letters of credit on the one hand, and faked resistance on the other. The county was occupied, and Soames intended to profit from it as long as he could. I was just his tool."

The sun had set. He couldn't see the expression on her face, didn't know what she was thinking.

"There was only that one small part of me that understood something was wrong." He gulped in a breath. "And so when I could—when peace came in March, and Soames lost the threat of martial law and summary execution to expand his empire—I escaped. It took me months to regain my reason, such as it was."

There were still some memories he had of those months that he doubted, and he'd never know if they were real or not.

"I had thought I was so brave before the war started, refusing to bow under my father's persuasion. But I no longer had the strength of any convictions. It had all been lies, a fantasy I told myself so I'd believe myself superior. I wasn't. I begged like any man when threatened with a dire fate. A little pain, and I lied, no matter who was hurt. That was the point when I vowed that I'd not flinch from the worst that I was. I have to know who I am, what I am—or I'll let the next fellow who comes along make me into far worse."

She laid a soothing hand against his shoulder. "Now you're not alone in that any longer. I know who you are, too—all of it, the good and the bad. And I won't let you be anyone but yourself."

But she didn't know. She didn't know who he was. She didn't know that it was his own brother who was making idle plans to hold her—and far, far worse.

No matter what, that would never happen to her—not while he had breath in his body. He'd seen to that today, no matter what else he had done.

"No," he said gravely. "I'm not a good man. But you had it right: I'm your scoundrel."

"Shh," she said.

"You don't know what I've done."

She turned to him, coming up on her elbow. "You're not to blame," she said. "I can't even imagine what you've gone through. You aren't awful. The world has been awful to you."

"Those things are not mutually exclusive, love."

"If you hadn't noticed, I started my career as a reporter by falsifying a report that I was infected with syphilis. I've presented my share of false references in my time. You may not be *good* by the standards of the rest of the world. But you're perfect for me, and I won't let anyone hurt you again."

Oh, he wished that were true.

He looked over at her, at the fierce expression on her face. Her hair spilled around her shoulders in little curls, tickling his arm. And he felt a sense of unimaginable wonder. He'd thought to keep her safe, and yet here she was, insisting that *she* would protect him. He couldn't wrap his mind around what this could mean.

He didn't realize he was shaking until she set her hands on his shoulders. He didn't know how cold he felt until she curled up against him, her body so warm.

God. He didn't know what he was going to do when she left him.

"For what it's worth," he said, "when I asked you to marry me, I thought I loved you."

She stilled in his arms, turning to him.

"I've thought I loved you ever since the evening you told me you weren't trying to empty the Thames with a thimble, that you were watering a garden instead. I felt like you changed my entire world from futility to hope over the course of one conversation."

"Edward." She turned to him, placing her hand on his shoulder.

"You can't know what it's like to have no hope," he said. "To believe that the best you can manage is survival. I wanted you so much." His fingers slid over her bare shoulder, down her hip. "I wanted you so much I thought it was love. I stopped being able to envision a world without you in it to light the way."

"You keep speaking in the past tense."

"That's because I was wrong. A desperation to possess at any cost—that's not love." He leaned over and brushed a kiss against her lips. "This is."

The kiss felt like a slow awakening, a sensation of warmth, a steady glow that enveloped the two of them.

But she drew away from him. "Edward. I—"

He set his finger on her lips.

"No. Don't say it. It's hell enough realizing that I want only to protect you from harm." His voice dropped. "That I'm the one who will hurt you."

She shook her head. "I wish you wouldn't talk like that. I know you better than that."

He smiled sadly. She didn't.

"One of these days, you'll understand," she said. "I love you, scoundrel and all. And I've known you could never hurt me. Ever since that same day."

He kissed her again. "Tell me that tomorrow."

It was particularly sweet—stomach-churningly sweet—when she nodded her head.

"I will. And the next day, and the day after, and the day after. I'll tell it to you day after day, night after night, until finally you believe it's true."

⌘ ⌘ ⌘

FREE AWOKE IN THE MIDDLE of the night in a cold sweat, flailing her arms, trying to escape—

"Shh," she heard Edward say. "Shh. Free. It's all right."

Her heart was racing away from her. Her mouth was dry, and it took her a moment to understand that she was in bed with her husband of…several hours, not being held in place, not tied down in a government hospital.

Her pulse slowed. Her muscles loosened. She let out a long, slow breath.

"You're safe," Edward said. "I have you."

"It was only a nightmare." She couldn't bring herself to look at him.

"Of course it was," he said. "And now I'm only holding you." He folded his arms around her. "See how that works?"

Marrying him had been impulsive and foolhardy. She hadn't even had a chance to inform her family of her marriage—and after she told them, there'd be many explanations demanded.

But if they could just see this, just *feel* this moment—the warmth of his arms around her, the comfort of his touch, those cold fears washing out of her as he stroked her face—why, they'd all understand why she'd done it.

The morning would bring a demonstration, a reunion with Amanda, and a trip to gaol—but it would also bring him. And once everyone she loved grew to know him, they'd understand. Edward was the best thing she could ever have impulsively grabbed for.

Chapter Nineteen

"I'M SO GLAD YOU COULD spare a few moments," Genevieve said.

The morning had dawned crisp and cool, with scattered clouds obscuring the summer sun for once. Amanda shifted a bag on her shoulder and smiled at Genevieve.

"Of course I did," she said. "Don't I always?"

Always. It was hard to remember that *always*, when it came to Genevieve, meant only a handful of months. They now met when Amanda came into town, and at this point, that meant they saw one another nearly twice a week. It seemed as if they'd known each other longer than that.

Amanda caught a glimpse of herself in the mirror over the side table. It had taken her months to learn not to wince and look away from her own reflection, and there were times…

"Ah, ah," Genevieve said.

Amanda looked at her. "It's nothing," she said. "Just noticing that I still have ink stains on my fingers."

"Those," Genevieve said loftily, "are more by way of a badge of honor than a stain. They're war wounds."

Amanda couldn't help but smile. But there was the rub: the more comfortable Genevieve made her feel, the more *uncomfortable* she grew. Weeks of becoming familiar with Genevieve's sly, understated sense of humor—and trusting that Amanda was not the butt of it—had helped ease her sense of awkwardness.

And yet Genevieve was still as lovely as ever, sweet as ever, and…sadly, as innocent as ever. Hence Amanda's dilemma.

"I can't stay long today." Amanda indicated her bag. "I've the demonstration to attend, and everything will only become more complicated from there on. There's the possibility that I'll be arrested, and…"

Genevieve interrupted her with a hand on her arm. "That's precisely the reason I asked you to come this morning. You see, I know some ladies who would like to participate in the demonstration. I thought we might all walk to the park together."

Ladies. Amanda tensed. As if to emphasize what Genevieve meant, a burst of laughter—light and airy—came from the other room.

Amanda had been doing better since that first gathering back in April. She'd even gone to a handful of small parties since then—ones where she was sure her family would not be in attendance. Still, she'd always needed time to steel herself before going out in company. Today, she wasn't sure she had the extra energy to make the effort.

"Oh, Genevieve." She shook her head. "I'm on edge enough. You know how I feel about this sort of thing."

She expected Genevieve's face to fall, for her to be disappointed. Instead, the other woman looked at her, her eyes shining with determination. "I've planned this for over a month. I'm not letting you walk away."

"But—"

Genevieve took a step toward her. "No, I am not."

"But—"

"My own sister, Geraldine, has just come up from the country for the first time in months. She's heard so much about you, and she wants to meet you."

That made Amanda more nervous rather than less. What if Geraldine didn't like her? She knew how close the two sisters were. She didn't want Genevieve to be ashamed of their friendship.

"Have I ever led you astray?" Genevieve demanded.

She hadn't. "That isn't the point."

"Then just this once, Amanda." Genevieve threaded her arm through hers. "This once, I'm going to ask you to trust me."

Looking down into her friend's blue eyes, the determined set of her chin... She couldn't say no. She didn't dare disappoint Genevieve.

Genevieve turned her in the direction of the parlor and guided her to the door. She disengaged Amanda's arm only long enough to wrestle the door open. "Ladies," she announced. "She is here."

Amanda recognized Geraldine instantly. She looked so very like her sister—blond, blue-eyed, a sweet smile on her face—but with a little more of the plumpness that came from bearing children. But it was the woman sitting at her side that made Amanda's heart stutter.

She was tall and dark-haired. She was also plump and smiling a little. But her smile had a sadness to it.

"Maria?" Amanda could not make herself move into the room.

Her next-youngest sister. The last time she'd seen her, Maria had told her she wanted nothing to do with her. Amanda couldn't believe that Genevieve had done this to her. All her old fears assailed her. She wanted to turn on her heel and run away, before Maria could do the same in response.

But Maria didn't run. She stood, raising one hand to her mouth. "Amanda." And then she held out her arms.

Amanda didn't know how she managed to cross the room and navigate around the table. Her gown caught on a teapot; she was dimly aware of Genevieve behind her snatching it gracefully before it upended itself.

But her sister was in her arms. Maria didn't hate her forever. She hadn't ruined absolutely everything.

"I'm sorry," she whispered in her sister's ear. "I'm sorry. I'm so sorry."

"I'm sorry, too."

Amanda gulped back a sniff. She wasn't going to cry. She *wasn't*. But when she pulled away from her sister, she saw Maria's eyes wet with tears, and found she couldn't help herself.

Genevieve handed her a handkerchief.

It was some ten minutes later—ten minutes of incoherent exclamations, of taking her sister's hand and being unable to let it go—before she no longer needed to dab at her stinging eyes.

"Maria," she said. "Why are you here? I thought…"

Her sister blushed. "You thought I hated you. I did. At first. Mama and Papa told me it was your fault I didn't find a husband that first Season. I thought you had ruined my life."

"It was," Amanda said seriously. "I did."

Maria didn't respond to this. Instead she looked out over Amanda's shoulder. "That's a matter of opinion, I suppose. I *did* marry down. I resented you and Aunt Violet for years. And then… One day, I realized that the scandal you caused meant that the man I had married truly loved me. He'd married me for *me*, not for what I could bring him." Her lip curved up in a smile. "I discovered I loved him, too, and I stopped feeling so bitter."

"I'm glad."

"But I don't think I understood how badly I had erred until I had my daughter. She's so…so *bright,* Amanda. She's only five now, and the other day, I found her reading *Pilgrim's Progress* aloud to her younger brother. I want you to know her." Maria's eyes glistened once more.

"Oh, Maria. I would love to know your daughter."

"I started listening to what I said to her. When she was three, I told her that she couldn't contradict the boy next door, even when she's right, because it's indelicate for a lady to disagree with a gentleman. I told her that she mustn't run, because ladies never hurry. Every day, from the moment she took her first step, I've told her to stop: to stop thinking, to stop speaking, to stop moving about. And I didn't know why

I said any of it. Those words kept coming out of my mouth, passing through me."

Amanda reached over and gripped her sister's hand.

"I think that's when I understood that you only ruined my life because my life needed ruining. Because the life you rejected demanded that I spend all my time telling my daughter to be less and my son to be more."

"I wasn't trying to save anyone," Amanda said. "Just myself."

Maria gave her a wavering smile. "Well. I started reading your paper a year ago. I would sit at breakfast with your essays and imagine that you were sitting across the table from me. That you had forgiven me for the horrible things I said to you. And then Miss Johnson came to me."

Genevieve and Geraldine were sitting across the table from them, both silent. Geraldine wiped a demure tear from one eye. But Genevieve was smiling—a fierce, brilliant, perfect smile, one that Amanda could feel from three feet away.

"I'm wearing black," Maria said. "I sent my number in for the demonstration and black is what I was told to wear. I brought…" She rummaged in a little bag. "This. For the gag." She held up a dark kerchief. "Do you think this will do?"

"Maria, they've quashed the permit for the demonstration. We might all be arrested. You don't have to do this."

Maria's smile faltered a moment. She looked at her kerchief. "Are you still going?"

"Yes," Amanda said.

Maria looked at Amanda and raised her chin. "Let them just try and hold me, then," she said. "I'm pregnant. My husband might not be the duke I dreamed of as a girl, but he can still make himself heard if necessary."

Geraldine sniffed again. "Sisters," she said.

Maria took Amanda's hand. "Sisters," she repeated. "I walked away from you years ago. I'll be damned if I let you stand alone today."

ℋ   ℋ   ℋ

BY THE TIME EDWARD and Patrick were called into the small, stuffy chamber behind the room where the Committee for Privileges met, the proceedings had already begun. Most of the lords on that committee likely hadn't noticed the last-minute alteration to the agenda submitted by Baron Lowery, nor the extra witnesses that he'd had sworn in at yesterday's poorly attended Parliamentary session.

The entire proceeding had an unreal quality to it.

It seemed impossible that Edward should be here now. Just last night, he'd married Free. Just this morning, they had come down to London on the train together. He'd not been able to keep himself from touching her, public though the ride had been. His hand kept stealing into hers, his leg had brushed hers. They'd parted ways at the station—she to go to her demonstration, he to find his solicitors. He'd had his hair cut respectably short, and he was now garbed in a severe, dark suit, tailored to his form.

She was likely already in the park where they were to gather, issuing placards to the women. Preparing for arrest. She thought he had only a little business to do before he returned. She had no idea who he was about to become.

A man was reciting the substance of James's claim to the viscountcy in the other room—a dry, dull, monotonous stream of facts about parentage.

He doubted the full committee was in attendance. Likely, they all thought this a fairly routine matter. After all, they were merely seating a lord who had presented his claim to the queen and had the particulars duly approved by the attorney general. Under ordinary circumstances, there would be nothing for them to do but vote at the end. Half had probably sent their proxies by way of one or another member.

Edward was about to make matters deviate from the ordinary.

In the back chamber, a man came up to the two of them. "You're on the list of witnesses?" He brushed his thinning hair away from his eyes and peered at a page in his hand. "Your names?"

"Edward Clark," Edward said. "And Patrick Shaughnessy. We were sworn in yesterday morning."

The man nodded, checking them off the list he held. "If they need you, you'll be called. Until then, you can have a seat." He gestured at a handful of chairs and bustled off.

Edward recognized the names that were being recited in the other chamber, loud enough for them to hear even in here. There was a deposition referenced from the vicar who'd baptized his brother. A family servant attested to a continuing acquaintance. He wondered if James had noticed the additions to the witness list, or if he'd brushed them aside.

The man droned on. "As to the immediate family, the eldest son of John Delacey, the fourth Viscount Claridge, was Peter Delacey, who died an infant on August 2, 1849. The second eldest son, Edward Delacey, was born on March 15, 1850. He was in Strasbourg at the time that hostilities broke out between France and Prussia; all attempts to discover him after the region once again became stable were fruitless. Hundreds were killed, the bodies not all recovered. The last letter received from Edward Delacey, presented to this body as evidence by James Delacey, was dated July 6, 1870. Under our law, after seven years have passed without word, Edward Delacey is presumed dead. That brings us to the third rightful son of John Delacey, James Delacey, who is before us now."

There was an indistinct murmur, one that Edward could not make out.

Then a different voice spoke up. "The chair recognizes Baron Lowery."

"Thank you. As I understand the law, Edward Delacey is merely *presumed* dead at the moment. Is that correct?"

"For all legal purposes, yes."

"But that presumption can be rebutted for legal purposes. Including, I suppose, right now."

There was a pause and then another murmur.

"Do you believe that presumption can be rebutted?" someone asked.

"I believe I am honor-bound to rebut it," Lowery said. "You see, it has come to my attention that Edward Delacey is alive."

Edward's hands were shaking. He pressed them against his trousers, but it didn't help. He'd avoided this as long as he could. The thought of being called by that name again, of taking his father's seat…

Yet here he was. It was too late. Even if he stood and left the room, they'd know now, and he'd never escape again.

There was a long pause in the other room.

"I have been presented with evidence to that effect," Lowery continued, "which I shall present to this body, if I am so allowed."

He could hear murmured voices in the other room—his brother, no doubt, coming alive and objecting. He couldn't hear their words, didn't care about the objections James lodged or the matters of procedure he argued. He just wanted this over with.

After five minutes, the man who had been reciting facts before spoke again, loud enough for him to hear once more. "Lowery may proceed."

"But—" That was James, speaking loudly enough that Edward was certain of the identification.

"James Delacey, you are not a member of the committee, and may only speak before it when duly called upon."

Silence. And then, the voice of Baron Lowery. "I call Patrick Shaughnessy, my stable master, to testify."

Beside him, Patrick shut his eyes and heaved a great breath.

"Go," Edward said. "It will be all right."

The man who had greeted them eyed them with a far more avid interest now. The door to the hearing room had been scarcely ajar; he opened it wide and gestured Patrick forward. Patrick stood, clenching his fists. He had never been easy speaking to a crowd. But he marched forward bravely into the high-walled hearing room in the House of Lords.

The greeter didn't close the door this time. Through the opening, Edward could see Patrick make his way slowly to the front. He lowered himself gingerly into the seat that had been pulled forward.

"State your name, sir."

Patrick leaned forward; Edward could see his lips moving, but nothing more.

"Loud enough for the lords to hear, if you please."

"I'm Patrick Shaughnessy," his friend said more loudly. "If it please you."

"Can you tell us where you were born?"

"I grew up on the estates of Viscount Claridge." His back was a rigid line. "My father was stable master there. My mother was a seamstress."

"Did you know Edward Delacey?"

"We met when I was five, when my parents came over. We became friends almost instantly. My father taught Edward how to ride; Edward taught me how to read. From the time we were young until the day he was sent to school, we were inseparable."

"Did that friendship continue after he went to school?"

"His father didn't wish it to," Patrick said slowly. "But Edward wasn't the sort of child to turn his back on a former friend. We would sneak out together when he was home on holidays—going to boxing matches and the like."

"Do you have any proof of this friendship?"

"Edward Delacey was accounted a competent artist," Patrick said. "He painted a miniature of the two of us when we were thirteen. I've brought it with me." Patrick groped through the bag he carried and handed over an item.

"Did Edward maintain this friendship with you?"

"We got into a spot of trouble when we were seventeen," Patrick said. "My father was injured." The line of his back bowed momentarily. "Our family was sent away. Edward protested the treatment and was sent to Strasbourg in punishment."

That was one way to describe what had happened—a way that left out the radical sentiment and Edward's own foolish choices. But Patrick's revelation had caused another murmur in the adjoining room. The men out there likely hadn't heard that Strasbourg was a *punishment*.

"Did he write you while he was there?"

"A few letters, yes. And then hostilities broke out, and I heard nothing for months."

"For months," the man said, sounding somewhat perplexed.

"Months," Patrick repeated. "Not quite a year. He sent me a letter in April of 1871 saying that he was in a bad way. At the time, I was only a groom for Baron Lowery."

Patrick had become more easy as he spoke on, but Edward grew tense. That April had been awful. He'd been wounded. Desperate. Destitute. He hadn't known who he was, had only known that he'd done some terrible things. His entire world had been ripped to shreds. He'd had nothing at all.

"He asked me to help. So I sold everything I had and got on a steamer."

"Everything you had, even though you were only a groom?" the man said dubiously. "Really?"

No, Edward realized. He'd never had *nothing*.

"We're that sort of friends," Patrick insisted. "He's like a brother."

Even at his worst, there had been constants in his life: Patrick. Stephen. People he couldn't eradicate from his heart and hadn't wanted to. He'd always had that much.

The questions continued on. "And did you find him?"

"I did. He was alive, but..." Patrick shook his head. "He barely talked, and he'd been hurt. Badly. He wasn't well."

They would no doubt imagine that Patrick spoke of physical harm. But the physical harm had been minimal—his fingers, a lingering cough in his lungs from the water. It was his mind that had been splintered.

"So I took care of him for a few weeks, and reminded him..." Patrick stopped, coughing.

Edward knew what he'd been about to say. He'd reminded Edward that he wanted to live. But while Patrick was no liar, even he wouldn't announce to the House of Lords that Edward had harbored thoughts of suicide.

"I reminded him," Patrick said, "that war had ended and life went on. When he was well enough to be left on his own, he told me to get back to England, but that he was not coming with me. His family had left him in Strasbourg, you see. He felt they'd abandoned him, and he had no wish to return to them."

This was met with a longer pause. "So the last you heard from Edward Delacey was when you left him in 1871 then? Do you have proof of any of this remarkable tale?"

"Oh," Patrick said. "I have that letter he sent me in 1871. I've kept all his letters."

There was a pause. "*All* his letters?"

"Yes. We've corresponded ever since."

A clamor arose at that. Edward let out his breath and put his head in his hands. There truly was no going back after that proclamation, no pretending any longer.

"When was the last time you received a letter from Edward Delacey?"

"Two weeks past," Patrick said. "But—"

"And how do you know that Edward Delacey has been writing these letters, and not some other man?"

"I know," Patrick said, "because he saw those letters yesterday morning as we were compiling the evidence, and he did not disavow them."

That was met with deafening silence. There was not even a shocked whisper in response.

"You saw him," the questioner finally said. "Two days ago. He's in England?"

"Yes," Patrick said. "He is. He's—" He gestured at the room behind him. "He's there. Waiting in the back chamber. I had to half-drag him here, your lordships."

That much was true. Edward smiled sadly.

"James Delacey, would you recognize your brother?"

There was a long pause. "Of course I would," his brother said, his voice sounding a little too hearty.

"Let Edward Delacey come forward, then."

Edward stood. Some part of him wanted to run away, to escape England and leave Patrick to face the wrath of the lords on his own. But he wouldn't do that to Patrick...and he couldn't let Free linger on in a cell, at his brother's nonexistent mercy.

He came forward. It had been a long time since he'd tried to walk like a lord—arrogant, occupying space as if all the room in the world belonged to him. These men were watching him, judging him.

He sat, hoping that his dazed state came across as bored arrogance.

"Are you Edward Delacey, the eldest living son of John Delacey?" the speaker asked.

"I am," he said. "Although I have been called Edward Clark these last years, and I prefer that name."

That got another murmur.

"James Delacey, is this man Edward Delacey, your brother?"

He looked over at James. James was watching him, a confounded expression in his eyes. No doubt he didn't realize that this was not the only one of his plans that would unravel today. He'd understand it soon enough.

"I don't know," James demurred. "He—well—that is..." He trailed off.

"There's no point lying now, James," Edward said. "Whatever you claim, they'll make you swear it under oath. You'll not want to perjure yourself before the House of Lords."

"Ah... If only I..."

"The alternative to your admitting this now," Edward said, "would be to find the British consular secretary from Strasbourg, the one you wrote to. I suspect this body would find his testimony *most* instructive. Do you want that?"

He'd do it, too, if need be—expose his brother's treachery to the world. He didn't give a damn about gossip; he cared about Free. He could see the moment his brother gave in. James lowered his head, his skin pale. "I don't understand. You said you didn't want it. You said..."

Edward could now see the face of the man who had been asking the questions. He was the attorney general, the man tasked to present James's credentials to the House of Lords. At this, the man hissed.

"Delacey," he said, "are you telling me that you not only know this man is your brother, you *spoke* to him before these proceedings?"

James winced. "I. Ah."

"You sent a letter to the queen detailing your claim two weeks ago. And you knew it was false?" There was a dangerous note to his voice.

"I—that is one way of looking at it, of course. But—"

"There is only one way of looking at it," the man said severely.

And like that, there was nothing to do. Edward could scarcely pay attention. The proceedings were wound up, the vote taken. The committee decisively agreed not to refer James's petition to the House of Lords.

Edward sat in place, barely hearing anything, unable to contemplate how his life had changed. The only thing he could think of was Free. She'd be furious once she found out.

But then, she'd not be in gaol. She wouldn't be tortured. And that would be enough for him—it had to be.

He stood when the committee adjourned and began to leave.

"Claridge," a voice called.

It took him a moment to understand that *he* was Claridge now. Not confirmed yet, but recognized. It was only a matter of time until he received all the accolades he'd never wanted.

Edward looked over. A man was striding toward him— thin, blond, and smiling.

"The majority of them are too shocked to say anything. I thought I'd say... Welcome to Bedlam." The other man winked. "Don't listen to a word they say. It really *is* as bad as you fear."

"I hardly need instruction on that point." Edward shook his head.

"Come by sometime and we'll talk about what we can do about it." The man held out his hand. "I'm Clermont, by the way."

Clermont. It had been years since he'd memorized his peerage, but he knew that name. He didn't remember the title from his dimly remembered lessons as a child; he remembered the man because Free had mentioned him just yesterday. This was her brother's brother.

After Free realized how he'd misled her? This man would be his enemy.

Edward frowned. "You're not on this committee."

The other man shrugged one shoulder. "When my wife tells me that there's been an interesting pair of witnesses sworn in for a routine hearing, I try to make it my duty to sit in. Now, shall I send a note around for dinner someday?" His hand was still outstretched.

Edward looked regretfully at the other man's hand. "I won't take you up on that until I'm sure you mean it."

"I mean it."

"Now, yes," Edward said. "In a day? Your Grace, what you just witnessed is not the worst mess I've made in the last twenty-four hours."

Clermont raised an eyebrow. "Ah. You've been busy."

"Yes. Now if you'll excuse me, I have to go retrieve my wife from gaol."

His Grace lifted his other eyebrow, but all he said to this was, "You'll find that substantially easier now, I'll warrant."

As if rescuing women from prison cells were a part of a duke's regular affairs. And hell, if Clermont had any acquaintance with Free at all, it probably was.

Chapter Twenty

IT TOOK EDWARD THIRTY-THREE MINUTES to convince the sergeant on duty of his identity. In the end, the man sent a runner to the House of Lords to ascertain the truth. When the boy came back, breathless and wild-eyed, Sergeant Crispin became substantially more helpful.

"A rough business," Crispin said. "Rough indeed. I—uh—know your brother."

"Oh, do you?" Edward asked in a low voice. His brother had worked out an arrangement with Crispin with regards to Free, and God help the man if he'd done anything to her in the hour and fifteen minutes he'd had her in his custody.

"We'd an arrangement." The sergeant licked his lips. "I don't suppose you're here to, ah, agree to the same thing?"

"I don't know." Edward said blandly. "What sort of arrangement did you have?"

The man blanched. "Um. Nothing, really. Why are you here, my lord?"

My lord. People were already calling him *my lord*, and it would only get worse from here.

If he had to take the reins, he might as well get all he could from the part. Edward stood straighter. "Your arrangement with my brother is of little importance to me. Carry on with that as you will."

The man looked faintly relieved.

"I'm only interested in a prisoner who is being held here."

"Ah?" The sergeant looked about. "In these front cells?"

"No." He'd glanced through them when he came in.

"Are you sure he's here, then? We've only a handful of cells in the back, and those won't be of much interest to you."

"Well, show me them, if you would." Edward did his best to look bored. "I'll judge whether they're of interest; you needn't decide for me." God, that was exactly the sort of self-indulgent tripe that a lord spouted—as if he were the center of the universe.

But the man didn't punch him in the face for his condescension. Instead, he ducked his head. "Of course, my lord. I only wish to be of assistance. But there's nobody back there but the suffragettes."

"Nonetheless."

The man neither sighed nor rolled his eyes at this. Edward was conducted through a maze of desks, down a back hall, into a back room containing a handful of holding pens filled with women in black gowns. Edward scanned them quickly, his eyes coming to rest on the very one he was looking for. She sat on a bench talking to another woman. She glanced up as he came in, but then looked away.

It took him a moment to realize that she didn't recognize him. Since he'd left her at the station, he'd cut his hair close. He'd shaved. He'd donned a fine wool coat and a gentleman's top hat, and he carried a gold-topped walking stick. If she'd heard him talking to the sergeant, she'd have heard his sleekest, poshest accent.

He wasn't anyone she knew any longer.

"What was it you said you had back here?" he asked the sergeant.

"Just some suffragettes," the sergeant replied. "Nobody important or dangerous. They were making a racket earlier, and we're having them cool their heels until their men can come get them. You understand how it is."

"I thought that's what you said." Edward felt a smile tweak his lips. "That's why I didn't understand you at first. You're mispronouncing the word."

"What word? Suffragettes?" The sergeant frowned. "It's my accent, my lord—a thousand pardons, I know it's low, and I *do* try to talk proper, but—"

"It's not your accent."

"It's not?" Bafflement flitted across the sergeant's eyes.

"It's *definitely* not your accent."

His voice carried, and this time, Free did look up. Her eyebrows came down; her lips narrowed. She came half up from her seat, staring at him.

Edward spoke a little louder. "It's the way you're saying it. Didn't you know? 'Suffragette' is pronounced with an exclamation point at the end. Like this: 'Huzzah! Suffragettes!'"

Behind the sergeant, Free glowed. He could see the smile taking over her face, lighting her until he wanted nothing more than to wrap his arms around her. It was the first thing he'd seen all day that had given him hope—hope that once she understood the lies he'd told, she might forgive him yet. That he might spend tonight in her arms, and tomorrow, and the day after.

"Huzzah," the sergeant repeated in confusion. "Suffragettes?"

"That's a question mark," Edward said sharply. "Try it again: Suffragettes!"

"Suffragettes!"

"That's it. You've got it!"

"Oh, excellent!" The sergeant smiled in pleasure—a pleasure that lasted only a few seconds. "My lord, why are we huzzahing suffragettes?"

"That requires a little more explanation." He turned and extended his hand toward Free. "Bring that one here."

There was a long pause. "If my lord insists."

Free's eyes widened, and Edward realized that this was the first time she'd noticed the sergeant calling him "my lord." She glanced down, almost demurely—she'd have fooled him, except he knew there was nothing demure about her—and then looked up at him. She didn't quite quirk an eyebrow; that would have been too obvious. Still, he could make out the words she didn't say writ in her expression. *Edward, what on earth are you playing at?*

Edward kept his face fixed in an expression of bland, arrogant superiority. The sergeant nodded hastily. "Yes, yes. Of course." He turned and clapped his hands. "You heard his lordship. Fetch that woman at once."

"Gently!" Edward admonished.

His lordship? Free mouthed at him. The palms of his hands grew clammy, but he ignored her. A guard fumbled out a set of keys and motioned for Free to step forward.

"Let's see," the sergeant muttered, fluttering pages. "She's number 107, and that makes her…ah, 105, 106, here she is. Miss Marshall." His eyes narrowed. "Are you sure you know nothing of, ah, my arrangement with your brother?"

Edward didn't bother to answer that. She'd given her name as Marshall? She'd called herself Miss? He'd have raised his own eyebrow at her, except that it would ruin the patrician lines of his profile. And right now, he was too busy playing a role to do that.

Instead, he frowned and crossed his arms, glaring at the man in front of him. "Well, now you've done it again. That's not how you pronounce her name. That's not how you pronounce it at all."

"Ah." The sergeant frowned. "Um. Is it… Let me guess. Huzzah! Miss Marshall! With an exclamation point?"

"No," Edward said. "It's not Miss anything."

Free seemed as surprised by this as the sergeant. She'd not remembered it, then. She'd given her maiden name the same way that one kept writing last year's date well into February. For that matter, did suffragettes even change their name upon marriage? He'd have to ask Free. If she was still willing to talk to him after she realized what he'd done. Edward kept his attention firmly on the sergeant.

"Married, eh? Who's the unlucky sod, then? One of your tenants, I suppose? Tell him he needs to do a better job of keeping her under his thumb. You should leave her with us for the night. Let us soften her up."

Edward managed not to shiver at the thought.

"Nonsense." Edward smiled grimly. "Now you're mispronouncing everything, Sergeant. She'll do better with me. As for her husband…" He savored every moment of the sergeant's expression—the shift from confused to surprised to appalled, the blood draining out of his face. "Let me tell you how to pronounce her name. You say it like this: Lady Claridge. And I'm her husband."

⌘　⌘　⌘

LADY CLARIDGE.

For a moment, Free's world stood still. She felt very high up, her lungs unable to gasp for air. He couldn't—she wasn't—that thing Edward had said, it was entirely impossible. But then reality asserted itself, and she remembered the plan they'd sketched out together.

He'd been supposed to come up with a brief note of release—the sort with a muddle for a signature, one that wouldn't be traceable.

He'd apparently changed tactics, and not for the better. A forged order of release from a harried bureaucrat was already pushing things. But this? This was an utter disaster. He might as well have waltzed into a bank and announced his intention to empty the vault.

But she could hardly argue with him in front of the sergeant. That would just get them both thrown back in that cell.

Instead, she narrowed her eyes at him, willing him to change his story. *Did I say Lady Claridge? I misspoke. Clark. I meant Mrs. Clark.* That's what he needed to say next.

He kept silent, looking down his nose at the sergeant.

The man had gone goose-fat pale; his eyes were round. Behind him, one of the guards—the one that had shoved her against a wall—whispered, "Oh, bugger me."

"Your wife," the sergeant said weakly. "Number 107 is your *wife?*"

Edward inclined his head to Free. "How was your stay in gaol, dear?"

So they were going to play it this way. Free managed a bored little shrug of her shoulders. "Passable, love. I've had better."

"Well, then." Edward smiled, letting his teeth show. He turned to the sergeant. "You know perfectly well you can't hold my viscountess."

"I'll…" The sergeant swallowed. "I'll just release her to your custody, then?"

"No, you'll release her to her own. While we're at it, you might as well release the lot of them."

Oh, he was absolutely going to hear from her about this lie. And how they were to avoid the inquiry that would result afterward, she didn't know.

"All? But they hadn't a lawful permit!"

Edward gave him a supercilious little smile. "Come, sergeant. We've had this discussion already. When I say 'all,' you don't add a question mark at the end. You say, 'yes, my lord,' and you snap to it."

Free could hardly believe her eyes or her ears. He played the role of viscount so perfectly. His accent… God, if he'd spoken to her like that, with that snobbish public-school-affected mouth full of mush, she'd never have married him.

"Yes, my lord," the sergeant said. And then he raised his voice. "You heard his lordship. Let them go. Let them all go!"

"My lady?" Edward smiled at Free. There was nothing of the rascal in his smile. It was highborn and stuffy, and she wanted no part of it. Especially since once this mess caught up with them, they'd *both* be arrested. And this time, there would be real cause behind it, not just some ridiculous quashing of permits.

This was not the time to have that argument.

"My *lord,"* Free said.

He held out his arm to her and she took it. He conducted her through the station like the best of stuffy husbands—

guiding her around debris with a gentle touch, as if she couldn't figure out not to step in refuse on her own. Her teeth ground, but if this was the act they had to put on...

Of all the lords to impersonate, why on earth had he chosen Claridge? James Delacey hated them enough as it was. It was a good thing that the sergeant knew nothing about the rarified heights of the *ton*. Delacey would never marry a suffragette, and if his wife had expressed a wish to attend a demonstration, he'd have starved her into compliance rather than fetched her from gaol. Delacey would never joke about exclamation points. He didn't have a puppy-cannon. He'd never declare his affection for her by saying that he gave a very small damn about her. Edward was nothing, absolutely *nothing* like Delacey, thank God, because that man made her skin crawl.

Except...

Now that Edward had cut his hair, now that he was wearing that stiff suit of navy superfine...

He looked like him. A little. And she'd mistaken James Delacey for him once. While it had seemed ridiculous at the time, it no longer seemed so impossible. With that stance, with his hair cut in that sober, respectable way, he looked a bit like an older, thinner version of Delacey.

She shook her head, dispelling that awful illusion.

Edward conducted her outside, handed her into a carriage marked with, of all things, the Delacey family crest: a hawk clutching a rose. Stealing, or more forgery? It had to be forgery, she told herself. Had to be. But if so, he must have planned this for longer than a few hours. Why hadn't he told her?

She entered the carriage and found the family crest tooled in the butter-soft leather of the squabs.

"Edward," Free said dangerously. "Edward, I don't know what you've done, but this is madness."

He nodded to the footman—the footman! As if she'd ever want anything so ridiculous as a man to do nothing but open and close doors for her!—as insouciantly as if he were a lord, and the kind who sprung his wife from gaol on a regular basis. He followed her into the carriage and waited until the door was shut.

"Impersonating a lord," Free continued, taking the seat across from him. "That has to be a felony. And Claridge, of all people—now *there's* a man who will press charges, if ever I saw one. What on earth do you think you're doing?"

"I'm not impersonating James Delacey," Edward said. He'd dropped that false, stuffy tone, thank God. She'd have hit him if he hadn't.

"Oh, really." She frowned at him. "I was with you back there, recall. You're doing a very bad job of not impersonating him. Next time you try not to impersonate a man, don't give out his title as your own."

He folded his hands. "If I were impersonating James," he explained, "I would have introduced myself as the Honorable James Delacey. I would not have called myself Claridge."

She shook her head. "A technical matter of forms of address. Besides, Delacey was supposed to have been seated…soon. I'm not sure when. There may not even be a technical difference at this point."

"I told them I was his elder brother," he said.

"His elder brother?" That flustered her for some reason. "He doesn't have an elder brother." No, but Stephen had mentioned there was one awhile back. She frowned in memory. "His elder brother is dead."

Edward shrugged and looked away. "I did promise you necromancy. Here you are."

She was beginning to have a headache. "This is a terrible idea. Claridge will still come after you. If Edward Delacey were really alive, his brother wouldn't be the rightful viscount any longer. He would tear an impostor to shreds."

"True," Edward said simply. "But I know James well enough to goad him into admitting the truth of who I am before the Committee for Privileges."

None of this was making any sense. She blinked at him, trying to decipher those words. They'd sounded as if…as if…

She must have misheard. "But you're not his brother. You're…"

Edward Clark. Who was sent abroad—into a war zone—by a father who had hoped for more from him… Her whole mind froze.

"You're too old to be him," she said. "You're…what, thirty-six?"

"Twenty-seven." His lips firmed. "It's the hair; I got all that white in a matter of weeks. I look older than I am."

No. No.

"It wasn't really a lie." He didn't look at her. "I *did* mention that you wouldn't like my younger brother."

"You're not Edward Delacey." Her voice shook.

"I've tried my damnedest not to be him. My solicitor says I can keep the name Edward Clark, and I will. But…" He swallowed. "I was him. Once. And I may have misdirected you in some minor fashion in that regard."

Minor? Her hands were beginning to tremble.

"No," she said. "No. You're not."

And, oh, God. Last night. For all the columns she'd written, all the horrible stories she had heard about what marriage might mean to a woman, she had never imagined that *she* might end up in one of them.

"For God's sake." She swallowed. "Do you know what this means? We're married. We can't annul it, we're unlikely to be granted a divorce, not unless…"

Not unless she was unfaithful to him, a prospect she found even more disgustingly distasteful than having Claridge as a husband.

She shifted away from him.

"Oh my God. *James Delacey* is now my brother by marriage." And that wasn't the part that hurt the most. "You didn't tell me. You knew, and you didn't tell me—you with your necromancy and failed logic. Why?" She could feel her eyes begin to sting. But she wasn't going to cry. She wasn't.

"I did tell you once that if you knew everything about me, you'd not want me."

"You're Claridge," she said, feeling a little sick to her stomach. "You weren't some low-level scoundrel out to get revenge for some minor slight. It was *your brother* scheming against me. You could have stopped this whole thing—quashed their quashing of our permit, silenced your brother for good, taken your place. You could have done all that without marrying me." She let out a little noise.

"I wasn't sure I could do it in time." His lips had gone white. "It might have taken another day—paperwork and all. I wasn't sure that mere bluster would have worked. If you were going to be arrested, you needed to be a viscountess. They'd have to let you go then as a right of peerage. I couldn't risk them holding you—not with what James might have had planned."

She turned away from him. "It wasn't your risk to take. It was *mine.*"

He shook his head—and then he shrugged. It hurt, that expression of indifference. As if all her emotion, her care, meant nothing to him. "I have always known you would come to hate me eventually. What's a little sooner?"

"Why didn't you tell me?" She was almost desperate. "You could not have kept it from me, and once I found out, I…"

He gave her a wintry smile. "It's that simple. I've never expected that I would be able to keep you with me. All I could do was keep you safe."

That steadiness in his gaze… She still remembered last night. The way their bodies had joined, the way their hands had intertwined. It had been one of the sweetest, loveliest experiences of her life. If she let him do that again…

No. She slid into the corner of the carriage, her shoulder pressing against the door.

"I'm sorry, Edward," she said. "I can't. I can't do this."

"I know. I never expected you would."

Somehow, his acceptance cut her more deeply than if he'd demanded her submission.

"If I stayed…" she started.

But she could not continue on. If she stayed, she'd let herself be seduced. She was being seduced now by the sudden hope that flared in his eyes. God, how he'd smile if she kissed him now. And all she would have to do was…no.

Free slid her hand up the leather of the seat until her fingers met the side of the carriage. She traced a figure eight against the side, and thought about all the reasons she'd married—bad ones, it turned out. And yet not so bad.

"But I can't," Free said. "I can't stay."

God, she hated that the one person she wanted to comfort her at this moment was…him.

The carriage rumbled on. She had no idea where it was taking her—Claridge House, perhaps? Was there such a thing? The only thing she knew was that she had to get away before she did something foolish. "I can't stay," she repeated. Her fingers found the latch on the door.

"I know," he said calmly. "We'll work it all out, darling. I'll leave you to your work, if that's what you want. You won't ever have to see me again."

It *wasn't* what she wanted. She wanted everything she'd lost back—her scoundrel, her Edward Clark. She couldn't listen to this man who seemed to be that same person and yet answered to *my lord*. She couldn't bear to sit down with him and plan a future apart. She'd break down if she did.

She turned the handle in one smooth motion. The door tumbled open. The carriage was moving at a stately clip through a residential area. She could see no more than a blur of passing houses. One second since she'd opened the door; he was staring at her in confusion. Two, and he began to reach forward.

"I can't," she said one final time. But she understood now why she was saying it. She was saying it because she *could*. If she remained here, she *would*.

She stood. He reached for her, but he was too late. She jumped through the door. Her feet hit the cobblestones; her ankle nearly gave way beneath her. But she caught her balance, if not her breath, and as quickly as she could, she darted down an alley.

"Free!" she heard him calling. "Free!"

She scrambled through a mews, and then down another side street.

"Free!" he called once more, but he was farther away now. So long as she kept going, he'd never discover her again.

Chapter Twenty-One

IT BEGAN TO DRIZZLE while Free found her bearings.

By the time she made her way to the cemetery, it was full-on pouring rain. She had no umbrella, but it didn't matter. It was summer; the rain was not that cold, and the water obscured the tears on her cheeks.

She traversed the graves carefully—up three rows, then down the line, until she found the simple stone her family had erected years ago.

Frederica Barton
1804-1867
Beloved sister
Devoted aunt

Her family had added a line after her funeral, when they had all discovered the truth.

Author of twenty-nine books of high adventure.

Free bowed her head. She couldn't yet face the living; she couldn't stand to deliver those convoluted explanations. Her Aunt Freddy would have to do. Some people thought she'd named her paper the *Women's Free Press* as a sly reference to herself. In a way, she had. But she shared her name with another woman—a woman whose bequest had made this all possible.

It had felt like her Aunt Freddy's posthumous blessing on Free's life. She'd tried to use it wisely: to never back down, to never let fear stop her from moving forward. Aunt Freddy's money from those twenty-nine novels had paid for Free's education, her home, the press she loved.

Every time Free was afraid, she thought of her aunt. But until now, Free had only feared what others might do to her. This was the first time she'd feared herself.

She sank to her knees beside the grave. "Hullo, Freddy."

She could almost hear her aunt's annoyed response. *You're far too casual. Don't call me Freddy. And what are you doing, kneeling in all that mud? Get up before you dirty your gown.*

"Right. Aunt Frederica. I suppose I ought to call you that." But she didn't stand. Instead, she trailed her fingers through the wet grass. There were a few stray dandelions sprouting up. She pulled them, making a pile of green leaves and white roots. That was how you got through life: one weed at a time. It was how she'd get through this.

When she was done here, she'd take the train back to Cambridge. She would write to Edward. They could handle the details of their separation through the mail.

Even the thought of that smarted.

And, she realized, her plan had one terrible flaw. The constables had confiscated her coin purse at the station, and she'd been too distracted to demand its return. She had no money for a ticket. Or—her stomach rumbled—even for a meal. Night would come all too soon.

Edward would no doubt be willing to remedy all that. For a moment, she imagined herself waiting on his doorstep, imagined his reaction at finding her there. He'd pull her to him and hold her tight, and she'd never feel alone again.

The thought was far too alluring to contemplate. It was a good thing she didn't know where his doorstep was.

She had other friends in London. Genevieve was here. Amanda. Violet Malheur. Her brother's house might not be completely shut up. There were any number of people who might take her in.

But for some reason, her thoughts slid back to the last time she'd visited Freddy, back when her aunt was alive. She'd been with Oliver, then, and he'd brought her to the place where he'd been staying at the time—his half-brother, the duke's house. That had been before Oliver had married and purchased his own home. Free had gawked at the surroundings, laughed at her brother's casual acceptance of luxury.

Now that same casual luxury had come for her, and she was afraid.

She was afraid of herself. Not just that she would accept Edward back and forgive him. She was afraid of who she might become if she did that. Oliver lived in a massive home. He tried to do almost everything right. She was afraid that she, too, would start caring about propriety and stop caring about her newspaper. She would back down and make herself small to fit into the role of viscountess.

She was afraid that she'd bite her tongue and swallow her nausea when presented with James as her brother. She might keep her newspaper, yes, but in what form?

If Frederica Marshall turned into Lady Claridge, she might stop being the person that would make her Aunt Freddy proud.

"Freddy, what do I do?" She trailed her fingers in the grass.

But her aunt didn't answer, and the rain continued on.

If Free wanted to not be afraid—if she wanted to truly look that potential future in the face, and make a real decision, it wasn't Amanda or Violet Malheur she needed to speak with.

It was someone else entirely.

⌘ ⌘ ⌘

THE DOOR OPENED and a waft of warm air, perfumed by beeswax and lemon, drifted out. Free stood frozen on the doorstep, already doubting her choice.

But it was too late. She was already here, garbed in a dripping wet gown, trying to figure out what to say to the manservant looking down his nose at her.

He barred the way between her and that wide expanse of marble tile in the entryway. She could see chairs upholstered in luxurious cream-colored velvet just beyond. A painting larger than her two arms outstretched graced the entry wall.

Meanwhile, Free's hair dripped water down her back.

To his credit, the man did not slam the door in her face. He simply raised an eyebrow. "Are you in need of assistance, madam?"

That gentle tone suggested that the duke had a charity policy, and that Free appeared so bedraggled that he'd judged her a beggar.

"No." Free said. "I mean, yes. I'm here…"

Oh, it had been stupid to think that she should come here, stupid to imagine that simply because she'd met the duke a handful of times and he'd been polite, that he'd take her in for the night and answer a few questions.

Free raised her chin. "I'm here to see the Duke of Clermont."

The man's eyebrows rose. Wordlessly, he held out a silver salver.

She dipped one chilled hand into her pocket and pulled out… Well, it *had* been her card once. The rain had turned the cardstock to near-mush; the ink was bleeding into incoherence. She set it gently on the silver plate and tried not to wince.

He peered at the almost-dissolved ink. "Miss…Felicia? Perhaps you could provide some assistance on the pronunciation of your family name."

He was being too kind. The card was an unreadable mess.

"It's Frederica Marshall," she said hopefully. "Oliver Marshall's younger sister. I *do* know His Grace. A little."

The man's expression went from kindly charitable to understanding. "Of course," he said, although his tone suggested that there was nothing *of course* about it. "I missed the family resemblance. Would you care to wait in the…"

A beat passed as he considered the available options. Free felt sorry for him. He couldn't very well put her in the front parlor with all that near-white velvet. She looked like a dog that had run through a field of mud; she wouldn't allow herself in that stately room even if she were dry.

"Don't worry," she told him. "I can drip in the entryway. But I wouldn't mind a towel."

He nodded and gestured her in. It took a scant few moments for not one, but two towels, to be brought by a maid. The woman helped her take off her cloak; she opened the door and unemotionally wrung the article of clothing out on the front step, before taking it off to drip dry in some more appropriate place. Free was doing her best to rub warmth back into her limbs when steps sounded above her.

She turned to see the Duke of Clermont standing at the top of the staircase. He was tall and thin, his blond hair fluffed up as if he'd been ruffling it.

God, this had been a stupid idea. His waistcoat probably cost as much as her rotary-press drum. His eyes fell on her; he frowned, and then he was striding toward her, taking the stairs two at a time.

"Free," he was saying. "Good God, Free, what on earth happened to you?"

She shook her head, sending droplets flying. One landed on his upper lip, but he didn't seem to notice.

"Louisa, fetch her some tea. And you should be in front of a fire." He set his arm about her towel-draped shoulder and pushed her into the parlor. She tried to dig her heels in. The carpet beneath her feet seemed to glitter with gold threads, and she could hear her shoes squelch with filthy water with every step. She refused to look down, for fear that she'd find a string of muddy footprints across that white expanse.

But he was determined. He pulled a chair up for her, one of those gorgeously embroidered chairs. She didn't dare do anything so brazen as to sit in it, but then her knees stopped working and she did anyway. He took a towel from her and started rubbing her hands.

"You're freezing," he told her in an accusing tone of voice.

"I'll be a-all right." There was a tremor to her speech. "I just n-need to get a little warm, ask you a few questions, and then I'll be out of your h-hair."

He made a reproachful sound. "It's eight at night. Have you a place to stay? Any money at all?" He glowered at her. "Do you even have an umbrella?"

"I—that is—I was arrested, and I seem to have misplaced my coin purse."

He clearly knew enough of her that he didn't find this surprising or even unusual. He clucked instead and kept rubbing her hands.

"Have you had supper? Tea?" He was shaking his head at her, but he abruptly stopped. "Have you been crying? What has happened to you? How can I help?"

She shook her head. She'd come here to talk to him, and now she didn't know how to do it. She had hoped to ask a few impersonal questions, but he wasn't treating her impersonally. If she started her story now, under the weight of all his kindness, she would burst into tears. And she'd already left water everywhere. "I'm so sorry," she heard herself say, "so sorry, Your Grace. I won't be a bother. I'll leave first thing in the morning. I never intended to presume on so slight an acquaintance. I just didn't know where else to go."

His hands froze on hers. He was on his knees before her—which seemed impossibly strange given that it was *his* cream carpet that she was befouling. He looked up at her, and let out a long, slow breath before he sat back on his heels.

"You're not a bother," he said.

"You're busy. You're important. You have a wife and children, and—"

"And I have a brother," he said.

Her throat closed up. "Yes, but—"

"No buts." He gave her a short smile. "*You* may have a slight acquaintance with me. I suppose I should be calling you Miss Marshall. I suppose we should even keep Louisa here in the room to safeguard your reputation. But as strange as it might seem to you, Oliver is my brother, and I am deeply grateful to you for sharing him with me."

Free let in a breath. "Yes, but—"

"As I said, *you* have a slight acquaintance with me." He looked away. "I know you somewhat better. He used to read me all his letters from home when we were at school together. I didn't have any of my own, you see."

She felt a faint flush rise in her cheeks.

"It's how I knew what I wanted." He wrapped her feet in the towel, tying it off. "It's how I knew what it looked like to have a loving family and a little sister who sent her brother her first scribbles before she could write. I remember the first letter you sent him."

"Oh, God." She put her head in her hands. "This is going to be embarrassing."

"You dictated it to your father," the duke continued. "And you said: 'Dear Oliver, please come home. What are you going to bring me? Love, your Free.' And I remember thinking…"

Frederica felt herself blush. "How mercenary."

"I remember thinking," he said, as if she hadn't spoken, "that I would give everything that I had for a little sister."

The heat died away from her cheeks. She found herself staring at the top of his head in surprise and puzzlement.

"For anyone," he continued, "who rejoiced when I came home for any reason at all. I would have sent you a million presents if you would have agreed to be my little sister, too." He sighed. "Alas, after the way my father treated your mother, I didn't think the offer would go over well. So I never made it."

She searched his face for signs that he was joking. Perhaps poking fun at her a little. He looked serious.

"But you have a family now. Everyone respects you."

He raised a dubious eyebrow.

"Well, they may call you names," she amended, "but they're mostly respectful names. You have a wife, and unless Oliver is completely wrong, it's a love match. You have children who must adore you. And…" She trailed off and looked at him.

He looked away. "I spent *years* imagining you were my little sister. Love is not a finite quantity." He smiled at her. "And yes, I know you're not my sister—you're Oliver's. Still, I'm glad you came to me. Whatever it is you need…" He spread his hands. "It's yours. Even if it's just a towel and a room for the evening."

She hadn't known quite what she'd been hoping for. She'd imagined posing him a few abstract questions, receiving a few desultory answers. She certainly hadn't expected…this.

She swallowed hard and looked away.

"I was hoping you'd have dinner with me," he said. "Minnie is out for the evening with some friends; she'll be back in a few hours. London is dreadful in the summer, and the children are with Minnie's aunts for the next two weeks. I'm at loose ends and was just feeling a mite lonely."

"Your Grace—"

"I wish you'd call me Robert. If you keep Your-Graceing me, I'll have to stop thinking of you as Free, and as much as Oliver has talked of you, I don't think that's possible."

"But—"

"Or call me Your Grace, if you must, and I'll invent you a title of your own to match. Something that fits you. If you call me Your Grace, I shall have to call you…" His finger tapped his lip in contemplation.

She felt an unaccountable urge to laugh. She had a title now. She was Lady Claridge, a stuffy, stupid peeress. She'd never wanted anything to do with the nobility. And yet here she was, accepting a duke as her brother and a viscount as her husband. The entire day was completely impossible.

"I shall have to call you Your Fierceness," he was saying. "Like this: Would you like anything to eat, Your Fierceness? You must be starving, Your Fierceness."

"Stop, Your Grace."

"As Your Fierceness wishes." His eyes twinkled at her.

"Have it your way. But I'll have to go in stages." She took a deep breath. "Can I just call you…*you* for the next little bit?"

"Yes, Your Fierceness," he said. He stood. "Louisa, is Miss Marshall's bath ready?"

"Yes, Your Grace," the maid, who'd been standing in the corner, said. "Mary signaled to me not a minute past."

"Very well, then," the duke—Robert—said. "If you could conduct Miss Marshall there?"

She wasn't Miss Marshall any longer. She didn't know *who* she was.

The maid bowed her head and then turned to Free. "If you would care to come with me, Your Fierceness?" There was a glint of a smile in the woman's eyes, just that tiny hint of a sense of humor. And somehow, it was that—that tiny indication that the Duke of Clermont's servants felt free to express humor in their employer's presence, rather than turning into empty shells of themselves—that decided her.

Free pushed herself to her feet and wobbled across the room.

"Come along, miss," Louisa said to her indulgently. "Come along."

# # #

A WARM BATH AND DRY CLOTHING did a great deal to restore Free's good humor. When she came down the stairs, back into the parlor, the Duke of Clermont—Robert, she reminded herself with a strange feeling—was sitting in front of the fire, slicing bread. It was such an odd thing to see: a man of his stature wielding a knife. He cut a thick, clumsy slice of bread as she watched from the doorway, the crumbs spilling haphazardly onto the carpet.

She paused, not sure what to say.

"Come," he said, motioning to her. "Sit down."

She drifted toward him.

"I don't know anything about cheering up sisters," he said, sliding the bread onto the waiting tines of the toasting fork. "I don't know anything about cheering up anyone except children between the ages of six and fourteen. But maybe this will work on you."

She glanced over at him curiously. "What are you doing?"

"*We,*" he corrected her. "We're making dinner. We'll toast bread and cheese over the fireplace and have some tea." He gestured with the toasting fork, and the bread dipped perilously close to the flames. He shrugged guiltily. "Oh, dear. I'll take this one."

"No, it's better singed," Free heard herself say. "I always like that extra smoky flavor."

His smile grew. "Come on, then." He patted the cushion on the other side of the fireplace. "Have some toast."

She'd known she was hungry, but her stomach growled in anticipation at the aroma of toasting bread. After he'd singed one side—only a bit black—he added cheese to the top and leaned in again. The cheese on top began to bubble and drip off the edges. He seemed to have infinite patience for waiting, turning the toast this way and that to try and get an even melt.

He handed her the slice of bread when he was satisfied.

"Don't wait for me," he told her and speared another piece of bread.

She wished she could be polite enough to demur, but she was too ravenous to think. Instead, she broke off a piece and put it in her mouth. The cheese was the perfect temperature— hot enough to be glorious, barely managing to escape burning the top of her mouth. The bread crunched between her teeth, soft in the middle, toasted to a crisp on the edges. She almost let out a moan.

"I know," Robert said beside her. "I've had toast for breakfast made ingloriously on the racks of the kitchen oven. That's just browned bread. It's not really toast if it hasn't been cooked over an open flame."

"Mmm."

A cup of tea was put into her hand. She took a sip— liquid that was sweet and milky and bitter all at once filled her mouth.

"How often does the Duke of Clermont make himself dinner?" she asked.

"Not very often," he replied. "Maybe once every month or so, the family gets out the toasting forks and I do my best to wrangle up toast and cheese."

"Mmm." She wished she could say more, but her mouth was full again.

He poured himself a cup of tea one-handed, juggling the fork skillfully. "The trick," he said, "to getting good toast is to try not to be too perfect. You won't want to brown it too evenly, or to avoid singeing it. You don't want to cut the bread too perfectly, either. It's better if it has lots of jagged edges to blacken nicely."

"That's the problem I always have, too," Free said. "I have to try so hard not to be perfect."

He grinned at her.

His cheese was beginning to bubble, and he was eyeing the piece with a hungry look. And that was when they heard a noise in the hall.

They turned. A door was opening; voices murmured in the distance. For a moment, Free had the wildest idea that Edward—no, she couldn't think of him that way—*Viscount Claridge* was here. He'd hunted her down. He was going to apologize, tell her how badly he'd treated her, and she was going to...

She had no idea what she was going to do. Her tea sloshed onto her skirt, and she realized her hand had begun to tremble.

But the figure who came into the room was a woman— the Duchess of Clermont, no less. She didn't blink at the sight of her husband sitting before the fire. She didn't ask what Free was doing here. She simply came into the room and took off her gloves.

"Oh, good," she said. "A toast and cheese night. I need one of those."

Her husband looked longingly at the slice on his toasting fork, but he didn't even hesitate. He handed the bread to his wife.

She slid down to sit on the floor beside him. "Want half?"

"God, yes."

Maybe it was the toast, managed in so perfectly imperfect a fashion. Maybe it was the companionable silence. Maybe it was the fact that she'd expected to be treated like some distant, grasping relation, and now she was sitting on the floor with the duke and duchess, eating burned bread and dripping cheese. Maybe that was what prompted her to finally speak.

"I got married," she confessed.

Robert's hands stilled. He looked up at her, his eyes widening.

"It was…it was a whim," she said, speaking faster. "Or more than a whim. I don't know what it was. We've corresponded for months. Maybe I was feeling reckless." Maybe she'd thought herself in love. She didn't say that, though. She shut her eyes. "I got married yesterday night."

Across from her, the duchess took a genteel bite of toast and looked down. "You married by special license, then?"

"I should have asked how he'd obtained one so quickly." Her hands were trembling again, so she set down her teacup. "I knew he was a scoundrel, you see. I knew that. But he had always been there for me. I thought I could trust him."

She felt sick to her stomach.

"And then I went to the demonstration, and was arrested, and he…he…"

Neither the duke nor the duchess spoke. They just watched her intently.

"I was arrested," she repeated. "As I'd known I would be. We were all crammed into the station. He came to get me out."

It didn't sound awful when she told the story. It sounded sweet. Almost romantic.

"But he didn't forge papers falsifying my release." And oh, *there* was a complaint for the ages. There wasn't a wife in England today complaining about her husband's failure to commit crimes. "He *told* me he was Edward Clark."

The duchess twitched at that name, her eyebrows lifting. She turned to her husband, but he set a quelling hand on her knee.

"He told me he was a scoundrel and a metalworker," Free said. "He's a forger. I've seen him do it myself. But he didn't tell me everything. He was..." She gulped.

"Edward Delacey," Robert said, his voice low.

Beside him, the duchess let out a long, slow breath. "Huh. I was right."

"No." Free's hands balled into fists. "He doesn't want to be called Delacey." That much, at least, they agreed upon. "But he's Viscount Claridge."

The duchess tilted her head to the side, to contemplate the ceiling, not quite looking at her husband. "There should be a rule somewhere that lords ought to act like lords. When they engage in forgery or, ah, general skulduggery, it can be very confusing to the rest of us."

Free nodded vigorously.

"You start to think of them as normal people," the duchess said. "And then the next thing you know, they're being introduced."

"Hmph." Robert snorted beside her.

"And all you can think is, surprise! A lord!" She shook her head and patted Free on the shoulder. "I hate it when that happens."

Chapter Twenty-Two

EDWARD FOUND THE LITTLE FARM at the end of the road. After he'd looked for Free last night—looked for her everywhere, with no hope and a feeling of sinking dread—he'd purchased a ticket out here. He'd spent the night in a tiny inn, and then come out in search of... Well, he wasn't sure what he had hoped to find.

Fields of lavender waved purple heads in the wind, wafting a delicious scent around. A kitchen garden closer to the house was coming up cabbages. Daisies planted at the edge of the path lifted their heads into the morning sun as if they had no thought but to rejoice in the moment. Foolish flowers; someone would come along to cut them down before long. Even if they didn't, winter would freeze them out, leaf and root alike.

But the flowers didn't care about his dark mood. They rustled softly, swaying in a light breeze, whispering that this was a quiet, peaceful place. That frost could not come here unless Edward brought it himself.

It was a cheery, homey place, not at all the sort of abode where he'd imagined the Wolf, the mighty pugilist of his childhood imagination, retiring.

Edward walked slowly forward. Not reluctantly; he had a damned good idea what was about to happen to him, and quite frankly, he welcomed it. But there was something about the air that sparked his imagination, something that made him think of other possibilities. He might have been treading this path with Free by his side. She'd have interlaced her hand with his, looked up at him with that air of totally unwarranted trust...

Ah, hell. He was tormenting himself. He shook his head at the daisies beside him, rejecting their foolish optimism.

The front door opened. Edward looked up to see a man standing there, his head tilted as he contemplated Edward. Edward felt every muscle in his body tense.

This. This was the Wolf. He'd imagined himself at the side of a ring with this man at the center. When he was a child, he'd pictured this man absorbing blow after crippling blow. He'd painted that long-ago fight in oils.

But the Wolf—Hugo Marshall—didn't look anything like the mighty fighter of his imagination. He was no Hercules; he wasn't even handsome. He was much shorter than Edward. There were no patrician lines to his face; he was the sort of man who Edward had passed on the street a thousand times and never given a second glance. He was wearing a loose cravat and a jacket with faded patches over the elbows. His hair was steel gray.

"Good morning," the other man said politely. "You've been dawdling outside my house for the last fifteen minutes. Is there some way I can help you?"

Edward took his hat off. He wasn't sure if he intended it as a sign of respect, or if he simply wanted to hold something. All he knew was that he was turning it in his hands, end to end, his mouth so dry, he was unable to speak.

"What is it?" Mr. Marshall took a step closer. "Are you well, sir?"

No. Edward was not well. He didn't know how he was ever to be well. "You..." He'd managed to get only the single word out. He could do a few more, surely. "You...you must be Mr. Hugo Marshall."

"I am." Marshall looked him over and frowned. "And you have the look of... Ah, my memory isn't what it used to be. It's been years since I had to sort out high society." His eyes were sharp and penetrating, flickering over Edward's features. "No. I don't know you, although you remind me..." He shrugged. Then his gaze traveled to Edward's coat—badly pressed—and his unshaven cheeks. "Hmm. Why am I so sure that you're high society?"

Oh, how Edward wished he could lie. "I am."

"Are you here about some dimly remembered family scandal that I ferreted out years ago? If so, go away." The man waved a hand. "I don't remember a thing from that time—as I've just amply demonstrated."

"That's not why I'm here, sir."

Marshall's eyebrows rose on the *sir.*

"You see, I'm..." He took a deep breath and then raised his chin. "I'm Edward Clark." He didn't even know if Free had mentioned his existence to her parents.

Apparently, she had. An amused grin swept over Marshall's face. "Are you, then? That explains the nervousness. But don't tell me you've come to ask for Free's hand. She didn't speak of you as if you were a stupid fellow. You must know she'd never forgive either of us, if we..." He paused. "Wait one moment. Free never mentioned to me that her Mr. Clark was high society."

Her Mr. Clark. God, those words cut him.

"I'm Edward Clark. Born Edward Delacey. Now, apparently, Viscount Claridge." He shut his eyes. "You can address me by my preferred title: *you idiot.*"

Marshall's eyes were narrowing on this. "What have you done to my daughter, you idiot?"

"To my great regret, I..." Edward's hands were clammy. "It's..." God, it would be better if lightning could just strike him now. "I can't—that is, I seem to have married your daughter."

Marshall looked about the yard, as if searching for Free. When he didn't find her, he turned back to Edward.

"You regret marrying my daughter." His voice sounded calm, if one could call the cold, black embers after a fire had burnt out *calm.*

"No," Edward said. "Never that. *She* regrets marrying *me.*"

"Ah, then." There was steel in the other man's words, an edge so sharp that Edward could almost feel it slicing into him. "That's worse."

"It is." Edward shut his eyes and tensed. But nothing happened—no blow to the stomach, no fist to his face. He waited, his muscles growing taut, but instead, a bird chirped merrily off in the distance. He finally opened one eye to see Marshall watching him quizzically.

"Aren't you—that is—having confessed what I just did, aren't you going to…?"

"To rough you up a little?" Marshall asked.

"Yes."

"I'm imagining it right now. Give me a moment, and I'll get through it. Then we can talk like rational beings."

Edward blinked. "Pardon?"

Marshall shrugged. "Come now. All you've said is that my daughter regrets marrying you. I don't know if she'd regret marrying you *less* if I beat you to a bloody pulp. She might not; she might feel sorry for you if you were laid up with your ribs broken and your eyes blackened. Then she might end up saying things she doesn't mean and find herself in a worse spot than she is now. I only strike other men when I think there's a chance it'll do some good."

"That's…that's…" It was alarmingly rational.

"Besides, if Free wanted you to have a black eye, you'd have one. When she was twelve, she used to get into fistfights with the boy next door, and we were always being called upon by Mrs. Shapright to come see what Free had done to him."

Edward felt the corner of his lip twitch.

"So tell me. How is it that a viscount came to marry my daughter without my knowledge?"

"I hadn't been in England for a long while. I never intended to return, and when I did, I didn't plan to make myself known. I didn't want to be a viscount. I just wanted to finish my business and go away."

"I see."

"And then my business brought me into Free's way." He swallowed. "And… And…"

"And she bowled you over." There was a glint of a smile on Marshall's face.

"Precisely. I don't even know how it happened. One moment, I was standing there, utterly cynical about everything in the world, and the next… I was standing there, utterly cynical about everything except her. It was the most ridiculous thing."

And yet it wasn't ridiculous at all. He could remember every instant of their first weeks together. When she'd first told him about the Hammersmith-Choworth prizefight. When she'd knocked on the door of Stephen's room, ushering in the charwoman, and he'd jumped for the window. When she'd looked him in the eyes and told him that he saw only the river, not the roses. It wasn't ridiculous that he loved her; it was the most reasonable thing on the planet. He hadn't realized that he was rifling through those first memories until Marshall gestured for him to continue.

Edward shook his head. "The only thing I knew was that if she knew the truth—if she knew everything about me— she'd never have me. So…I didn't tell her. And…" He swallowed. "Your daughter can be a bit impulsive sometimes." He cleared his throat. "Hypothetically, if a man returns from a long absence with a special license and a terrible reason to marry, well…" He shrugged and steeled himself for what was to come. "Mr. Marshall. I don't know what Free would want, but for God's sake, don't let me off. I lied to your daughter. I married her by trickery, and she's miserable now. It would be much easier if you could just beat me into a bloody pulp."

Marshall shrugged. "I'm getting old. I never beat a man into a bloody pulp before breakfast anymore. It will do you some good to stew. Come on in and meet my wife."

Edward stared at him in confusion. "Don't you understand? I spent the night with your daughter under the color of lies."

Marshall inhaled, shaking his head. "Have you spent any time at all talking to Free? If I pummeled a man for spending the night with her, she'd be furious with me. She would tell me that it implies that a father owns his daughter's body, and we've had that fight twice already. I'm not about to repeat it."

"But—"

Mr. Marshall made an annoyed noise. "Think of things from my point of view. I've only your report to go on, and by your own admission, you're a liar. So I can hardly trust your account of the matter. You may be going through a rough patch in your marriage, but you might also make it up to her. I'm doing my damned best not to wound you permanently, because it could make Christmases awkward for many years to come. If she tosses you to the side, well." Marshall gave him a not-quite pleasant smile. "Then I'll have my chance."

For just a moment, Edward felt as if his head had burst into flames. This was not how he'd envisioned this conversation proceeding. Not at all.

And that, strangely, was what made him finally feel as if he knew what he was doing, because that feeling of being utterly turned about was all too familiar.

He screwed his eyes shut. "Free gets that from you, I see."

"Gets what?"

"That ability to set the world on its head."

There was a long pause after that. "No," Marshall finally said. "You should come in and meet her mother."

$$\mathcal{H} \quad \mathcal{H} \quad \mathcal{H}$$

"SO YOU'RE HEADING BACK to Cambridge." Genevieve sat next to Amanda on the long sofa. Their skirts did not quite touch—Amanda had twitched hers out of the way when Genevieve sat down. But they were close enough that Amanda's heart was pounding in a low, insistent rhythm.

"I must," Amanda said. "Alice was running the paper all by herself yesterday, and if I'm not back by this afternoon, she'll get no rest at all."

"Has Free returned yet?"

Amanda considered this. She'd felt almost guilty yesterday when her sister had harangued the officers at the arrest. They'd been on the other side of the park from Free—and Maria had taken hold of Amanda's arm with one hand, and Genevieve's with the other. She'd pleaded fatigue, pointed out her state of being with child—and consequently, Amanda had not been dragged to the station with those closer to Free.

Amanda had used her unencumbered state to send a messenger to the station. Free had been released a scant few hours later, and so there were no worries on that end.

"Free didn't say anything about when she was returning," Amanda said. "But she's newly married. I suspect she was otherwise occupied last night."

"Married!" Genevieve's eyes widened. "I'd heard nothing at all of that. Does her brother know yet? Does Jane?"

"It was…sudden," Amanda explained. "Although, not precisely sudden to me. We do share a house, after all. She's been besotted for months, smiling every time one of his letters arrived, acting as if she'd won top prize in a contest. It will be great fun teasing her when…"

It was at that point that Amanda realized something very important. Between planning for the demonstration, reconciling with her sister, and the enjoyment of spending a little time afterward with Genevieve, she'd failed to notice one thing.

"Oh, no," she groaned, putting her head in her hands. "I was going to say, when we're both back in Cambridge. But I just realized."

"Oh dear." Genevieve caught on, too, and she too grimaced. "You live with her. Will she…" She paused delicately.

"Will Free throw me out?" Amanda shook her head. "No. She wouldn't. But I'm not sure how I feel about living with a newly married couple. Things might be a little awkward."

More than a little, she suspected. Free had kissed Edward in public. God only knew what might happen behind a door.

"What will you do?"

"Spend more time in London. It would make sense, given what I write about." Amanda swallowed. "But I suppose it's just as well. It will mean seeing my sister more. And Maria says Toby wants to see me—I haven't seen my eldest brother in ages."

But it wasn't the thought of Maria that had her heart pounding. She didn't look at Genevieve, but she blushed anyway.

"You could see me more, too," Genevieve said.

Her tone was light and…and…

And no, oh *no*, Amanda was not going to even think of what else it was. Unbidden, though, the word whispered in her mind.

Flirtatious.

It was almost flirtatious, and Amanda had been trying her best to see everything Genevieve did in the light of friendship, not flirtation. It wasn't working so well any longer.

"That would be very nice." That sounded rather too stiff.

Genevieve reached out and set her hand on Amanda's knee. It was a light, gentle touch. A *friendly* touch. That's all it could be. "Good. Then that's settled. I should like to see more of you."

Amanda's mouth had gone dry. And Genevieve's hand didn't move. It rested there, poised on her leg. "Yes," Amanda said awkwardly. "I'd like to see…more of you, too." That pause made her sentence sound like a double entendre. Which it was. Mostly unintentionally done, on her part. She felt her face flush violently.

And then Genevieve moved her hand up a few inches— a distance so meaningless to her, so burningly painful for Amanda. That inch transformed the place her hand rested from the knee to the thigh.

If Genevieve had been at Girton College with Amanda, among women who regularly whispered of such things, Amanda would have known precisely how to take that hand. She'd have taken it in her own and kissed it.

But Genevieve had gone to an elite, proper finishing school. She'd spent all her time in polite society with ladies who were…well, *ladies*. The possibility that Amanda might have been burning with unrequited lust quite likely did not occur to her.

"Do you think," Genevieve said, "that you might ever want to stay with me while you're in town?"

Amanda jumped up, pulling away from the heaven of Genevieve's touch.

"No!" Her voice was a high-pitched squawk. "No, I do not think that is a good idea. You're very sweet. And a good friend—a wonderful friend. But you're so…ah…"

Genevieve sat in place, a faint blush on her cheeks.

"So innocent," Amanda finished.

Genevieve snorted. "I've spent the last ten years as social secretary to Mrs. Marshall, who runs a hospital and a charity on medical ethics. What about that position makes you think that I'm *innocent?*"

Amanda swallowed. "I don't mean *innocent* innocent. I just mean… That…" She swallowed. "Not all women are alike. Some of us don't wish to marry because we want other things from life."

Genevieve stood and came toward her. "I haven't married," she said. "I want other things from life."

"*Different* other things," Amanda muttered.

"I try to dress demurely and speak politely." Genevieve was coming close—too close. "I don't do those things, Amanda, because I'm *too innocent.*"

She stood so close that Amanda could see that her skin wasn't really perfect. She had faint freckles on her nose—three adorable, kissable freckles.

"I do them," Genevieve said, "because you have to pretend to be proper on the outside when you aren't. When you want *different* other things."

Oh, God.

It was too much. She'd been trying *not* to see Genevieve in this light for months now—trying and failing. She'd never failed so badly as she did now. She'd never hoped as painfully as this, either. Her heart was racing.

"You see," Genevieve said, "I've always admired you. But these last months—listening to you talk of Parliament, watching you slowly gain confidence as you returned to society. I've found myself admiring you more. And more. And hoping that maybe…you might admire me, too."

There was no mistaking her meaning now. Not when Genevieve took Amanda's hand in her own and pressed it to her heart.

Amanda swallowed. "How did you know what you wanted? I didn't truly understand it myself—not until Girton, until someone else explained."

Genevieve simply looked at her. "I understood," she said, "because I met you."

Amanda felt all aflutter—foolish and happy, giggly and alight.

"I met you," Genevieve said, "and suddenly everything my sister had ever said to me about her husband—it all made sense."

Amanda couldn't help herself. She reached out and cupped Genevieve's cheek, running her thumb along those freckles on her nose.

"So let me repeat my question," Genevieve said. "I know that I do my best to be proper. But do you think there's a chance that you might want to be improper with me?"

Amanda's thumb found Genevieve's lips—pale pink, so perfectly sweet. She swept her fingers over them. Genevieve's lips parted.

Amanda leaned down. "I'm mad for you."

Genevieve smiled, looking up. Amanda could feel her breath against her lips, warm and sweet.

"Good," Genevieve breathed.

Their lips met. Genevieve dropped her hand, but only so she could bring her arms around her. And all Amanda's last fears came to a thundering, crashing, delicious halt.

"Good," Genevieve murmured against her lips once again. "I'm mad for you, too."

❁ ❁ ❁

THE CARRIAGE ROBERT HAD HIRED from the station pulled up to a stop in front of Free's parents' house.

"Well then," Robert said. "Shall I wait here?"

It was ridiculous. Free was a grown woman. She ran her own business, managed fourteen full-time employees and many more writers. And right now, she wanted nothing more than to go home and curl up in her mother's arms.

But now was not the time for that. She turned to Robert. "Come in," she said simply. "And thank you for last night and this morning. I feel…"

Not better, not by a long ways. But she felt more at peace.

Robert and Minnie had given her a long explanation of how they spent their time. Minnie had stayed awake with her until one in the morning. Minnie had her own set of difficulties: She felt anxious in crowds and being a duchess hadn't cured that. So they'd adapted. They had made it work.

Free didn't want to be a viscountess, but it was rather too late for that now, though. The only questions were what sort of viscountess she wanted to be…and how she would get on with her viscount.

Robert was watching her, wondering how she would end her sentence.

"I feel more important," she said.

He turned his head away and smiled—a shy smile, as if he were actually embarrassed by her gratitude. "You're welcome, Your Fierceness."

For a second, she wondered if he would mind if she hugged him. Then he shifted in his seat, looking down at his hands, and she was fairly certain he wouldn't.

She slid across the seat and put her arms around him. "Thank you," she said again. "For being my brother when I needed one."

He brought his hand up to pat her back. When she pulled away, he coughed into his hand. "Of course," he said. But his voice was just a little too rough. "Of course."

"Come in," she said. "My parents will be happy to see you."

He sat up straight. "I don't know... That is... It's a little more complicated than that. I don't want to impose, and given the rather odd history between our two families..."

"Come on," Free said, with a roll of her eyes. "If you're not by my side, I'll burst into tears when I see my mother, and that will be very embarrassing. After all that I've been through in the last few days, you can't subject me to that."

He looked at her for one second. Oh, the man definitely did *not* have younger siblings if he actually believed a word of that. He was far too susceptible to a touch of guilt.

"Oh, very well," he said in a put-upon voice. "If you insist."

But he didn't look put upon. He looked pleased. He handed her down from the carriage, unhitched the horses, and tied them up. When that was all taken care of, he offered her his arm and conducted her up the path to the house.

It occurred to her, as she knocked on the door, that something was amiss. In all the time they'd been dawdling on the road, somebody ought to have seen them. But neither her father nor her mother had appeared.

Too late to wonder. She heard a noise inside, and then her mother opened the door.

Free's heart stopped. Her mother—oh, God, her mother. Her eyes were dark. Her face was lined. Free hadn't seen her look like that since Aunt Freddy passed away years before. It had taken her mother a few months to lose that look about her, that grief-stricken look that said the world had betrayed her. Now it was back, and the only thing that Free could think was that something awful had happened. She gasped.

"Oh, thank God," her mother said.

"Oh, no." Free spoke atop her. "What on earth is wrong? Is it Laura and her baby?"

Her mother gasped and put one hand over her heart. "What's the matter with Laura?"

"It *isn't* Laura? Then…"

There was a moment while they stared at each other in confusion. Another moment, when her mother let out a breath. "Free. I was worried about *you.*"/

"Me." Free looked around. "Why me? I'm…" *Perfectly fine*, she had been about to say. But she wasn't. She didn't know what she felt any longer.

And then her mother put her arms around Free, pulling her close. It was utterly ridiculous. Free had made her own way for years. She was far too old to bury her head in her mother's apron and bawl. But somehow, when her mother held her, the sound of her breath, the feel of her shoulders, the distinctive smell of her soap… They all combined to mean something like comfort. Comfort had been in short supply in recent times.

And then her mother whispered in her ear. "I don't care what your father says. Say the word, and I will walk back into the kitchen and stick a knife in his back."

Free pulled back. That sense of comfort withdrew, leaving her uncertain. "Who are you planning to kill?"

"He's in there." Her mother gestured to the house with her head. "Claridge."

Free's hands turned cold.

"And I swear to God," her mother continued in that low voice, "I did not raise my daughters to become some filthy lords' playthings. I have no idea what happened, what hold he has over you, but if he's done a damned thing to hurt you, he'll pay. They can hang me. I—" She stopped, took a deep breath, and looked to her right.

Just as well that she'd stopped talking. The thought of someone stabbing Edward in the kidneys didn't make Free feel any better.

But her mother was looking at the man standing next to Free. "Oh," she continued, in an entirely different voice. "Your Grace. How…ah… How unexpected to see you." She brushed at her skirts and grimaced.

What flitted through Free's mind was nothing rational. She had nothing to say to comfort her mother. What occurred to her instead was this: *What's the difference between a lord and a bit of algae?*

She'd never heard that particular joke. Still, she didn't have any difficulty coming up with her own answer.

One of them's a slippery, slimy, disgusting thing. The other is necessary to the proper functioning of freshwater ponds. It was deeply, impossibly inappropriate. She was fairly certain that this was proof that her tenuous hold on calm rationality was slipping from her grasp. Another five minutes, and she'd start staring off into space, laughing at nothing at all.

What's the difference between a lord and a pile of horse manure? It was too easy. *One of them smells terribly; the other, applied judiciously, increases the productivity of fields.*

But then, she could have said the same thing about ladies. And now she was one.

Next to her, her mother and Robert were still talking. "You mustn't talk that way," the duke was saying. "I'll do it, if it must be done. They'd have to go through the Lords to hang me, and there are extenuating circumstances. Such as the fact that Claridge is a lout. They'd never convict me. But…" He frowned. "No, sorry. Before I agree to commit a crime with witnesses present, I really ought to talk to Minnie. She'll have a better idea."

A smile touched her mother's face. "You are a handy person to know. Would you…two…care to…"

Come in? Abscond? Free wasn't certain what she wanted. She didn't want them to kill Edward—even though they were probably joking. Robert was, at least; she wasn't entirely sure about her mother. But she didn't want to see him. She didn't want him near almost as much as she wanted him close. She was afraid that if she caught sight of him, he'd charm her into compliance.

She drew a deep breath. "We can postpone Claridge's inevitable demise," she said. "At least until we've spoken with Minnie. And until I've…"

Behind her mother, Edward came into the hall. He caught sight of her and came to a halt.

Or maybe it was Free's world that stopped instead. Her heart ceased to pound. Her breath ceased to circulate. Every atom of her being seemed to slow and come to a standstill.

What's the difference between a lord and your husband?

None. There was no difference at all.

Chapter Twenty-Three

FREE STOOD ALL OF FIVE FEET from Edward, real and solid and safe. He'd spent the night worrying about her. She was separated from him now by a mere two paces on the one hand, and a gulf of lies on the other. Edward didn't know if he could reach her if he tried.

"Free," he said. "I'm sorry."

Her eyes seemed an impenetrable wall. At least she didn't turn on her heel and walk away.

"I'm dreadfully sorry," he said. "I ruined everything, absolutely everything. What I did was unforgivable."

She didn't move.

"Inexcusable," he kept on. "I know you'll want nothing to do with me. Whatever it is you want—a sworn statement that I'll not interfere with your business, a promise to keep my distance—whatever you want, Free. You can have it. I owe you that much."

She opened her mouth once, closed it, shook her head, and then opened her mouth again. "Why did you do it?" she managed to get out. "Why didn't you tell me? Why didn't you let me know?"

"Because I'm stupid," he said. "And selfish. I should never have asked you to marry me."

Free held up a hand. "That isn't what I meant. You had to know I would find out—and find out soon. Why didn't you tell me the truth before?"

"Because…" He frowned. "Because I knew you wouldn't marry me. I wanted to make sure you'd be safe—and as I said—there was a hefty dose of selfishness involved." He didn't have any good reasons to offer her—just that feeling of sickness at heart, of panic at the thought of losing her, at what might happen to her if he didn't have her…

"That doesn't make any sense," Free said. "*I* don't know that I would have walked away if you'd told me the truth. How could *you* know I would?"

He swallowed. His heart beat a painful rhythm against his chest.

"You had to know there was no future in what you were doing," she said. "So why did you do it that way? Wasn't it worth the chance that I would say yes?"

Everything hurt. He shook his head. "I don't know anything of planning for futures. I always assumed…"

She raised an eyebrow.

"That whatever happened to me was going to be awful, no matter what I chose."

She let out a long breath and looked about. And that was when Edward realized that they stood in her parents' hall, surrounded by her father, her mother—good God, that man standing over there was the Duke of Clermont, and what he was doing here, Edward didn't want to know.

Free let out a long breath. "Come. Walk with me." She gestured.

Her mother twitched, frowning, but didn't say anything.

Free turned and went out the front door into the sunshine. He followed. She didn't wait for him outside, though. She turned to the left and began picking her way along a path. He trailed after her, feeling as if he were Eurydice following Orpheus out of hell. Except that he had the strangest feeling that if she looked back, *she* would disappear, not him. She took him over a faint path worn through the fields, over a hill, down an embankment, to a line of trees along a stream.

A few massive rocks lined the bank. Free seated herself on one of them, smoothing her skirts before looking up at him.

God, her eyes. He never wanted to see her eyes like this again—so hurt, so uncertain. *He'd* done that to her.

"If it helps," he said, "I've always known I didn't deserve you."

"How odd. I've only begun to doubt that in the last twenty-four hours."

He seated himself across from her. "Yes. You'll only doubt it more the better you know me."

She shut her eyes. "How could you be so certain?"

"Because I hurt everyone I love. My best friend as a child—I convinced him and his brother to speak, and my father had them whipped in front of me." Edward glanced down. The next words came out low. "And that's not the worst of it."

"What is the worst of it?"

The worst of it was a dark, echoing memory, one that at odd times seemed to have happened to someone else. "I told you that I stayed with a blacksmith near Strasbourg," he said. "That was my father's punishment for my earlier choices."

She nodded at him.

"It was a lovely punishment," Edward said. "I was there for two years. He was paid to look after me, but I expect my father thought of me 'laboring' and imagined I would hate it. I didn't. He taught me things like how to shoe a horse. He'd lost his own son years past, and he never treated me as a burden. I loved him." His voice roughened on those last words, but he shook his head. "He showed me how to work metal. His name was Emile Ulrich."

She nodded again.

"And then Strasbourg was taken. I thought to get the two of us out of occupied territory. I failed, and I was taken in by Soames after my first attempted forgery. Ulrich found out what had happened, and he came to Soames, determined to get me out. He started to raise a stink about what Soames was doing, holding me in a cellar."

Edward swallowed and looked away.

"He was the first person Soames made me implicate as part of the resistance. They shot him summarily in front of me."

She inhaled slowly. Her eyes reminded him of storm clouds on the horizon: dark and impossible to read. "What did you do?" she asked.

"What else could I do? I had no way to escape, and I was so turned around in my head that I wouldn't have known what to do with one if it were offered. I stayed as Soames's pet forger, believing what he told me to believe. People say sometimes they've lost hope for themselves." He shrugged. "They rarely mean it the way I did. I lost all sense of myself for months. There was no future, no past. Only him and the prospect of pain. He kept me until the French lost Paris and sued for peace."

She looked at him.

"Eventually, I got away. My friend Patrick came and took care of me until I was well enough to send him off. I spent several years wandering about Europe, honing my craft as a forger, learning how to commit crimes and not get caught at it." Edward couldn't look at her now. "It took me years to untangle what had really happened. When I did, I went back to Strasbourg. Soames was still there—and he was rather successful, in fact. I knew enough about him to change all that. So I forged the right letters and took control of his accounts. I left evidence that he'd played both sides during the war. And then I took his money and left him to account for what he'd done. That's how I established myself." He shrugged. "I always expected, every day, to be uncovered. There are times I wonder if everything is not a lie after all, if maybe I'm still in that cellar, so terrorized that I cannot bear the truth."

She had sat, listening, as he spoke, scarcely interrupting. "Is that why you haven't asked me to forgive you?"

"I don't see how you can." His voice dropped low.

"No?" She looked into his eyes. "Don't you?"

"I try not to lie to myself."

"You walked into my life," she said slowly. "You found evidence proving that other papers were copying my columns. You saved one of my writers from certain embarrassment and possible imprisonment. You saved me from fire. You rescued me from gaol. And, yes, you hurt me, too. But you think you would be lying to yourself if you believed I could forgive you?"

Edward shook his head. It wasn't a denial; he wasn't even sure what it was.

"Do you think I could hear what you just told me, and not bleed for you?" Her voice was trembling now. "Do you think I would condemn you if I heard that story, or that I would agree that you were hopeless? I have never given up hope so easily, and no matter how you hurt me, I love you too much to do it now."

"Free." He could scarcely speak.

"So." She stood, brushing her hands off briskly. "You don't think you can have forever with me. You don't things can be lovely with the two of us. I will admit that we have some things we must discuss about our future." She dismissed those *things*—their entire way of life—with a toss of her head. "But if you think that the two of us cannot resolve our differences, you *are* lying to yourself. Not all truths are bitter, and not all lies are sweet."

His whole heart jolted. "Free. I don't know—"

She came toward him. And then, to his shock, she took his hands.

"I understand," she said. "I understand why you did what you did. I understand why you didn't tell me. Your entire life has taught you that you can't have anything good unless you steal it. You wanted me; you stole me. You never expected to keep me." She shook her head. "I can even forgive you for that."

His heart, cold and shriveled thing that it was, came to life, thumping in a way he didn't understand. He couldn't quite bring himself to look her in the eyes. She seemed so brilliant, so untouchable.

And yet here she was, touching him in defiance of all his expectations. This couldn't be happening; it couldn't be real.

But her fingers were truly laced through his, warming him from the outside.

Her features softened. "You lied to me about the family that rejected you. I knew you hadn't told me when I married you, and I married you anyway. *They* rejected you. I was hurt when I found out the truth. But it hurt just as much that you thought *I* would reject you."

Her other hand came up and brushed against his cheek. He let out a breath.

"I still know who you are, Edward. And if you recall, I didn't fall in love with a man who represented himself as the most honorable fellow in all of England. I fell in love with a scoundrel."

It felt like forgiveness—sweet words that he didn't dare believe in.

"So, yes, Edward. I think I could forgive you." Her voice trembled. "But you can't keep telling yourself that I am a lie, one that you must walk away from. If we're to do *this*, whatever this ends up being—we'll need to do it together."

He almost couldn't hear her. She had said *if*. She'd said she could forgive him. He didn't know what to do with that confused, painful jumble of his emotions.

Her fingers trailed along his chin. She tilted his face up so that he met her eyes. "Come find me when you're willing to do that."

He'd never thought of the future until now. He'd flinched from it all these years. It had seemed as impossible to unravel as his past.

But when he shut his eyes, he didn't think of a dark cellar. He remembered himself in the back chamber at the committee hearing just yesterday morning.

We're that sort of friends, Patrick had insisted.

And they were. Stephen and Patrick had been the constants in his life, the two people he had never forgotten. They were fixed. They were not a lie. They'd not betrayed him, and he…

How odd. He hadn't betrayed them either. It took him minutes to understand that, and more time beyond that, turning that bewildering thought in his head, over and over, trying to imagine what it meant.

Maybe pessimism was as much a lie as optimism.

He got out the notebook he always carried. He drew to remember—to recall all the details that his inconsistent, unreliable memory washed away. Over the months, he'd drawn a hundred sketches of Free. He started one now—one of her standing in front of her press as she'd greeted him—was that just two nights past? It *was*. He drew her skirts, ruffling in a breeze, her eyes, brightening in recognition.

Like every other sketch he'd made of her, this one was missing something—something so fundamental, so necessary, that he knew he'd never get anything right if he didn't figure it out now.

He wracked his memory, searching. There she was, a lone silhouette against the doors of her business. That was wrong. Empty.

She hadn't been alone. Slowly, he drew in the lines of his own trousers, the tilt of his head as he'd walked up to her. His outstretched hands—that brilliant smile on her face now seemed to make sense.

It had never been *her* that he'd drawn incorrectly.

The thing that he had been missing was…himself.

He sat sketching on that rock in the sunshine long after she'd gone back to the house. He worked until the sun switched from his left to his right side. The breeze came and went, the water rippled past.

When he was ready, he stood and went back to the house. Marshall let him in; he found Free sitting at the table.

She didn't rise as he approached her. She didn't frown at him, but she didn't smile either. He wasn't sure how he made his way toward her, if anyone else was in the room. He couldn't see anyone but her, couldn't think any thought except that he no longer wanted to be towering over her, looking down.

It was a simple matter to get on his knees before her, and an even simpler matter to bend his head.

"Free," he said. "I want to make you happy, but I don't know how."

For a long, fraught moment, she didn't respond. And then, ever so slowly, she reached out and took his hands in hers.

"We'll figure it out," she told him.

Chapter Twenty-Four

FREE DID NOT KNOW what she was doing in this house, if one could call something so vast by so unassuming a name. The ceilings reached high over her head. Her footsteps in the huge, echoing space seemed to belong to a much larger creature. A horse, perhaps, or an elephant.

And the man at her side… She stole a glance over at him.

Edward strode beside her. He seemed as uneasy in this place as she felt, and maybe that was the only thing that kept her from running in horror.

Yesterday, he'd told her he wanted to make her happy. Today, she'd come with him to his estate in Kent. Because— she still didn't quite believe this—the man she married had an estate in Kent, and that was now an inextricable part of her life. She'd married him for richer or poorer, but quite frankly, at the moment she would have preferred poorer.

He'd made every effort to make her feel comfortable. He'd not yet announced the marriage. He'd wired ahead and sent the servants away on holiday, because he knew that she'd be overwhelmed by a procession of people all wanting to meet her needs.

Yet somehow the absence of servants made the tour Edward was giving her even more bewildering.

This was what he'd kept from her: this vast empty space screaming of responsibility. This was what he hadn't told her, because he'd feared she wouldn't want it.

"The grand hall," he told her. Then a few minutes later: "The blue parlor to the right; the yellow parlor to the left."

"The zebra-striped parlor," Free muttered as he paused at the door of the next room.

He glanced down at her, and the half smile on his face slowly died. "You...hate this."

She'd been trying her best to imagine herself in any of these rooms, in any role except gawking seer of sights. She'd failed.

"It's not really filling me with delight," she admitted.

He turned from the room. "I'm doing this all wrong. Come with me. Let me show you the good parts." He marched down the hall to an unobtrusive door set in the wall. He wrenched this open and led her into a bare hall, one not floored underneath by marble. Here, no massive portraits looked down in snooty disapproval.

"Oh, thank heavens," Free said, breathing in relief. "I was going mad out there."

"Here." Edward jiggled a door to a room and then opened it wide. "The seamstress's work area. Patrick Shaughnessy—he's that friend I told you about—his mother was a seamstress."

Free blinked. "Patrick *Shaughnessy?* Is he any relation, by chance, to..." She trailed off, and then she glanced up at him. "Of course he is. Of course. Stephen Shaughnessy—he's why you came back in the first place." She looked around the room. A small, dingy window let light spill onto the bare wood floor. A simply made chest of drawers stood against one wall.

"Yes. He is. He's like a little brother to me."

She frowned, recalling... "He lied to me about you. That little..." But she couldn't muster up anger over it.

"Clod," Edward suggested. "It's what Patrick and I always called him. We referred to him as 'the clod.' But only when he was present. You're not angry at him for lying, are you?"

"He hardly knew you were going to marry me," she said dryly. "But I'll have words with him." It made sense of everything Edward had done in the beginning. "Then it wasn't entirely about revenge when we first met, was it?"

He gave her a look. "It took about five minutes before it was about you, too. You've been the one easy part in all of this. If I didn't ask you to join this uneasy future with me, it's because I love you too much to ask you to come into this." He gestured around him.

She turned away from him to hide the emotion that swept through her. Yes. She knew he loved her. She'd known it almost from those first five minutes. He was just learning how to do it properly.

She blindly opened a drawer. "Let's see what we have in here." The drawer didn't stick as she'd expected from her own household drawers. It slid open smoothly on a clean, oiled track. "Linens," she said coolly. She slid that drawer closed and picked another. "More linens. Good heavens. If we sewed the sheets end to end, we could reach the ocean from here." She shut that drawer, too, and put her hand on the topmost drawer. "Let me guess what's in this one: yet more linens." Free yanked it open.

But this drawer rattled as she pulled it open.

And when she looked inside, it wasn't linens. It was a collection of thimbles, large and small. Some were old, weathered iron; some were new and shiny tin. There were *hundreds* of thimbles there. For God's sake, why would anyone ever need so many thimbles? Even the servants here ran to excess.

Free stared at the drawer, blinking in confusion. And somehow, that was what broke her—not the four parlors or the vast grounds. It was thimbles.

She began to laugh. Not just a little giggle, but a helpless, unladylike belly laugh. She should have been able to stop, but after the last few days, somehow she couldn't. It almost hurt to laugh like that. Edward watched her in confusion.

"Well," she said, wiping tears of mirth from her eyes, "if your brother ever comes to visit, I know *just* what to slip under his mattress."

Edward let out a crack of laughter. "The needles are in the drawer just over."

Somehow, after that, the tour got better. Not that it became any less overwhelming; it was still utterly ridiculous that any human beings would spend their lives surrounded by this kind of wealth. But the visit started to be something that they were doing together.

There *were* a handful of servants in the gardens and stables that he hadn't sent away—those whose duties could not bear a few days' neglect—but they slipped away when Free and Edward approached. Edward showed Free around the farrier's station. He explained how to shoe a horse, demonstrated how to work the bellows. That, she could accept. After that, he took her up to the ruins on the hill.

He pointed out the boundaries of the estate—hazy and indistinct, thousands of acres, hundreds of tenants. She could scarcely believe it.

"One of the early skirmishes in the battle for Maidstone took place just down there," he told her. "Back when my forefather was a mere Baron Delacey. People come constantly to see this place for historical reasons. My father hated it."

"Let's put up a monument," Free suggested. "Open it to the public."

He sat on one of the broken battlements and smiled. "Better. We could charge admission. That would be so crass that my father would turn in his grave." His smile widened, and he turned his finger in a lazy circle. "Which would also be useful. We could attach his coffin to some kind of an engine and use the power of his outrage to…I don't know, grind corn."

Free found herself smiling. She came to sit beside him. "Is that how we'll sully the family name then?"

"Oh, we've already made an excellent start on that. But why limit ourselves to just the one option? I might expand the farrier's station so I can do some metalwork here. If we decide to stay here." He glanced over at her. "That would employ some of the men, too. And the way I see it, the more people we employ in an actual productive scheme, instead of supporting our degenerate ways…" He swept his hand, indicating the house below. "Well, the better it will be."

She took his hand. "The massive palace and the ridiculous estates are a significant problem. But I want to run my newspaper." She hugged her knees. "That's the one thing I insist upon. Everything else, I suppose we can work with, but my newspaper is not negotiable."

"Very well, then. We will make that happen. I promise."

They stared off into the distance. It was really an excellent hillside for a ruined castle. She had a vantage point on the slow, lazy river making its way through the trees. On the far horizon, she could see the sea—sparkling blue waters fading into indistinct sky.

"Someone," Free said, "is going to have to do the things the lady of the manor is supposed to do."

She didn't go on. She was really considering this. She was considering *him*, considering what she would have to be, have to do, to become his viscountess.

She wasn't sure who took whose hand, whose fingers twined with whose.

"On the benefit side," Free said, "that house leaves a *lot* of room for me to hide the bodies of my enemies."

His thumb caressed her palm. "We'll put them in the zebra-striped parlor," he told her.

"Can't we just do this instead for the rest of our lives?" Free asked. "Just the two of us. Together. The rest of the world can disappear. I like it like this."

"No," he said. "We can't. You'd be bored in half a day. And how will we fill the zebra-striped parlor with the bodies of your enemies if we never sally forth and slay them?"

She was laughing at that, when she saw a wisp of dust rising from the road. It was still more than a mile distant. "Someone's coming."

Edward glanced upward—and then slowly stiffened. His hand pressed into hers. "Yes," he said slowly. "And…I rather think I recognize the carriage. It would be lovely if it were just the two of us, Free. But it isn't. That's my brother."

Chapter Twenty-Five

EDWARD WAS WAITING WITH FREE in the blue parlor when James Delacey arrived. Free didn't move as the carriage pulled up on the gravel ring outside the house. But still, it felt as if she drew farther and farther away—as if she were drifting from him on every breath.

Through the gauzy curtains of the parlor, they could see the horses coming up to the house. A footman jumped off the back of his conveyance, setting out a step. Another appeared and opened the door. The first one held out a hand, steadying his brother as he stepped out.

Beside him, Free shook her head. "Are *we* supposed to have all those footmen?" she whispered in shocked tones.

"Yes," he whispered back. "But we can flout propriety as much as we like, remember. *Supposed to* is not a necessity, just a consideration."

She frowned and folded her arms.

James strode forward confidently, marching up to the house at an even pace.

The front doors remained obstinately shut. James came up short, inches from the wood panels, and frowned at the doors in confusion. Slowly, he retreated a few steps. Then he walked to the doors more tentatively. They still didn't open.

There were no servants to open them after all. James no doubt had no experience with the concept of *no servants*.

His brother reached out and, with a quizzical expression on his face, touched the door handle.

"Do you think he'll be able to figure it out?" Free said beside Edward.

Edward wasn't sure. Some evil part of him wanted to pull out his pocket watch and see how many seconds would elapse before his brother decided to take on the arduous task of exerting pressure on the handle himself. Instead, he sighed. "It's your home, Free, whether you accept me or not. With all that my brother has done to you, can we even let him in?"

Her eyes narrowed and her nostrils flared. "With all that he has done to you, can *you* let him in?"

For a moment, they exchanged glances. She sighed and looked away first; he blew out his breath.

"I suppose we'll have to have this out with him sooner or later," Edward said.

Her hands went to her hips. "Sooner," she said with a growl. "Let's finish this sooner."

"Then I'll show him how hinges operate."

He left her behind. The front door opened easily, letting afternoon sun spill into the darkened entry.

James was standing there, the strangest expression on his face. When he saw that Edward had opened the door himself, his face turned pale. He put one hand in his pocket.

"Edward," he said. "Where the devil are all the servants?"

"On a seaside vacation," Edward replied. "They'll be back in a few days."

"*All* of them?"

He hadn't come here to talk about the servants. Edward stood to one side and gestured his brother into the house. Not so long ago, James had thought this house his. It must burn him up to have to demand entrance. But if it bothered James, he made no sign of it. He simply followed Edward into the blue parlor.

He didn't notice Free sitting on a chair on the opposite side of the room. James turned to look at Edward as soon as he came through the door.

"We must talk of the future," James was saying. "I don't like what you've done. You lied to me and have set the most intense scandal brewing. Everyone in London is talking about your claims at the hearing. There are the most unbelievable rumors about what happened after."

"Is that so?" Edward asked, not quite politely.

"But it's not too late." James gave Edward a decisive nod. "If we are to make it through this affair with some semblance of dignity, you and I must be seen to be on friendly terms."

"Must we? I should think that would be impossible."

"Yes." James sighed, completely misunderstanding. "It will be difficult for me to pretend after what you've done to me, but I can do it for the sake of the family name. I'll start by offering a little advice. You must stop doing ridiculous things like sending all the servants to the seaside. You'll get a reputation as an eccentric if you keep that up, and you're laboring under enough of a burden as it is."

"I don't mind having a reputation as an eccentric."

James waved this off. "You say that now, but give yourself a few months and you'll come around." He crossed the room to find a decanter and poured himself a glass. This he raised. "You've a name and title to live up to, Edward. The burden changes you. We can waste time snapping at one another, or we can handle this as gentlemen and brothers."

"Ah. How do gentlemen and brothers handle things, then?" Edward asked.

His brother still hadn't seen Free. She sat frozen in place, watching the two of them.

James went back to Edward, glass in hand, and punched his shoulder in what Edward guessed was meant to be a gentlemanly, brotherly fashion. "You look positively middle class in that garb, and we can't have that. So I'll drag you back to town and introduce you to my tailor. After that, I must show you around to all the right people. You'll have to marry—the right wife will open doors, no matter what your past. In fact, I know just the woman, if you'll trust me."

Ha.

"You'll make me an allowance that befits my station. We'll smile at one another in public. That will tell everyone that no matter how unusual your past might have been, you've agreed to play by the proper rules."

"I see," Edward said gravely. The allowance, he suspected, was his brother's primary object—and the only reason he'd not yet turned ugly. "There are numerous flaws with that plan, but one problem seems insurmountable."

James raised an eyebrow.

"I'm already married."

His brother's chin jerked up. "*That* was one of the rumors from yesterday that I had hoped was not true. Surely, what I heard must have been garbled in some fashion. Even you would not stoop so low as to marry—"

"Oh, I didn't stoop to marry," Edward said. "Rest assured on that count."

"Ah." James looked visibly pleased.

"In fact, you can meet her yourself. Turn around."

James did. Edward could tell the moment he caught sight of her. The change that came over his brother was absolutely electric. He almost snarled, and he took two steps back.

"This is a joke," he said. "The rumors, her here… It's a joke."

Free stood.

"It's not a joke," Edward told him.

"Oh." James swallowed. "My God, Edward. This is bad. Really bad. Worse than anything I feared yesterday."

He hadn't said a word in greeting to Free. He'd not acknowledged her beyond that bulging of his eyes, and Edward felt his anger begin to come to a boil.

James turned back to Edward. "You can't marry her. For God's sake, Edward. Think about what the Delacey family name means. We'll figure out…something. I promise. We'll have her…"

"I go by Edward Clark," Edward said. "I have been called Clark for the last seven years. I'm not going to be a Delacey again, and I sure as hell won't ask my wife to take on that name. If it comes down to it, I'll take *her* name before I take on Delacey."

James sputtered. "That's absurd. And so is she. I know that she"—he pointed accusingly toward Free—"can utterly bewitch a man. God knows I've experienced it myself. But—"

Edward's hand clenched on his brother's shoulder. "A piece of advice," Edward said. "Don't insult my wife. Whatever you're about to say? Swallow it."

"Why, because she's so utterly seduced you that you'd strike your own brother? That's proof enough that you need to hear what I'm saying, however hard those truths must be for you."

"My own brother?" Edward said. "This is the brother who tried to have my wife's business burned to the ground? The brother who had lawfully issued permits quashed, who conspired to have her thrown in gaol and assaulted with who knows what sorts of torture?"

Free stood and took a step toward James. "This is also, I take it, the brother who wrote the British Consul in Strasbourg claiming that you were an impostor."

"Yes. That." Edward scowled.

James raised his hands placatingly. "I'll grant you, that last was a misstep."

"No, James, I know how a brother acts. The man who is truly my brother risked his life to save me when I needed him. He told me I could be someone good, instead of telling me I was an embarrassment for engaging in trade. He would never sneer at my wife, let alone threaten to put her away. I know what it's like to have a brother, and you're not mine."

James drew himself up. "Very well, then. Make your own way into society. Court scandal, if you wish. I only came here to help you." He sniffed. "Much good that has done me. You can talk to my solicitor about an acceptable allowance."

He turned to leave.

Free spoke again. "Do you really think, after everything you've done, that you'll be getting an allowance?"

James stopped once more. His shoulders tensed. He turned to her, his lip curling.

"I'm a gentleman," he said stiffly. "Of course I will."

"You think that we should provide you with enough money so that you can continue to hurt others." She snorted. "That seems unwise. You were a horrible plague before. Why on earth should we give you the opportunity to go on like that?"

"I…because…" James trailed off. He looked as bewildered as if he'd walked up to a house and had the doors remain stubbornly closed. "Because," he repeated, "I'm a gentleman. Because it would be scandalous to do otherwise." His teeth ground. "Because my own funds will run out in a few years' time. Think what having a destitute brother-in-law would mean for our family reputation. I don't think I need to discuss anything else in mixed company. Even if the company in question is hardly ladylike."

Free simply shrugged off that insult. "I told you once that everything you tried to do to me, I'd bring back to you a thousandfold. Now, maybe you'll believe me."

James stared at her, his teeth grinding, his face turning red. Then he turned away, jerking his head toward Edward. "You need to control your wife."

"Haven't you figured it out?" Edward said quietly. "I married her to unleash her on the world, not to keep her under wraps."

James blinked, as if trying to understand that.

"I married her because she made me believe in her," Edward said. "Because I wished her beyond your power, not under mine. You have no idea of the debt I owe her. For her I'd do the unthinkable."

He glanced back at Free.

"If she asked me to do it," he told James, "I'd even forgive you."

He let that settle in, let his brother understand it. He watched as James turned to Free, his jaw working. He wondered if James would find the words to beg, or if, as he'd done with the door, he'd be brought up confused and short.

He never would find out.

"Don't bother," Free told his brother. "Whatever you have to say, I'll not be moved. You're young. You've a good education and several years of funds. It's never too late to learn a trade."

James let out an inarticulate cry of rage. "A trade!"

"A trade." Edward found himself smiling. "It's what most men do. Try it sometime; it might agree with you."

James's hands balled into fists. "You'll regret this. You shall truly regret this. There will be a scandal, I tell you."

Free came forward. "Yes," she said simply. "We are going to make the most massive scandal. We're good at scandals, you see. And if you think that what has happened to you will be the extent of that scandal, think again. You are going to be the smallest, the most forgettable, part of what we do."

Her fingers crept into Edward's hand, and he grasped hold of her. She felt real and solid. She felt as if she'd come to his side not just for the moment, but...for good. Forever.

She drew up her chin. "Now get out of our house," she said.

And James left.

⌘ ⌘ ⌘

THE DOOR CLOSED BEHIND Edward's brother.

Free stared after him, hearing her own words echoing in her mind. *Get out of our house.* She'd just accepted all of this.

"Free." Edward's hand clenched in hers. He turned to her, slid his other arm around her waist. "Are you all right?"

That was when she realized she was shaking. "Yes. I— it's just—"

"I know," Edward said. "It's just."

Free took a deep breath and looked around the blue parlor. She still didn't *fit*. She didn't know how to take on this role.

"Ah," Edward said. He smiled at her—that smile that she'd learned to read as vulnerability rather than wickedness. "When I said we, of course, I didn't mean to imply—"

She took hold of his shoulders. He stopped midsentence and then shook his head.

"I meant," he whispered, "me—and—if you should decide—"

"Oh, you idiot," Free said. "You're the only one who would make all this worthwhile."

And then she did what she'd been wanting to do since she first saw him at her parents' house: She kissed him. Not lightly. Her hands dug into his coat, her fingers tangling in the fabric, and she pushed up to him. His mouth met hers.

"Free," he groaned. "God."

They *would* make it work. Somehow.

"I have to believe this," she told him. "I have to believe that with the jokes about thimbles—the way we have been able to weather every crisis that has come our way together…" She took another kiss from him. "I have to believe that with all of that, that we can figure this out, too. I don't know how yet. But if you believe in *us*, then I will, too."

His thumb traced down her throat, a sensual line. "I love you. How could I not believe in you? But—"

She brought him close. "Don't say it," she said. "Don't tell me how little you trust yourself, Edward. I've had enough of that. Tell me I can believe in you. That I can trust you. That you'll never let me down."

He let out a long breath. And then slowly, his lips came down to hers. "I…" His voice was rough. "I…"

"Because when I look at what you've done for me, I can believe in you. You saved my newspaper from the fire. You rescued me from prison. You gathered evidence so that I could prosecute a suit against your brother."

His lips were rough against hers. "Free."

"And I haven't even mentioned the puppy-cannon."

He kissed her. "Sweetest, I have another confession to make. This may be almost as bad as the last one."

She pulled away, looking up at him, almost afraid to hear what he had to say.

He leaned down and whispered. "I don't have a puppy-cannon."

"No puppy-cannon?" she echoed.

"No. The physics of cannons are actually really unkind for dogs. I can't endorse the idea, however cuddly it sounds in principle. Although I have to admit that it would make an excellent parliamentary tactic. You could sit in the Ladies' Gallery. On my signal, when someone said something ridiculous…" He made a noise that sounded something like a rocket.

"Arf, arf," she added, half-smiling. "Will it shock you to hear that I believe in you, even *sans* cannon? I do, Edward. I believe in you. And I wish you would, too."

He let out a long, ragged breath. "I…I believe." His voice was harsh. "I believe in us." And then he pulled her to him.

His kiss consumed her. His hands were hot against her body. She wasn't sure whether she undid his trousers, or if he did; she wasn't sure if she wrapped her legs around his hips, or if he lifted her against the wall. But when he joined with her, his hands strong against her waist, she let herself fall into the feel of him, the sweep of his kiss. The thrust of him inside her, building—joining.

Roughly though they'd come together, her climax came slowly—not a sudden wave, but a slow, rolling gentleness, one that built until it overwhelmed her senses, taking over her. He came shortly after, thrusting hard, holding her in place against the wall as he did.

When he'd finished, he smiled. "God," he rumbled. "It's worth it. It's all worth it, just for you."

She couldn't disagree.

He took her up to bed afterward.

Even that seemed odd and unfamiliar. She smiled at him as he helped her into her nightrail. She curled up in the bed. But she felt small in that vast expanse of linen. Even when he joined her, curling his body around her, all that empty, extra space surrounded them like hostile territory.

"We'll make it work," she told him. "If any two people can make this work, it will be us."

He let out a breath, his hand slipping around her waist. "We will. But this isn't what you wanted from your life."

"There is some parity," she told him. "I doubt you ever said to yourself, 'I want nothing more than to marry a woman whose radical press garners death threats and arson attempts.'"

"A failure of imagination on my part." He kissed her shoulder. "I had only to see you and know I wanted nothing else. You, on the other hand…"

"Everyone tempers their dreams over time, Edward. We'll figure out the future tomorrow. For tonight…"

He let out a breath.

"For tonight," Free said, "I finally want to have that conversation you promised me about how attractive I find your muscles."

"Ah," he rumbled against her chest. "Do you?"

She slid her hands down his side. "I do."

And so she did.

❋　❋　❋

AFTER THEY'D FINISHED the second round, after Free had fallen asleep by his side, Edward slid his arm around her. He could feel her chest rise and fall, slowly at first and then more slowly still.

It was so close to sweet that he could almost accept it as his future. So close, and yet so far.

Everyone tempers their dreams sometimes.

But not Free. He'd wanted to give her a thousand things. Sizing her dreams down to fit in his life had not been on his list. And yet that was what this all would mean, would it not? She'd live in this house, think about his tenants. Even if she moved her newspaper here, the estate would always make extra work for her, sapping her energy from the causes she loved.

Her breath evened out beside him, deepening, coming to a steady rhythm. The evening darkened from blue to purple to black.

"I don't want you to compromise," Edward said. "I want you unbowed."

But Free was asleep and she didn't even mutter in response.

"I love you," Edward told her. "I want to give you your heart's desire, not spend the rest of my life knowing that I stole your dreams from you."

Still she didn't move. Years with her stretched out in front of him—years of *almost,* years where she felt happiness with him nearly as great as if they'd never met. Years watching her look out the windows of this great big house, remembering what she'd once had.

This estate, this title, this life…for her, all of this would be a constant bruising, an eternal source of pain. He couldn't do that to her.

Slowly, he drew himself from around her. Even more slowly, he stole from her bed.

He didn't dare look back. He simply walked out the door and down the stairs before he lost his nerve.

Chapter Twenty-Six

THE SOUND OF BIRDS pulled Free from sleep. Happy summer chirps filtered through the open window. She woke, opening her eyes to a spill of sunlight across the carpet. It was still scarcely morning; dawn came early in summer.

Now, that early morning light illuminated the pattern of some rich carpet, imported from who knew where. Hand-carved mahogany furniture stood against the walls. The window framed the rolling hills of an estate that she didn't want but was going to have anyway. After last night, though... After last night, that feeling of disconnectedness had faded to a dull ache. In another month, she might even be satisfied.

The one consolation—the only thing that made it worthwhile—was that they would be doing this together. She shut her eyes and turned in bed, reaching for her husband.

She found cold sheets instead. That woke her right up. She got out of bed and fumbled for her robe.

He wasn't in the dressing room, nor in the library next to it, nor in... She didn't have names for all the rooms that she looked in. Why did anyone need *three* sitting rooms, all in different colors?

Where was he? Why hadn't he woken her up? He wouldn't leave her entirely, she told herself. She wouldn't panic. The thud of her heart had nothing to do with fear.

She rushed down a stairway wide enough to host a stampeding herd of cattle. In the normal course of things, she might have been able to ask the servants where he'd gone. But there were no servants—except in the stables. Surely they'd have seen him there, if he'd left.

She dashed outside. The dew on the grass soaked into her slippers. But as she came up on the stables, she heard voices—just audible over a loud, soughing sound. She heard *Edward.* She hadn't realized how she'd worried until she staggered in relief, knowing that he hadn't disappeared.

"Just like that," he was saying. "Yes, we'll need it a bit hotter than you'd use for a shoe. Wait until it glows orange."

That heavy soughing sound repeated, and now she recognized it as a bellows working. He'd showed her a bit of that yesterday. She dashed up to the stables, turned the corner to the farrier's station.

Edward was holding a thin piece of metal over a fire. He'd donned thick leather gloves, removed his coat, and rolled up his sleeves. He turned the iron in his hand, slowly, with great precision. Free found herself unable to breathe at the sight of him—at those lovely muscles she'd admired up close last night, displayed to such lovely advantage, at the intent concentration on his face.

The metal went from dark gray to dull red, coming up on orange. He picked up a tool—something that looked like a pincers—and then tapped the metal with it, shaping it with light, gentle touches, coaxing it into a graceful curve.

"There," he said to the man working the bellows. "Now to heat the end. This will have to be damned hot, Jeffreys—work the bellows hard, until the iron is almost yellow." He held the tip in the fire, watching. "Yes. Precisely like that."

Before she could understand what was happening, he'd set something on the table, something small and shiny. He touched the heated end of his iron to that thing, holding it in place for a moment.

"There. That's the last one, Jeffreys."

The man left off working the bellows. "You know your way around a forge, sir. My lord, I mean."

Edward's nose wrinkled at that last, but he didn't say anything. Instead, he crossed to a barrel. He slipped the thin metal inside and steam rose in clouds.

"There." He pulled it out, turning it from side to side, considering.

She'd not had a good view of the thing before. She could see it now. It looked like a flower. A flower made of iron, the base sporting graceful leaves, the stem rising up in a gentle curve, leaning into some unseen wind. It terminated in what looked like a tiny iron bell.

No. She leaned forward squinting. That wasn't a bell.

He nodded at his handiwork and then turned around. That was when he saw her. His eyes widened slightly. "Free."

"Edward." She looked at him. "You awoke early."

"Not precisely." He gave her a small, tired smile. "I've not slept yet. Now shut your eyes, Free. And Jeffreys—you can take yourself off. Thank you for your help." Edward jerked his head, and the man who'd worked the bellows smiled slightly, bowed, and slipped away.

"Shut my eyes?" Free didn't comply. She looked around instead. "Why would I—" And then she stopped, her breath taken away. Because there were *others*—an entire pail of these plants, stems rising gracefully to belled flowers. It was like looking at a meadow of metal flowers waving in some spring breeze.

She took a step forward.

No, those really weren't bells. They were thimbles—he must have taken a handful from the seamstress's room. He'd made all these flowers from those.

She could suddenly feel the pebbles beneath her slippers, hard, gritty little dots pressing into the soles of her feet.

"Last night," he said, "after you fell asleep, I kept thinking. Of all the things you said, of all the things I know you want. You told me that everyone tempered their dreams over time—eventually."

"I did." What this had to do with a sheaf of iron bluebells, she didn't know.

"You told me you wanted to believe in me," he said. "And—here's the thing, Free. What I remembered most was that day in your office. The day I fell completely, irrevocably, head over heels in love with you. I was a complete ass to you, and I told you that you were trying to drain the Thames with thimbles."

She smiled faintly. "I remember that."

"You told me I'd had it wrong. That you weren't trying to drain the Thames—you were watering a garden, drop by drop. You made me think, for the first time in my life, that there was a way to win against all of this." He stretched his arms wide.

Her throat felt scratchy.

"So that's what I was doing last night." His voice was low. "You told me to believe in myself, and so I made you a garden of thimbles. A promise, Free, that we won't compromise. That our marriage won't be *almost* what you wished for, that your dreams will not be tempered. That I will not be the one who holds you back, but the man who carries thimbles to water your garden when your arms tire."

A breeze came up, swirling between them, and the stems danced in the wind, the flowers clanging merrily together.

"That's how I thought I could make it up to you," he said. "Drop by drop. Thimble by thimble. But about halfway through making these, I knew it wasn't enough. I couldn't ask you to become another viscountess. I'd be miserable; you'd be miserable. And you'd do a bang-up job, but there are a hundred women who could be viscountesses. There's only one of you."

She was feeling almost hazy. Her knees felt weak. But he was the one who took her hand. "So I'm asking you, Free. *Don't* be my viscountess. Don't throw my parties. Don't run my estate. Let me be your thimble carrier. Be *you,* the most wonderful woman I have ever known. I'll be the one making sure that you never run out of water."

"How?" Her voice cracked. "You have a seat in Parliament, an estate that needs care. Your wife needs to make sure that..."

"No," he said softly.

"I mean, it, Edward. I have no patience for those lords who neglect their duties."

He came up to her and touched her cheek. "The lovely thing about being a complete and utter scoundrel is that I don't have to accept everyone else's reality. I had this idea last night. This strange, incomprehensible idea. Why do *we* have to make decisions about the estate? I've spent the last seven years of my life blackmailing people and forging letters. I know nothing of estate management."

"You could learn."

"Why should I? Neither of us want this. Why should we change our entire lives when there are people who already know this place better than I ever would? Let them run it."

Free blinked. "Who do you mean?"

"All the land I showed you yesterday? Those hundreds of tenants, all the people in town who rely on the estate? They know what they need, and they surely don't need us to explain it to them. Let them decide how to manage this all. It's their life. Imagine what would happen if we simply got out of the way."

Free let out a breath. She'd been trying to figure it all out—how to have *this*, and have her newspaper as well. It…it might be possible.

"Take this house, for instance," he said. "We don't want it. So why not find a better way to use the funds to keep it open? Ask the tenants what they'd want. Maybe they'll choose to rent it out. Maybe they'll convert it to a hospital or a school."

"You're right," Free said slowly. "Would we choose a board of tenants, then?"

"Choose?" He smiled at her. "Come, my dear. It's time you stopped being so acquisitive and started being more political."

For one moment, her heart stopped. And then—as the future truly opened up to her—she began to smile.

"I rather think," he said, "that they're competent to vote on a board themselves."

"They could." She couldn't breathe. "And who will get to vote, do you think?"

He reached out and took her hands. "Must you ask? It's our estate. Our board. We can set any rules we wish."

The bluebells shifted as another breeze ruffled them, thimble after thimble ringing out.

"So," he finished, "I had rather assumed the women would vote, too."

She couldn't stop smiling. She reached out and pulled him to her. He was solid and real in her arms. And he was right—there was no need to compromise. Not with him. From here on out, there would be no almost—just more, and more, and more.

"That's where we'll start," he said. "When the fabric of society fails to unravel in response... Well, we'll take on the rest of the world."

She pulled him down for a kiss. "They don't stand a chance."

Epilogue

IT WAS LATE AUGUST, and the archive room at the *Women's Free Press* was miserably hot. In part that was because the weather was deucedly warm. In part, it was because no breeze came in through the window, even though they'd opened it as wide as it would go. But mostly, it was because there were seven people—counting Edward—crammed into the tiny space.

The chair and the desk that had once stood here had been pressed into service in the adjacent meadow, bearing food and drink.

That meant that everyone sat on the floor.

To Edward's left, Oliver Marshall's knee jammed into his thigh. On his right, Patrick Shaughnessy sat, quietly contemplating his cards. Violet and Sebastian Malheur sat shoulder-to-shoulder across the room. Opposite them sat the Duke of Clermont, with Stephen Shaughnessy at his side.

"So is someone going to explain to me," Edward asked, "why we must all play cards in a closet?"

"Tradition." That came from Sebastian Malheur.

Sebastian Malheur was precise and amusing. He'd glanced once at each card as it was dealt, and then never looked at them again. Edward had met him first a few weeks ago, when Free had taken him down to London on her brother, Oliver's return.

"Tradition?" Edward looked dubiously around the space.

They were crammed in every which way. Marbles—which Clermont had insisted were the only tokens to be used—took the place of cash bets. Clermont had explained the matter of those tokens solemnly. Apparently, marbles were a serious business in these parts.

Edward shook his head. "You lot have terrible traditions."

"The cramped space is not part of the usual way of things," Clermont said. "It's more that when one of the Brothers Sinister gets married, we get together the night before and play cards."

"Discomfort, however, does seem to be the norm." Sebastian grinned. "*Particularly* on the part of the groom." He looked off in distant memory. "And Oliver did say you could use a little discomfort."

Edward pushed back against the wall—as much as he could in these maddeningly close quarters—shaking his head. "Oh, no," he said. "Just because I'm left-handed and married to Oliver's sister doesn't mean I'll join your ridiculous organization of entirely non-sinister proportions. I will not be dragooned into such a thing."

"Don't worry," Robert said. "We're not dragooning you. You're not really a Brother Sinister. You're just a convenient excuse."

"That's a relief."

"And Stephen and Patrick may be left-handed, but they're not even relations. So unfortunately, we can't include them." That came from Free's brother.

"Also you're not really marrying Free today," Violet pointed out. "You're just holding a late wedding breakfast."

"While we're at it, it isn't even the night before." That was Sebastian. "So you see, it all comes out right. All the ways in which this is *almost* the right circumstance, and yet not, cancel one another perfectly. Ergo, we must all sit in this closet while I win at cards."

"You will not," his wife muttered.

"While the Malheurs win at cards," Sebastian corrected smoothly. "Speaking of which—how do we fare? I know that Oliver and Robert have both already crossed twenty-one. But what do the rest of you have?"

"Seventeen," Patrick said, flipping over the card he'd kept facedown.

"Nineteen." Violet turned over a nine and a seven to go with the three she had on display.

"Ah." Sebastian flipped his single card over, showing a pair of kings. "I'm at twenty. Can anyone beat that? I think not." The man smiled beatifically and glanced at the marbles in the middle of the room.

"I've only got eighteen," Stephen said, "but I don't think that your *almosts* do cancel out. You see, I'm not really left-handed."

"No!" Robert and Oliver spoke together in joint outrage.

Sebastian's eyes widened. "An infidel! Stone him!" He looked wildly around, found a scrap of paper on the floor, and hurled it ineffectually at him. "Die, fiend, die!"

Stephen watched the paper flutter to the ground, and then shook his head. "Are you mad?"

"No," Sebastian said. "I'm not even angry, but it's more fun this way. You set everything off balance. If I can't get a little amusement in return, what's the point?"

"Ah," Stephen said with a wave of his hand. "You lot were asking to be lied to. Gathering a bunch of men, muttering something about being left-handed." Stephen shrugged. "Of course I'm going to say, 'Yes, I'm left-handed.' Why wouldn't I?"

"Ah, well. At least tradition was upheld on the most important point." Sebastian leaned forward and began to gather up the marbles in the center of the room. "I won."

"No," Edward said. "You didn't."

Sebastian froze. He glared at Edward, who had a string of cards showing. "You can't have won," he said. "Not unless you have a three under there. The chances of that are—"

Edward smiled blandly and flipped over the card, revealing the three of spades.

Silence met this proclamation. Sebastian blinked at Edward's hand, frowning. "Did you cheat?" he finally asked.

"I lie. I forge. I blackmail." Edward shrugged. "But cheating at cards? I'd never stoop so low."

"Good to know you have some principles," Oliver said with a roll of his eyes.

"Indeed," Edward said. "Cheating at cards is too easy. I'd be vastly bored if I let myself do it."

Beside him, Patrick—who knew Edward's sense of humor rather better than the others—let out a crack of laughter.

But at that moment, the door opened behind him. A draft of cool air swept over him. Edward turned and glanced around.

"Ah," he said. "Speaking of principles. Here comes my principle now."

Free stood in the doorway, her hands on her hips, dressed in a gown of brilliant blue and white. She glanced over them all—crammed into the too-tight space—and shook her head in exasperation.

"Why is half my wedding party hiding in the archive room?" she asked.

Edward reached forward and gathered up the scattered marbles. "Ah, Free. How lovely to see you. Did you know that every one of these marbles represents a favor owed to me by these fine men and women?"

Free tilted her head, contemplating the marbles. "Yes," she said slowly. "I did know that. Jane mentioned these to me once. Apparently she's still holding one in reserve."

"It's a high-stakes game," Edward said, "but I was willing to play. And now look what I have for you." He reached up and poured the marbles in her waiting hands. "Here," he said. "I know I gave you a puppy for a wedding present, but these are much better."

Free smiled down at him. "Dearest. You shouldn't have. A duke *and* an MP, both in my pocket? It's everything I've always wanted."

Oliver began to struggle to his feet. "See here," he said sharply.

Edward stood gracefully and kissed his wife on the cheek. "Enjoy."

"I'm fairly certain they're joking," Sebastian stage-whispered.

Edward ignored this. "Now we've taken care of two of them," he told her. "How many more do we need?"

"I don't know." She linked her arm in his. "Shall we go find out?"

Other Books by Courtney

The Worth Saga
Once Upon a Marquess
Her Every Wish
After the Wedding
The Return of the Scoundrel
The Kissing Hour
A Tale of Two Viscounts
The Once and Future Earl

The Cyclone Series
Trade Me
Hold Me
Find Me
What Lies Between Me and You
Keep Me
Show Me

The Brothers Sinister Series
The Governess Affair
The Duchess War
A Kiss for Midwinter
The Heiress Effect
The Countess Conspiracy
The Suffragette Scandal
Talk Sweetly to Me

The Turner Series
Unveiled
Unlocked
Unclaimed
Unraveled

Not in any series
What Happened at Midnight
The Lady Always Wins

The Carhart Series
This Wicked Gift
Proof by Seduction
Trial by Desire

Author's Note

THIS BOOK STARTS WITH the Cambridge/Oxford boat race of 1877. In reality, the boat race of 1877 was judged a dead heat (with Oxford probably a hair ahead of Cambridge). I changed that for purposes of this story: sorry, Oxford!

When I first started working on this book, I had this vague idea that Free (who I already knew was a suffragette) would get paired with some dude who was opposed to women's rights, and they would have explosive chemistry et cetera blah blah blah. It turns out that I did not want to write that book: I couldn't make myself believe that Frederica Marshall, suffragette, would fall for a man who fundamentally didn't believe she was his equal. I also realized that book, if I wrote it, would be one where the theme turned out to be, "Aw, if women just put out long enough, men might decide they're actual worthy human beings!"

And so instead of figuring out how to pair Free with someone who was trying to drag her down, I started to ask myself an interesting question: What was the most that someone like Free could hope to accomplish in her time?

And so I started exploring what women—extraordinary women—did in the late nineteenth century. The answer surprised me.

When I chose to make Free an investigative reporter, I modeled her after a real nineteenth century investigative reporter, Nellie Bly. At the age of 21, Bly (who was the daughter of working-class Americans) went to Mexico, where she lived for six months, reporting on the regime there. In 1887—at the age of 23—Bly faked insanity so that she could be admitted to the Women's Lunatic Asylum in New York. She stayed there for ten days, and when she got out, she wrote the story of the women she met in the asylum—women who were, for the most part, *not* mad when they went in.

Like Bly, I sent Free undercover—in her case, to a government lock hospital in Britain. Like Bly, Free reported on the conditions she found. The government lock hospitals really did exist—and they did more than just lock up prostitutes, although that's all they were ostensibly supposed to do. The Contagious Diseases Act—which established the lock hospitals—said that if anyone said a girl was a prostitute, she would have to submit to fortnightly examinations by a doctor. The purpose of the Act was to try and stop the spread of syphilis in the British Army and Navy.

That brings me to another nineteenth century woman— Josephine Butler. Butler was a devout Christian who abhorred sexual immorality. You might think that a woman like Butler would keep silent about something like the Contagious Diseases Act. But she was outraged by the double standard in the Acts—a standard that allowed the men who spread the disease to walk free while imprisoning only the women.

She was furious that the burden of the Act fell disproportionately on the poor. She found evidence that officers were specifically targeting milliners and flower girls— on the theory that all lower-class women were of low morals and thus inherently suspect.

Butler spoke out repeatedly—at gatherings and demonstrations, in newspapers and in books. She was labeled "indelicate" and when she was referred to in Parliament, men scoffingly said she was no "lady." That didn't stop her. Mobs that came to hunt her down did not stop her.

She insisted that the examinations the women were subject to constituted what she called "surgical rape," and that holding them without a trial by their peers was a violation of their rights under Magna Charta and other sources of British

Constitutional Law. She called for civil disobedience on the part of women in response to the acts; in 1870, in her book *The Constitution Violated*, she wrote: "If the breach in the constitution be effectually repaired, the people will of themselves return to a state of tranquility; if not, MAY DISCORD PREVAIL FOR EVER."

This came from a married, upper-class, evangelical Christian.

And so if you're wondering if women in 1877 could really *do* the things that Free did, or think the things that she did—the answer is yes, yes, yes. They did.

Amanda notes to herself at one point that she used to believe that poor women shouldn't be allowed to vote, either. That was also—sadly—fairly representative for the time. The dark side of suffragette history is a horrible prejudice against people who didn't fit their mostly white, middle-class mold. In England, that prejudice was predominantly class-based; in the U.S. (which we didn't see at all in this book), there was some deep-seated, awful racism. I don't think we can separate the harm of that prejudice from the good that those women did, and I tried to present that time in all its equally problematic and glorious history.

One last point: If you read Josephine Butler's memoir, one of the things that comes through is how many vicious, deeply personal attacks she suffered. Her husband (who never asked her to quit) had a career that also suffered as a result of what she was doing.

I knew when I was writing the book that many of the things Free hoped to achieve are things that are still in doubt today. Today, 137 years later, we've had one female prime minister in Britain and precisely zero female presidents in the United States. And so one of the most important questions I felt I had to grapple with was this: Why bother? Why work for a goal that will not bear fruit in over a century? Why do people work to change things today?

I found the answer in Melissa McEwan's Shakesville (http://www.shakesville.com). McEwan describes her work as follows:

Sometimes it feels like it's all I ever write about; sometimes it feels like I can't possibly write about it enough to do the issue justice; often, those feelings exist within me simultaneously. *All I ever do is try to empty the sea with this teaspoon; all I can do is keep trying to empty the sea with this teaspoon.*

Her analogy inspired me to write Free's defense of what she does:

"But we're not trying to empty the Thames," she told him. "Look at what we're doing with the water we remove. It doesn't go to waste. We're using it to water our gardens, sprout by sprout. We're growing bluebells and clovers where once there was a desert. All you see is the river, but *I* care about the roses."

I've said in every Author's Note since the beginning of this series that this is as much an alternate history as it is a historical romance. I like to imagine that between Violet's accomplishments in *The Countess Conspiracy* and what Free was doing in this book, that some of the human rights violations that suffragettes experienced over the next decades—the imprisonment, the resulting hunger strikes, the force feedings—might have been averted.

I still hope that the things we do today will make a difference.

And I hope that explains this book's dedication:

> *For everyone who has carried water*
> *in thimbles and teaspoons throughout the centuries.*
> *And for all those who continue to do so.*
> *For as many centuries as it takes.*

Finally, a note on the word "suffragette": When I started writing this book, I did a preliminary check to see if the word was being used in period literature (namely, a date-restricted search through Google Books). The answer seemed to be yes—it was mentioned in a handful of plays that came up first—so I didn't pursue the question any further. It turns out that the Oxford English Dictionary attributes the word to

1906, and the plays I checked aren't as conclusive as my first glance suggested. But by the time I checked it seriously (which was not until someone questioned the usage shortly before publication), the word was so baked into the book (including a title change!) that there was no way to change it. So that was absolutely my bad.

That being said, the OED dates words from the first printed use, and does not document (or attempt to document) informal uses, which usually predate the OED—and often by some margin. It's clear from the use first listed in the OED that the suffragettes had already been calling themselves suffragettes for some time before the press started doing so. How long that gap between the informal verbal use and the formal recorded use was is impossible to say at this point. In some instances, I've found words (in private, written correspondence) that are not attested in the OED until some 50 years later. So it's *possible* that the word "suffragette" was used in 1877 in the limited circles that this book discusses. Is it likely? Enh... I'm not going to insist it is. Let's stick with "possible."

So I am taking something of a liberty in using the word—and I'm doing so in part because there was no way to change it at the point when I discovered the issue, and in part because there is no replacement word in our vocabulary that conveys the same meaning to a modern audience ("suffragist," which is clearly period, is not specific to women). I hope that if this really bothers you, you can imagine Free coining the word herself. Since I already have her coining "chromosome" in *The Countess Conspiracy*, I don't think this achievement is beyond her.

Acknowledgments

I'm a terrible person to work with—I never know when I'll be done and want things turned around immediately—and I'm deeply grateful to have such fantastic people to help me out. As always, this book would not have been completed without the tireless help I received from Robin Harders and Keira Soleore, my editors, Krista Ball, whose eagle eye kept me in the clear, Martha Trachtenberg, my copy-editor, Maria Fairchild and Martin O'Hearn, my proofreaders, and Rawles Lumumba, my project manager, who did all of the above and more. Melissa Jolly, my assistant, has managed to keep me sane and focused.

There are too many friends who have helped me out with this book in some way or another for me to thank by name, but I'll try it anyway: Tessa Dare, Carey Baldwin, Leigh LaValle, Brenna Aubrey, Elyssa Patrick, Carolyn Jewel, Sherry Thomas, all the Peeners, the entire Denver lunch bunch, but especially Thea Harrison, Pamela Clare, and Jenn LeBlanc, my husband, my family, and last but not least, both of my wonderful creatures, Pele and Silver. I'm also indebted to innumerable author loops and boards for offering strategic advice and the ability to blow off steam.

I also want to acknowledge Rachel Chrastil's *The Siege of Strasbourg*, which was invaluable for giving me a sense of how horrible the siege actually was.

I'm also grateful to all the librarians who have read my books and recommended them for institutional purchases, to library patrons, to friends—basically, to anyone. Finally, if you're reading this as a library borrow, you can thank my agent Kristin Nelson, and her staff, particularly Lori Bennett, for helping me make this book available to libraries everywhere.

Women the world over have inspired me by standing up and speaking out, even knowing the consequences that could come. Every time I thought of making Free back down, or dream smaller, I thought of you, and you inspired me to write her as more. I can only hope I managed to make her live up to your examples.

Finally, to you my readers—who have stuck with me through four full-length books and several novellas in this series—thank you so much. This series has been so much more because of you. It's not quite over yet—there's one novella left—but without you, I would never have gotten this far or written this much. Thank you.